MW01316974

Follow the Money

AN SJPD NOVEL

PHYLLIS

ENJOY THE STORY

BOB [illegible]

2513

PHYLLIS

ENJOY THE STORY

Bob

Follow the Money

An SJPD Novel

Bob DeGeorge

iUniverse, Inc.
Bloomington

Follow the Money
An SJPD Novel

This is a work of fiction. All of the characters, names, incidents, organizations, and dialogue in this novel are either the products of the author's imagination or are used fictitiously.

iUniverse books may be ordered through booksellers or by contacting:

iUniverse
1663 Liberty Drive
Bloomington, IN 47403
www.iuniverse.com
1-800-Authors (1-800-288-4677)

ISBN: 978-1-4502-9914-5 (sc)
ISBN: 978-1-4502-9913-8 (dj)
ISBN: 978-1-4502-9912-1 (ebk)

Library of Congress Control Number: 2011903048

Printed in the United States of America

iUniverse rev. date: 09/27/2011

To Detective Cindy Calderon,
a partner who always had my back.

Acknowledgements

I would like to thank Rob Rossler for being so patient and proofing my drafts.

I would especially like to thank the brave men and women of the San Jose Police Department who I worked with for many years. Without the hard work and dedication of the men and women in patrol and investigations, San Jose would not be as safe as it is today. It is these dedicated officers that work harder at keeping San Jose safe than its citizens realize that deserve so much credit. They are the backbone of the department, and they are the ones who make it the fine department that it is.

Chapter 1

Rex pulled the gold Chevy Impala to the curb of South Seventh Street and parked. He looked up the street and could see a dark green Plymouth Voyager van pulling in to the curb. That would be Five-O and his partner from the U. S. Postal Inspectors.

Rex picked up the mike and keyed it. "Mitch, you up?"

"We're in the back and set."

"Five-O, you ready?"

"Roger that."

Rex reached down and switched the radio to another channel.

"5 King 10, 24-0-2."

"Go ahead to 5 King 10."

"24-0-2, we're in position and starting our surveillance."

"10-4. All units have been told to stay away from your op."

"Thank you. We'll be back on channel 9."

Rex turned to Kat as he put the mike down. "Go ahead and call the grandson."

Kat picked up her cell phone and punched in a number. When the caller answered she spoke to him briefly and then disconnected. Five minutes later, her phone rang. She spoke briefly and disconnected.

"The grandson says that she's on her way. She told him she would be here in five minutes.

Rex picked up his handpac and hit the transmit button. "Heads up everybody, she's on her way."

They were staking out an old Victorian house on South Seventh Street just south of San Jose State University. Back in the 1920's and 1930's, when these houses were first built they were the homes of San Jose's upper middle class. Now they were converted into one-bedroom apartments for college students, single-room apartments for pensioners on Social Security, and half way houses.

Still, the neighborhood was pleasant. The streets were lined with mature trees that had grown tall and stately. Some of San Jose's new rich had bought the houses and were restoring them to their original splendor. It was a quiet neighborhood, but not dead. People were walking on the street or sitting on their front porches.

Today they were hoping to collar the Black Widow. She was the suspect in a case that Kat was working with the US Postal. They had dubbed her the black widow because she was preying on old men. She would befriend them, offer them sex, and then get them to sign over their social security checks.

Just then, Rex heard Kat swear, "Damn, can you believe this? Look at the Postal van."

A meter maid had just pulled up behind the undercover Postal van in her Cushman and was getting out with her ticker book. She walked up to the front of the van and looked at the windshield.

"What the hell is she doing?" asked Rex.

"Look at the sign," Kat said pointing to a street sign they were parked in front of that said you could not park on this street without a permit.

Rex keyed his handpac, "Five-O, just flash your badge and she'll go away." There was no response, but a couple of seconds later Rex and Kat saw the Meter Maid do a double take and quickly get in her Cushman and drive off.

As they watched the Meter Maid drive away, Kat spotted their suspect walking up the street towards the old house. "There she is, across the street walking up to the house."

Rex keyed his handpac, "Suspect approaching from the South, standby."

The suspect walked past the driveway and up onto the front porch where she stopped and talked to two elderly men who were sitting out there.

Rex keyed his handpac again, "Suspect on the front porch, standby, wait until she goes in."

The suspect spent a couple of minutes talking to the two older men then turned and walked into the house. Rex keyed his handpac, "She's in the house, Five-O move in."

Rex and Kat got out of their car and started toward the house. There was still no movement from the Postal van. Then Five-O and his partner jumped out of their van and ran for the house. They hit the steps just in front of Rex and Kat and continued through the front door.

The two old men just sat and watched. First two people with guns drawn had run past them. Next came Kat and Rex in dark blue raid jackets that said police with their guns' drawn. Rex winked at one of the old men and gave him thumbs up as he hurried past. The old men just stared back with that look that only old people can give, that look that says I have seen it all and nothing surprises me anymore. Rex and Kat cleared the front door, they heard Five-O shouting "Federal Agent, stop." They heard a sharp cry and some thumping sounds. Kat was down the stairs first.

Rex hit the bottom of the stairs. He saw Agent Cunningham wrestling in the cramped hallway with the suspect. The suspect screamed and yelled, "Get off me you fucking bitch."

Cunningham and the suspect were sprawled in the middle of the hallway. The suspect had a knife in her right hand, and Cunningham was desperately trying to keep the suspect from stabbing her. Cunningham had both of her hands around the suspect's right wrist, and she was smashing the back of the suspect's hand against the wall. Meanwhile, the suspect was trying to claw Cunningham's face with her left hand.

Cunningham was on top of the suspect and in the narrow hallway, there was no way to take a shot. Out of the corner of his eye, Rex saw Kat holster her weapon, move up, grab the suspect's left hand and arm and twist it up behind her back forcing the suspect face down on the floor.

The suspect yelped in pain, the knife fell to the floor, and she said, "All right, all right, I give up. You don't have to break my fucking arm."

Kat pulled the suspect's right arm behind her back and cuffed her.

Then she picked up the knife. "Honey, don't you know you don't bring a knife to a gun fight? You're lucky you didn't get shot."

As Kat and Agent Cunningham searched the suspect, Rex thought back as to how this morning had begun. He was sitting in the Financial Crimes Unit at his desk.

* * *

"Good Morning Kat," Rex called out as his partner walked in and dumped her briefcase at her adjacent desk.

"Good morning Cowboy. Did you get the Op Order done?"

"Yeah, I got it done last night before I left." Rex handed her a copy of the Operation Order for their Surveillance/Arrest Operation that was going down this morning.

"Sorry I couldn't stay and help you with it last night, but I had to pick up the kid from school," Kat said.

"No big deal. It was a simple thing to write up and besides, family comes first. I got a call from Postal just before you walked in. Five-O said he'd be here in about fifteen minutes."

Kat looked around the still empty office. "Are we going to have a supervisor to go with us?"

"Yeah," Rex said, "The Burglary Sergeant, Pike. He's in his cube waiting for everybody to get here so we can brief. Since your Sergeant decided to take the morning off the L. T. assigned him to us. I already gave him a copy of the Op Order."

Kat made a face. "Can't we get somebody else besides Edward the Lump? I'd almost have Sergeant Alvarez over him."

"Nope, he's the only supervisor in this morning and we have to take a supervisor with us."

"Well, hopefully he will stay out of our way," Kat said.

This was such a basic operation that neither Rex nor Kat saw any reason to bring along a Sergeant. They were seasoned senior officers entrusted to investigate cases involving millions of dollars. In the old days, you just grabbed up some people, went out, and did your thing.

However, in this new era of hand wringing, ever since Robbery shot a suspect down in Salinas, you could not do a thing without a Sergeant. It had gotten so rediculous that the Chief of Detectives had made it an order. You were not even supposed to leave the city to interview a witness without notifying your Sergeant, who then notified the Lieutenant, who then notified the Captain, who in turn told the Chief of D's that a couple of his Detectives were "out of town."

Rex and Kat ignored this rule on a regular basis. Crooks did not pay any attention to city limits especially in financial crimes. Their investigations would start in San Jose, but often took them all over the Bay Area. If they were out in the field doing follow up investigation on a case and it took them out of town, they were not about to stop and call in to the office to find a supervisor to ask permission to go out of town.

Five-O walked into the office. He was a senior US Postal Inspector in the San Jose office. His real name was Harry Ho, but he was affectionately known as "Five-O" after the TV cop show because he was from Hawaii and usually wore Hawaiian shirts to work. Today he was dressed in tactical 5-11 pants and shirt, and a black raid vest that said Federal Agent on the front and back in gold letters. His nine-mil pistol was strapped to his right leg in a tactical holster.

Kat flashed him a smile and said, "Five-O, welcome to the party. I see you dressed for the occasion. Who's your friend?"

Behind Five-O was another Postal Inspector also dressed in tactical gear.

"Kat, Cowboy, I'd like you to met Susan Cunningham, she just transferred to the San Jose office from El Paso. Thought I'd bring her along so she could see how we operated."

They shook hands all around. US Postal and the SJPD worked closely together, primarily on financial and identity theft crimes. Rex and Kat liked working with Postal. With Postal, everybody was equal. The FBI always acted as if they were better than the locals were and did not share anything. Secret Service was good, but they were constantly being pulled off cases to work some protection detail, so you could not count on them. However, Postal was always there, especially Five-O. They had worked several joint investigations together.

Mitch and Terry walked over and joined the group. They were two Burglary Detectives that were going to help today.

"O.K.," said Rex, "Looks like we've got everybody, let me get the Sergeant and then we can have our briefing."

A couple of minutes later Rex walked back to the group with Sergeant Pike in tow. "This is short and sweet, so we can brief right here." Everybody grabbed a chair or parked it on the edge of a desk.

"Kat, this is your case so why don't you bring us up to speed," Rex said to Kat.

Kat took over. "Five-O and I have developed a joint suspect. She's a little crankster who hustles elder single men living in low-income apartments for their social security money. She also gets them to take out life insurance policies where she is named as the sole beneficiary. One of our victims is in the hospital, but our suspect has continued to try and reach him. His grandson is cooperating with us. The suspect has mail coming to the victim's apartment, and she is anxious to retrieve it. This morning the grandson will lay in a call to the suspect telling her she can come over to his grandfather's apartment and get her mail. We'll be waiting for her with arrest warrant in hand."

Rex took over. "Five-O, since you and your partner are dressed for the occasion; you guys will be our arrest team. Take a position just north of the target house. Follow our suspect in and take her down. We've got an arrest warrant for her, so we don't need her to do anything else, just take her as soon as you can.

"The house is an old Victorian that's been carved up into a bunch of one-room apartments. The victim's room is down a hallway on the left of the entrance hall that goes down a short flight of steps.

"Mitch and Terry, you take the back of the house. There is a wide driveway and parking area back there that gives you a place to park where you can eyeball the back door. If our suspect comes out the back, take her.

"Kat and I will set up out front to the south. We'll follow Postal through the front door. The Patrol District Sergeant has been notified and will keep his marked units out of the area. Radio channel 9 has been reserved for us."

When Rex had finished the briefing, he asked if there were any questions. Nobody had any. It was quiet for a minute while they all looked at Sergeant Pike who sat looking at the Op Plan.

Finally, Rex leaned over and said to Sergeant Pike, "I think this is the point where you're suppose to say, 'O.K., if nobody has any questions, let's go.'"

Sergeant Pike looked startled, gave Rex that deer-in-the-headlights look and then said, "O.K., let's go, see you out there." He got up, turned, and walked out of the room.

Rex just shook his head. "Right, I'll go ahead and call radio and log everybody on. You guys can head on out there. Kat will call our victim's grandson as soon as we are set and have him lay in the duped phone call. Hopefully our suspect will take the bait."

* * *

Kat and Agent Cunningham helped the suspect to her feet and marched her down the hallway towards the front door. Rex followed along smiling at Kat.

Kat looked over at Rex and asked, "What?"

Rex, still smiling, said, "I guess that Grab My Crotch stuff paid off."

Kat made a face, "It's called Krav Maga, a form of Israeli street fighting, and you should try it."

Rex said, "No thanks, I'm too old fashioned. I just prefer ramming the dirt bag's head into the nearest wall or car fender."

Kat just shook her head and continued outside with the suspect.

Cunningham and Kat walked the suspect over to the detective's car and sat her in the front passenger seat, putting her seatbelt on to secure her in the car.

While the girls were taking care of this, Rex pulled out his cell phone. He punched one of the speed dial numbers.

"Dawn Summers, KTVU Channel 2 News," she answered after two rings.

"Hi Dawn, this is Rex, perp walk picture show in ten minutes," he said and then hung up.

Dawn Summers was a television reporter for the local Fox affiliate, KTVU Channel 2. A while back, she had done a real favorable story on Kat and Rex's investigation of a con artist couple that preyed on the elderly.

Cops usually did not like reporters because they were trying to make the cops look bad, especially in San Jose. It was said of the local newspaper, the Mercury News, that their editor only believed in two kinds of police stories, police corruption, and police brutality. That was why the cops called it the "Murky News." The cops usually felt that the Murky News slanted their stories and tried to put the cops in a bad light.

Still, the news media were useful, if you knew how to use them. Getting the story of an investigation or an arrest out could help you find additional victims or witnesses. Rex and Kat were old hands at using the news media. You had to understand that the media had different deadlines they were up against. If you gave them enough information with enough lead-time to get their story into the next day's paper, or on the five o'clock news, they could be your friend. If you were prepared before you talked to the press, knew exactly what you were going to say, and how many facts you were going to give out, it went a lot easier and the press did not make you look like a fool.

Because Dawn was an honest reporter that had not tried to screw them yet, Kat and Rex had developed an unofficial relationship with her. It also helped that she worked for the local Fox News affiliate, which was known for its fair and balanced reporting.

By Department policy, all news stories were supposed to go through the Public Information Officer, the PIO. This usually meant that the story did not get to press for a couple of days unless it was some significant event. Television reporters did not like doing old stories; they wanted the news that was happening now. If a TV reporter could include film of something that was happening now, that usually meant that the story got on the evening news.

Rex genuinely liked the "Perp Walk." This was the shot of the suspect being taken out of the police car and lead in handcuffs into the police station. It was tremendously popular with TV news people too. Rex was not above getting a little positive publicity for him and his partner and the department. He just had to be a little cagey in how he did it.

He had Dawn's cell phone on his speed dial, and whenever they were bringing in some criminal they had just arrested, Rex would make that cryptic call to her cell phone. It told her that if she could get her cameraman in place on West Mission Street, in front of the police department, he could get a telephoto shot of the suspect being taken from the back seat of the police car and marched into the San Jose PD Pre-Processing Center, San Jose's mini jail. This let Dawn know that she needed to get a hold of the Public Information Office and ask about any recent arrests. The deal was that Dawn would not burn Rex. In return she got live footage of the arrestee. She had an action shot that would almost guarantee the story would be on the evening news.

After the suspect was secured in the detectives' car with Agent Cunningham and Kat guarding her, Rex asked Five-O what happened.

Five-O handed Rex his handpac and said, "Our radio quit working. I thought that was her but I wasn't sure until you guys jumped out of your car. When Susan and I caught up with her in the hallway, I yelled for her to stop and she started to run. Susan was faster and took her down with a flying tackle and the fight was on."

"Great," Rex said sarcastically. "SJPD, the finest police department in the universe and we don't even have radios that work. Well, at least none of our people got hurt. We'll take her to Pre-Processing if you want to follow us down." He turned to Mitch, "Thanks for the help guys."

Rex got behind the wheel of their car and Kat got in the backseat behind the suspect. Kat asked, "Where's Sergeant Pike?"

"I don't know," said Rex.

"Think you better tell him it's over?"

Rex tried to raise Sergeant Pike on his handpac, but there was no response so he tried the car radio. "24-20, 24-0-2, you copy?"

"24-20, go ahead."

"Did you copy any of the last traffic?"

"Negative."

"I guess your handpac also died. We're Code 4, 10-15 with one and on our way to PPC."

"10-4, need me for anything?"

"Negative, we got it handled."

Rex looked at Kat, "Well, you got your wish; he stayed out of our way."

Chapter 2

Rex pulled their car into the fenced in the parking area of the Pre-Processing Center. He looked South across the parking lot to West Mission Street and saw a KTVU Channel 2 News van parked there. As Kat got out of the back seat, she followed Rex's gaze and saw the news van. Kat did not say anything. Kat took the prisoner out of the front seat and passed her over to Rex.

Rex, holding the suspect by her left arm, walked her down the side of the detective car until they were even with the trunk. He stopped her there facing across the trunk of the car while Kat searched the front passenger seat to make sure the prisoner had not dumped anything on them. Rex knew that she was perfectly positioned for a full-face shot on the news camera's telephoto lens. When Kat had finished her search, and found nothing, the two of them walked their prisoner across the small parking lot and into the tunnel that led into the Pre-Processing Center.

San Jose PD's Pre-Processing Center, known to the cops as PPC, was like a mini jail. It was complete with holding cells/interview rooms. You took your prisoner there to have them fingerprinted, photographed, and entered into the SJPD database. They could also be strip searched if necessary. In addition, you could interview them before taking them over to the County Main Jail.

When Kat had gone through their suspect's pockets during a search incident to the arrest, she had found a small baggie of dope. They thought it was Meth, and they would test it at PPC.

After pictures and prints, Kat and Five-O entered the interview room to talk to the suspect while Rex had one of the PPC officers conduct a Valtox test on the dope. Sure enough, it tested positive for Methamphetamine.

Just then, Sergeant Alvarez came into PPC. "There you are," she said to Rex sounding a little flustered.

"Here I am," Rex replied.

"Why didn't you tell me you and Kat were going to make a major arrest today?" she asked.

"What major arrest?" Rex asked innocently. "We just went out and grabbed a suspect in a case we've been working with Postal."

"Well it must be something big because the Lieutenant just got a call from PIO asking for a press release on a major arrest you guys just made. He asked me what was going on and I couldn't tell him because I had no idea. You know how embarrassing that is? It makes me look like I don't know what's going on in my own unit. I've asked you before to keep me informed," ranted Alvarez.

"Sorry Linda, but last night, after you had gone home, we caught a break on Kat's Black Widow case. The grandson of one of the victims called Kat and said he had just talked to the suspect. The suspect wanted to come by his grandfather's room and pick up her mail. We figured if she really did show, it would be the best time to grab her. I ran it by Lieutenant Wong and he told me to write up the operation plan for the stake out and he would have Sergeant Pike go out with us."

"O.K., but I wish you would have kept me in the loop."

"It wasn't that I wasn't trying to keep you in the loop. I let the L.T. know what was happening and he decided there was no reason to call you."

Alvarez pursed her lips and frowned. It was obvious to her that she could not pin anything on Rex much as it would have pleased her. He had informed Lieutenant Wong and the lieutenant had cut her out of the loop.

"So what happened?" asked Alvarez.

"Sergeant Pike, Postal, Terry, and Mitch from Burglary, and Kat and me set up on the house this morning. We had the grandson make the call to the suspect and tell her to come over and pick up her mail. A few minutes later, the suspect showed up and we took her down. Kat's in interviewing her now."

"Why is the press all over it?"

"I don't know. Maybe it's a slow news day."

At that moment, Sergeant Rick Comstock from the Public Information Office walked into PPC.

"Hey Cowboy," he called out to Rex, "thought I'd find you down here. I understand you made some kinda bust that the press is all interested in. I need to get some info for the press release. Hi Linda."

"Sergeant Alvarez was just explaining to me how you were all over my Lieutenant for information on our little bust and how you needed the information ASAP," said Rex.

"Nah," said Comstock looking at Alvarez like she had just grown two heads, "I've just got one call from Channel 2 News so far, but I figured there would be more, so I thought I'd just get ahead of the game and be ready to go. I called Lieutenant Wong to see if he knew anything. He didn't and said you weren't in the office so the next logical step was PPC and here I am. So, what have you got?"

"Well," said Rex, "Kat is the lead detective on this and she's in there," indicating one of the interview rooms, "talking to the suspect now. This is an elder fraud case being jointly investigated by the US Postal Inspectors and the San Jose PD. It involves a young female crankster that has been leading elderly single men on with promises of sex to get their social security checks signed over to her. We call her the Black Widow. In one case, she even got one poor old guy to take out and insurance policy naming her as the beneficiary. We were not sure if she was willing to wait for him to die of natural causes or not. In exemplary agency cooperation, we placed the victim's residence under surveillance this morning and were able to apprehend the suspect."

Sergeant Comstock made some notes on what Rex had just said. "The Black Widow, I like that."

Kat and Five-O came out of the interview room. Kat said, "She's not talking. She says she doesn't know what we're talking about. She said she's just friends with my victim and then she lawyered up." She turned to

Five-O, "Cowboy and I will take her over to the main jail and book her. I'll get with you tomorrow and coordinate on all the follow-up reports we have to get to the D.A. so we can combine all of our cases and make sure you get a copy of her booking sheet." She looked at Alvarez and Comstock, "Hi Linda, hi Rick, what's up."

Comstock replied, "It seems your little arrest has generated the interest of the new media, at least Channel 2 News, and if they go with the story, the rest of the news outlets will be all over it. I want to get a press release together and Channel 2 News wants a stand up. Look Kat, you and Cowboy have more time in front of a camera from when you working sexual assaults then I do in PIO. Would you mind doing the on-camera interview as a favor to me. They always like to see the Detectives rather than the press guy anyway." Sergeant Comstock was right; Kat and Rex had so much time in front of news cameras that they had it down pat. They could give their answers in brief five-second sound bites that were easy to edit.

"As a special favor to you, Sarge, I'd be glad to do it," Kat said with a smile.

Rex turned to a uniformed officer in PPC that he knew and said, "Hey Fred, you've got a female prisoner, would you mind taking ours over with you and booking her in too? We'll do all the paperwork; you just have to deliver her."

Fred said, "Not a problem Cowboy."

Rex turned to Sergeant Comstock, "That takes care of that, Kat can do her stand up any time you say."

Rex then turned to Alvarez, "I guess you can go tell the Lieutenant that everything is taken care of."

Alvarez's lips tightened into a thin line, and Rex could tell she was upset with him. However, there was nothing she could do at this point. She turned around and left PPC.

As she was walking out, Rex looked at Kat and very quietly said, "Don't go away mad Linda, just go away."

Sergeant Comstock was on his cell phone. He stopped his phone conversation and looked at Kat. "Channel 2 News is upstairs now, can you do your interview in front of PAB? That will give them time to edit and get the story on the evening news."

"Sure can," said Kat. "Let me just print off a booking photo for them."

"Good idea," said Comstock. "I might as well print out a bunch for the other news media to go along with the press release. Thanks guys, come by my office after the interview to look over the press release."

Sergeant Comstock left. Rex turned to Kat and said, "Come along my dear, your audience awaits."

Kat looked at Five-O and said, "Come on Five-O, the press is waiting." Kat stuck her tongue out at Rex as she walked out of PPC with Five-O.

Rex gave Fred the Pre-Booking Sheet and Felony Affidavit on their prisoner then turned to Special Agent Cunningham and said, "Come on, let's go on up and watch the press conference. We can be the peanut gallery."

As Rex and Agent Cunningham walked over to the grassy area in front of PAB, he saw Dawn Summers talking to Kat. Her cameraman was setting up his shot, and Five-O was standing beside Kat.

They made a good picture for the camera. Kat still had on her dark blue police raid jacket with her badge hanging from a chain around her neck. At a very trim five-foot six inches tall, with jet-black hair and intelligent dark brown eyes, she was the perfect recruiting poster picture for the new San Jose PD, a young, vibrant, intelligent Latina.

"This morning, in a joint operation involving the San Jose Police Department and the U.S. Postal Inspectors, an arrest was made in an elder fraud abuse case. The police have dubbed the suspect the Black Widow. Detective Sanchez, what can you tell us about this arrest?" said Summers.

As Summers held her mike towards Kat, Kat looked into the camera and said, "This morning we arrested Jennifer Bates on theft and fraud charges stemming from an on-going investigation conducted by the San Jose PD and the U.S. Postal Inspectors. We dubbed her the Black Widow because Bates sought out single elderly men living alone and befriended them. After gaining their confidence and affection, she would induce them to sign their Social Security Checks over to her. In one case, one elderly gentleman even changed his life insurance policy, naming the Black Widow as his new beneficiary. Over the past month, Bates has successfully preyed on six victims that we know of, and we are sure that there are more victims out there. We are asking that if anyone has any information concerning Jennifer Bates they contact me or Detective Johnson at the Financial Crimes Unit."

"In the case of the life insurance policy, what do you think her intentions were?" asked Summers.

"We are not sure at this point if Bates was willing to let nature take its course or if she was going to help things along," replied Kat.

"Thank you Detective. This is Dawn Summers reporting from the San Jose Police Department for KTVU Channel 2 News." Summers waited for her cameraman to signal that they were through filming. Then she turned to Kat. "Thanks, that was great. I think we should be able to get this on tonight. We'll edit in Bates' booking photo and run a scroll with your telephone number."

"Thanks Dawn," said Kat. "With any kind of luck we will get some more people to come forward on this."

"Hi Dawn," said Rex as he stepped forward with Cunningham. "I'd like you to meet Special Agent Cunningham who also helped us on this morning's arrest."

Summers shook hands with Cunningham and handed her a business card. "So nice to meet you. Can I get one of your business cards?"

When Cunningham seemed to hesitate a little Summers said, "It's all right, I'm one of the friendlies, just ask Rex."

"Yep," said Rex, "she is all right for a reporter."

As Summers took Cunningham's business card, she said, "Well, gotta run. We got some editing to do to get this story ready for the evening news. See you all latter."

As Summers and her cameraman walked back to their news van, Kat said to Five-O, "Thanks for standing there with me, I guess we'll see you guys tomorrow morning. You and I can go over all of our reports and make sure this case is ready for the DA's."

Five-O said, "Sounds good to me, coffee and bagels at our shop tomorrow morning then." He and Cunningham walked away.

* * *

Rex and Kat stopped by Central Supply to book in the narcotics evidence from the Bates arrest and then went on up to the PIO looking for Sergeant Comstock. He had already completed the press release. Kat looked it over and said that it looked all right to her. Sergeant Comstock said that there had not been any calls from other media, but he suspected to start getting calls after Channel 2 News aired their story.

Rex and Kat went back to their shop and sat down at their desks to write up their reports. They had only been there about ten minutes when Sergeant Alvarez came over and told them Lieutenant Wong wanted to see both of them in his office.

As they walked into the lieutenant's office, he was seated behind his desk. He motioned towards the two guest chairs and said, "Please, sit down." Sergeant Alvarez had followed them into the Lieutenant's office and stood against the wall.

Lieutenant Wong said, "I understand you two had a pretty busy morning."

Rex looked at Lieutenant Wong and said, "Not really L.T., we got lucky and were able to catch a bad girl Kat's been after."

"Sergeant Alvarez tells me that you failed to keep her informed about your arrest."

"Sir," said Rex, "with all due respect, I did no such thing. If you remember, I briefed you on this last night. Sergeant Alvarez had already left for the day and showed on the board that she would not be in until 1000 today.

Lieutenant Wong got a pained look on his face as he looked over at Sergeant Alvarez. He was getting the impression that he was being used. He was still relatively new as the commander of the unit and had not figured out all of the personnel dynamics. Still, he knew enough to know that he did not want to be in the middle of a fight between one of his sergeants and one of his senior detectives.

"That's right, I did. Well, why didn't you let Sergeant Alvarez know about your arrest when you got to PPC?"

"Sir, Sergeant Pike was our assigned supervisor in the field and he knew we had made the arrest. We came straight back to PPC and were in the middle of processing and questioning our prisoner. I had not been back up to the unit and did not know that Sergeant Alvarez was even in yet. Besides, I figured Sergeant Pike would have told you. Where is he anyway?"

"Uh, Sergeant Pike hasn't come back in yet," replied Lieutenant Wong. "O.K., it's not a big deal. Why is the press all over this arrest? I don't appreciate being called by the PIO and not knowing what's going on."

"The press interest was news to us too," said Rex. "I don't know how Channel 2 News got wind of the arrest."

"Look," said Lieutenant Wong, getting a little heated, "you two are senior Detectives and know the need to keep your superiors informed of what is going on. I expect you guys to set the example."

"Look Lieutenant," said Rex, "we had Sergeant Pike with us when we made the arrest. We brought our prisoner straight back to PPC. Kat was interviewing the suspect, and I was processing the paperwork when Sergeant Alvarez and the PIO caught up with us. What do you want? You want me to personally call you every time we make an arrest?"

"No," said Lieutenant Wong, "but from here on out I expect you to keep your Sergeant informed of all of your activities."

"Whatever you say Lieutenant," sighed Rex. "This is not worth fighting over. I promise we will keep Sergeant Alvarez informed. Is there anything else? Because if there isn't, we have paper to write so we can get our arrest complaint over to the DA's Office on time."

Neither Lieutenant Wong nor Sergeant Alvarez said anything, so Rex stood, opened the office door and walked out.

Kat stood, looked at Sergeant Alvarez, and said, "This is my case. I'm the lead detective. All I was doing was my job, following leads and making an arrest. Do you have a problem with the way I'm doing my job?"

Sergeant Alvarez did not say anything.

"I didn't think so. And another thing, Rex is the best detective in this unit, maybe even on the whole third floor. He makes quality arrests and brings good press to the department. He's also taught younger detectives a lot of things about how to do a top-notch investigation, including me. He works harder than anybody up here and he's the best thing you've got going in this unit." Kat turned and walked out of the Lieutenant's office.

Rex and Kat spent the next couple of hours writing their reports and putting an "in-custody" package together for the DA's Office. They finished about 1600 hours.

"There," said Kat as she finished stamping DA COPY on one set of reports. "Let's walk this over to the DA's Office and drop it in the in-custody basket tonight. That way, they can get to it first thing in the morning and, with any luck, we can walk the complaint over to the court before 1130 tomorrow morning."

"Sounds good to me," said Rex as he watched Kat put a hefty clip on the copies of the reports to hold them all together Kat also clipped her business card to the package and wrote her cell phone number and 'call when ready' on the card.

As they were walking back to their office from the DA's Office, Rex said, "Hey, it's quitting time. You want to go over to the Bistro for a drink? I could sure use one."

Kat said, "Sounds good to me. Let me call John and let him know I'm going to stop off for a drink."

They went back up to their office and signed out for the day. Alvarez was there making sure they were not signing out early, still the ever present clock-watcher. She did not have anything to say to them, and they definitely did not say anything to her.

The Bistro was a newly remodeled bar and restaurant on North First Street. It was owned by a Greek named Georgie, a guy who had been a friend of the police for ages. If Georgie knew you were a cop, then you always ate at half price at his place whether you were in uniform or not. His head bartender, Bruce, was the cousin of retired San Jose PD Captain. Bruce was also known for his ability to make the perfect martini.

Shortly after Georgie had opened the Bistro, it had become the upscale watering hole for detectives and attorneys. Strategically located just a block away from the PD, The Sheriff's Department, the DA's Office, and the Public Defender's Office, it was the perfect place to go after work.

Most days after work you could find a few detectives from both San Jose PD and the Sheriff's Department in the bar along with attorneys from the District Attorney's Office, the Public Defender's Office and even a brave private defense attorney or two. It made for quite a mix during happy hour. No matter what battles had been fought and won or lost in court, the unwritten rule was that everybody played nice at the Bistro. It was not uncommon to see a detective buying a defense attorney a drink or vice versa.

As Rex and Kat walked in, Georgie was at his usual post at the maitre d's station. "Rex, Kat, how good to see you. Are you eating tonight or just drinking?"

"Just dropped by to get a couple of beers after work Georgie," said Rex.

"You know where the bar is, Bruce just came on duty."

Kat and Rex turned right towards the bar. They grabbed a couple of bars stools, and Bruce walked down the bar to greet them.

"Hi guys, what will it be tonight?" asked Bruce.

"I'll have a John Courage and Kat will have a Gordon Biersch," ordered Rex.

After the beers were poured and placed in front of them, they clinked glasses in a toast. Then Kat looked at Rex and said, "You came pretty close to getting in trouble today, you know that."

"Yeah," sighed Rex, "but I can't help myself. Dumb and dumber just set me off."

"Look," said Kat, "I don't mind the little game you're playing with Summers, tipping her off so she can get film of the perp walk and all, I mean I like the perp walk, but maybe you should cool it for a while."

It was not in Rex's nature to cool anything, especially when he was toying with supervisors he did not respect. That was why he and Kat made such good partners. She was always able to keep him in check and from stepping over the line.

"O.K., Kat, I'll tone it down and mind my p's and q's."

"So, how are you going to handle Sergeant Alvarez the clock watcher now that you've been ordered to keep her informed of our every move?" asked Kat.

"I haven't quite figured that out yet," said Rex, "but I'll come up with something."

One of the flat screens in the bar was tuned to Channel 2 News. Kat saw a shot of their Black Widow suspect being led into PPC.

"Hey Bruce," she hollered, "turn that up."

Bruce found the remote and turned up the volume just as Summers was asking her lead in question of Kat. As the bar watched, Kat's interview went on uncut. After the interview, the screen filled with their suspect's picture again and the Financial Crimes Unit's phone number scrolled at the bottom. Summers did a voice over saying that the police were calling the suspect the Black Widow because she preyed on old men. Summers continued with the information that even though an arrest had been made the investigation was still ongoing, and police were asking anyone who had any knowledge of the suspect to call.

When the story ended, Bruce turned down the volume. He then placed two more beers on the bar in front of Kat and Rex.

"Hey Bruce," said Kat, "We didn't order these."

"From the gentleman at the end of the bar," said Bruce.

Kat and Rex looked down the bar and saw Deputy District Attorney Jose Martin raise his glass in their direction. Kat and Rex raised their glasses back in gratitude. As they drank the beers Jose had bought them, they engaged in small talk and took some more congratulations on their arrest with some of the other people in the bar that they knew. It was an enjoyable way to unwind.

Chapter 3

When they got back to their desks the next morning they had several messages on their voice mail and email that needed responses. Even though the two of them worked their cases together, there was no official partnership. All of the cases were assigned individually, and each detective carried a caseload of about twenty to thirty open cases at any given time. There was just too much white-collar crime going on in San Jose and the Department did not allocate that much man power to it.

The entire Financial Crimes Unit consisted of ten detectives, who were suppose to investigate everything from forged and counterfeit checks and credit cards, to real estate fraud, financial elder abuse, identity theft, and any theft of money or goods over $400. With a population of nearly one million people, at least 100 police reports a day came into the Financial Crimes Unit.

The fourth email Rex pulled up was from Porter Jones, the head of security for Costco in the Bay Area. Porter was a recently retired Oakland PD cop and a good guy. Shortly after retiring he had landed his current gig as director of corporate security and loss prevention for Costco. His territory was the San Francisco Bay Area. Rex had met Porter at a monthly California Financial Crimes Investigators Association (CFCIA) meeting a couple of months ago. Porter wanted to know if anything had been done about a series of reports that had been turned in from the San Jose Costco stores concerning large purchases of cigarettes with counterfeit American Express credit cards.

Rex had not heard of any of the cases. He emailed Porter back asking him to provide the case numbers and said that he would look into it. Porter emailed back the case numbers within half an hour, and Rex got busy.

Rex first checked the assigned case database for each detective and found that none of the cases were assigned or being worked. Then he checked the entire case log database, which showed all of the crime reports that had come into the unit. It was tedious because it was not a searchable database. If was just an excel spreadsheet with the reports listed in numerical order by date of report.

Rex found that all of the reports were designated "NM" which meant "No Manpower." The official status of each report was "Not Assigned due to a Lack of Manpower." About 90 per cent of the reports that came into the Financial Crimes Unit daily were closed out this way. The only way they got a second look was if someone asked about them as Porter had in this case. Rex spent the next half hour pulling the reports from the "No Manpower" file cabinets.

After reading through each report, a pattern emerged. The crooks had gone into Costco with a business membership card and made a large purchase of cigarettes. Because the purchase was so large, they had to show a California State License for the re-sale of cigarettes, which they had. They paid for the cigarettes with a counterfeit American Express credit card. Since it took 30 to 120 days for the fraudulent use of the credit card to be discovered, the crooks were long gone with little chance of ever being identified.

"Look at this," Rex said to Kat as he dumped twelve crime reports on her desk. She just looked up at him and waited, knowing he would give her the Readers' Digest version. "All of these reports are related. The victim in every case is Costco and each one involves buying large quantities of cigarettes with counterfeit American Express credit cards. All of them were No Manpowered because that idiot Sergeant of yours was too stupid to see the pattern."

Kat started looking through the crime reports. "Now you know I'm not a real supporter of Sergeant Alvarez, but you have to admit that individually there is nothing in each report to go on. There is almost no suspect info and no physical evidence. The discovery of the crime was so far after the actual crime occurred that all of these reports are just bare bones counter reports that look like they were filed for insurance purposes only."

Rex was still wound up. "That doesn't make any difference. You and I both know that if it is a counterfeit credit card it is going to take at least thirty days to show up. And since it is a compromised credit card that was used, that means there are at least two real victims, Costco and the credit card holder. It's just that she seems to read through each report and forget about it as soon as she has finished reading it. She's not looking for a pattern in anything. She's not an investigator and doesn't look at the reports with an investigator's mind. All she's worried about is case assignment. One case number, one case assigned, one case investigated and closed. No one around here seems to be capable of seeing beyond that. No one seems to be able to grasp the fact that multiple crime reports can be tied to the same crook. This is investigations for crying out loud, we are supposed to investigate."

"So what do you want to do?" asked Kat, but she already knew the answer to that question.

"Let's look into this further," said Rex. "If things pan out we'll take all of these cases and assign them to ourselves. I have a feeling there is something bigger going on here. Like we always say, follow the money."

"O.K.," said Kat, "we'll follow the money."

Rex fired off an email to Porter telling him they were going to look into the cases. He asked Porter to forward all of the information he had. Rex then called the San Jose Office of the Bureau of Alcohol, Tobacco, and Firearms. He and Kat had never worked a cigarette case before, and ATF would be an excellent place to get some information. The ATF agent he talked to said that re-sale of stolen cigarettes that already had the tax stamp on them was a big thing, especially back East. Usually the cigarettes were stolen from a truck or a warehouse. He had not heard of any cases of buying them with counterfeit credit cards.

Finally, he told Rex that ATF could not get involved because as far as they knew no state line had been crossed so no federal crime had been committed. The agent did give him the number of a California Department of Justice Special Agent that might be able to help him.

Rex placed his call to Agent Mills at DOJ in Sacramento. Agent Mills told him that every store, from the corporate giants to the small mom and pops were issued a license by the state to sell cigarettes. Agent Mills said it was common for mom and pop stores to buy in bulk at a discount from stores like Costco. He had not heard of any buys of cigarettes with counterfeit credit cards either. Agent Mills told Rex that if he could send him a copy of the license presented to Costco, he could tell Rex if it was legitimate. Other than that, there was not much more he could do for him because DOJ was swamped and had an even greater manpower shortage than San Jose PD.

With the wheels set in motion, Rex decided he had done all he could to move the ball forward on this case for today and set it aside. He could do nothing more with the investigation until Porter got back to him. "Oh well," Rex thought, "there were plenty of other cases to work on."

He pulled another 'Open Case' folder from his file drawer and went to work on it. Managing such a large caseload meant doing a little bit on each case daily and trying to keep it all straight in your head. This was one of the reasons that the criminal justice system worked at a snail's pace. There just were not enough detectives to go around.

Chapter 4

At 1015 hours, Rex and Kat walked into the US Postal Inspector's offices on the second floor of the Main Post Office on North First Street. The post office was a stately brick and stone building built in the 1930's. It was across North First Street from Saint James Park. The park covered two square city blocks of manicured lawn and stately trees with a statue of President McKinley.

The park also had a tragic history. On the Sunday evening of November 26, 1933, it had been the scene of the last lynching in California. While some 5,000 to 15,000 people looked on, fellow citizens of San Jose had stormed the county jail using building materials from the post office building site. They took two men accused of the kidnap and murder of young Brooke Hart from the jail by force, hauled them across the street to Saint James park and hung them from a Mulberry tree and Elm tree. No one was ever arrested for the lynching.

They stopped outside Five-O's open office door and knocked lightly on the doorframe. Five-O was seated at his desk on the phone. He was dressed in his usual Hawaiian shirt today. He looked up, covered the mouthpiece, and said, "Bagels are in the conference room, I'll be right there."

Rex and Kat went on down the hall to the conference room and found Inspector Cunningham and Supervising Inspector Roger Young, the Special Agent in Charge of the San Jose Office already there. Young waived at them as they entered the room. "Cowboy, Kat, how are you guys? Do what do we owe the pleasure of a visit from two of San Jose's finest?"

Kat replied, "Hi Roger, I'm here to go over yesterdays arrest with Five-O and get our reports ready for the D.A."

"And I'm here," Rex chimed in, "strictly for the free bagels and coffee."

Young got up and started for the door with his coffee and a bagel. "Yeah, I saw the news report on Channel 2 last night, good job. Thanks for sharing the spot light with the Postal Inspectors. Well, I've got some paperwork of my own to get to. Does Five-O know you're here?"

Kat nodded yes.

"O. K. then, I'll see you guys later. Cowboy, I'd say help yourself, but I see you already are."

As Rex was deciding which spread to put on his bagel, in walked Five-O. "Hey Cowboy, only one, I don't want you to get fat."

Rex smiled and replied, "The day I get fatter than you, you little pineapple, is the day I turn in my badge."

Five-O laughed and turned to Kat. "Let me get a cup of coffee and then we can go over our reports in my office. Susan can entertain Cowboy. By the way, did you guys park in the lot out back? I need to give you a placard for your car so the security guard won't tow it." Rex and Kat both laughed.

Rex said, "We don't have a car, we came by light rail."

Five-O got a strange look on his face and said, "You did what?"

Rex said, "We are down to one car for four detectives in our unit, but the sergeant and lieutenant have permanently assigned cars even though they don't have a case load. When it came time for our meeting this morning, there were no cars. Rather than try to beg a car off somebody we just took the train down." Five-O walked out of the conference room just shaking his head.

Rex finished spreading the smear on his bagel and sat down at the conference table with Susan.

"So, if I remember right from yesterday you just transferred from El Paso," Rex said to Susan.

"That's right," she replied. "I not only worked there, but I was born and raised there. Five-O tells me that you and I have a Texas connection, but he wouldn't tell me what it was."

"Well," said Rex, "I got ancestors that came from El Paso. My great-great grandfather was a Texas Ranger."

"Really," Susan said, "how neat. Were you also born in Texas?"

"Nope, great-great granddaddy Johnson left El Paso hunting an outlaw that killed his partner in 1880. He wound up trailing him all the way to Trinidad, Colorado where he killed him. Bat Masterson was the town marshal at the time. According to old family stories, it was a straight up gunfight on Main Street right out of High Noon. He also won a small gold mine in a poker game so he quit the Rangers and stayed in Colorado. He became sort of a frontier private investigator. There are some old family stories about him getting into it out there, but those are best told over a cold beer or a shot of whiskey. You know, like the Toby Keith song, 'Whiskey for My Men and Beer for My Horses.' "

Susan said, "I'd like to hear some of those stories sometime. So what about you, sounds like law enforcement runs in the family."

"Well," Rex slowly drawled in his best impression of a Texas accent, "as my great, great grand pappy once said, "if you have tried and failed at every other job, there's always law enforcement." Rex and Susan chuckled over that little pearl of wisdom.

"So why do they call you Cowboy?"

"I guess its part my Texas Ranger connection and part the way I dress."

Susan looked him up and down. He was six feet two inches tall, and she guessed he weighed in at a remarkably fit two hundred and twenty-five pounds. He was wearing a dark blue western suit, white shirt, and red tie with black cowboy boots. A gold Texas Ranger belt buckle and a white cowboy hat topped off the whole look. The suit did not hide the fact that he was in superb physical shape, with broad shoulders and muscular arms. Then she saw the gold ring on his left hand and thought, it was a shame how all the good ones always seemed to be taken already.

"Well, you definitely look the part. So is this all for show or do you really cowboy?"

Rex smiled and hooked his thumbs in his belt, "As a matter of fact little lady, I do know my way around a horse. I've got four of my own and on weekends I even do a little jack pot team penning. Do you ride?"

"Yes, but it's been a while."

"Well then, we'll have to have you down to our little ranch. The wife and I can take you out on a trail ride. I find trail riding a great way to reduce the stress of the job."

"That sounds like fun. You're on."

"He's on for what?" asked Five-O as he and Kat walked back into the conference room.

"Rex just invited me to go horseback riding with him and his wife."

"Yeah?" said Five-O. "He tried to get me on a horse once but I told him I wouldn't even get on a hobby horse as a kid."

"Well," said Rex, "we'd better be getting back to our office."

"Before you go I have another question for you," said Susan. "That lapel pin you're wearing, the letters K. M. A., what does that mean?"

Kat stifled a laugh as Rex looked at Susan in his most serious manner. "That Inspector Cunningham is part of a long standing San Jose PD tradition. You see, when you have been on the force long enough to be eligible to retire you are awarded this pin. It signifies that you have put in your time, and you can now retire any day you want. It lets everybody know that if things don't work out you could leave today without any regrets."

"But what do the letters stand for?" asked Susan.

"Kiss My Ass."

Chapter 5

Rex was relaxing on the back patio of his ranch home. It was a warm evening in Hollister. Frank Sinatra was playing on the XM Radio, and his lovely wife had just walked out onto the patio with two martini glasses and a shaker. It was Sunday evening at the Johnson's and that meant steak and martini night.

"Ah," said Rex looking at his wife with a smile. "Here comes my favorite bartender."

"You know I spoil you way too much," said Carmella with a twinkle in her eye. She put the glasses on the table and poured. "There you are sir, the perfect Chairman of the Board."

Rex took a sip. "Ah yes, the martini named after Frank Sinatra himself. Oh, that is good. What goes into these again?"

"One part Grey Goose and one part Bombay Sapphire. Mr. Vermouth just gives a wave as you pass by. Shaken, not stirred."

"That is pure rocket fuel, but it goes down so smooth."

Rex had already selected a CAO Brazilia cigar to go with his martini. After he had it lighted, he leaned back in his chair and said, "This is the life."

"So how are things going at work honey?" asked Carmella. "You looked a little tense this last week.

"Oh, you know. It's the same old crap. That idiot sergeant we've got just drives me up the wall. We opened a new case this week that she had totally missed when she was reviewing incoming reports. Kat says I shouldn't get so worked up over it and not let her get to me."

"Kat is right."

"Yeah, I know she is. It's just that I can't help myself. Kat and I do a really good job. We care about what happens. And then we end up having to work for some idiot that has not a clue about what's going on. Worse yet, she acts like she does. I mean if she would just stay out of our way and let us do our job that would be fine. No. She has to act like she knows what she's doing and try and tell us how to do our job," said Rex.

"So why don't you just do your job and ignore her as much as possible?"

"That's what I try to do. But some days I can't help myself. She does something that just sets me off."

"Well, don't do something stupid yourself that is going to get you in trouble," said Carmella.

"Don't worry my sweet, Kat makes sure that I don't."

"Dinner should be ready by the time you finish you cigar and martini."

Monday at the office always seemed easier to handle after a Sunday steak and martini night. Rex was stuck at his desk all of Monday morning because he had house mouse duty. One detective from the unit had to be in the office at all times during business hours to handle any official calls that came in. Some days it was quiet, and other days you ran around like a mouse chasing after the cheese in a maze. Porter Goss, director of Costco security, called Rex back late Monday morning just as Rex was finishing his half-day tour as house mouse.

"Hey Cowboy," said Porter over the phone, "How's it hanging?"

"Not bad my friend," Rex replied.

"Hey, I've got just about everything you want, so how's about I come down to San Jose and take you and Kat out to lunch."

"Porter, you don't owe us lunch."

"Look, that's what I've got an expense account for. Don't give me any arguments. If I don't use it they are liable to take it away from me."

"O.K., you win. When and where?"

"How about the Fish Market in Santa Clara tomorrow, say 1130?"

"You're on; I'll let Kat know when she gets back."

When Rex got in the next morning, Kat was already at her desk. She looked up as Rex walked in and said, "I've already snagged us a car. If you're ready we can go get some breakfast and then I've got an appointment with a victim in South San Jose."

"Sounds good," said Rex, "Give me a minute to check my emails and then I'll sign us out on the board. Where to for breakfast?"

"I told Mitch we'd meet him over at Bill's Cafe," Kat said.

The meeting with the victim in South San Jose took longer than expected. The case involved an office manager for a construction company that had been ripping off the company for years. Since she was the only one keeping the company books and a friend of the owner, who he trusted like a daughter, it was hard establishing the paper trail. The owner of the company knew nothing about bookkeeping and had not paid any attention to anything the suspect had been doing. His books were a mess and Kat and Rex had to play forensic accountants to try to find enough evidence to get an arrest warrant.

As they were getting into their car Kat said, "We don't have enough time to go back by the office and change our sign out time. And if we don't you know the clock watcher will get upset and then your Sergeant will be calling you to see where you are."

Rex looked over at Kat, "How come she's 'my Sergeant?' She's your Sergeant too you know. I'll just call Sally or whoever's up front and have one of them change the board."

"You gonna have them tell your Sergeant our new destination too?" Kat asked with a wry smile. "You know that we are not suppose to leave the city without letting your Sergeant know, and you are also under direct orders to keep her updated on your every move."

Rex smiled back with an impish grin, "I told you I would come up with a solution for that, and I have." Rex pulled his cell phone off his belt and waived it at her. "My new Blackberry Storm Smart Phone. Watch and learn. What I am going to do is email your Sergeant from my new phone. I am going to inform her that 'unless otherwise directed' we will be meeting a confidential source in Santa Clara. Knowing her, she has probably already left the office for lunch herself, so she won't even get this email for a couple of hours. But that is not my problem. I have followed orders. I have not only informed her, but I have informed her in writing via a date and time stamped email so there can be no questions as to when she was updated. So shut up and drive, I'm hungry."

When they walked into the Fish Market, Porter was waiting for them. They were just in front of the lunch crowd, so they got a table without waiting.

After lunch, Porter pulled a fat folder out of his briefcase and spread it on the table. "The state requires us to photocopy the cigarette sales license whenever a large purchase is made, so I've got copies of all of those. Also, since you have to swipe your Costco Membership Card, I've got printouts of the account info on each card. I've also got some surveillance pictures of the latest transactions, but the photos aren't that great. No photos of any of the earlier buys because we don't keep anything past thirty days. And I've got copies of the fraud alert notice the banks sent us telling us that the cards were compromised." This was what was nice about working with a corporate security guy who was a retired cop. He knew what you needed and got it all put together in a neat little package.

Porter continued, "I also have a print out of the date, time, and store of each hit. This has not only been happening in San Jose, but they have hit the stores in Mt View, Sunnyvale, Santa Clara, Gilroy, and Fremont. We've made police reports to all of these agencies. The case numbers for the other agencies are on the print out."

"Well," Rex said, "Fremont is out because that's not in Santa Clara County, but the rest are so we can check with the other agencies and see if they have anything going on. I smell a task force coming on."

"All right Cowboy," said Kat, "don't get too carried away. You know how the department hates the term 'task force.' The powers above are not going to like us opening up a multi-jurisdictional case; it's too complicated for their simple little minds."

Rex got that look in his eye that meant he was already figuring how to con their superiors, and get the investigation going without them actually knowing what was happening. "Well, we have worked around the administration before with our 'informal' task forces. No reason we can't do that again. Our Sergeant isn't going to know or understand what we are doing and the Lieutenant is afraid to come out from behind his desk. He hasn't understood what we are doing from the day he took command of the unit. We don't put all of the case numbers on our active case log, just one each. And then we make sure we keep the deaf, dumb and blind in the dark until we get our arrest warrants."

Kat looked at Rex a minute. "You're evil and that's why I like working with you. Let's do it."

Back in the office, Rex made calls to the other police agencies that Costco had made reports to, while Kat called her contact at American Express. The guy was a former Secret Service Agent who she had worked with before. He would be able to give her all the information on the compromised cards, where they were compromised, the name of the cardholder and their contact information. Then she would have to call each cardholder to verify the circumstances of how their cards had been compromised. Besides having their American Express card compromised, they might be the victim of additional identity theft, but had not known or not reported it. It took them three more days of playing phone tag with everybody to get all the information they needed together.

Including the twelve San Jose PD crime reports there were six reports in the other cities. That made it eighteen times these crooks had pulled off their scam and gotten away with about $475,000 worth of cigarettes. Of all the police agencies, only Santa Clara PD had an open investigation going. The Santa Clara Costco had been hit twice. None of the other agencies had even started anything.

Since the monthly Santa Clara County Fraud Investigators' meeting was coming up next Wednesday, Rex suggested to each detective he talked to that, they come to the meeting, and after the main meeting they could all get together and discuss the cigarette case. They all said they would be there.

As luck would have it, the meeting was being hosted by Santa Clara PD. Sergeant Sam Capalini was the detective handling their cigarette case. He had been a cop longer than Rex and had been investigating financial crimes for years. He was a real good cop and both Rex and Kat liked working with him. The three of them had worked on several cases in the past that had crossed city lines. Sergeant Capalini was not the sort of guy that was out to make a name for himself. He already had a well-established reputation. His primary goal was to see the crook went to jail. He did not care who took credit for it.

Kat had excellent luck with her phone calls too. She had gotten hold of each of the credit card holders in the twelve San Jose cases. Because of the low-dollar amount charged on the compromised cards, American Express had not made any police reports. If the amount of fraud was not over $10,000.00 per card, the company usually did not report it, but just wrote it off and issued a new card.

Kat had gotten her contact at American Express to make the theft reports of the compromised cards and theft of money with American Express being the victim, so it bolstered the case. Even if American Express had filed reports, they would have been "No Manpowered," and stuffed in the non-worker file because there had been nothing there to indicate they were related to the Costco caper and there was no suspect information.

This was how it usually went. The cases were not worked until the bank fraud investigator put something together that showed a pattern or pointed to a suspect and brought the new information to the PD. Not the best way to do business, but it worked, eventually.

Fortunately, almost all of the local, state, and federal law enforcement agencies and all of the bank fraud investigators, credit card company investigators and corporate fraud investigators were members of the California Financial Crimes Investigators Association (CFCIA). This was a statewide information sharing organization that brought all of the law enforcement and private fraud investigators together in a regional monthly meeting where they could share information and the cases they were working. It was also a chance to get together over a decent lunch.

Through CFCIA and some cases they had worked on together, Kat had gotten to know the American Express Investigator pretty well. Once she had pulled the police reports for San Jose, she had called Larry White at American Express. Larry had been able to run a computer search program that showed that all twelve of the credit cards in all the Costco cases had been compromised at high-end restaurants in Los Gatos, San Jose, and Santa Clara. Larry had emailed all the information to Kat.

Rex call Five-O and ran down the Costco leads and his theory that it involved Asian Organized Crime. Five-O agreed and offered the services of the Postal Inspectors.

"Through one of my confidential informants I have learned that someone has turned the Loving Cup Coffee House at Capital Expressway and King Road into a sort of hiring hall. The word is, if you go hang out there, you might get tapped to pass some counterfeit checks. I'm gonna talk to my tech people about putting up a couple of light pole surveillance camera so we can see who is coming and going. Who knows, we might get lucky and find a tie-in with your case."

"Gotta love it," said Rex. "I'll see you at the county meeting tomorrow and you can fill us in."

Chapter 6

At 0630 hours, Wednesday morning, Rex parked his pickup truck in the employee parking lot across the street from the PD. Both he and Kat liked getting into work early. For one thing, coming in this early meant you were in front of the morning commute, and generally got to leave before the evening commute was at its worst. Since they worked ten hours days, anything you could do to avoid the morning or evening freeway parking lots were worth it. People did not believe it, but the San Jose freeways were more congested than Los Angeles.

Rex walked up the outside stairs to the third floor. He always used the stairs, taking his exercise wherever he could get it.

The Police Administration Building, simply known for its initials as P. A. B., was a dreary, unpainted, cement building that looked more like a bunker than an office building. The third floor was the Detective Bureau. Rex used his key to open the South door. While not a modern building, some upgrades had been made over the years. Even so, it was still like working on the set of "Barney Miller."

Rex walked down the hallway past the Robbery and Intelligence/Vice Units. Next was the office of the Chief of Detectives. Across the hall from the Chief of D's was Homicide. Their motto was 'our day begins when your day ends.' Then there were the framed photographs of the eleven San Jose PD officers who had been killed in the line of duty during the 160-year history of the department. Seven of those officers had died since Rex had joined the department and he knew all seven.

You could not pass by those framed photos without stopping to reflect on the ultimate sacrifice that these eleven men had made to their community. Yes, eleven men. Thank God, they had not lost a female officer yet. The police department was like a family, sometimes a highly dysfunctional family, but a family nonetheless. You could have your squabbles with each other, but you were all brother and sister officers whose blood ran blue.

Rex always said a silent prayer of thanks that he was still in one piece after all these years as he passed by. "There but for the grace of God," thought Rex. He remembered that fateful winter night many, many years ago.

He had been with San Jose for a couple of years and was working swing shift patrol in District Tom. Just the day before a Sheriff's Deputy had been killed responding to a disturbance call in the Burbank area. He had gotten his gun taken away from him by the suspect. The suspect had then shot the Deputy in the head, killing him.

Rex had been dispatched to a home where the parents were having trouble with their 24 year old live at home son. As usual for San Jose, almost all of the patrol cars were one-man cars. Dispatch had assigned a fill unit, but he was coming from some distance.

When Rex arrived at the residence, the parents informed him that their son was mentally ill and had quit taking his medications. He had not been violent towards them this evening, but he had been violent in the past. Their son was down in his basement bedroom. He had been there ever since last night and would not come out. They were concerned for his safety and wanted an officer to talk to him.

This type of call was so typical of what a police officer responded to most. They were not calls of crimes in progress, but rather social service calls. A family was in crisis. They had a problem they did not know how to deal with. They wanted someone to make it all better. That someone was the police. Twenty-four hours a day, seven days a week, 365 days a year, the police were the only ones who still made house calls.

Rex headed downstairs to talk to the son and see what was going on. As he headed into the basement, the only light came from the one light bulb over the stairs, the rest of the basement was dark. He called out the son's name but got no response. Rex identified himself as a police officer and said that he just wanted to talk to him and still got no response. As he moved his flashlight around the basement, he saw an unmade bed and a nightstand lamp lying on the floor. The door to what he thought was the bathroom was closed.

As Rex moved further into the room to get a better view, there was a sudden movement to his left. Out of the corner of his eye, he caught the figure of a man charging at him with a raised arm. Rex turned and swung his left hand up, which was holding his Stream Light SL 20 metal flashlight. The flashlight struck flesh and there was a yelp of pain. Rex's flashlight was knocked out of his hand, and a hammer fell out of the suspect's right hand.

The suspect kept coming. He crashed into Rex and they went down on the floor in a heap. Rex felt the wind go out of him, but he could not give up. Somewhere in the back of his mind, he heard his old training officer telling him, "Remember, there is always one gun at every call, the one you bring."

They struggled on the floor, fighting desperately. Rex was scrambling trying to get behind the suspect so he could put a carotid restraint hold on him and end the fight quickly by putting him to sleep. The suspect was a big man and he was very strong.

Then Rex felt a tug at his holstered gun. He knew what was happening, the suspect was trying to get Rex's gun out of his holster. Immediately Rex clamped his right hand over the suspect's left hand and tried to get a finger or a thumb, so he could peel the hand away from his gun. The suspect now had his hand wrapped around the pistol grip and was tugging at Rex's gun. All Rex could do was pin that hand against his side.

The suspect had his right arm wrapped around Rex's back and now he started punching Rex in the back of the head with his fist. Each blow made Rex see stars. Rex was fighting for his life now because he knew that if he ever let this guy get hold of his gun he would kill him.

Rex reached up with his left hand, grabbed a fist full of the suspect's hair, and pulled with all his might. The suspect howled and quit hitting him. They rolled around on the floor with the suspect still jerking at his gun trying to get it out of the holster. Rex got his left arm between him and the suspect and pushed. This opened up enough space to get his left shoulder into the suspect's chest.

Rex now had both hands on the suspect left hand as he was still trying to jerk Rex's weapon out of the holster. Rex was on top of the suspect now. He managed to lift himself up a little and pile-drive his left shoulder into the suspect's chest slamming him to the floor. The air went out of the suspect along with a little of the fight, but he still held on the Rex's weapon trying to get it out of the holster. Rex raised up a little again and again was able to slam his shoulder into the suspect's chest as he drove him into the floor.

The suspect loosened his grip a little and Rex was able to get hold of his thumb. Rex started pulling the thumb back ready to break it. The suspect howled in pain and pulled away from Rex.

They both came to their feet. They circled each other in the small room. Rex's left hand slipped down to grab his nightstick. It was not there, it must have come out of the baton ring when they were rolling around on the floor. Rex thought that it was a good thing he had boxed some in the army. That Koga arrest and control stuff they taught was all right if you could take the suspect by surprise, but it was not worth a crap in a toe-to-toe fistfight. That is exactly what this was going to be.

The suspect gave out a sound that was something between a growl and a shriek; it sounded more animal than human, and charged Rex. Rex stepped in and hooked a left to the mouth that smeared it to bloody shreds against the suspect's teeth. The suspect swung his right fist and Rex ducked, catching it over his left eye instead of on the chin. The blow cut to the bone and blood started to run down the left side of Rex's face and into his left eye.

Shoving the suspect away, Rex started to swing again, but the suspect brought up a knee aimed at Rex's groin. Rex turned to avoid the knee, but he turned too far. The suspect got behind him and threw an arm around his neck. Grabbing the suspect's hand and elbow, Rex dropped to one knee and threw the suspect over his shoulder.

The suspect bounced back up, he must be operating on pure adrenaline now. Rex stabbed a left into his face breaking his nose and showering both of them with blood. Rex followed through with a belt in the stomach that took the wind out of the suspect. As the suspect stumbled forward, Rex grabbed a handful of hair and jerked the suspect's head down to meet his upcoming knee.

Just then, Rex's fill unit came thundering down the stairs. Rex yelled for him to grab an arm. The fill officer grabbed the suspect's left arm by the wrist twisting up and forward forcing the suspect down to the floor on his face. Rex grabbed the right arm at the wrist and twisted it down and into the suspect's back as he also put his knee into the suspect's back. All the fight had gone out of the suspect, and he just lay there. Rex pulled his handcuffs from the cuff case on his duty belt and put the cuffs on him.

"Yes," Rex thought, "there but for the grace of God. I could have died in that basement that night, and my picture could be up on that wall."

Policing a big city, especially working patrol, was a rough and dangerous business. Rex had spent many years on the mean streets of San Jose learning how to survive. It was calls such as this one that had made him the tough, hard nosed cop who was not afraid to get his hands dirty.

When Rex joined the San Jose Police Department, it was a very aggressive force. Rookies learned quickly that they were expected to handle violent situations quickly and by themselves. He remembered a Patrol Lieutenant had once told them at a briefing that if it looked like someone was going to take them on he expected his officers to hit them first, hit them hard, and hit them continuously until they went down. If somebody wanted to fight the police, he would be booked into jail via the hospital.

That night was not the only night he had almost been killed doing his job. That sort of thing stayed with you. If you were going to do your job, you had to put that out of your mind and not be afraid to jump into the middle of it with anyone out there on the streets that challenged you.

Opposite the pictures, a large framed American flag hung on the wall. Here and there on the hallway walls were some historical pictures of the department and the men and women who had served before.

As Rex got to the North end of the hallway it branched left and right in a T intersection. To the left were the Gang Unit, Video Unit, and Briefing Room 314. To the right was the Sexual Assaults Unit and Juvenile/Missing Persons. Straight ahead were the Court Liaison Unit and the Fraud/Burglary Unit, Rex's current home.

As he walked into the Fraud/Burglary Unit, there was a high counter on his right behind which the three civilian support staff sat. Almost straight ahead were Kat's and Rex's desks. A few years back the Department had finally bought modular partitions and desks.

Unlike the private sector though, they were trying to cram too many people into the space they had. The only ones that got real cubicles were the sergeants. The lieutenants got offices with real walls and a door. The only high partition walls were around the perimeter of the unit to mark off its territory. All the other desks were put in facing each other in islands of four with only a short wall just a little bit higher than the desktop separating them. The desks were placed so close to each other that in the aisles between the desks, the detectives sitting back to back could not both push their chairs out at the same time without running into each other.

Chapter 7

The Fraud/Burglary Unit was one big open bay with the desks for sixteen Detectives, three Civilians, three Sergeants, one Lieutenant, and various other file cabinets and work stations. All of which was crammed into an area that OSHA said only half that number of people should be working in.

Yep, gone were the old gun metal grey government surplus desks and the old 5-drawer file cabinets. Computers had replaced the typewriters and the phones upgraded, but it still had the look and feel of the set from that old TV cop show, "Barney Miller." The joke was that here they were in the "Heart of Silicon Valley" in the 21st century, and the police department had advanced all the way to the 1980's.

Kat was not in yet, so Rex put his briefcase down at his desk. The first thing he did was check his voice mail for messages. There was one from the Gilroy PD detective saying he was not sure if he was going to be able to make the meeting. Rex then fired up his computer and checked his email. There was nothing except a couple of personal emails that they were not supposed to get, but everybody did.

Kat walked into the office. "Did you get us a car yet?"

"No," said Rex, "I just got in a little ahead of you, the Clock Watcher is in her cube, and I just don't want to deal with her this morning. You get the car keys."

Kat made a face and said, "Oh, O.K."

Each unit had its own cars assigned. The problem was there were not enough cars for everybody. There should have been at least one car for every two detectives, but there were not even enough cars for one for every four detectives. The city was not buying unmarked cars anymore because they could not understand why the detectives ever had to leave the building. After all, none of the employees in City Hall had to leave their desks once they got to work. When a car broke down or had to go in for routine maintenance you did not get a replacement, you had to make do without.

To try to be fair about the cars, they were not assigned to individual detectives. The sergeants kept the car keys in their cubes and you had to go in and ask for the keys. To Rex, this always felt like he was a grown man being treated like a teenager having to beg to take the family car out.

He hated getting the keys to a car when Sergeant Alvarez was in her cube. It always turned into a game of twenty questions about where was he going, how long would he be gone, and did he put the correct return time up on the board. It was their Sergeant's feeble attempt at showing she was the boss and in charge. She did not really know how to investigate a case or what it was the Kat and Rex did. She did know how to watch the clock to make sure you got to work on time and did not leave early and she had the power of issuing out cars.

Kat came back with the car keys. She waved them at Rex and said, "Sign us out and let's go get breakfast."

They took the elevator down to the basement floor and walked out the back door to the West parking lot where the fleet of detective cars was parked. They found their car; a 2001 tan Chevy Impala parked in the area reserved for the Financial Crimes and Burglary Units cars.

While Rex got in on the passenger side, Kat slipped into the driver's seat. When Kat turned over the ignition key New Age rock blared out of the radio speakers. Kat and Rex reached for the volume at the same time.

"I guess some of the kids must have used the car last," said Kat.

By kids, she meant some of the young detectives in the unit. Rex just smiled and tuned the radio to KSFO Hot Talk 560. He and Kat liked listening to conservative talk radio as they drove around town. Brian Sussman was on now with Officer Vic.

Rex liked Officer Vic's guitar picking and the little ditties he wrote and played on the air about whatever the current political issue or target was. Later in the day, they would catch parts of Rush Limbaugh, Mark Levin or Sean Hannity as they drove around town.

When talk radio got too much and they found themselves yelling at the radio about some stupid politician, they went back to country music. Rex had introduced Kat to country music a few years ago, and she liked what she called the "lyin', cheatin', drinkin' songs."

Twenty minutes later, they were sitting down with Mitch and Terry from the Burglary Unit at Bill's Cafe on The Alameda. Bill's was a long time San Jose restaurant that had a mixed clientele of defense attorneys, contractors, retired people, and cops. As Rex looked around the room, he could see San Jose cops at different tables from three other units. The food was good, the waitresses friendly and they still gave the cops "h. p." or half price off on their meals. Breakfast was also a time to catch up on Unit and Department gossip. Mitch was also a police union representative, so it was a good time to talk to him about the latest union issues. Sometimes they would even discuss a case.

After everybody had ordered breakfast, Rex turned to Mitch and asked, "So Mitch, how are contract negotiations going?"

"This is going to be a really rough year."

"What do you mean?" asked Kat.

"Well," said Mitch, "as you well know, every time we start contract negotiations the city claims it is broke and can't afford to give us a raise."

"Yeah," quipped Rex, "and after we sign the contract they find sixty million dollars in a shoe box under the mayor's bed that they didn't know they had."

"Exactly. That's why the union always pays for a forensic accountant to go over the city's books, so we can find out where they are hiding the money."

"So what's different this year?" asked Rex.

"The economy for one thing," said Mitch. "This is the year of making the public employee unions public enemy number one. The city conveniently forgets about the millions of dollars they lost in a bond debacle. Or the hundreds of millions of dollars they spent building themselves that new taj mahall of a city hall. How about all the money spent on building a new police sub-station that can't be opened because the city says it can't afford to hire enough officers to staff it.?

"No, the city would rather jeopardize the safety of every citizen and officer and blame it all on the greedy police and firefighters who are demanding too much money for their retirements."

Rex shook his head. "Have you ever known a politician to apologize or take the blame for a mistake? No, of course not. As far as they are concerned, they don't make mistakes. And what about this crock we always hear from the city about every department must share the pain? That we have to make equal cuts across the board? Haven't they ever heard of prioritizing?"

"That," replied Mitch, "is just so much political speak for don't cut my special program. If they had any balls, which they don't, they'd provide for public safety first and then fix the pot holes. If there was any money left over, then they could spend it on their pet welfare projects."

After breakfast, Rex and Kat made a couple of stops at some banks, so they could interview witnesses and collect evidence on some of the other cases they were working.

At 1000 hours, Kat parked their Impala in the visitor parking lot of the Santa Clara Police Department. This was the new Santa Clara Police Department building on El Camino Real, just across the street from Santa Clara University. The building itself was in that modern California Mission architect style. It was a cool looking building. It was a good location because there was a Starbucks and a Bagel Shop just on the other side of the parking lot. They would not need either today as coffee and goodies were always provided at these meetings by the hosting agency.

As they walked into the lobby, they showed their badges to the desk officer and told him they were there for the county fraud meeting. He asked if they knew where the conference room was which they told them they did, and he buzzed them through the security door.

At the conference room, they saw Five-O talking with Sergeant Sam Capalini by the coffee pot. There were about fifteen other people already in the room.

As Rex and Kat walked over to Five-O and Sam, they were intercepted by Special Agent Barbara Harris of the FBI. "Detective Johnson, Detective Sanchez," she said, "I was wondering if you two had gotten anywhere on that counterfeit credit card case involving Asian Organized Crime? If you had any new information, it would be nice if you could share it with the Bureau."

In fact, they had made some headway and had a new address of a coffee house where some of the Vietnamese players were meeting. But sharing information with the Bureau was always a one-way street. They wanted information from the locals, but they never wanted to give the locals any information. Then, when the locals had solved the case, the Bureau would call a press conference and take all the credit for solving the case and making the arrests. If the locals were lucky, they got to stand in front of the press cameras behind the FBI.

Rex looked Special Agent Harris up and down and coyly said, "Why no, Special Agent Harris, we seem to have hit a dead end. How about you? Has the Bureau come up with anything?"

Special Agent Harris replied in typical FBI speak, "We are continuing to investigate and don't have anything we can share at this time."

As Rex and Kat walked away Kat said to Rex under her breath, "That's why I can't stand the FBI."

As Rex poured himself a cup of coffee, Five-O asked him, "What did the FBI want?"

While reaching for a cheese Danish Rex said, "The Furniture and Bedding Inspector wanted to know if we had made any progress on our Asian Organized Crime case. You know, the one we're working with you. It would appear that your fellow Fed hasn't come up with anything and is trying to steal any info us poor, unwashed, uneducated local cops might have."

"What did you tell her?"

"That we had hit a dead end," Rex replied.

"Sweet. You're learning how to play this game. By the way, our tech unit is installing pole cameras at the Loving Cup Coffee House today. We should start receiving pictures today. My tech guys will run them through a facial recognitions software program that they have tied into the San Jose PD Photo Data Base and the DOJ Photo Data Base."

"That's why I like working with you. You have all the fun toys, and you share."

Sergeant Capalini called for everyone to take their seats. After Sergeant Capalini made the usual introductory comments, they went around the room so that those detectives and bank investigators present could share information on their current investigations and see if anyone else had information about the case or their suspects.

In the world of financial crime, the suspects did not believe in minor things like city or county limits. They traveled the Bay Area and beyond in the pursuit of their crimes and cases often overlapped jurisdictions. They were also repeat offenders, and a detective could be working a new case and find out that a detective in another city had worked the same suspect, doing the same crime a couple of years ago.

These cases were not like most assaults or even homicides where you had one assault or murder and you chased that suspect down. These were complex and sophisticated frauds. These were the bright criminals. Long gone were the days of the simple $200.00 forged check. These guys were the local "Bernie Madoffs." They were con artists and counterfeiters. These guys were so good that they could lie to a bank manager and make him believe they were telling the truth. They did not use a gun; or fear and intimidation, they used their brains. Their whole purpose was to take other peoples' money and not get caught. They were quite good at it, and they took millions of dollars from people and banks every year in the Bay Area.

Since Asian Organized Crime was moving up from Westminster, they were getting even better and harder to catch. They were into all kinds of financial crime, counterfeiting credit cards and business checks, identity theft and stealing from the elderly. They were well organized and improving their scams faster than the police could keep up with them.

That was why these county meetings and the CFCIA meetings were so important. It was the best way of sharing information and collaborating on investigations. Santa Clara County was not the only county in the Bay

Area that held these monthly meetings. All of the counties did, and Rex and Kat had been to their share of meetings in other counties to make presentations and look for help in some of their past cases.

A few of the investigators attending had some new crimes to share with the group. There was another rash of counterfeit checks hitting the check cashing stores in Mt View and Sunnyvale. The detectives had some surveillance photos and handed them out. The Russian Mob was suspected of buying high-end lap top computers with counterfeit credit cards at the Fry's Electronics store in Campbell. Another family of gypsies was moving through the area doing a home repair scam. And of course, Identity Theft reports were up in all of the jurisdictions. Everybody shared and discussed cases except for the FBI, who as usual asked for information but gave none in return.

Chapter 8

After the county meeting ended, Rex, Kat, Five-O, Sergeant Capalini and the detectives from Mt View, Sunnyvale and Gilroy sat down to go over the Costco case.

"Well, I'm glad everybody could make it," said Rex. "Look, I know that 'task force' is a dirty word among most Chiefs of Police so let's just call this an informal working group."

There was a chuckle from everybody as Rex took a sip of coffee.

"Look, it's early in this investigation and we don't have any solid leads, but we do have some information to share with you. The bad guys enter Costco right after it opens for the regular members at 1100 hours. This is when the store is the busiest. There are usually two of them. They contact a floor manager and let them know that they want to buy several cases of cigarettes, usually between ten and twenty cases. The manager asks for a copy of their state cigarette license and makes a copy of it. Then they go to a register, and the Costco membership card is swiped and the purchase is rung up. They pay for it with an American Express credit card. The embossed name on the credit card matches the name on the Costco membership card and the owner name on the state license. Everything looks legit and the card transaction goes through without a hitch, so they load up a cart and are out of the store in less than thirty minutes." Rex nodded to Kat.

Kat stood up and continued the briefing. "All of the Amex cards were compromised accounts. According to Amex the points of compromise are high end restaurants in San Jose, Santa Clara, Los Gatos, and Saratoga. We believe that they are getting the cardholders info by use of a skimmer. For those of you that are not familiar with these devices, they are a card reader about the size of a small cell phone, and this is what they look like."

Kat held up a small black box with a slot to slide a credit card through running down one side. She handed the skimmer to the nearest detective to pass around the room.

"When the waiter or waitress takes the credit card from the customer to the register to ring up the sale, they swipe the card twice. The first time is to pay for the meal, the second is through the skimmer. The skimmer captures all of the information on the mag stripe on the card. The latest skimmers can hold the information for up to 50 cards.

"Later, the skimmer is plugged into a lap top, and the information is downloaded onto the computer. Another device is then plugged into the computer that will transfer all of the information on to the mag strip of a counterfeit card. You have a new counterfeit credit card ready to go in minutes. It is usually our pals in Asian Organized Crime that provide the counterfeit cards with the blank mag stripes. These cards look exactly like the real thing right down to the hologram. The counterfeit card is embossed with the name that matches whatever ID the passer is using so that even if the store clerk asks for ID like they are supposed to do, the names match."

Rex took back over. "I talked with the ATF and found out that this sort of thing is really big back East. Only back there the cigarettes usually 'fall off the back of a truck.' Apparently, there is real money to be made in the resale of cigarettes that already have the tax stamp on them, especially if you are buying them with other people's money in the first place. What these guys are probably doing is selling the cigarettes they get from Costco to local mom and pop stop and robs at a big discount. Even if they sell them for half off that still gives them a profit of about $450,000.00, for just the cases we know about in Santa Clara County.

"Can the ATF help us out on this?" asked one of the other detectives.

"The ATF can't help out with anything other than general information because right now no state lines have been crossed so it is a local problem and not a federal one. I also talked to a guy from DOJ whose job it is to license all the stores that sell cigarettes in California. He had me fax him a copy of the resale license that Costco had recovered and told me that it was legitimate. The license was issued to a Korean mom and pop store in Westminster but the name and address of the store on the license was bogus. The Westminster connection and the quality of the counterfeit credit cards leads me to believe that we might be looking at another con cooked up by our old friends in Asian Organized Crime."

There was a murmur of agreement that went through the assembled detectives.

"Now I know what you are going to say, 'but my Chief says there is no organized crime in our city.' At least that is what our chief says. The next thing he would tell me is if it is Asian Organized Crime then I should turn the case over to the FBI Asian Organized Crime Task Force. See what I mean about 'task force' being a dirty word? Since we haven't definitely established said connection to Asian Organized Crime, it is still a local problem, and I think we should run with it.

"What I propose is that Kat and I take the lead in this and work with you to make one case to take to the DA. Since these crimes all appear to be the work of the same group of people at this time, there is no sense in each of us stepping all over ourselves running down the same leads and talking to the same people. Again, I'm not talking about a 'task force,' I'm just saying it would make sense to work together on an informal basis and share information and leads and then put together one big case to take to the DA. Questions? Comments?"

The Gilroy Detective spoke up. "Look, as you guys know. Gilroy is not big enough to specialize like San Jose. We just break it down into crimes against persons and property crimes. I'm working all the property crimes; burglary, theft, fraud; with one other detective. Financial crimes are not really my thing, and I've got too big a case load to learn about cigarette fraud. So, if you guys want to run with it, that's fine with me. Besides, we only have one case. If you need something run down in my city or help on a search warrant or something like that give me a call. Otherwise, I'd be happy to turn the whole thing over to you." The detectives from Mt View and Sunnyvale agreed with Gilroy. All they asked was that they be kept in the loop.

Sergeant Capalini did not say a thing. He just sat there with a pensive look on his face. "Rex, you sure you are not going to get in trouble with your boss by putting together this unauthorized working group?"

"Sam, as far as I'm concerned we are just a bunch of detectives talking about mutual cases. Who said anything about an unauthorized working group? In the full spirit of cooperation, we are just sharing information on the latest crime spree that has affected all of our cities. Oh, and since Santa Clara has the next highest number of cases and since you are the man when it comes to financial crimes investigations, I'd like for you to be an active participant in our cigarette fraud discussion group."

Sam Capalini laughed and said, "You know, one of these days you are gonna go too far and get in trouble with your bosses."

Rex smiled back, "What are they going to do, send me back to patrol?"

Sergeant Capalini looked at Kat, "That's one crazy partner you got there. What else do you guys have on this?"

Kat said, "We've got Costco Security going over all the surveillance video from all of the Costco stores to see if we can get any decent pictures of these guys. That's about it for now. The leads are thin, and there isn't much to follow up on. We've got the point of compromise for the cards but haven't come up with a plan on how to proceed with that."

"Has Costco put out a fraud alert to all of its stores?" asked Sergeant Capalini.

Rex answered, "I'm not sure, but I will check with Porter and make sure that he does."

Sergeant Capalini nodded, "Also, how about an alert to Patrol in all the affected cities?"

"That would be a good idea too," said Rex. "Let me get a copy of the fraud alert Costco puts out, add in any information we have, put it on a TRAC flyer, and email it to everybody so we are all putting out the same info."

Everybody nodded in agreement, and Sergeant Capalini added, "You might want to send that TRAC Flyer state wide. We know they hit Fremont, so who knows where else they will hit."

Rex, "Duly noted and consider it done. You know, I should probably ask Porter to check with Costco Corporate Security nation-wide. Let's see if anything like this has happened in Southern California or any other state. I'll also talk to Fremont PD and see what they are doing."

There being nothing else to discuss the meeting broke up.

Chapter 9

The two men sat together at a small table in the empty balcony section of the Loving Cup Coffee House on Capital Expressway at King. They each had a small cup of espresso coffee in front of them. One man was Vietnamese, and the other was Filipino. Even though they were alone, they talked in low voices to avoid being over heard. It was mid-morning, and there were only a few other customers in the coffee house. All of them were down on the main floor.

The Filipino man said, "The previous documents were as excellent as you said they would be. Do you have new ones for me?"

The Vietnamese man nodded and pulled an envelope from his briefcase. "As you requested, twelve sets of Costco membership cards and American Express credit cards with matching names. Also, twelve cigarette sales license."

The Filipino man inquired, "The price is still the same?"

The Vietnamese man nodded.

The Filipino man handed an envelope to the Vietnamese man, which he put in his inside coat jacket. He then handed over the envelope of documents.

The Filipino man said, "You will be able to pick up the merchandise in one hour. It will be in a white Chevy van parked in the Lyon's Plaza at King and Tully." He put a second envelope on the table. "The keys to the van and the license plate number of the van are in this envelope." He then stood, nodded at the other man and left.

The Vietnamese man continued drinking his espresso. A few minutes later anther Vietnamese man came up from downstairs and sat down at the table.

"You can pick up our cigarettes in one hour at the Lyon's Plaza. They are in a white Chevy van. Here are the keys to the van and the license plate," the first man said handing over the second envelope. "Take the cigarettes to our warehouse and then get rid of the van. I'm assuming it is stolen although our friend did not mention this."

The other man nodded and left.

No one in the coffee shop had paid any attention to the utility truck and crew working on the parking lot light poles close to the coffee shop earlier in the day.

As the Filipino male walked out the front door, he was unaware that a digital camera had just taken a picture of his face.

A second camera on another pole had also been set up to take pictures of the cars parked in the immediate area of the coffee shop. These images could be blown up to read the license plates of each car in view. After all the faces had been run through the software recognition program, the pictures and information would be forwarded to Five-O. Five-O would then run the vehicle license plates through the DMV computer for the registration information.

If any known gang members or other people with criminal histories turned up, Five-O would provide that information to Rex so he could run it through additional databases at the San Jose PD.

Chapter 10

It was a pleasant Spring morning in Willow Glenn. Rex and Kat were having coffee at Peet's with Five-O. They were sitting at a table outside enjoying the fresh air and watching the people go by. Willow Glenn was a pleasant, upscale neighborhood in San Jose. The central business district was lined with coffee and bagel shops, boutique shops and upscale restaurants and bars. In the morning, people were out walking their dogs or roller blading or just enjoying the tree-lined street. Shop owners were getting their morning cup of coffee before opening up for business. Other people were just meeting friends. At 0900 hours, Peet's was packed as it always was.

"Cowboy, where are you with the cigarette case?" asked Five-O.

Rex scowled and said, "Nowhere." Rex and Kat had gone to Fremont and checked with the Fremont Detective handling that case but had come away with nothing. The Fremont Detective did not have any leads yet either. About the only thing they could agree on was that it appeared they were chasing the same suspects. They agreed to keep in touch and share information on their respective investigations.

Rex continued, "There haven't been any more purchases, so far as we know. We haven't any more leads to go on than we did last week. I mean we know where the Amex cards are being compromised, but I can't figure out what to do with that piece of the puzzle. It has to be one of the wait staff who are carrying the skimmers, but I'm at a loss as to how to figure out which one without tipping our hand. You know we are not going to get any support for a big operation. Oh well, as my great grand-pappy use to say, 'If at first you don't succeed, try something else.' "

"How about getting a phony card from American Express?" asked Five-O.

"We could do that, we've done it in the past with House Hold Finance," said Rex. "The problem is what we do then. We can't keep going to the restaurant and using the card hoping to learn which wait staff is running it through the skimmer."

"No, I guess not," Five-O mused.

"You know how these things work," Rex said to Five-O. "The wait staff person with the skimmer runs however many cards through the skimmer as they think they can get away with in a night. The skimmer stores all of the information on each card. Somebody higher up in the gang provides the skimmer. They usually have two or three people with skimmers at various high-end restaurants. They come around every couple of days and swap out the full skimmer with an empty one. They then take the skimmers back to their house, or wherever they are set up, and download all the information onto a computer. Then they upload the card info from the computer onto the mag stripes on the counterfeit cards. We need to find the guy that is distributing the skimmers and collecting them and follow him and see who he leads us to. That's my problem, how to get to him."

They sat drinking their coffee's in silence for a few minutes, thinking. Then Kat said, "I've got an idea. Five-O, you remember that ICE Agent you brought to the last CFCIA meeting? How about you talk to him and get him to get a copy of the I-9's of all the employees at the restaurant. You know, tell them it is just a routine immigration inspection or something like that. That way he would be dealing just with the owners, who we don't suspect are involved in the skimming, and the restaurant staff would not be tipped that an investigation was going on. Then we could run the names and see if any of them have been arrested and for what.

"We could also run the names through the gang database to see if they are affiliated with any gangs or known gang members. That might give us something to go on."

Rex was nodding his head in agreement as Kat outlined her plan and said, "Yeah that just might work. How about it Five-O?"

Five-O gave his lopsided smile and said, "You two are devious. Yea, I'll talk to him and see if I can't get a favor, one fed to another. I've also asked for some more info on that coffee house. We have been seeing the same two cars come there almost every day. Both are high-end jobs. One is a red Lexus ISC, and the other is a yellow Acura NSX. The plates come back to a TVN Enterprises on both. Here's the print out." Five-O handed Rex two sheets of paper.

"We also got a facial recognition hit on this guy," Five-O continued handing a photo to Rex. "He is a low-level enforcer out of Westminster. His rap sheet shows he's been busted for some petty thefts and misdemeanor assaults."

"What's a low-level enforcer from Westminster doing in San Jose?" asked Rex looking at the photo and the rap sheet.

"That's a good question."

"All right, you go talk to your ICE guy, and Kat and I will check out this address for TVN Enterprises."

Chapter 11

"Well that figures," said Rex with a little disgust in his voice. They were parked in front of the address Five-O had given them for TVN Enterprises. It was a UPS Postal Annex store.

"A mail drop."

They went inside and patiently waited for the clerk on duty to finish with a customer. Then Rex discreetly flashed his badge at the clerk.

"We'd like to see the application for Box 1719, please."

The clerk hesitated just a moment before going to the back office to get the paperwork for them. The application and postal form required to be filled out for every private mail box showed them the box owner was one Tran Van Nguyen. It also showed an address that was supposed to be Tran Van Nguyen's real address. More importantly, there was a photocopy of Tran Van Nguyen's California Driver's License. Rex copied down all the information and thanked the clerk.

Back in the car Rex said, "Well, let's see where this address leads us."

"I'll bet you it's another mail drop," Kat said.

Rex just grunted as he drove off.

Twenty minutes later, they were parked outside another UPS Postal Annex store in Milpitas.

"At least he's consistent," said Rex. "He stays with UPS."

"Must be the service."

They were just getting out of their car when Rex's cell phone rang.

"It's Five-O," said Rex as he checked the caller ID. Answering the phone he said, "Five-O, tell me some good news."

"The good news," said Five-O, "is that I talked to the ICE Agent, and he said he could do it under what they call a routine immigration audit. He checked his files and some of those restaurants have employed foreign nationals in the past, so it would look normal to the owners if he asked for a copy of the I-9's. He is going to pay them a visit tomorrow afternoon, and he will call me as soon as he has the documents."

"Super," said Rex, "we owe you one."

"How's it going with you guys?"

"The address you gave us was a UPS Postal Annex. The box is rented by a guy named Tran Van Nguyen. Ring any bells?"

"No, nothing."

"We just pulled up to the address on the application that was supposed to be his real address, but it's another UPS Postal Annex."

"He's definitely trying to cover himself than. I'll get a mail cover going on the first address, so we can see what mail he is receiving."

"Sounds good. He doesn't want to make it easy to find him. The application at the first store also had a photo copy of his CDL. I'll run it when we get back to the office and see what pops out."

"Sounds like a plan, Cowboy. I'll give you a call tomorrow as soon as I hear back from the ICE Agent."

Rex disconnected and told Kat the good news.

"Well," said Kat, "at least we are moving the ball forward."

The following afternoon found Rex and Kat at their desks doing paperwork when Five-O called. Five-O had just left the ICE Office on Monterey Road and wanted to know where he could meet them. Rex told him they were at their office and to come on by.

Forty-five minutes later Five-O walked into the Financial Crimes Unit. He had with him the copies of the I-9's for all the employees at the restaurants in question. Kat took the sheets and logged onto the CJIC computer. She started running the names for a criminal history. On the third name, she got a hit. Lisa Nguyen had been arrested two years ago for passing counterfeit checks. Kat copied down her PFN and CII and then switched to another mask to run a complete criminal history. She was also able to pull up a copy of the booking sheet from when Lisa was arrested on the fraud charges. One thing about booking sheet information was that it showed the name and address of the person the arrestee wanted contacted in case of an emergency.

After printing out all this information, Kat went back to checking the rest of the names on the I-9's. None of the other people showed having a criminal history. Kat then went back to the printouts on Lisa and ran the name of her emergency contact person. They did not have a date of birth to go with this name, so it was a harder to narrow down. The search came up with eight possible subjects. Kat ran each person and narrowed it down to two based on their age. Since they were assuming that Lisa's contact person was most likely a boyfriend, they could come up with an approximate age that was close to Lisa's age.

"Well," said Kat as she brought the paperwork back to her desk, "it looks like the employee we should be looking at is a Lisa Nguyen because Lisa has a prior fraud conviction from two years ago. She also listed a contact person on her booking sheet that I am assuming is or was at the time her boyfriend, a Nick Pham, and I've come up with two possible subjects that also have prior fraud convictions as well as theft and assault."

"Looks like your idea paid off," said Five-O.

"Give me the names of the two possible boyfriends and I'll go down to the Gang Unit and see if they have anything on either one," said Rex.

Rex came back in fifteen minutes. "Both of these guys are in the Gang Unit data base. One is affiliated with a gang known for auto theft, and the other is with a gang they think is involved in selling protection to Vietnamese store owners."

Kat said, "Give me the one involved in auto theft, I'll go see my buddy John in auto theft and see if he can tell us anything more."

"And give me all three names and addresses," said Five-O, "and I'll start a mail cover on each one and see what we can find out. I'll also talk to the postal carrier on their routes and see if he can give me any information."

"Good idea," said Rex. "Hey Kat, can you run all three through the Photo Data Base and print out their photos?"

"Yeah, no problem. I'll also run them through DMV to see if their CDL address matches the CJIC printout."

"I can also run the names and addresses through a Lexus-Nexus search and see what other names come up associated with the addresses," said Five-O.

"All righty then," said Rex, "looks like we got some leads to work on."

Five-O came back an hour later. He had found out that the houses where the two Vietnamese males lived were both owned by TVN Enterprises. The address given for TVN Enterprises was the same UPS Postal Annex Rex and Kat had check out the previous day. So that meant the owner of TVN Enterprises had to be Tran Van Nguyen.

Rex got back on the DMV computer and punched in the CDL number for Tran Van Nguyen. The print out gave Rex Tran Van Nguyen's date of birth. It also showed a prior address in Westminster and a current address in San Jose.

Armed with Tran Van Nguyen's DOB, Rex ran him through CJIC looking for a criminal history. He found a couple of assault charges when Tran Van Nguyen was a juvenile, but there was no PFN and no adult criminal record.

Rex told Five-O that Kat had found out that the Regional Auto Theft Task Force (RATTF) was working on a rash of stolen Toyota Camrys, and they thought a crew of Viets was doing it, but they did not have anything concrete yet. Rex also told Five-O that they were about to take a drive by each of the addresses, take pictures and copy down the plates of any cars parked there. He would call him when they had any new information.

The next morning Rex and Kat were printing out Registration information on the license plates they had taken down yesterday. As they compared the information, an intriguing pattern emerged. All of the cars were salvaged vehicles, and they all showed the same previous address. A quick on-line phone book check showed that this address belonged to the P & L Auto Repair on Lincoln Avenue in San Jose. Kat and Rex knew they were on to something.

Auto repair shops were a frequent cover for chop shops for stolen cars. The cars were brought in to the shop and cut apart or "chopped." The parts were sold, or two cars were put back together with a VIN from a wrecked one, and sold as a salvaged car. Kat called her friend in auto theft with the information, and thirty minutes later a San Jose officer assigned to Regional Auto Theft Task Force (RATTF) was at her desk.

Kat and Rex explained to the officer that they were working a counterfeit credit card case. This case had led them to the P & L Auto Repair. He explained how they believed that the counterfeit credit card case was probably part of a greater Asian Organized Crime effort in San Jose. Since RATTF was currently working a rash of stolen cars that they believed was being done by a Viet crew, there just might be a tie in between the two cases. Rex believed that they may have just found the chop shop for the stolen cars, and the auto theft detective agreed.

The task force was briefing at 1400 hours that afternoon, before hitting the streets. The auto theft detective wanted Rex and Kat to attend the briefing, and bring their photos and any other information they might have to share. They told him they would be there.

They spent the rest of the morning printing out the photos of the residences they had taken the day before, made copies of the photos and printout information for each subject, and assembled all of this into a briefing packet for each member of the RATTF team. Rex also called Five-O and told him what was going on and asked him to come to the briefing.

Chapter 12

At 1400 hours, Rex, Kat, and Five-O were on the second floor of the Santa Clara County Sheriff's Office on Younger Avenue in the RATTF office. Kat handed out the packets they had made up, and Rex started the briefing.

When Rex was through with the briefing and had asked if there were any questions, the Sheriff's Sergeant in charge of the task force, Sergeant Webber, stuck his hand up and said, "Yeah, where are you guys going with your investigation and how do we keep from stepping all over each other?"

"Like I said," Rex replied, "we are just getting started with our investigation. We believe that the two are connected and that it is all part of an increase in Asian Organized Crime here in Silicon Valley. However, you won't get the powers that be to admit that.

"For right now, I would say that both investigations should go forward independently, but we should share all of our information. When we get to a point where either one of us is going to conduct a search warrant or make an arrest, I think the other team should be notified and given a chance to be there. For instance, if you guys develop enough to get a search warrant on this possible chop shop we would like to go in with you. There may be evidence there in the files that would help in our case.

"You guys are the experts in doing surveillance in these types of cases. I would say that if you are going to surveil any of the houses or the shop just let us know what the game plan is. We'll make sure we stay out of your way. And, if we come up with anything on the mail cover or anything else in our investigation we will be sure to pass it on to you right away."

"That sounds good for right now," said Sergeant Webber. "Can you give us an idea of the kinda of stuff you would be looking for? This skimmer for instance, what does one of those look like?"

"Glad you asked," said Rex as he reached into his briefcase and pulled out a small black box. "This is a skimmer we got a hold of about a year ago. Pass it around. But make sure I get it back.

"The ones out there today are even smaller. You see the card slot on the top? All you have to do is run the credit card through there, and it captures all of the account information on the magnetic stripe. The new ones will hold the info on up to fifty cards.

"You then download the information onto a lap top computer. With another card reader plugged into the computer, you can transfer the card info to a blank card. The counterfeit cards are usually manufactured in Southern California and brought up here by a courier.

"The blank white plastic cut into the size of the credit card with the mag stripe attached come from China. Asian Organized Crime in Southern California has the equipment to turn the blanks into any credit card they want. If they are done right, you can't tell the counterfeits from the real ones.

"Since the latest counter measures at stores is to ask for I.D. to make sure the name embossed on the card and the I.D. are the same, they have had to make fake DL's for the passer. That is done up here. Again, all you need is a digital camera, a computer, and a laser jet printer, and you can make a CDL good enough to fool a quick look by a store clerk.

"If they need to make better CDL's they can because several reams of blank card stock for California Driver's Licenses have been stolen from the printer's warehouse in L.A. You probably won't see any of this stuff going in or out of the house or business. Maybe somebody carrying a lap top, but that's about it. You will see people coming and going at the houses, just like at a dope pad."

Rex and Sergeant Webber exchanged business cards and cell phone numbers. They agreed to work closely on the two investigations and keep each other fully informed. Sergeant Webber told Rex that they would be setting up a surveillance of the suspected chop shop in the next couple of days. He would let him know what happened.

Chapter 13

When Rex and Kat got back to their office after meeting with RATTF, they found Officer Sonny Tam waiting for them. Rex had been Sonny's Police Academy Training Officer.

There was always a bond formed between training officers and their recruits that went further than just friendship or the fact that they were both police officers. An Academy Training Officer introduced the recruit to police life. The San Jose Police Academy was part Marine Corps Boot Camp and part college campus. It was the responsibility of the training officer to take civilians fresh out of college and some still even living at home and mold them into police officers.

Police Departments are para-military organizations. They have a chain of command and the recruit has to learn to follow orders. On the other hand, the recruit has to learn how to take charge of any situation, to think on his feet and become a problem solver for the rest of society.

As Rex was fond of telling his recruits, there was no more awesome responsibility than wearing that gun and that badge. In a free society that valued individual rights and freedom, only the police officer was granted the authority to take away a person's freedom. When a police officer walks into a situation, he has to determine if and what law has been broken. He has to decide on the spot if someone is going to jail. It is not the district attorney or the judge; it is the police officer who decides to take away a person's freedom, and put them in jail.

The Police officer has to do this without having all of the facts. He better be right because those attorneys and that judge will spend a lot of time tearing apart his split second decision. A police officer does not have the luxury of arguing and analyzing his actions for days. He has to make his decision now. A police officer is there to protect society, to keep the peace. When everybody else is running away, it is the police officer that has to walk into that dark alley and take on the monsters of the night.

Sonny looked up as Kat and Rex walked into the office. "Senior Training Officer Johnson, how are you sir?"

"How many times do I have to tell you that we're not in the Academy anymore and you don't have to call me sir?" Rex shot back.

"I know, but old habits die hard," said Sonny.

"Is this a social visit or do you have a real reason for being here?" asked Rex.

"A little of both," replied Sonny. "Can't an old recruit just stop by to say hello? And I think I might have something for you about your cigarette case. I saw your bulletin in the briefing binder."

"Well," said Rex, "in that case sit down and tell us all about it."

Rex rolled up an empty desk chair, and Sonny sat. "I'm working swing shift out in District Paul. My beat is the Tully and King Road area. I got a lotta small shops in there owned by Vietnamese.

"I've been working with the Violent Gang Enforcement Team trying to talk to these shop owners, and get them to trust the police more. For a long time, we have suspected that local Vietnamese gangs are selling protection to the store owners, but nobody will come forward.

"I've got this one old guy, Mr. Pham, owes a little Stop and Rob. I've been working on him for almost a year now. I stop in his shop two to three times a night and drink a coffee and have a pastry with him, and I even pay for it. We talk about Vietnam, his family and how they got to the States. He's a tough old bird. Use to be an interpreter for the U.S. Army during the Vietnam War. Anyway, all my work may have just paid off.

"He told me last night how he is getting shaken down for protection. He said he didn't mind paying the protection to be left alone and just go about his business, but something new has come up and he doesn't like it.

"Two nights ago, during my days off, this gang banger comes to his store and tells Mr. Pham that he is now going to supply him with cigarettes. Mr. Pham says no, he has his own suppliers he buys his cigarettes from. This guy tells him that he can still buy from his legitimate suppliers, but he is also going to take what the gang bangers give him and sell them. And all the money he makes selling those cigarettes, he is going to give back to the gang banger.

"When Mr. Pham still refused, he was reminded that he had a granddaughter at Silver Creek High School. When I came back to work last night and stopped in to see Mr. Pham he was mad and upset. He told me all of this and asked me what I could do to help him."

Kat whistled, "Wow, that's quite a story. We always knew they were selling protection out there, but this is the first time we had anybody come forward. And the cigarette deal. Do you think it could be the same guys from Costco?"

Rex nodded his head. "It makes sense. We knew they had to be peddling the cigarettes somewhere. Asian's are heavy smokers and stocking a Vietnamese grocery store with smokes is a perfect way to get rid of them and make your profit.

"This can't be the only store either, there has to be others. Sonny, did Mr. Pham tell you anything else? Is the guy that told him he was going to sell the cigarettes the same guy that has been collecting his protection money? Does he know who he is? When is Mr. Pham supposed to take delivery on the cigarettes?"

"It is the same guy he pays protection to, but he doesn't know his name. Mr. Pham says he looks like a typical Viet gang banger, dark glasses, leather jacket, and open neck shirt. The guy told him he would deliver the cigarettes tomorrow night."

"That doesn't give us much time to come up with a plan," said Rex. "O.K., are you going on duty right now? Because I need you here. Who's your Sergeant?"

Sonny told Rex that he was in fact on his way out to his beat but had stopped in to tell Rex what he had. Rex called Dispatch and asked them to send a message to 6P10, the District Paul Swing Sergeant, to call him ASAP. He sent Kat and Sonny down the hall to the Detective Conference Room and said he would be joining them there in a minute.

Rex called the Violent Crimes Enforcement Team (VCET) office hoping someone would still be there. He got lucky and found Sergeant Anderson in the office. Rex told him he was brainstorming a possible take down and would need VCET's help. He asked Sergeant Anderson if he could come over to the Detective Conference room to sit in on an initial planning session. Sergeant Anderson said he would be right over.

VCET was the natural unit of choice to help in this surveillance. They were a highly trained unit that had no beat responsibilities. They roamed the city in search of gang members. They had made hundreds of arrests for homicide, robbery, stabbings, shootings, illegal weapons, and explosives. They had validated a multitude of gang members and they knew the gang culture of the city. Their motto was "*Iis minamur qui aliis minantur,"* We Intimidate Those who Intimidate Others.

Rex walked down the hall to the Gang Unit to see if Detective Phong, who was in charge of Vietnamese Gangs was in. Since it was almost the end of the workday, he found Detective Phong at his desk. Rex asked him to join the party.

The District Paul Patrol Sergeant had also called Rex back. Since he had not left police headquarters yet, Rex invited him to join their conference.

Ten Minutes later they were all assembled in the Detective Conference Room. Rex ran down the Costco cigarette case to everybody by way of background so they knew the origins of the case. He then briefed them on the information that Officer Sonny Tam had brought to them.

While he had been setting up this meeting, Rex's mind had been racing. He had the basics of a plan in mind. He now told everybody in the room what he was thinking about. Provided they could get Mr. Pham to assist, he wanted to lay a trap. He wanted to have VCET stake out Mr. Pham's shop and take down the gang banger as he made the delivery.

To make the case even tighter, he wanted Mr. Pham to wear a wire and get the gang banger to tell him where the cigarettes came from if he could. At least get the gang banger to instruct Mr. Pham again that all the money he made was to be turned back over to the gang banger. Sonny thought that he could persuade Mr. Pham to do this.

Sonny described the store for Sergeant Anderson and the Sergeant made a rough drawing of the store, the parking lot, and the street. Sergeant Anderson said he would have to see the store, but tactically thought it could be done it they could get the crook to come in the front door and not the back delivery door. If they could do that, they could set up in the back storeroom with an arrest team. They would also set a chase car and a backup team out on the street.

Everybody agreed that it was feasible, but that the timing was going to be tight. What they needed to do now was get approval from the command staff to go ahead. An operation like this meant they needed approval from the Chief of Detectives and the Chief of Patrol. The usual protocol in the Detective Bureau was to inform your Sergeant, who went to the Lieutenant, who then went to the Captain, who in turn notified the Chief of Detectives and the hand wringing began. This situation was worse because it involved two separate Bureaus, Patrol and Detectives.

Since it was going to happen on Swing Shift, Sergeant Anderson said he would start the ball rolling on his end by getting hold of his lieutenant and everybody on the Patrol side. He said that he would also write up the Operations Plan. Before leaving, Sergeant Anderson and Rex exchanged cell phone number.

Rex told Sonny's Sergeant that he would like Sonny in on the bust as well, and his Sergeant agreed. Rex also wanted to go with Sonny to talk to Mr. Pham tonight. Rex wanted to make sure Mr. Pham was willing to go along with the stakeout. Before they did that, he had to start the ball rolling for approval of the operation by the Chief of D's. Sonny's Sergeant told him to stay with Rex and help him however he could, and not to worry about his beat, the rest of the team would cover.

It was now after 1700 hours, and Rex doubted if any of the brass was still around. He walked back over to his unit and sure enough, both Sergeant Alvarez and Lieutenant Wong were gone for the day. Rex started back down the hallway to the Chief of D's office with Kat and they saw Deputy Chief of Detectives Ortiz headed for the back door.

Rex called out down the hallway, "Chief Ortiz, can you hang on a minute?"

Hearing his name the Chief of D's stopped and turned around. A faint smile crossed his lips when he saw who it was. The Chief of D's had a little soft spot in his heart for these two detectives. He knew them as hard working and smart investigators. "Hello Kat, hello Rex, why are you accosting me in the hallway when I'm trying to get out of here?"

"Sorry Chief," said Rex, "but something real important just came up and we're working against the clock here. I need your approval for an operation."

Chief Ortiz sighed. "Since it is so rare that you asked my approval of anything before the fact this must be good. Come on. Let's go back to my office."

It took Rex only fifteen minutes to explain what they wanted to do. Rex liked the Chief of D's. He was a good man and a man who was not afraid to make a decision. This was relatively rare in the command staff of the department these days. But the Chief of D's was a working cop. He had come up through the ranks like everybody else, but even though he was now an administrator he still liked putting bad guys in jail. When Rex was finished, the Chief of D's sat behind his desk mulling it over. Finally he said, "I like it. We know that these scum have been taking advantage of their own in the Vietnamese community for years. Finally, someone has the *huevos* to come forward. You go ahead and run with it. I'll make some phone calls and let everybody know that I approve. Now get out of here and get busy."

Rex and Kat left the Chief of D's office and walked back to their office to pick up Sonny. They followed Sonny out to Mr. Pham's store. After Sonny made the introductions, it took surprising little time to convince Mr. Pham to go along with what the police wanted to do. It seemed that he had already made up his mind to fight back and there was no stopping him now.

Rex called Sergeant Anderson and told him that they had just talked to Mr. Pham and gotten his full cooperation. Rex made arraignments for Sergeant Anderson to come out to the store and check out the lay out. Rex also told Sergeant Anderson that the Chief of D's had given the go ahead for the operation.

They decided to brief at 1400 hours the next day and would have everybody in place by 1600 hours. Since that was all they could do that night, Kat and Rex decided to knock off and go home. Since it was probably going to be a long day tomorrow, they decided not to come in until 0900 hours the next day. They noted the later start time on the sign out board before leaving the office. This would keep the clock watching Sergeant Alvarez happy.

Rex also got on his computer and fired off an email to Sergeant Alvarez with a courtesy copy to Lieutenant Wong. He informed them that he and Kat were planning an operation with VCET for the next night and that they would be in at 0900 hours the next morning to brief them on it.

As Rex hit the send button he said, “There, now everyone is officially informed as ordered and I have a record of doing so.”

Chapter 14

Rex was walking across the employee parking lot across the street from PAB the next morning when he caught up with Kat just as she reached the side gate to the police compound. They were both dressed down for the day in jeans. As they entered the rear stairway door to the third floor, they saw Lieutenant Wong coming out of the Chief of D's office. Unfortunately, he saw them as well.

"You two," said Lieutenant Wong barely controlling his anger, "in my office now."

Lieutenant Wong stormed off down the hall, and Rex and Kat followed at a leisurely pace. They dropped their briefcases and coats at their desks and then walked into Lieutenant Wong's office. He sat at his desk glaring at them.

"What's up L.T.?" asked Rex innocently, "you wanted to see us?"

"Why was I not informed of this operation of yours?" sputtered Wong. "Why wasn't Sergeant Alvarez informed? You were told to keep her informed."

"Well sir," said Rex in an extra calm voice, "for one thing this all came together very suddenly with a short window of opportunity in which to act. By the time, we had talked to the right people in the Department to see if what we wanted to do was even possible, you and Sergeant Alvarez had gone home for the evening. We were intending to bring you up to speed on it this morning. Also, I did inform Sergeant Alvarez and yourself in an email I sent out last night. By the way, where is the good Sergeant this morning?"

"According to the board she called in sick," said Kat.

"Oh, that is too bad," said Rex, "I hope it is nothing too serious."

"Never mind that," said Lieutenant Wong. "I don't appreciate being called into the Chief of D's Office and asked what my detectives are up to. Especially when I have no idea about what is going on. Now explain this operation of yours to me and I'll see if I approve."

"First off," replied Rex, "it is not our operation, its VCET's. We are working a cigarette theft case from Costco using counterfeit credit cards to purchase the cigarettes. Our investigation has lead us to the possible involvement of Vietnamese gang members, so we have informed the Gang Unit.

"A patrol officer brought us information that a storeowner he knows is being pressured to put stolen cigarettes in his store by a Vietnamese gangster that sells him protection. The delivery of those cigarettes is happening this evening, so we asked VCET if they could stake out the store and take down the gang banger when he makes his delivery."

Rex was thinking that there must be something going on between the Chief of D's and Lieutenant Wong. Rex had thoroughly briefed the Chief of D's last night. So why had he called Lieutenant Wong into his office this morning to ask him what his detectives were doing? Was the Chief of D's trying to embarrass Lieutenant Wong on purpose? It would not be the first time that a higher up had set things up to take out a subordinate he did not like. That was a little bit of department intrigue Rex did not care to be involved in.

"I don't know if I like that," said Lieutenant Wong. "Isn't that dangerous for the store owner? I don't like these buy-bust situations, too many things can go wrong."

"L.T.," said Rex with some frustration in his voice, "this is not our operation, this is not your operation. It is VCET's operation and the Chief of D's and the Patrol Chief have all ready approved it. All we are doing is tagging along so we can interrogate the suspect and hopefully catch a break on our case."

Lieutenant Wong screwed up his face and glared at Rex. He knew that Rex had gone around him and effectively taken him out of the decision process. He did not like it, but there was nothing he could do about it. Rex had played his cards right and had won this hand.

"All right then," said Lieutenant Wong through clenched teeth, "what time is this operation going down?"

"Early this evening," said Kat. "We brief with VCET at 1400 hours and want to be in place by 1600. The guy is supposed to be making his delivery sometime after 1700."

"Fine," said Lieutenant Wong, "get out of here. But keep me informed."

"Well, all righty then," said Kat as they walked back to their desks, "that went well. Did you really email Alvarez and the L.T. last night?"

"I certainly did," replied Rex with a grin. "I sent her one of my 'unless otherwise directed emails' with a courtesy copy to the L.T. I told you I was going to keep her informed and I have. It's not my fault she wasn't here to receive it last night or that she called in sick today."

Kat laughed, "You are too much, Cowboy. Come on, let's go get a cup of coffee and decide where we are going to lunch later. I already scored us a car."

After coffee, they came back to the office to work on paperwork on their other cases. They decided on Italian for lunch and went out to a late lunch at Pasta Pomodoro.

They liked the one on Race Street at The Alameda. Taking surface streets from the department it only took ten minutes to get there. Parking was always a little iffy, but since they were having a late lunch most of the lunchtime crowd had already left, and the rear parking lot was only half-full.

Rex enjoyed his usual order of spaghetti in marinara sauce while Kat had the three-cheese ravioli dish.

"So how was your weekend?" Rex asked Kat.

"Busy as usual. Saturday afternoon we had a little league game. Our team is all third graders, and we were playing a team that was all fifth graders. I thought we were going to be slaughtered, but we managed to hold them to a one run lead."

"How's your boy doing?"

"You know, this is the first year pitching for all of our boys. I've taken them all to just three pitching practices before this game, and I just wasn't sure how it was going to turn out. But the boy surprised me. We rotate pitchers, and he pitched one inning. He struck out one and walked one. Then the next two players hit singles, and the bases were loaded. His last out was a grounder right back to the pitcher mound. Thomas was able to field the ball and throw the force out at home plate. The catcher threw the ball down the line to third base, double play."

"Hey that sounds great. Too bad they lost, but it sounds like they held their own against the bigger kids."

When they got back from lunch, it was time for the briefing, so they walked over to the Special Ops building. Sergeant Anderson and his team were there along with the Special Operations Lieutenant. Detective Phong from the Gang Unit was there with the wire, receiver, and recorder. Officer Sonny Tam was also there.

Sergeant Anderson started his briefing. He had photos of the store inside and out. He also had a floor diagram. He put Kat, Rex, Detective Phong, and himself and his 2-man arrest team in the back storage room. The two-man arrest team would consist of one Metro officer and Officer Tam. Kat, Rex, and Detective Phong would be wearing raid jackets identifying them as police. Sergeant Anderson, his VCET officers, and Officer Tam were wearing tactical BDU's. He put another two-man backup team in a van in the parking lot in front of the store and a chase car in the parking lot of the shopping center across the street.

The officers in the van would be out of sight in the back of the van and were wearing BDU's. The officers in the chase car were wearing BDU's, but would cover the uniform top with a civilian shirt so they would not be so obvious.

The plan called for Mr. Pham to get the crook to bring the cases of cigarettes in the front door and leave them by the front counter. As he was doing this, Mr. Pham was to engage him in conversation and try to get him to repeat his instructions of how Mr. Pham was to sell the cigarettes and what he was to do with the money. If Mr. Pham could get anything out of him about where the cigarettes came from that would be even better.

Detective Phong would monitor the recording they were making of the conversation since he spoke Vietnamese.

It was Sergeant Anderson's call as to when to move in and make the arrest. They wanted to try and get the suspect just inside the store at the front counter. If they could not take him down inside the store, or he got spooked for some reason, the backup arrest team would take him in the parking lot. If the suspect got to his car and drove off, the chase car would follow, and they would try to make a car stop on him.

If it turned into a car chase, Sergeant Anderson would monitor conditions and have the final say on continuing the pursuit. Sergeant Anderson also went through which hospital was the closest, that the District Sergeant and Area Lieutenant were informed of the operation, and told them which radio channel they would be operating on. Sergeant Anderson concluded his briefing by asking if there were any questions. Since there was none, he told everybody to load up their vehicles and proceed to Mr. Pham's store and get set up.

Chapter 15

Rex and Kat drove out to Mr. Pham's store. They parked in the parking lot of the corner shopping mall across the street where they would not be obvious. Even though a gold Chevy Impala was a popular car, if one got close enough you could see the emergency lights in front of the rear view mirror through the windshield and the police radio mounted on the center console. They walked across the street and into the store. Mr. Pham was at his usual spot by the cash register, and he greeted them warmly. He told them the other police officers were already in the back of the store.

They all walked to the back of the store where Sergeant Anderson and his men along with Detective Phong were. Detective Phong explained the wire to Mr. Pham again and then hooked it up and taped the mike and transmitter under Mr. Pham's shirt. He had Mr. Pham go back out to the cash register and give him a sound check. The transmitter and recorder were working perfectly. Through his headphones, Detective Phong could hear everything that was being said.

Rex went over with Mr. Pham again what he wanted him to try and get the suspect to say. Mr. Pham had a clear idea of what was needed because of his experience of working as an interpreter for the U. S. Army in Vietnam. He had interpreted for many questioning and interrogation sessions and understood the importance of getting the right information.

Sergeant Anderson went over how they were going to make the arrest, and what he wanted Mr. Pham to do so he would not be in harm's way.

Sergeant Anderson explained that when the suspect was about ready to leave, Mr. Pham was to make some excuse, walk away from the suspect, and walk into his cooler and get down on the floor.

If something went wrong and the suspect started getting nervous or threatening Mr. Pham was given both a verbal and hand danger signal to use. Sergeant Anderson told Mr. Pham that if they had to come out before he could walk away from the suspect, than he was to drop to the floor and stay there until it was all over.

With everybody clear that Mr. Pham knew what was going on and what he was suppose to do and comfortable that they all knew what they were going to do, they sent Mr. Pham back out to the front counter. Rex and Kat put on their raid jackets and they all settled down to wait.

Rex hated this part of any sting or surveillance. They were now on crook time, and all they could do was wait for the suspect to show up. Everybody was set and in place. Nerves were keyed up, as everybody was amped up ready to make the arrest. All you could do was wait. You could not go anywhere, you could not move out of position, you just had to sit back and wait for the bad guy to show up. You had to stay alert because you did not know when the bad guy was going to show, or what he was going to do when he did show. This was what they meant when they described police work as hours and hours of boredom followed by moments of sheer terror.

Customers came and went. Mr. Pham busied himself at the front of the store. He did not look worried at all. They made regular radio calls to each other to make sure the radios were still working. Since they had reserved a channel strictly for themselves, the radios were quiet.

Then at 1725 hours, Rex heard over his earpiece, "Heads up, looks like the bad guy just pulled in driving a minivan."

There was a pause and then Rex heard, "All units it's show time. Suspect is wearing a black leather jacket. He just opened the side door on the van and is taking out large boxes."

Everybody in the back room seemed to get a little tenser. It was as if an electric charge had just shot through the room. Only Sergeant Anderson was positioned so he could see the front counter. He had made himself a duck blind out of boxes of merchandise with a small opening between the boxes where he could look out. Since the lights were turned out in the back room and he was not backlit, he could not be seen from the front of the store.

As he watched, Mr. Pham pushed and empty hand truck out through the front door of the store to the suspect. As Mr. Pham went out, he made sure he propped the front door open. Sergeant Anderson could see that Mr. Pham and the suspect were talking and he looked back over his shoulder at Detective Phong. Detective Phong gave him a thumbs up indicating that the wire was working.

The suspect stacked three boxes on the hand truck and Mr. Pham wheeled it back inside. He dumped the boxes on the floor next to the front counter but out of the aisle. Sergeant Anderson nodded to himself. Mr. Pham was good; he was making sure that the boxes were not put in the aisle where they would be in the way of the arrest team.

Mr. Pham wheeled the hand truck back outside, and the suspect stacked three more boxes on the hand truck. Mr. Pham wheeled these in, dropped them by the first boxes, and went back outside.

After the suspect loaded three more boxes onto the hand truck, he closed the side door on the minivan and followed Mr. Pham into the store. All of the officers knew what was happening because one of the VCET officers in the surveillance van had kept up a running commentary on the radio.

As Sergeant Anderson continued to watch, Mr. Pham and the suspect stood in front of the counter by the cash register talking. There were no other customers in the store. Sergeant Anderson snuck a quick glance over his shoulder at Detective Phong again. Detective Phong gave him another thumbs up.

Just then a customer came into the store and headed to the cooler at the back of the store. The suspect seemed to cut himself off in mid sentence, turned, and headed for the front door. Mr. Pham started walking quickly to the back of the store.

Sergeant Anderson keyed his radio, "Suspect is leaving the store, take him down outside, now."

With that order, Sergeant Anderson set in motion what could only be described as controlled chaos. Sergeant Anderson moved out with his arrest team just behind him. Rex and Kat moved out to cover and protect Mr. Pham and the customer. The officers in the van outside slid open the side door and jumped to the ground.

Rex and Kat got Mr. Pham and the customer to lie down on the floor as Sergeant Anderson and his men ran forward with their weapons at the low ready. Sergeant Anderson was carrying a Colt .45. Sonny Tam had his department issue Sig-Sauer 9mm. The other VCET officer carried a Remington 12-gage pump action shot gun.

The VCET van had taken the far left parking space in front of the store. The suspect had parked his van two parking spaces to their right, near the front door. The customer had parked in the parking space just to the right of the suspect's van. As the two VCET officers burst out of their van, the suspect was quickly coming around the front of his van with his keys in his right hand heading for the driver's door. One VCET officer was armed with a Sig Sauer 9mm pistol, and the other carried a 9mm Heckler & Koch MP5 submachine gun.

The two VCET officers confronted the suspect, pointed their weapons at him, and yelled, "San Jose Police, freeze, put your hands up."

The suspect skidded to a stop. He had not noticed the police officers before this. Inside the store, Sergeant Anderson held his team just inside the still propped open front door out of the line of fire from the officers outside. The suspect stood rooted to the ground for a second looking confused. He started to turn around as if he was going to head back into the store. The officers again ordered him to stop and put his hands up as he took a step back towards the front door.

Chapter 16

Nick Lueong was confused. He had just delivered the cigarettes to this little old man shop owner who he thought he had totally scared. The man had been quite subservient to him, bowing his head and listening to everything Nick had told him. Nick was the enforcer; he was the one in charge.

He had told the old man that he was to sell Nick's cigarettes first, and that he was to give all the money he made off the cigarettes to him. He told the old man not to try to cheat him because he knew exactly how many packs of cigarettes there were. Nick threatened the old man's granddaughter again telling the old man that he knew she went to Silver Creek High School. They could get to her any time they wanted. This seemed to make the old man even more afraid.

When a customer came into the store, Nick had decided it was time to leave. As he hurried to his van, two guys jumped out of a van parked next to him pointing guns at him and yelling. Nick's first thought was that it was a rival gang that was after him. He turned to run back into the store and saw more guys with guns just inside the front door.

Then the words they were saying started to sink into his brain. Nick realized they were the police, and they were there to arrest him. Nick thought of the promise he had made to himself that he would never be taken alive.

He was good for three murders in Southern California and was convinced that if he ever went to jail he would never get out. Nick had told himself many times it was better to go down fighting than go to prison for the rest of his life or worse yet, get the needle.

Nick's brain processed all of this in less than a second because Nick had another problem. Nick was high on Crystal Methamphetamine. He had just smoked some L. A. Ice before making his cigarette delivery. He did this, he told himself, because it helped him keep his edge. The way it made him feel invincible helped him put more fear into the shop owners he demanded protection money from.

Now everything seemed to be running in slow motion for Nick. He turned back towards the cops that had come out of the van with a crooked smile on his face. As he turned he dropped the van keys and reached inside his jacket pulling a 9mm Glock from his waistband.

The two VCET officers saw Nick turn back towards them. They saw his right hand reach across his body and go to his waistband inside his jacket. They saw Nick's hand come out from under his jacket holding a semi-auto pistol that he was starting to point at them.

As Nick's hand found the butt of his Glock on his left hip, he pulled the gun out of his waist band and started bringing it up sideways, across his body gangster style, towards the officers.

Seeing the handgun, the officers yelled, "Drop the gun."

Nick just smiled that crooked smile at the officers and started firing as soon as he got his gun out and was still bringing it up on target.

* * *

Unfortunately, for Nick, the officers were already on target and they had transitioned their fingers to their triggers ready to shoot as soon as they saw Nick's gun. Both officers fired at the same time. Two 9mm slugs caught Nick center of mass, right square in his chest. A short burst of five 9mm slugs from the MP5 stitched a line from just below Nick's sternum up to his left shoulder.

Nick went down still holding his Glock in his right hand. The officers fanned out to each side and approached, their weapons still trained on Nick. The officer to Nick's left kept him covered with his MP5, the officer on his right stepped on Nick's right hand pinning it to the ground and reached down and took the Glock from his hand. While his partner continued to cover him, the officer holstered his own weapon, took out his handcuffs, and handcuffed Nick behind his back. He then made a quick search of Nick's waistband and jacket pockets to make sure Nick did not have any more weapons.

The officer then called out loudly enough for the officers in the store to hear, "Code 4, suspect down."

As Sergeant Anderson and the other two officers emerged from the store, the VCET officer was checking Nick's carotid artery for a pulse. As Sergeant Anderson walked up holstering his weapon, the officer looked up at him and shook his head.

Sergeant Anderson bent down and also checked for a pulse. He did not find one either. "Yep, he's dead."

Rex and Kat came out of the store. Kat looked over the scene and said to no one in particular, "What happened?"

"He pulled a gun and tried to shoot it out with us," said the VCET officer with the MP5.

"Dead?" Rex asked looking at Sergeant Anderson.

"Yep."

"Damn. O.K., your scene, what do you need us to do?"

Sergeant Anderson started giving orders to secure the scene. Rex got their detective car from across the street. Sergeant Anderson called in the chase car. They used the two cars to block the entrance to Mr. Pham's parking lot. The other officers strung crime scene tape. While they were doing this, Sergeant Anderson got on his cell phone and started making notifications. He used his cell phone instead of his radio because the press routinely monitored the police frequencies. He wanted to keep them from knowing as long as possible.

Sergeant Anderson called Dispatch and talked to a supervisor. He told the supervisor that there had just been an officer involved shooting at his location, the suspect was dead, and no officers were injured. He asked the supervisor to send messages over the computer, not in the clear over the radio, to the Area Lieutenant and the District Sergeant. Then the

Dispatch supervisor was to notify Homicide. As the supervisor was typing all of this into her computer, a notification message attached to Sergeant Anderson's detail flashed. The message said that the Chief of D's was to be notified. She told Sergeant Anderson this, and he asked that she take care of that notification also. Now all they had to do was wait for all the troops to arrive.

The first to arrive was the District Sergeant. He got with Sergeant Anderson to see what help he needed. They decided that they needed four more officers for perimeter security. The District Sergeant said he would handle that and would take over crime scene security. Next to arrive was the Area Lieutenant. He checked that Sergeant Anderson had made the appropriate notifications. He then checked with the District Sergeant to make sure that the crime scene was being properly secured. Other officers arrived, and the crime scene was expanded. With so many cops at the scene now, they were starting to draw a crowd of onlookers. Whenever something big happened, the people just came out of the woodwork. It was better than live TV. They had to be there to see what was happening.

Because of the growing crowd, the District Sergeant decided to close King Road in front of the store. He radioed the on-duty traffic team to come over and divert traffic. He also pushed the perimeter to the other side of the street. That would leave the street in front of the store clear for the Crime Scene Van and the Homicide Detectives.

Since it was 1740 hours when the officer involved shooting notification went out, the Homicide Detectives and Crime Scene Officers had already left for the day. That meant that the on-call teams had to be contacted and called back. Since it was an officer involved shooting, the on-call Internal Affairs Investigator and the on-call DA Investigator also had to be notified and be called back. The PIO was also notified so that he could respond out and handle the press that was sure to descend on the scene any minute now. Notifications went all the way up the chain of command to the Chief of Police.

Rex was anxious to get a look in the suspect's van. He wanted to get an ID on the suspect. This might lead them to other addresses that they would want to hit. The longer they had to wait, the greater the chance whoever the dead guy was working for would find out, and start covering their tracks.

However, he had to wait until Homicide got there. The scene was now frozen for them. While they were waiting, Rex called the RATTF Sergeant to let him know what had gone down. He wanted him to know that the shit had hit the fan and to go ahead and move on that chop shop if they could. If it was all connected, as Rex suspected, the bad guys would be closing that place down as soon as news of the shooting got out.

The on-call Homicide team showed up a few minutes later followed by the PIO, Sergeant Comstock. Sergeant Comstock got there just in front of the first news van, which happened to be Dawn Summers from KTVU Channel 2 News. Sergeant Comstock set up a briefing area for the press on King Road inside the road closure but outside the crime scene perimeter. Sergeant Comstock would have his hands full because TV stations would want to put up something live on their 6 PM news.

Finally, the Crime Scene Van arrived. As the Crime Scene Officers and the Homicide Detectives huddled to make a game plan, Rex went over to talk to them.

Chapter 17

The on-call Homicide team was Sergeants Harris and Long. Rex knew them well and they were two senior no nonsense investigators. Rex gave them a quick overview of his case and what the op was. Rex explained his need to search the van as soon as possible to see if there were any other addresses that they should lock down and get search warrants.

Sergeant Harris looked over the crime scene and decided it would be all right to start the search of the suspect's van. Sergeant Long told Rex that after they got some photos of the body, they would check it for ID. Rex thanked them for their cooperation, and walked back to Kat to tell her the good news.

As Rex and Kat stood looking at the suspect's van with their backs to the perimeter, they heard the growl of a familiar voice directed at them. "Detectives Johnson and Sanchez, get over here." It was Deputy Chief Ortiz.

Rex and Kat cringed a little and turned around to see the Chief of D's standing on the other side of the crime scene tape. As they walked over to him, Kat put on a smile and said, "Hiya Chief, how you doin?" in her best New York accent.

"Don't how you doin me," the Chief of D's growled back. "What kind of a five star cluster fuck have you two created here?"

Sergeant Anderson, who had been talking with Sergeant Harris, heard and saw the Chief of D's and started over to them. "Chief, don't blame your detectives, this was my operation and my guys who did the shooting.

Your detectives stayed in the background where they were supposed to be. They did their job of protecting the storeowner and a customer that came in just before the take down. Besides, it was a clean shoot. The guy pulled a gun on us."

This seemed to calm down the Chief of D's. "O.K. Anderson, if you say so. Are all of your people all right?"

"Not a scratch, they'll be just fine."

"What about the shop owner and that customer you mentioned?" asked the Chief.

"They're both fine. Detective Phong is in the store with them mainly keeping the customer calm. He doesn't speak English, so I assigned Phong to him to keep him calm until we're through with him. Mr. Pham is doing fine too. Not only did he get the suspect to say a lot of good incriminating stuff, he's in there right now brewing fresh coffee for all the cops out here. That old boy is one tough bird."

One of the Crime Scene Officers called Rex over to the suspect's van. He had the van's registration and handed it to Rex. "I've taken all the pictures of the van I need so you are free to look through it if you want."

Rex thanked him and pulled on his latex gloves before he opened the side door. It was a standard Toyota minivan with the rear seats removed. Rex could see that the back of the van was empty. Rex searched the driver and passenger areas up front but also came up empty. Then Rex looked at the Registration. The van was registered to TVN Enterprises.

As Rex walked back to where Kat and the Chief of D's were standing, he pulled out his cell phone and called Five-O. Rex gave Five-O the Reader's Digest version of the stake out and shooting and then told him about the van being registered to TVN Enterprises.

"Didn't you say that the homes where the two other Gang Bangers we are looking at were owned by TVN Enterprise?" asked Rex.

"That's right Cowboy," said Five-O. "We've got a mail cover on the post office box that is the address for TVN Enterprises but so far we haven't gotten anything."

"O.K., thanks."

"Whatcha got?" asked Kat.

"Apparently a dead end," said Rex. "You remember Five-O coming up with a TVN Enterprises as the owner of those two houses? Well it seems that this van is also owned by TVN Enterprises. The only problem is, TVN Enterprises is a post office box. Five-O already has a mail cover on the box, but no mail has come in."

Sergeant Harris walked over and handed Rex a 3 by 5 card. "That there is the CDL number, name, DOB and address from the suspect ID. Now we would be going over there eventually, but that's going to take some time and probably wouldn't happen until tomorrow. How about you seeing about getting a search warrant tonight on that place and we can piggyback in on your warrant if we need to. Since you guys were inside during the shooting, I can get your statements latter."

Released from the scene, Rex explained to the Chief D's that he and Kat were going to go back to the department, write up a search warrant for Nick Lueong's house, and serve it tonight.

Kat explained to the Chief of D's that it was looking more and more like they were dealing with some kind of Continuing Criminal Enterprise that was somehow tied to a company called TVN Enterprises. She told the Chief of D's how their investigation showed the bad guys were involved in selling protection to Vietnamese businesses, stealing and re-selling cigarettes, and auto theft. The Chief of D's took a cigar out of his cigar case and studied it, rolling the cigar in his fingers.

"You two get your search warrant and go over the suspect's house with a fine tooth comb. You find out everything you can about this guy and this TVN Enterprises. If this is all tied in to some sort of criminal enterprise, I want to know about it. I want a full briefing on what you find in the morning. And Detective Sanchez, sorry I growled earlier. You and your partner are doing a fine job. Keep up the good work."

Back in their car, Kat radioed dispatch for a jurisdiction check on the Lueong address. The address was in District William. Kat saw that the area lieutenant was still on scene, so she walked over to him and told him what was going on with the search warrant. She wanted to see if he could clear it with the District William Sergeant to have a unit sit on the address until they could get their search warrant. The area lieutenant said that he would take care of it.

As they drove back to the Department Kat said to Rex, "The Chief of D's apologized for growling at us. He said we were doing a good job and to keep up the good work."

The Chief of D's was a sharp supervisor and a smart cop. Rex had worked for him years ago when he was a lieutenant in command of the Field Training Unit; the unit charged with training rookie cops fresh out of the police academy how to survive on the street. Back then and now, Chief Ortiz knew right away when one of his officers was doing the right thing, and he would just get out of the way and let them do their job.

Chief Ortiz had explained it to Rex once. The job of a supervisor was to facilitate the officers under him. The good supervisor made sure his officers had everything they needed to do their job, and all the roadblocks were removed. Unfortunately, not too many supervisors thought like that anymore.

"He's a good man," Rex replied. "One of the few in the command staff that still care about doing good police work and not just furthering their own career. He gets it. He sees the big picture. It is not just one case number, one clearance with him. He understands about how all of this, the car thefts, stolen cigarettes, counterfeit credit cards and protection shake downs could all be tied together."

"I hear ya," said Kat. "It seems that most of command staff wants to bring it down to the one case number, one investigation, one case closed level, probably because they are so worried about stats and case closures. If you string a bunch of cases together, that means that you have a bunch of cases open longer. They just want them closed. It almost seems like they are telling us don't dig to deep, don't investigate too much, don't look for connections. Just take each case as it comes and get it off your desk as soon as possible and on the next one."

Chapter 18

When they got back to the office, Rex jumped on his computer. Thank God for computers. On his computer, Rex had every search warrant he had ever written and examples from a search warrant class he and Kat had attended. Kat had the same thing on her computer. Instead of having to write out the entire search warrant it was just a matter of cut and paste. He and Kat had gotten so good at writing search warrants that they taught the new detectives in the unit how to write them. They could write up an unusually complete search warrant in a matter of minutes. Also, neither Rex nor Kat bothered to have their search warrants reviewed by an Assistant District Attorney. Their work was good, and they knew it. They knew as much if not more than most ADA's about search warrants. There was no requirement to have an ADA review, so they did not bother; it was just a waste of time.

While Rex was putting together, the search warrant Kat got on the phone with Dispatch to page the on-call Superior Court Judge to her cell phone. The on-call judge called Kat back in fifteen minutes. It turned out the on-call judge was Judge Tobias. This was good because he was the judge that Kat and Rex would have gone to in the first place.

Judge Tobias was fair and honest. He liked cops, and better yet, he liked Rex and Kat because they always brought him quality stuff. Kat explained their need for a search warrant, and asked the judge if he wanted to do a telephonic search warrant, or if they should bring it to him. Since it was only 1900 hours, the judge told them to come to his home in Los Gatos. Kat told him that they would be there in half an hour.

They took Interstate 880, the old Highway 17, to Los Gatos. Traffic was light because the evening commute was winding down. Almost exactly one half hour later, they were knocking on the Judge Tobias' front door. The judge invited them in, and they exchanged pleasantries. The judge also wanted to know about the shooting so Kat filled him in as much as she could.

Judge Tobias read Rex's search warrant. He found the search warrant to be in good order, so he swore in Rex, had him swear that the fore going was true and accurate, and then signed the warrant. As he handed the warrant back to Rex, he wished the two of them good luck and admonished them to be careful. The whole thing took about ten minutes, and Rex and Kat were back on the road headed for Lueong's house.

As Rex drove back to the East side of San Jose and Lueong's house, Kat told Rex she thought they should call Five-O and see if he could meet them there. After all, Kat reasoned, this was as much Five-O's case as theirs, and since they were dealing with a Vietnamese suspect they were bound to find documents written in Vietnamese and Five-O could interpret. Rex agreed so Kat made the call and Five-O said he would meet them there.

Kat then called Dispatch to get the cell phone number for the District William Sergeant. She called the Sergeant and told him that they had their signed search warrant and were in route. The Sergeant told them that he had Six One William One sitting on the house. There were no lights on and no signs of life. He told Kat that he would meet them at the residence with two more units and assist in the serving of the warrant.

"Who is the District William Sergeant anyway," asked Rex

"It's a guy named Dorn," Kat replied. "I don't know him, but I think he just got promoted."

Rex shook his head. "Must be a fairly young officer promoted to a really young Sergeant. I don't recognize the name at all."

When they arrived and met Sergeant Dorn face-to-face Rex still did not recognize him. That was not too uncommon in a department the size of San Jose. After all, there were about 1200 officers from Chief on down.

Rex looked at the Sergeant's badge to see the number, so he could figure out his seniority. All San Jose badges were issued only once and sequentially. No badge number was ever repeated. You could see how senior someone was by his or her badge number. Judging from this young Sergeant's badge number, he had been on five or six years.

Rex told the young Sergeant that he wanted him to send two officers to the rear of the house and then Rex, Kat and the young Sergeant would enter and clear the house. The third officer would remain out front for security. The young Sergeant did not offer any argument and assigned his men accordingly.

They gave the two officers assigned to the rear of the house a little time to get into position and then Rex, Kat, and Sergeant Dorn moved up to the front door. Rex was on one side of the front door, and Kat and Sergeant Dorn were on the other. Sergeant Dorn had called for Code 33 on the channel, meaning that nobody else was to speak on the channel except those units involved in the entry.

Rex reached out, pounded loudly on the front door, and yelled, "San Jose Police, we have a search warrant." The idea was to make the knock and notice loud enough so that the officers in the back of the house could hear it. If they could hear the announcement, then you could argue that anybody in the house should have heard it.

Rex waited about fifteen seconds and pounded on the door again. "San Jose Police. Open the door, we have a search warrant."

Sergeant Dorn started to move out from behind Kat and into position to kick in the door. Rex motioned for him to hold his position. Rex reached for the doorknob and tried it. The doorknob turned, the door was unlocked. Rex pushed the door all the way open while remaining to the side of the door. He called out a third time, "San Jose Police, come out with your hands up."

Rex then nodded to Kat, and they made a crisscross tactical entry into the residence. They had been to several tactical classes together, and had made this type of entry for real several times. The entry went smoothly. Since the house was dark, they came in with their guns up in a shooting position with their flashlights held beside their guns. The idea was to enter quickly through the door so you were not silhouetted in the kill zone. Then you both swept your half of the room visually to see if there was anybody in there.

Kat and Rex did this in a matter of seconds each calling out "clear" as they cleared their area of the room. They moved deeper into the house with Sergeant Dorn following them and providing rear security.

It was a small single story two-bedroom house with an attached garage. They cleared each room and closet and finally the garage as they systematically searched the house for anybody hiding there. When they were done, Sergeant Dorn radioed that it was Code 4 and the house was clear and that the radio channel could go back to normal traffic.

When Sergeant Dorn cleared the channel the officer in front of the house radioed that he had a federal agent with him . Kat told Sergeant Dorn that would be a U.S. Postal Inspector they had asked to assist them in the search.

They met Five-O in the living room. He was also wearing a raid jacket that said "Federal Agent" on it. "Hey Cowboy," called out Five-O smiling his usual lopsided grin, "I thought I should put this on," fingering his raid jacket. "You know, these cops see some Asian brother coming up to the house and they are liable to shoot first, and ask questions later."

"That was probably the smartest thing you ever did you old shit for brains," replied Rex with a smile.

Sergeant Dorn stood to one side looking nervous.

"Relax," said Kat. "They're old friends; they talk to each other like this all the time."

"Well," said Sergeant Dorn, "if you don't need us anymore , I'll leave one unit out front for security, and the rest of us will get out of here."

"Sounds good," said Kat. "Thanks for all your help." She turned back to Rex and Five-O and said, "Shall we get to it?"

In order to preserve the chain of evidence, Kat was designated as the finder of the evidence. This meant that Kat would be the one signing the inventory form of all evidence they seized, and she would be the person to pick up the evidence and put it in an evidence bag.

Rex brought in a Search Warrant Kit, which consisted of evidence bags and tags and they all pulled on their latex gloves and got started. To make it go faster, they each took a room. Rex started with the living room, Kat took the kitchen, and Five-O took the second bedroom which had been turned into a makeshift office.

Rex found a Smith and Wesson Chief's .38 Special tucked down in the cushions of the couch. The serial number had been filed off. Kat found two baggies of what looked like crystal methamphetamine in the refrigerator. Finding nothing else, they went to the bedroom/office to see how Five-O was doing.

Kat stuck her head in the door and asked, "Hey Five-O, how's it going?"

"Looks like we hit pay dirt in here, I've got a lap top computer with a mag stripe imprinter hooked up to it. I'll bet this is where the credit cards are being made up."

"Good," said Kat. "We'll seize all of the computer stuff and take it over to the Hi-Tech Unit. They can do a search of the computer and tell us what they find on the hard drive."

"Yeah, and look at this," said Five-O holding up a small ledger book. "As you can see, all of the entries are in Vietnamese, so it was a good thing you called me. This is your boy's ledger book for all of the businesses he is running protection on. Everything is in here. Names, dates, and amounts collected. This is great."

"Good," said Rex. "We'll turn that over to the Gang Unit and let them run with it. You know the brass isn't going to like this. All these years of denying that any sort of Asian Organized Crime was here in San Jose, and now we have hard evidence. Find anything yet that would tell us who our dead guy was working for or who might be working for him?"

Five-O shook his head, "Not yet, but I'm still digging."

"Kat," said Rex, "why don't you take the bedroom next and I'll take the garage."

"You got it," replied Kat.

In the bedroom, Kat found an AK-47 under the bed with a fully loaded 30-round magazine and one round in the chamber. She also found a loaded Glock 9mm in the drawer of the nightstand. When she ran the serial numbers, they both came back stolen in Southern California. The closet was full of upscale men's clothing, mostly from Nordstrom's.

In the garage, Rex found a 2004 yellow Acura NSX. He found the registration in the glove box, and it showed registered to TVN Enterprises. Rex remembered one of the cars photographed at the Loving Cup Coffee House they had under surveillance had been a yellow Acura NSX.

Since this was about a $50,000 car, it seemed out of place. Rex checked the VIN plate against the registration and it matched, but he still was not satisfied. He called Sergeant Webber of RATTF and told him what he had found. Rex felt that it was too much car to be where it was. Sergeant Webber agreed. He told Rex where to look for a secondary VIN. Rex found it, and the secondary VIN did not match the registration.

When Rex told Sergeant Webber that the secondary VIN did not match, Sergeant Webber said that meant that the car was stolen and had been through a chop shop. Sergeant Webber asked Rex if he could impound the car and have it towed to the San Jose Evidence Warehouse.

Rex called the uniformed officer into the garage. He asked him if he could fill out the CHP 180 Impound sheet and ensure that the car was towed to the warehouse.

Rex continued his search of the garage. Neatly stacked on some shelving along the back wall of the garage he came up with ten army ammo boxes. When he opened the boxes, he found them full of 9 mm ammunition and two boxes of 7.62mm ammunition. There was enough ammunition to start a small war.

Rex headed back into the house and met Kat coming out to get him. "This just gets better and better," said Rex. "I found a stolen and chopped Acura sports car in the garage and boxes of ammo. I think the car is the same one photographed at the Loving Cup Coffee House."

"Well," said Kat, "I found a 9mm Glock in the bed stand and an AK-47 under the bed."

They went back to the office/bedroom to tell Five-O what they had found. He was reading a file folder open on the desk. He looked up as they entered.

"This makes no sense," said Five-O as they entered. "I found this file that looks like some sort of background check on a John Paul Mercado Reyes in the file cabinet. It's got a DMV printout of his CDL and his vehicle registration and notes about where he lives and that he was an engineering student at San Jose State. There are also some photos. They look like surveillance photos to me. I can't figure it out."

Rex and Kat looked over Five-O's shoulder at the file.

Rex said, "He was obviously collecting information on this guy Reyes, but why and for whom?"

"That is the mystery," said Five-O.

"Find anything else that might tie Lueong in with anybody else?" asked Kat.

"Nothing in the files," said Five-O, "maybe there will be something on the computer."

"We can only hope," said Rex. "Let's bag it and tag it and go book it in."

Rex took out his cell phone again and called Sergeant Harris. When Harris answered, Rex filled him in on what all they had found. Sergeant Harris was particularly interested in the weapons find.

It took them another hour to photograph, tag, and box or bag the evidence from the house. The tow truck came and took the Acura. The uniformed officer followed the tow truck to the impound warehouse so the chain of custody would not be lost.

When they had everything they were taking loaded into their two cars, they used a set of keys they had found in the house to secure the place. They left a copy of the search warrant and the inventory sheet on the kitchen counter

At Central Supply Rex and Kat spent the next hour booking in the evidence. Some of the evidence would be sent to the Evidence Warehouse to hold. Some, like most of the paperwork and ledger, were TOT'd, which stood for 'Turned Over To', the case file so Rex and Kat could work with it. The computer would be sent to the Hi-Tech Unit, so they could make a search of its hard drive.

It was midnight before they were done. They agreed they should be back to work by 0800 hours the next morning to complete their paperwork, and take a fresh look at where the new evidence was sending them.

Rex sat down at his computer and opened up a new email. In the subject line he typed 'Cigarette Sting and Subsequent Search Warrant.' Then he typed the message. 'Cig sting lead to VCET Officer Involved Shooting which lead to search of dead perp's house. Here til midnight. Unless otherwise directed, Kat and I will be in at 0800 tomorrow. Will give you full briefing then.'

He addressed the email to Sergeant Alvarez with a courtesy copy to Lieutenant Wong and hit the send button.

Chapter 19

Rex stopped at the Starbuck's on The Alameda on his way in to the office the next morning. As he was walking into the store, he called Kat. As soon as she answered he said, "Good Morning Sunshine, are you on your way to work yet?"

"Yes I am."

"Well, what do you want for coffee this morning, I'm at Starbucks."

"Oh, get me a Grande Americano."

"You got it. What do you want to eat? I'm gonna go next door to the pastry shop."

"You can get me an apple strudel from there."

"One apple strudel coming up. Meet me at the side gate to PAB in about twenty minutes," said Rex and disconnected.

Kat was waiting for him as he walked out of the employee parking lot with his armload of goodies. "I figured we would be right in the thick of it as soon as we walk in with no chance to go out for breakfast," said Rex as he handed Kat her coffee.

They headed up the stairs to the third floor. As they passed the Chief of D's office, they saw that he was already at his desk, so they stopped at his door and knocked.

"Good morning, Chief," said Rex. "You wanted a briefing on what we found last night. Do you want it now or do want us to come back later?"

"Give it to me now. Just let me get another cup of coffee." Chief Ortega eyed their Starbuck's coffees and added. "I don't have fancy Starbuck's like you two. I'll have to settle for Homicide coffee. Be right back."

Rex and Kat settled into the guest chairs in front of Chief Ortega's desk and waited for him. He was back in a couple of minutes and sat down behind his desk nodding his head indicating they were to begin their briefing.

"Ken Lueong had quite an arsenal in his house," began Rex. "We found a Smith and Wesson Chief's .38 Special with the serial number filed off, a nine millimeter Glock and an AK-47 stolen out of Southern Cal, plus lots of ammo for all of the guns.

"We also found a 2004 Acura NSX, a $50,000 sport car, registered to TVN Enterprises. The primary VIN did not match the secondary VIN so we impounded the car. RATTF will be working on that.

"There was a mag stripe imprinter hooked up to a lap top computer, and a stack of credit card blanks, which means he was counterfeiting credit cards. There was also a hand written ledger in Vietnamese that showed all of the businesses he was shaking down, and how much their payments were.

"All in all what we've got is a guy who until now was known as a low level enforcer in Southern California Viet gangs who is now in San Jose doing high end credit card counterfeiting and extorting about half of the Vietnamese business community."

"Obviously somebody promoted him," mused the Chief of D's. "He obviously wasn't doing all of this on his own, any idea who he was working for?"

"Not yet Chief. We've got a lot of evidence to go through. We are going to take his computer over to Hi Tech this morning and see if they can pull anything off of it."

"I'll call Hi-Tech and tell them to put a rush on it."

"We're also going to work with the Gang Unit on the extortion angle."

"Good, keep me informed and let me know if there is anything you need."

They left the Chief of D's office and headed down the hall to Homicide. Sergeant Harris must have just beat them in as he was hanging up his suit coat as they walked into Homicide. They told him that they would have their Three's (supplemental police reports) on last night's shooting to him in the next thirty minutes. Harris told them he was fine with that.

They left Homicide and went on down to their unit. As they walked in, Sergeant Alvarez was waiting for them.

"I heard that you two had a busy night last night," she said as she followed them to their desks. When neither one of them said anything she continued. "Why didn't you call me last night?"

"Well," said Kat, "because it didn't occur to us to do so. You were out sick yesterday, so I didn't know if you were still sick and I didn't want to disturb you at home if you were.

"Besides, it wasn't our operation; it was VCET's, so there was no reason to call you even if you were over being sick. On top of everything, Chief Ortiz was on scene and we thoroughly briefed him about our role in the shooting, and we just came from his office where we updated him on the case.

"And Rex sent you an email explaining all this before we left last night. Don't you check your emails?"

Now Sergeant Alvarez was getting flustered. Rex and Kat used this standard tactic wherever they had to talk to her. Rex remained quiet and Kat did all the talking. It made Sergeant Alvarez extremely nervous when a smarter and stronger woman talked back to her in such a matter of fact way. She usually surrounded herself with weak people that did not stand up to her. She had come to hate the day Rex and Kat had come back to Financial Crimes.

Kat was a very strong independent minded woman. She could also be feisty if you pushed her too far. Kat had been a cop for fifteen years now. She had worked patrol and detectives. She was a smart, hard working, and very talented cop.

Rex stood there looking on with admiration at his partner. Dressed in a dark grey pantsuit today, she looked very professional and business like. She certainly sounded confident and in charge. An outsider watching this conversation would think Kat was the supervisor and Alvarez was the subordinate instead of the other way around.

"So where are you on your case?" asked Sergeant Alvarez

Kat answered, "We executed a search warrant on the shooters house last night with the aid of Postal. We recovered a lot of evidence. It looks like Lueong was tied in to many things, like extortion, stolen weapons, stolen cars, and counterfeiting credit cards for starters. We are going to be following up with Postal, RATTF, Gangs, Burglary, and Homicide. So, if you don't mind we have a lot of paper work to do and we should get to it."

Sergeant Alvarez just stood there blinking with that deer in the headlights look. Her morning got immediately worse because just as Kat finished, the Chief of D's walked up behind her.

Sergeant Alvarez physically flinched when the Chief of D's belted out, "Good morning Linda, great pair of detectives you've got working for you. Really top-notch investigators. Detectives, I just wanted to let you know that I called Hi-Tech, and they are waiting for that computer."

"We'll get it over there right away Chief, just as soon as we finish our Three's for Homicide," said Kat. She turned back to Sergeant Alvarez. "Was there anything else you needed Sergeant?"

Sergeant Alvarez just kept blinking that deer in the headlights look. Finally she turned, and walked away without saying anything.

Lieutenant Wong walked into the office. He saw the Chief of D's standing with Rex and Kat and almost fell over trying to stop and reverse direction to come over to them. As Lieutenant Wong came to a halt by their desks, Chief Ortiz said to Kat and Rex, "Great job, keep up the good work and keep me informed. Anything you need you let me know."

The Chief of D's turned around and saw Lieutenant Wong. "Good morning Calvin. Great detectives you've got here, looks like they really cracked a big one last night. This is turning into a multi-unit, multi-agency case. I want you, the Gang Lieutenant, the Homicide Lieutenant, and the Special Ops Lieutenant in my office, in half an hour. We need to see what kind of support we can give these detectives." Chief Ortiz called back over his shoulder as he left, "see you in half an hour Calvin."

Lieutenant Wong just stood there dumb founded for a moment. Then he turned to Kat and Rex and asked, "All right, what did you two get into?"

Rex then took Lieutenant Wong through the Reader's Digest version of the previous night again. As Rex went through his briefing, Lieutenant Wong looked more and more nervous. It was obvious that he felt out of his comfort zone with what was happening. Things were moving too fast for him, and there were too many moving parts.

When Rex was through Lieutenant Wong said, "Fine, fine. Is there anything you need right now?"

When Rex told him there was not, Lieutenant Wong disappeared into his office.

Rex looked over at Kat and said, "Don't you just feel all warm and fuzzy knowing what great leadership we have?"

Kat just made a face at him.

They finished their Three's from the shooting and took those down to Homicide. Next Rex worked on the Search Warrant Return that had to be signed and filed with the court. When Rex was finished with that, they walked the two blocks over to the Hall of Justice and went to Judge Tobias' chambers. Technically, they could get any judge to sign the return, but they always tried to find the same judge that had signed the search warrant. The judges appreciated hearing about the results of the search warrants they had signed.

Judge Tobias's court was in session when they walked in, so Rex walked over to the Deputy on duty and was about to ask when the judge would be taking a break.

Judge Tobias had seen Rex and Kat walk in and held up his hand, stopping a defense attorney in mid-sentence. Judge Tobias called out across the courtroom, "Do you have something for me Detective?"

"A Search Warrant Return, your honor," replied Rex.

Judge Tobias said, "We are going to go off the record here for a minute, thank you counselor. Detective, you may approach the bench." When Rex handed the judge the return he put a hand over his microphone and asked, "how'd you do?"

"Some dope, some stolen guns, a stolen car, a computer and other evidence that will substantiate extortion and counterfeiting credit cards your honor," replied Rex.

Judge Tobias said, "This all looks to be in order," while looking over the paperwork. He signed the return and handed it back to Rex.

As Rex turned to leave, he saw the female defense attorney the judge had cut off in mid sentence still standing behind the defense table with her mouth open. Rex winked at her as he went by and said, "Sorry for the interruption counselor."

Rex and Kat went down stairs to the Court Clerks window, filed both their Search Warrant and the Return, and then walked back to their office. Rex retrieved Lueong's computer from his locked desk drawer. They signed out on the board, and drove over to Hi-Tech with it. The Hi-Tech Sergeant was waiting for them. He signed for the computer and said that he would call as soon as they had anything.

Chapter 20

When they got back to PAB, Rex took the ledger book and walked over to the Gang Unit looking for Detective Phong. Rex explained to Phong what the ledger book was. He also let Phong know that the Chief of D's had now taken a personal interest in the case and was having a meeting with their bosses.

Phong looked through the ledger book. "Son of a bitch. We always knew there was extortion and the selling of protection going on out there, but we could never prove it. Nobody would ever come forward. Now with Lueong dead and this book, I might be able to get somewhere with the other shop owners. This is great man. If it's O.K. with you, I'm going to take it and run with it."

"That's exactly what I'd expect you to do," said Rex. "I don't think we will step all over each other's investigations as long as we keep each other briefed on what we are doing. Don't forget that RATTF will be running with the stolen auto portion of this case as well."

When Rex walked back into his unit, Lieutenant Wong and Sergeant Alvarez were standing by his desk waiting for him. Kat was sitting at her desk also waiting.

Lieutenant Wong said, "Chief Ortiz has decided to set up a task force to handle this investigation. You and Detective Sanchez will be the lead investigators on this with Sergeant Alvarez as the supervisor in charge. Detective Phong from the Gang Unit will be assigned, and RATTF and VCET will also be assigning people. Your first meeting will be at 1600 hours today in the Detective Conference Room to get everything rolling. Any Questions?"

Rex shook his head no, and Lieutenant Wong disappeared back into his office with Sergeant Alvarez.

"Great," signed Rex, "now what do we do?"

"Hey," said Kat, "you're the one that wanted a task force. Well now you got one, complete with your Sergeant large and in charge."

"I think I'm gonna call Capalini and invite him to the party," Rex said.

Later, Sergeant Alvarez came out of the Lieutenant's office and over to their desks. She gave them a complete list of what she wanted at the first task force meeting that evening. She wanted a full briefing of the case and what led up to the shooting. She wanted them to come up with a game plan as to where the investigation was going and who would be tasked with what assignments. She reminded Rex that she was in charge and that everything was to go through her.

Rex said that was fine and only had one thing to ask of her right now. Rex wanted to get Officer Sonny Tam assigned to the task force. He explained that Sonny had been working tremendously hard to win over the Vietnamese store owners that were being extorted. If it were not for Sonny, they would not have gotten the break they did. Besides that they could probably use his language skills since he spoke Vietnamese. Alvarez agreed and said she would get him assigned TDY from Patrol.

Sergeant Alvarez would posture about being in charge but she would still tread lightly around Rex. For one thing, she was afraid of him. He was a strong individual and an exceptionally smart detective. She realized that he knew what he was doing, and she did not.

For another thing, Chief Ortiz was personally interested in this case, and she did not want any screw ups pointed at her. As long as she kept the right amount of distance from the case and did not appear to be going too hands on, if anything went wrong then she could employ the tried and true save my ass method so well know within the PD of throwing down the investigating officer and putting all the blame on him. Of course if the investigation was a tremendous success then she would be there taking all the credit.

By now, it was lunchtime so Rex and Kat gathered up Mitch and Terry from Burglary and they all went out to Applebee's for lunch. Over lunch, Rex got Mitch and Terry caught up on the case and the forming of the task force.

Rex did not actually like big formal task forces. He liked to do what he did best, just work informally with other detectives. A formal task force meant formal briefings, like the one this evening. It also meant a lot of time wasted in meetings or preparing for meetings. However, they were stuck with it and so they would soldier on and make the best of it.

Rex asked Mitch if he would look into the guns they had recovered at Lueong's house. Two were in the system as stolen. The third one had had its serial number filed down. If Mitch could run down all the information on them, it would be immensely helpful. Mitch said he would do it when they got back to the office.

Back in the office, Rex made a few more phone calls and then got ready for the first task force meeting. By the time 1600 hours rolled around, he was as ready as he would ever be. He and Kat went on down to the Detective Conference Room.

Sergeant Alvarez was already in the room talking to Sergeant Capalini. Five-O walked in a few minutes later with Detective Phong and Officer Sonny Tam. Sergeant Anderson came in next along with Officer Owens, one of the SJPD officers assigned to RATTF. Finally, Sergeants Harris and Long walked in followed by the Chief of D's.

Deputy Chief Ortiz started the meeting. "Thank you all for coming. You are all here because of a major break in a case that is being worked by Detectives Johnson and Sanchez. It appears we have a continuing criminal enterprise operating in our city and throughout the South Bay Area.

"Because of last night's shooting, we know they play rough. Detective Johnson seems to think that this group is involved in many crimes including counterfeit credit cards, extortion and auto theft for starters. Detectives Johnson and Sanchez will remain the lead investigators on this case. They will coordinate the investigation. Sergeant Alvarez will be the Sergeant in charge.

"The PD will continue to work with the US Postal Inspectors on the investigation. The Gang Unit and RATTF will assist in the investigation in any way they can. VCET and MERGE will be our muscle. They will be in charge in the service of all search warrants and in making all the arrests. Any questions? No? In that case I've asked Homicide to give us an update on last night's shooting."

Sergeant Harris took over. "We've completed our investigation of last night's shooting and have determined that it was a justified shooting with the officers firing in self defense. Since there are no more loose ends to tie up as far as Homicide is concerned, that will be the end of our involvement in this case. Good luck in your investigation." They left the room.

Chief Ortiz said, "I too will leave you now to get on with organizing your investigation."

Alvarez started to go into how she saw the task force being organized and how the chain of command would work. Rex cut her off in a respectful way. Rex knew how to play the game, when to be abrasive, and when to be charming.

"Excuse me Sergeant Alvarez," said Rex, "I don't mean to interrupt but we sort of got the ball rolling last night, and we have some follow up investigation that is on-going and time sensitive that we should talk about right now."

Sergeant Alvarez hesitated a moment, "Oh, O.K., by all means, go ahead Rex."

"Officer Owens," said Rex, "did you get anywhere on the car we impounded last night and where are we on the suspected chop shop?"

"The car," replied Officer Owens "was stolen out of Newport Beach a year ago. The phony VIN tells us it went through a chop shop and a pretty good one. The VIN looks real right down to the rosette rivets.

"We are setting up surveillance on the chop shop tonight. We will photograph everybody going in and out and record the license plates of all the cars in and out or just parked in the shops lot. As soon as we get a car going in that is reported stolen, we will get a search warrant and hit the place."

He turned to VCET Sergeant Anderson, "I'll get with you after this meeting and coordinate so we can have a VCET Team on standby for the search warrant."

"Lueong was not the top of the food chain," said Rex. "This whole thing is apparently operating under a cover company called TVN Enterprises. Inspector Ho from U.S. Postal has been tracking that down. Five-O, what have you found out?"

"The address for TVN Enterprises in a mail box drop currently at a UPS Store. The application gives an address that turned out to be another mailbox store. The application there gave the Marriot Residence Inn in South San Jose as the home address.

"The renter of the box is one Tran Van Nguyen who is probably TVN Enterprises. The copy of the CDL shows an address in Westminster, which turned out to be another mailbox drop. I had a Postal Inspector in Southern California check out that application and he ran into the same dead end as up here.

"What is supposed to be the person's real address just comes back to another mail box store until the timeline gets too old for anyone to keep any more records. We have a mail cover on both boxes so we will at least know where all incoming mail is coming from. My hunch is that Tran Van Nguyen is our guy in charge up here, but he has no record and it will take some digging to find him."

"Thanks," said Rex. "I gave Phong a ledger we found in Lueong's house last night that shows all the Vietnamese business men he has been shaking down for protection and how much each paid. Phong is going to run with that and see what he can turn up there.

"The reason we are going to have VCET and MERGE handling all the entry work from now on is not just because of last night's shooting, it is also because of what else we found in Lueong's house. We found two handguns, a .38 Chief's Special tucked away in the couch cushions and a Glock 9mm in the nightstand. We also found an AK-47 under the bed as well as a fair amount of crystal meth. Because Lueong was so eager to shoot it out with us, we are going to assume the rest of them will be also go for their guns. We are going to adopt the concept of peace through superior firepower.

"There is also one wild card in this so far. We found a file in Lueong's house on a John Paul Mercado Reyes. The file was almost like a background check. We don't know who this Reyes guy is or why Lueong was checking up on him. We are going to go find him and ask him what he knows. So, if there is nothing else, let's get busy on our assignments.

"Oh, I'm sorry Sergeant Alvarez, did you have something more to say?" asked Rex.

The good Sergeant did have more to say. As it was Thursday, she set the next meeting for Monday at 1600 hours. She admonished everyone to keep her updated on all of their moves, and she reminded them that while Chief Ortiz had set this task force up, there were still budget problems within the department and they were to keep their overtime to a minimum. With that, the meeting broke up.

As they were drifting out of the conference room Rex made sure that he had everybody's current cell phone number, and they had his and Kat's. Rex also assigned Sonny Tam to work with Detective Phong for now. Sonny had spent almost two years cultivating the businessmen that were in Lueong's little ledger. They knew him whereas, they did not know Detective Phong. When Phong started contacting them hopefully Sonny could help break the ice.

Chapter 21

Dawn Summers was mad. She had just finished reviewing all the raw video tape that her cameraman had shot last night at the police shooting outside the convenience store. She had filed the story that PIO Sergeant Comstock had given them at the crime scene last night. The police department had been investigating a series of robberies of small Vietnamese owned stores. They had gotten a tip that this store was going to be robbed that night, so they had set up on it in an attempt to apprehend the criminal. The suspect had decided to shoot it out with the police and was killed.

As she reviewed the raw footage again, Summers decided that about the only thing true about what Comstock had told the press was that the bad guy had decided to shoot it out with the police and lost. Summers knew just about all the detectives on the San Jose Police Department by sight. It was what she was not seeing on the tape that was driving her crazy. She was not seeing any Robbery Detectives at the scene. She saw the Homicide Detectives, who she knew, and she saw Detectives Johnson and Sanchez. This was not a robbery. This was something else involving Financial Crimes.

A little bell went off in Summers' head. She remembered dropping in at the Bistro one night and finding Rex and Kat there. Summers knew all of the cops' watering holes and periodically made the rounds and bought drinks. It was not that she was trying to get them drunk and get information out of them. That would have never worked. As a group, they were too disciplined to fall for that. Besides, she had never seen such a group of professional drinkers as the cops. They could seriously put away the booze and not seem affected by it at all.

No, what she did when she made the rounds of the cop bars was to just cultivate some professional friendships. She would buy a couple of rounds, exchange pleasantries, and maybe pick up some general background information on current crime patterns in the city. The night she was remembering was a night when Rex was telling her, kidding her actually, that she ought to do an investigative report on organized crime in the city of San Jose. Asian Organized Crime to be exact. He said it was something no one in the department wanted to admit existed.

So that meant if Robbery Detectives were not at this crime scene, and the department's two leading financial crime detectives were, it was not a robbery. The storeowner was Vietnamese, the dead guy was Vietnamese, maybe there was something to this Asian Organized Crime story. At any rate, from where she sat it looked like the San Jose PD was trying to cover something up and she was going to get to the bottom of it. Summers felt a story coming on, not just a one-night story but a series.

Summers called Sergeant Comstock and told him that she had to see him right away about last night's story. He told her he would be in his office for the rest of the day, and she could come over anytime. One hour later Summers walked into Comstock's office.

Summers was all smiles and sweetness. After all, you could catch more flies with honey than with vinegar. Smiling ever so sweetly at Sergeant Comstock, she told him how she thought she was being lied to and why. She explained about reviewing all the video and which detectives she had seen and not seen on the tape.

Then she dropped the bombshell on him. Without revealing any sources, she said that she had information that led her to believe that the shooting and the investigation surrounding the shooting was about Asian Organized Crime in San Jose. She felt that the department was trying to cover up the level of Asian Organized Crime in the city and that she was going to do an in-depth, multi series report on it.

Comstock was pretty adept at holding a poker face too. He just sat there smiling back at Summers. "Well Ms. Summers, I've always said that the only three things a reporter wants is relevancy, access and accolades."

Sergeant Comstock went on to remind her that it was the policy of the San Jose Police Department to be entirely honest with the press. How he thought he had a close working relationship with the press. He reminded her that sometimes they could not disclose certain things to the press because it was an on-going investigation. Comstock then asked Summers if he could have a little time to look into this before she went ahead with her story.

Summers knew she had him at that point. There was something going on, and Comstock had just tacitly admitted that he had to check with the Chief of Police before he went any further. Summers knew that the PIO came directly under the Chief's Office. The PIO always cleared the really hot stories directly with the Chief of Police before he gave them to the press.

Summers told Comstock he had twenty-four hours before she started running with her story. She added that naturally, she would like the PD's view, but if they were not willing to cooperate with the press, she would go ahead without it.

As soon as Summers left his office, Comstock called the Chief's secretary and got the next available appointment.

The Chief greeted Comstock warmly as he entered the Chief's corner office. "Rick, how are you? Come on in, sit down. What can I do for you?"

"Chief," said Sergeant Comstock getting right to the matter, "we've got a problem with the press on last night's shooting. Specifically with Dawn Summers from Channel 2 News. I don't know how, but she saw through our story that it was a disrupted robbery. She thinks it involves Asian Organized Crime and smells a big story. She says that she is going to run with a whole investigative series on Asian Organized Crime in San Jose with or without the departments help or input."

The Chief's demeanor changed immediately. He slammed his fist down on his desk and said, "Damn it, who has she been talking to? For years, we have been saying there is no Asian Organized Crime here in San

Jose because of the negative impact it would have on the card clubs. Those card clubs bring this city a lot of revenue. Those card clubs were also going to throw a lot of money my way if I decide to run for mayor in two years. I don't need this fucking shit right now."

Just as quickly, the Chief had calmed down and leaned back in his chair. He continued in full campaign mode.

"I need to finish my tenure as chief of police showing crime is down, not that we've got organized crime operating under the radar. I need to be able to show that I have kept San Jose as the safest large city in America.

"I've done a lot to foster strong relationships with all of the groups in this city; the Vietnamese, the Japanese, the African-Americans, the Mexican-American, the Muslims and the gay community. As long as we don't recognize something like organized crime exists, then as far as the public is concerned it doesn't exist. Therefore, there is no problem.

The Chief sat forward and his eyes narrowed.

"Remember McNamara and the street gangs? For the longest time he said there were no gangs and no gang problems in San Jose and the public believed him. His idea was to deny the gangs publicity. It's the same thing here. I can't have some reporter going off half-cocked on some story about Asian Organized Crime. We don't have any organized crime here of any kind. Maybe a few street gangs have gotten a little more sophisticated, but that's all. This is a safe city, and my future campaign for mayor depends on me being able to say I kept it safe. People start hearing about organized crime and they start getting worried. I can't have that. I won't have that. We have to keep this under control."

"Chief," said Comstock, "I think we can turn this around in your favor if we cooperate with Summers. Let's give her an exclusive. We bring her in on the investigation, give her full access, but she can't put anything on the air until after the investigation is completed because of officer safety.

"That way the story comes out that you and the Department were quietly handling an attempt by an Asian street gang to infiltrate the Vietnamese community. We can spin it like you just said. It was just a street gang that got a little more sophisticated was all. We don't have any organized crime coming into San Jose because your reputation for being tough on crime is too good. And the evidence in that will be taking down this street gang and crushing them before they threatened the safety of the city."

"That doesn't sound half bad," replied the Chief. "Ortiz has already filled me in on this task force that he has Johnson and Sanchez heading up. Johnson's a good detective but a bit of a loose cannon. That's why I didn't promote him last time around, not really a company man. O.K., let's go with that. Get a hold of Summers and make the deal. I'll make sure Ortiz quietly controls Johnson behind the scenes and gets this investigation over quickly."

As Comstock walked out of the Chief's office, he liked everything except the part about controlling Rex Johnson. He liked Rex. He and Sanchez brought a lot of favorable press to the Department. Johnson and Sanchez were both smart and tough cops. It would be hard controlling them.

Chapter 22

The RATTF officers sat in their brand new surveillance van parked across the street from P & L Auto Repair. It was a mini-van, so it blended in with this neighborhood. The van had been purchased with a federal grant by the Sheriff's Department, and was a far cry from the broken down old undercover vans that had been used in the past.

No longer were they sitting on a lawn chair in the back of a stinking hot van, looking out a little side porthole window with binoculars, trying to see what was happening. The main operator sat in a captain's chair and operated the remote control periscope with a joystick. The cameras on top of the periscope were telephoto, night vision, infra red, and thermal. An image of what they were looking at was displayed on the flat screen monitor. The operator could view the images real time and could switch back and forth from still to video. All images could be recorded on the on board DVR. There was even a shotgun mike for recording conversations up to 150 feet away from the van.

The van was also equipped with counter surveillance measures. There were mini cameras and microphones hidden behind the parking and tail light lenses. These allowed the operators to watch and see if someone was trying to sneak up on them.

Inside the van, they had an on-board computer with Internet connection and the ability to log into any of the Bay Area police department CAD systems. They also had a police radio that allowed them to come up on any frequency of any of the police agencies in the Bay Area. Both of these units were programmable so that if they went out of the Bay Area, they could easily program new frequencies into the units.

The van was even designed with their needs and safety in mind. There was a carbon monoxide and oxygen level alarm installed and a heat exhaust. Surveillance usually meant long hours locked in the back of the enclosed van and the atmosphere could get a little thick. The van also had a small heater and air conditioner for the back end and a portable toilet and small refrigerator. Things had clearly come a long ways.

The operators could run any license plate they saw or run any name they heard through whichever dispatch center they were logged into. The only thing the van did not have was the newest computer soft ware that read every license plate, and told you if it was stolen.

The CHP in Oakland were testing this system now. Every day the computer was up loaded with all of the license plate numbers of all stolen cars and other cars of interest to the police. All the officer had to do was drive around, and the cameras on the police car would automatically check and run every license plate it saw against its database. If the car was stolen, or in the database for some other reason, the computer would alert the officer. The officer could then run the plate for further information. RATTF was hoping to add this system to their arsenal next year with another federal grant.

So, the RATTF officers sat back in relative comfort monitoring all that was going on around them and especially across the street at P & L Auto Repair. It was toward the end of the day, and a few legitimate customers were coming in to pick up their cars.

RATTF always surveiled a suspected chop shop at night because that was the primary time for car thieves to bring in the cars they had stolen, after normal business hours. As the RATTF officer watched, the owner closed up his shop for the day, but he did not leave.

Two hours later, the owner re-opened the bay door. A few minutes later a Toyota Camry was driven into the bay. As soon as the car was in the bay, the roll-up door was closed. The officers recorded the arrival of the Camry with their digital imaging equipment. They got on their computer and ran the license plate of the car. It came back clear and registered to an address on the East side of San Jose.

The RATTF officers called San Jose Dispatch and requested that they send a unit out to the address, make contact with the registered owner, and check the status of the vehicle. SJPD Dispatch called them back in forty-five minutes to let them know that a patrol unit had gone out to the residence, but no one was home.

The RATTF officer knew that they had struck out for now, but they were patient. They continued watching the auto repair shop. The lights stayed on in the work bay, and it was obvious that someone was working on a car inside. Finally, at 2215 hours, the lights went out and five Vietnamese men walked out of the shop.

The older man of the group stopped and locked the door. Three men got in to a Toyota pickup truck and drove off. The other two got into a BMW. The three in the pickup truck looked like auto mechanics; dressed in old, stained work clothes. The other two were dressed in the uniform of the Viet gangster, black leather jackets and slacks. They got pictures of everyone.

The RATTF officers continued their surveillance for another half hour and then called it quits for the night.

Chapter 23

Rex rolled over and shut off the alarm. His wife did not even move. Even the dogs did not stir in their beds on the bedroom floor. It was 0400 hours on Monday morning. Rex threw on his workout shorts and sweatshirt and stumbled down to the barn to feed the horses.

Back at the house, Rex grabbed a bottle of water and went to the bedroom they had converted into a workout room. Monday was a lift day. Rex went through his stretches and then started his weight lifting routine on the Bowflex. Staying in shape was important both mentally and physically. It helped keep the stress level down. Rex tried to lift three days a week and ride his stationary bike the other two or three days.

An hour later Rex stepped into a steaming hot shower. After he had showered and shaved, he came out of the master bathroom and gave his wife a wake up kiss. She stirred and smiled sleepily at him.

"Good morning sleepy head, time to get up."

Rex headed to the walk-in closet to get dressed, and his wife stumbled into the workout room to finish her morning workout. By 0600 hours, Rex, dressed in a light grey western suit, gun and handcuffs secured to his belt, was ready to go to work. He kissed his wife goodbye and told her he loved her.

Rex always tried to remember to tell his wife he loved her when he headed off to work. In this job it was always a possibility that this could be the last time they ever saw each other. Of course, you always thought that it would happen to the other guy, but you never knew. If his number was up, he wanted his wife to be comforted; knowing the last thing he had said to her was that he loved her. It wasn't much, but it might make things a little easier should the unthinkable happen.

Rex grabbed his large commuter mug of coffee, and headed out the door. It was fifty miles and about a one-hour drive at this time of the morning to work from his San Benito County ranch.

"Ah, Mondays," said Rex as he dove into his country breakfast of three eggs over medium, ham steak and pancakes, "the start of another great week catching bad guys."

"You're certainly chipper for a Monday morning," Kat shot back as she attacked her linguisa omelet.

"That's because we only had two in-custodies and were able to get out of the office before your Sergeant cornered us and started asking us stupid questions about the task force."

Every Monday morning, first thing, each detective unit usually had a stack of in-custody reports to take care of. These were people arrested over the weekend for crimes that their unit handled. In Rex and Kat's case, that would be any financial crime or grand theft.

This Monday morning there had only been two weekend arrests for them to take care of. They each took one and looked over the patrol officer's report to make sure all the elements of the crime were addressed. Then they ran the arrestee's name through all the computer systems and attach printouts of his criminal history to the file. Finally, they wrote up a single page summary cover report for the reviewing Assistant District Attorney. When they finished that, they made three copies of all of the reports and took the package over to the DA's Office. Failure to have an in-custody to the DA's Office by 1000 hours would mean that some Assistant DA would not have time to review the reports, the court complaint would not get typed up in time and sent over to the court, and the suspect would be released.

They buzzed through the paperwork and got it over to the DA's Office. Then they had hopped back in their car and hurried over to Bill's Cafe for breakfast before returning to the office.

As they were paying their bill, Rex's phone rang. It was Detective Phong. He told Rex he and Sonny Tam had found some entries in Lueong's ledger that did not make sense. He wanted Rex and Kat to look at them. Rex told Phong that they were on their way back to the office and would be at his desk in fifteen minutes.

When they got back to PAB, Rex and Kat went directly to the Gang Unit and found Phong. Sonny Tam was also there.

"What have you got?" asked Kat.

Phong opened the ledger book and pointed. "See these entries here? They are not like the entries for businesses that he was selling protection too. These are something different, but I don't know what. They are businesses, but they all seem to be restaurants."

Rex looked at the entries. Essentially, what he was looking at was an appointment calendar. The month was listed at the top of the page. Under that, the days of the week were listed across the top. Down the left side of the page was listed the first name of a person and the name of a business. There were twelve names is all. To the right of each name, in a box below a day of the week, were two dates and times. There were two appointments for each day of the week.

Rex pointed this pattern out to everyone. "Look here, on Mondays at 1900, he sees Lyn at the Silver Dragon and at 2000 he sees Hung at the Golden Pheasant. Then on Tuesdays, he sees Quan at the Snow Pea, and at 1800 it's Le at the House of Ming. And so on through the week.

"Son of a gun." said Kat. "Those have got to be restaurants where he has skimmers. The names are the wait staff people who have the skimmers and the dates are when he swaps the skimmers out. Phong, pull up Google Maps on your computer. Now enter all the address of the businesses."

When the map finished loading they had a clear picture of the pattern. The addresses clustered in accordance with the days of the week. The two restaurants visited each day of the week were close to each other.

"So," said Kat, "if he had a skimmer at each restaurant, that's twelve restaurants he had covered. Figure each person was catching four or five cards a night because they would have been told only to go for the platinum cards. That means that Lueong was collecting from forty to sixty credit card numbers a week.

"We need to put last names to these people listed in the ledger and get search and arrest warrants on them. I hope that we can catch some of them still in possession of the skimmer. That was a good catch Phong. This will probably break the credit card portion of this case wide open and put a stop to a lot of cards being compromised."

Rex photocopied the ledger entries on the restaurants and then he and Kat went back to her desk to start contacting the security people for each of the major credit cards. She wanted to check their point of compromise reports against the restaurants listed in Lueong's ledger.

Every month each credit card company security office ran tracking software, that pin pointed all the points of compromise. This way they could see if several cards were compromised at a specific location.

Multiple hits indicated a skimmer was probably being used there. The credit card security people then gave local law enforcement a copy of each month's report in the hopes of aiding in a criminal investigation and arrest. It was all part of the networking thing that went on between good financial crimes detectives and their civilian counterparts in the financial industry.

As he and Kat were going over the reports, Sergeant Alvarez came over to them and wanted an update. Kat started to explain about points of compromise and cross checking the reports against entries found in Lueong's ledger.

Sergeant Alvarez interrupted her, "What's that got to do with the stolen cigarettes?"

Kat sighed and continued, "What we are finding is that Lueong and whoever he worked for were into many different crimes including counterfeiting credit cards. The entries in his ledger should lead us to some of the people he had working for him."

"Now who is Lueong?" asked Sergeant Alvarez. "Why don't we just arrest him and see what he has to say."

Kat and Rex just looked at each other as if to ask could she really be that stupid?

Rex finally said, "We can't ask Lueong anything, he's dead. That's the guy VCET shot."

Sergeant Alvarez blinked back at both of them with her deer in the headlights look, turned, and walked back to her cube.

Chapter 24

"I swear," said Kat, "that woman is too stupid to live."

As they went back to the reports, Rex's intercom line buzzed. It was Grace telling him that Officer Kirby from Hi-Tech was on line two. Rex punched up line two and spoke to Kirby for about five minutes.

When he hung up, he turned to Kat and said, "Kirby said Lueong's computer was not password protected or encrypted, so they were able to get right into it. He said there was info on at least a couple of hundred credit cards on that computer. He knows about the task force and that this is a priority and said he should have a report and printout for us by close of business today."

Kat said, "That's great. So far I've found four of the restaurants listed as major points of compromise."

Mitch came over and told them he had some news on the Glock and AK-47 they had recovered from Lueong's house. It seemed that two gun stores had been hit in Los Angeles County a year ago. Twelve AK-47's and twenty-two various models of Glocks had been stolen.

According to the Los Angeles Sheriff's Deputy Mitch had talked to; two of the Glocks had turned up on dead guys. These were two Vietnamese gangsters that had been killed in a turf war that had been going on in Los Angeles County for the past six months. This was the first time one of the AK-47's had turned up.

The L.A.S.D. had very few leads on the burglaries of the gun shops. They had been remarkably sophisticated because they had by-passed sophisticated alarm systems at both stores. Word on the street was that the burglaries and the turf war were tied to Asian Organized Crime, but they did not know which family, group or faction was responsible for the burglaries.

The Deputy was surprised that one of the AK-47's had made it all the way North to San Jose. He told Mitch that heavy weapons like the AK's the crime families liked to keep for their own soldiers. If it was Asian Organized Crime, then whoever got the weapon in San Jose had to be known by, or connected to, one of the Asian Crime Families in Southern California.

Just as Mitch was finishing up with what he had found out about the weapons, Rex's cell phone rang. It was Sergeant Webber from RATTF.

"You remember that car my guys observed driving into the suspected chop shop on Friday night? Well the owner's were out of town for the weekend. They just got back this morning. That's when they discovered their Camry was missing. They filed a report this morning, and it just got entered into the system and popped up over here on our computer. That gives me enough to get a search warrant. I'm going to walk it through this morning, and we are going to hit the place this afternoon. Wanna come out an' play?" asked Sergeant Webber.

Rex told Sergeant Webber about the stolen AK-47's. Sergeant Webber agreed that where there was one there could definitely be more. After what happened with Lueong, they had to assume that they were dealing with a well-armed group that was not afraid to attack the cops. It was decided that they would use VCET and MERGE for the entry.

MERGE stood for Mobil Emergency Response Group and Equipment. It was the Department's SWAT team. San Jose could not call their SWAT team SWAT because that was what LAPD called theirs and SJPD could not copy LAPD. Besides, SWAT sounded too military, so someone came up with MERGE years ago and that was still the official name.

Everybody that was not a MERGE member or former member just called them the God Squad. That was because every officer on MERGE looked at all the other officers on the force with that distinct look that said, "I'm special, I'm above you. I'm the guy with the big gun that goes through the door first when things are really hairy. I'm a god."

There was a lot of joking about MERGE's holier than thou attitude and how long it took them to get to the scene of a barricaded suspect during a call-out. Or how long it took before they made entry. Or how once they made entry, how they usually found the suspect had killed himself hours ago, and if we had only known that we could have all gone home much sooner. After all, nobody liked standing around for hours securing a perimeter. Cops were not happy unless they were bitching about something.

However, when faced with a real threat like this one, a situation where you have a strong indication you will be going up against automatic weapons; you seriously wanted MERGE to handle it. They had the tools and the training to handle just this sort of thing.

So, while Sergeant Webber started walking his search warrant for P & L Auto Repair through. Rex called Sergeant Anderson in VCET and let him know what was going down. He briefed Anderson on the AK-47's, the confirmed stolen car seen going into the shop and that RATTF wanted to take the place down as soon as possible. Sergeant Anderson said he would start making calls and set everything in motion. He would call back when he had a time for the operations briefing.

Rex's next call was to Five-O. He brought him up to speed on the entries in Lueong's ledger. Rex also told him about the raid they were going to make later that day at the P & L Auto Repair.

"You know Five-O," said Rex, "those people in the ledger have to be the wait staff that has the skimmers, but without a last name we have no way to ID them. The only thing that I can think of is to go in to each restaurant cold and ask for the person and confront them right there. If we are lucky, we can get a consent search and find them still holding the skimmer. Then we can on-view them. At the least, we can invite them down to the police department for a chat. If we do it that way, I would like to have you along to talk to them. You can probably be more persuasive in their native language."

Five-O replied, "I know you want to get everybody you can, but remember these people are just the low-end worker bees and probably don't know that much. I'd be happy to help you out. Since we don't know their work schedules I would suggest that we show up at each restaurant on the date and time that Lueong would have showed up next and bag 'em that way."

"That sounds like a plan," said Rex. "You in on the raid this afternoon?"

"I wouldn't miss it, let me know what time the briefing is," Five-O replied.

Rex's intercom line buzzed again. Grace told him that Porter Goss from Costco security was on line one.

When Rex answered, Porter got right to it. "I think we got hit again this weekend. The assistant manager at one of the San Jose stores told his manager that they had a large cigarette purchase this weekend by a business member cardholder. He didn't think anything about it at the time because it was just one Filipino guy making the purchase.

"When his manager heard, he had enough sense to call me. I shot out an email to all the other stores in the Bay Area and Saturday we had a lone Filipino male making purchases at all three San Jose stores and each store in Santa Clara, Sunnyvale, Mt View, Foster City and Fremont.

"All were commercial buys using an Amex card. The first four purchases were all made around eleven AM. I've got loss prevention at each store going through the security tapes and pulling the footage on each transaction. I've got the store mangers emailing me copies of the tobacco resellers' license and the Amex card info."

"All right," said Rex, "get good stills if you can and get it all to me as soon as you can. We have some other stuff pertaining to this case breaking wide open too. It looks like it's all about to come together and we are about to take some major bad guys down."

When Rex hung up with Porter, he turned to Kat and said, "Come on, time to update your Sergeant."

Chapter 25

At 1400 hours, everybody assembled in the Special Operations Briefing Room. Both MERGE Teams and both VCET Teams were there along with the RATTF Team. Command Staff was well represented by Deputy Chief Ortiz from the Detective Bureau and Deputy Chief Osborn from the Patrol Division. Lieutenant Wong from Financial Crimes and Lieutenant Tufts who commanded the Gang Unit stood next to the Deputy Chiefs. Detective Phong, Officer Sonny Tam, Five-O, Rex and Kat took their seats in the back row.

Lieutenant Samson, the Special Operations Commander, stood up in front of the room and started the briefing.

"Thank you all for coming in. Our mission today is to assist RATTF in the service of a high-risk search warrant on the P & L Auto Repair Shop, which is a suspected chop shop. RATTF has had eyes on the place since 1000 hours this morning. Sergeant Webber informs me that they put their surveillance van in place as soon as he became aware of enough probable cause to support a search warrant.

"Detective Johnson has informed me that this chop shop is probably only one operation of an organized group. The chop shop was found during his investigation into a credit card counterfeiting and cigarette theft investigation.

"One of the suspected members of this group was shot and killed by VCET last week as they attempted to make an arrest. Since that suspect decided to shoot it out with the police, we are going to assume that everyone involved is armed, dangerous, ready, and willing to engage us.

"Detective Johnson also recovered an AK-47 from the shooters home. He has since learned that this was one of ten AK-47's stolen in Los Angeles County about six months ago along with several Glock handguns. Two of the Glocks turned up in the hands of two different Vietnamese gangsters killed in a turf war going on in Los Angeles County.

"So far, none of the other guns has turned up in Southern California. LASD found it very interesting that one of the AKs and a Glock from the gun store burglaries turned up here in San Jose. Because our detectives have developed a possible tie between the guy VCET shot and this chop shop, we are also going to assume that we could run into more of those AK-47's and Glocks on this entry.

"MERGE Teams 1 and 2 will be handling the entry with VCET Teams 1 and 2 handling the inner perimeter security and manning the chase cars."

Lieutenant Samson turned to an aerial view from Google Maps projected on the screen. It showed a close up view of the main building, surrounding buildings and the immediate surrounding streets as he continued.

"As you can see this is going to be difficult. The target is located in a metal row building less than half way down. There is a man door leading into the office and a single roll up door leading into the work bay. Since we will be doing this during business hours, we have to be extremely careful of other civilians in the area.

"Air Two will be up providing us our eye in the sky. We don't have any place to put our snipers, so Air Two will be our only over watch. Sergeant Webber has obtained a no-knock warrant, so we will be making a dynamic entry with the armored car through the bay door. If we are lucky, it will be open. If not, then we will crash through. MERGE Team 1 that is your job.

"MERGE Team 2, I want half of you to go into this adjacent yard and work your way around to the North end of the target building. You can see a fence here that you will have to go over, so take your ladders. Work your way south along the building until you are in position here where there is an L cutout that gives you some cover.

"The other half of Team 2 will approach from the South. You guys will go in through the office door at the same time Team 1 hits the bay.

"Team 1; watch yourself in the shop bays. You have a car lift, stacks of tires and car parts lying all around from what the RATTF surveillance team has been able to see. There will be grease and oil on the floor.

"Team 2; the office area includes a small waiting room with the actual office behind the waiting room. The bathroom is also off the waiting room so don't forget to clear that.

"For the VCET Teams, I want two officers each in marked chase cars. There is only one way in, but I want this thoroughly contained. Right here, is the only driveway into the complex. As soon as MERGE goes in I want the two chase cars pulled across the entrance blocking it.

"Once we have moved in and secured the entire building and the people we find there the RATTF Team and the Detectives will come in to execute the actual search warrant. Three of the detectives coming along with us, Detective Phong from the Gang Unit, Officer Tam on special assignment and Inspector Ho from U.S. Postal speak Vietnamese, so use them if you have a language problem.

"Also, depending on what is uncovered by the detectives in their search we may be tasked to hit other places immediately in search of other suspects. This is going to be a long evening, and I need everybody to stay sharp all the way to the end.

"We will stage here in this parking lot on Industrial off Gish. As soon as MERGE Team 2 is in position, we will move out. The order of movement will be the armored car, two SUV's with the MERGE officers, the two unmarked cars with the other half of the MERGE Team 2, and the two marked chase cars with the VCET officers. The detectives will remain at the staging area until I call you up."

Lieutenant Samson then went on to give out the radio frequency they would be operating on. He let everybody know that the District Sergeant and Area Lieutenant had been notified of their operation and gave them the location of the nearest trauma center.

Lieutenant Samson then asked the Deputy Chiefs if they had anything to say. To his surprise, Deputy Chief Ortiz, the Chief of D's, said that he did.

Deputy Chief Ortiz stood and addressed the assembled officers. "As some of you know, what started out as a routine investigation into cigarette thefts has turned into a major operation to take down what we believe to be a well organized Vietnamese street gang.

"Detectives Johnson and Sanchez, with the help of the Postal Inspectors have developed information that this gang is involved in the counterfeiting of credit cards, the theft of cigarettes by use of those cards resulting in probably a half million dollar profit on that scam alone. This gang is also involved in extortion through the selling of protection to Vietnamese business owners, and the operation of a major car theft ring.

"So far we have been able to keep this out of the press so that our hand would not be tipped. Unfortunately, one reporter did stumble on to the story. We made a deal with that reporter. She would sit on the story as long as she got an exclusive on it. To honor that deal we have also placed two guys from our video unit in the RATTF Surveillance Van. They will be filming your entry, and we will share that with the reporter.

"This raid should bring a close to this gang's operation. We will be holding a news conference about it in the next couple of days. I just wanted you all to know about the camera. Thank you and stay on your toes throughout this operation." With that, Deputy Chief Ortiz sat down. The room was silent.

Lieutenant Samson then asked if there were any other questions. There were none, so he told everybody when they were supposed to be at the staging area and ended the briefing.

As they walked out of the Special Operations building, the Chief of D's was waiting for them.

"Rex, Kat, can I have a moment of your time?"

"Sure," said Rex. "What is it Chief?"

"You guys are exceptionally good detectives. You are also two of the smartest people I know in the detective bureau. By that, I mean you cannot only solve complex cases, but you are both well aware of the current philosophy about organized crime from the office of the Chief of Police.

"Certain people have certain political aspirations. They are going to get what they want by telling the people of this city what they want to hear. It would not be wise to go against that. Both of you have sterling careers going for you. You are both highly thought of by a lot of people on this department. You both still have several years to go before retirement. Don't do anything foolish. You can accomplish almost all that you want to accomplish and still appear to go along with the program if you get my drift."

"Yes sir," Rex replied. "We understand perfectly.

The Chief of D's turned and walked away from them.

"I think Chief Ortiz is looking out for us," Rex said to Kat. "Our Chief of Police is still looking for a way to say that this is street gang activity and not organized crime. One of the worst kept secrets on this department is that he wants to become mayor of San Jose. If he declares victory against gang activity and doesn't have to admit that it was organized crime, that's another feather in his cap.

"They are going to shut our investigation down after tonight. Oh sure, we will be tying up loose ends and chasing down a few more bad guys, but you watch, after tonight it's over. They are going to declare a win. The San Jose Police Department, the greatest Department in the Universe, took charge of a dangerous situation where a street gang was threatening the safety of the entire Vietnamese community, and the rest of the city. The department poured assets into the investigation, and took them out before they could grow. The Chief is going to stand in front of the cameras and declare a victory."

"Yeah, but we still get to take down some major bad guys Cowboy. It doesn't matter how the Department or the Chief want to spin it, it's still a good arrest. I think that's what Chief Ortiz was telling us. We still got to do our job and we did it well. Let the Chief have his moment in front of the cameras. It won't hurt us to look as if we are going along with the program."

"You're right," Rex said with a sigh. Then he smiled at Kat. "Hell of a case, huh?"

"Don't worry; it will all be better when you are Chief."

"Like I got a snow ball's chance in hell of ever doing that."

Chapter 26

An hour later everyone was assembled in the parking lot that was the designated assembly area. Half of MERGE Team 2 had already taken off to work their way into position on the North side of the building. As soon as they radioed that they were in place everybody else would move.

The RATTF surveillance team was still in place in their van parked just inside the gate at the front of the parking lot. They had a good angle view down the parking lot to the chop shop. They reported that the bay door was open, and it looked as if people were working on at least one car inside. They could not see into the building from where they were at, but reported that they had seen at least four people in the shop. It seemed to be business as usual at all the other business. People would step outside for a smoke, or an occasional delivery truck had come and gone, but right now, all the workers were inside all the shops.

Air Two, the SJPD Helicopter, checked in with Lieutenant Samson. They were orbiting overhead and had a clear visual on the area. Everything on the ground appeared to be business as usual.

MERGE Team 2 radioed that they had scaled the back fence and were in position. As they had worked their way down the building, they had stopped just long enough to tell each shop to keep all their people inside. Seeing police in full tactical gear with automatic weapons left no room for argument. As they passed each shop, they could hear the bay doors closing behind them.

Lieutenant Samson checked with the RATTF surveillance team and Air 2 once more and was told that everything was still quiet with nobody moving about outside. The Lieutenant gave the order to move out.

As the MERGE Armored Car turned the corner from Industrial on to Kings Row, two workers sauntered out of the shop on the front end of the row of the buildings, facing Kings Row, for a smoke. They were just starting to light their cigarettes when the armored car roared through the open gate and down the parking lot, followed by the two marked SUV's with two MERGE officers in full tactical gear and weapons at the ready standing on the running boards on each side of both vehicles.

Right behind them, the two marked police cars slide to a halt parallel to the gate, blocking it. The four VCET officers in the cars, also in full tactical gear, piled out and took up positions behind the cars with automatic weapons at the ready facing North up the parking lot.

The two workers stood there dumfounded for a moment and then turned and ran back into their shop. Whatever was going on, they wanted no part of it. They never did get their smokes lighted.

As the MERGE Armored Car approached the chop shop, the driver turned on the spot lights and light bar, and hit the siren. As the armored car turned into the bay entrance and stopped with the front bumper just barely inside, the two SUV's broke left and right behind the armored car, and screeched to a halt. The MERGE officers hanging on to the sides bailed off at a run and converged on the bay door with their weapons up in the ready position. The two unmarked units came to a halt just to the South of the chop shop. More MERGE officers piled out of the back of the armored car. At the same time, MERGE Team 2 moved up from their position to the North.

As the MERGE officers started to enter the shop, you could hear shouts of "San Jose Police, get down on the ground."

Inside was chaos. They had not known what was coming and were taken totally by surprise. Two guys had been working on a car just inside the roll up door. The car was backed into the bay facing out. The hood was up, and the two mechanics were working in the engine compartment. Farther into the bay another car was parked. Just to the left of that car was a small table and two folding chairs. Two Vietnamese men sat at the table playing cards and smoking.

The two mechanics did not know what to do. They looked up, and all they saw was the silhouettes of what looked like giants coming through the bay door right at them. It was darker in the bay and bright sunshine outside so when they looked out the bay door they were partially blinded by the sun. The two mechanics just froze where they were bent over each fender.

The first two MERGE officers to reach them grabbed them and threw them on the ground pointing their MP3's at them, telling them to stay there and not move. The two mechanics were scared and not about to move.

As other MERGE officers moved past the first two into the shop, the two men who had been frozen in their card game when they first heard the siren and the rush of men coming through the bay door, came back to life. They each had a Glock handgun stuffed in the front of their pants. Almost simultaneously, they started to stand up and go for the weapons.

A MERGE officer saw them reaching for their weapons and shouted out "Gun." Four MERGE officers opened up with a controlled burst from two MP3's, a Colt .45 caliber handgun and a Remington 12-Guage Shotgun. In less than a second, eleven rounds slammed into the two gunmen. They went down in a heap. While two MERGE officers covered the downed gunmen, the last two MERGE officers moved farther into the shop searching for anybody else that might be there.

The other half of MERGE Team 2 had hit the office. There was no one in the small waiting room. The door to the office was closed. One MERGE officer kicked the door in and two officers button holed into the small office. A highly surprised and frightened middle-aged Vietnamese man sat behind the desk, a cigarette dangling from his mouth. The MERGE officers told him to keep his hands on the desk and not move.

Since they were pointing guns at him that was exactly what he intended to do. One officer came around behind him, brought his arms behind his back, and handcuffed him. Just then, gunfire erupted in the bay. The officer threw the man down on the ground and fell on top of him. The other officer also hit the ground looking for something to get behind. There was only a thin sheet rock wall between them and the service bay`. It would not even slow a bullet down.

Then the officers heard over their earpieces, "Two bad guys down, search continues." The officers in the office held their position protecting the man they had taken into custody. In a few more minutes, the all clear from the officers in the bay came over their radios. The two officers in the office hustled the man they had in custody outside.

The other two officers stopped in the waiting room and looked at each other.

Officer Morgan said, "I think we forgot something," as he nodded toward the closed bathroom door.

They moved over to each side of the bathroom door. Officer Morgan tried the knob and it was locked. He stepped back and kicked the door in. A Vietnamese man wearing glasses sat on the toilet with his pants down around his ankles and his eyes as large as saucers.

He held his hands out in front of him and yelled, "You no kill me."

Morgan and the other officer looked at each other. It was all they could do to keep from laughing. Officer Morgan told the frightened man, "Wipe your ass, and pull up your pants."

The MERGE officers turned the four people they had taken into custody over to the VCET Officers outside. The MERGE officers went back in and made a slow search of the chop shop, making sure that there was nobody else hiding in there. When they declared that the shop was secure, Lieutenant Samson radioed Rex that he and the rest of the detectives could come up.

When Rex drove up, he saw that the VCET officers at the front gate had not pulled back and were controlling entry to the site and not letting anybody in or out. One of the VCET officers told him that they had an officer involved shooting, and this was now and active crime scene.

"Great," Rex said to Kat, frustration seeping into his voice, "we are really stacking up the bodies on this one. We only have one or two officer involved shooting a year, and now we have had two in the course of this investigation in less than a week. The Chief of D's is not going to like this."

As they walked down to chop shop, Rex saw that officers were putting crime scene tape up around the outside of the shop. He saw Lieutenant Samson standing outside talking on his cell phone. Rex walked up to him and waited for him to finish his call.

"Two dead inside," said Lieutenant Samson to Rex. "They apparently were here to guard the place. They came out with Glocks as my guys moved in, so they got taken out. I've just finished making all the notifications. Homicide is on the way, so the scene is frozen until they get through. Sorry Rex, your search is going to have to wait."

Rex said, "That is not a problem. Nobody on our side got hurt right?"

"Right," said Samson, "all our people are fine. We got four live ones for you, but I guess you'll have to wait until Homicide interviews them first." Then Samson cracked a small smile and continued, "Morgan tells me they even caught one on the crapper with his pants down around his ankles."

Rex walked back to the group of detectives and RATTF officers standing nearby the two marked units at the gate and told them what was going on. He told Sergeant Webber about the two dead guys with guns that were apparently guards. Sergeant Webber agreed with Rex that that pretty much indicated they had hit the right place.

About twenty minutes later Rex saw another unmarked car approaching as he talked with the VCET Officer at the gate. It was Sergeants Harris and Long again. Rex went over to Sergeant Harris who was driving and shook hands.

"Hello Stan," said Rex, "I see you caught this one too."

"Yeah," said Sergeant Harris, "we are still on call. Was this another one of your operations?"

"It was MERGE's operation," replied Rex, "they were serving a high risk search warrant for RATTF that was tied in to my investigation."

"Is it the same investigation that you had going at the other shooting?" asked Sergeant Harris.

"That's right," said Rex.

"You're playing with some rough people," said Harris.

Chapter 27

They had been standing outside the perimeter for about forty-five minutes. The Crime Scene Unit had arrived shortly after Sergeants Harris and Long. RATTF had pulled their surveillance van out and parked it on the street. The SJPD Video Unit guys continued to film some long shots of the on-going investigation.

Homicide had the shop owner, the two mechanics and the guy found in the bathroom transported down to PAB for further interviews. Rex asked Five-O and Detective Phong to go along to help with translation. Rex also told Five-O that he wanted him to take a run at Bathroom Guy after Homicide was through with him. He had a hunch that he was more than just a customer.

The media circus was in full swing. Rex counted five news vans with their satellite masts up and broadcasting. The various news personalities were doing their stand-ups at the top of the complex driveway with the two marked police cars as their backdrop.

Rex took out his cell phone. As he did, he looked over at Kat.

"You better call your husband and tell him you're all right. This shooting is going to be all over the news. You also better let him know that we are going to be working late tonight."

Kat nodded and took out her cell phone.

Rex hit the speed dial on his cell phone for his wife. Carmella answered after two rings.

"Hey sweetheart, in case you've seen the news I thought I'd better call and let you know that I'm fine."

"Yeah, I'd heard about the shooting. I'm glad you called. Everybody else all right?"

"Yeah, everybody's fine. Kat and I were not involved in the entry, that was MERGE's show. Two bad guys down and no good guys hurt. We are just waiting now for the O.K. to go in and search the scene."

"Does this mean you are going to be working late?"

"I'm afraid so."

"Well, if you get a chance call me back with an update."

"I will hon. I love you."

"I love you too. Bye bye."

As they stood there, Kat looked over Rex's shoulder and said, "Oh-oh."

"What?" asked Rex.

"The Chief of D's just pulled up, and he doesn't look none too happy," she told Rex.

As Rex looked around Deputy Chief Ortiz picked him out of the crowd and walked over.

"Got a minute, Detective Johnson?" asked the Chief of D's. "You too, Detective Sanchez."

"Sure thing Chief," replied Rex.

They walked away from the crowd of RATTF officers. When Chief Ortiz figured they were out of earshot, he started in on Rex and Kat.

"What the fuck have you two stepped into? You have stacked up more bodies in a week than we get all year in gang shootings. This investigation of yours had better be producing something spectacular and fast. We need to be able to give the Chief and the press something solid, because they are both going to eat us alive over these shootings."

Rex knew that the Chief of D's was upset. He also knew that he was right. The Murky News, as the officers liked to refer to the local newspaper, and the other news channels liked nothing better than to second-guess all SJPD shooting and editorialize how they were not justified, how trigger happy the cops were and how they could have handled the situation better.

"Look Chief," said Rex, "both shootings were righteous. The bad guys pulled guns on our guys, and they had to take them out.

"As far as this place is concerned, just the fact that they had guards here proves that it is a chop shop and who knows what else. As soon as Homicide clears it, we are going in there to take the place apart with a fine tooth comb and see what we can find.

"These guys are tied to stolen cars and who knows what else. We are going to find evidence that will connect them. This is going to be a big thing and in the next couple of days the Chief can stand in front of the cameras and tell the world how the PD took down a major criminal enterprise that was threatening the safety of the community."

The Chief of D's seemed somewhat appeased by that. "O.K. Rex, I know you and Kat are two of my best detectives. Just put this together and show me that it was all worth it." The Chief of D's turned and walked off.

A few minutes later Sergeant Harris came walking down the parking lot looking for Rex. "We're all through in there Rex. You and the RATTF people can have the scene now. Long and I are going back to the PD to interview the other people from the shop."

Rex thanked Sergeant Harris and reminded him that he had sent Detective Phong from the Gang Unit and Five-O from the Postal Inspectors down to the PD to help with the Vietnamese translations. Rex also reminded Sergeant Harris that he wanted Five-O to interview Bathroom Guy.

Rex said, "I just have a feeling that there is more to him. I don't think he was a customer, and I don't think he was here by accident. I'll be interested to see what Five-O can get out of him."

Rex and the RATTF team pulled their cars inside the perimeter and up near the auto shop. Rex pulled an evidence kit out of the trunk of his car and then he and Kat went over to talk to Sergeant Webber.

"Sergeant Webber," said Rex, "if you don't mind why don't you guys take the work bay. That's more your area of expertise. You and your guys know what to look for when you're looking at a chop shop. Kat, Sonny, and I will start on the office and see what kind of paperwork we can find."

Sergeant Webber, who already had a Dell XFR armored laptop computer in his hand, said, "That's just what I was going to suggest. I've got my computer and my guys will go through every car part in there that has a serial number or a VIN. I'll be able to run them all to see if they belong to anything stolen. As you go through the office look for any ledgers or bill of sales, registrations, or pink slips that would show what cars went through here."

"Sonny here can read Vietnamese, so we shouldn't miss anything," said Rex. "Whatever paperwork we find that looks like it has anything to do with cars we will put aside for you." Rex looked at Kat and Sonny and added, "Well, let's go see what we can find."

The auto shop's office was small, dingy and reeked of stale cigarette smoke. There was an overhead fan, but it didn't work. There was a cheap wood laminate desk in the middle of the room with papers strewn all over the top of it. An overflowing ashtray acted as a paperweight for some of the papers. On one corner of the desk was a lap top computer standing open. There was a four-drawer metal filing cabinet in one corner. In the opposite corner was a small safe with the door standing open.

The first thing that caught their attention as they looked around the office was the open safe. It was full of neatly stacked bundles of money. As Kat looked closer, she could see that they were bundles of twenty dollar bills.

"Somebody was doing a land office business," said Kat as she looked through the bundles of bills. "All twenties. Assuming these are bank bundles, that's one hundred bills per bundle, there's about thirty bundles in the safe, so that makes it around $600,000.00. Look on top of the file cabinet. That's a counting machine. I'd say a lot of cash flowed through here."

Sonny was looking at the computer. "This thing is still on," he said. "It's just in sleep mode, which means somebody was using it just before the raid."

"Yeah," replied Rex, "but look where it is sitting. It's at the corner of the desk facing the edge with that folding chair in front of it. The owner of the shop who was sitting in that chair behind the desk when MERGE busted in. He wasn't using it. Another person was in this room with the shop owner, working on that computer just before the raid. I'll bet it was Bathroom Guy. The question is, what was he working on?"

Sonny reached over and hit the space bar on the computer, and the screen flashed to life. It was an Excel spreadsheet.

"Looks like somebody was having their books audited," said Sonny.

"Bathroom Guy must be the book keeper," said Rex. "O.K., don't touch anything else. We'll take the computer to Hi-Tech and have them do a complete search of it."

Rex got out his phone and called Five-O. He told him about the lap top find, the cash, and his suspicions that Bathroom Guy was the organization's bookkeeper.

"As soon as you get a crack at him work him," Rex told Five-O. "He's the accountant, and he knows what is going on. Get him to talk."

While Rex was on the phone, Sonny had been going through the papers on the desk. He had found a desk calendar which he was leafing through.

"Hey Rex," said Sonny, "look at this."

Rex looked over Sonny's shoulder at the calendar. All the entries were in Vietnamese.

"O.K. wise guy, so what's it say?"

"That's why you brought me along," replied Sonny, "not only for my good natured charm but my linguistic skills."

As Sonny pointed to the various columns, he continued. "All of the entries seem to have something to do with cars. You have dates when cars were delivered. Dates when parts were sold. Dates when some cars went to a paint shop. And dates when cars were shipped to Oregon and Nevada."

"Something for the RATTF boys," said Rex. "You'll have to do a complete translation for them."

Rex, Kat, and Sonny continued their search of the office for another hour. They found documentation for salvage titles and more paperwork on parts sales to various auto repair shops in the greater San Jose area. They also found a folder that had detailed descriptions of the make, model, color, and VIN on some decidedly high-end automobiles. Rex called Sergeant Webber into the office and told him what they had found.

"That checks with what we are finding out there," said Sergeant Webber. "There is a ton of stolen parts out there. It's all sorted out and stacked on shelves. Also, that car they were working on comes back stolen. Since a car is usually worth more for its parts, the thieves steal it, and then bring it to a chop shop like this one to strip it. They dump the frame and sell the parts to any auto shop that wants to make a cash deal. From what you found in here, I would say that is only one thing they were into.

"It sounds like they're also into car cloning. What they do there is steal a high-end car. You know, a Corvette or a Mercedes, or something like that. Then they go and find a legal car on the street that is the exact same make model and color. They copy down that cars VIN and then they make a phony VIN plate using the legal one and put it on the stolen car.

"They dummy up a bogus title application and certificate of salvage. The car passes through one or two straw buyers before they sell it to the real buyer. This would be someone who had put in an order for a specific high end car. They get their car at a significantly reduced price, and it comes with a clean title.

"The third thing it sounds like they are into is title fraud. They steal a car and strip it. But, they don't sell the parts, they put them aside. They abandon the frame on the street where it will be easily found by the police.

"After the insurance claim is settled, the car ends up in a salvage yard. The crooks buy the frame from the salvage yard gaining a clear salvage title. They put all the parts back on the car and the car is just like it was when they stole it. Next, you take the car out of state, exchange the salvage title for a regular title, and sell the car.

"This group is quite sophisticated. I've never seen an operation that was running all three scams at the same time. Rex, I'm beginning to believe more and more in your theory of Asian Organized Crime."

Chapter 28

Rex's cell phone rang, it was Five-O.

"Hey Cowboy," Five-O greeted him. "I've had that Bathroom Guy down in an interview room in your pre-processing for about an hour now. I think he is about ready to talk. You were right, he is a player in the organization. You should get down here as soon as possible."

"O.K.," said Rex, "Kat and I are on our way."

After Rex disconnected he told Sergeant Webber that the guy they had caught in the bathroom was not just some unlucky customer, but was apparently a player, and he was just about ready to talk. Rex suggested that since all of the evidence in the office seemed connected to the auto theft part of the investigation, he would leave Officer Tam behind to help process the evidence. Webber agreed. Rex turned the crime scene over to Sergeant Webber. They set up a meeting for 0900 hours the next day so they could compare notes.

Rex and Kat arrived at the SJPD Pre-Processing Center thirty minutes later. They secured their guns, ammo, and knives in the trunk of their detective car and went in to see Five-O. They found him engaged in a conversation with the Pre-Processing Sergeant.

"Hey guys," said Five-O, "I was just giving Sergeant Black my recipe for teriyaki BBQ sauce."

"Oh man Al," said Kat, "you gotta try it. Five-O's sauce is to die for. The way you like to bar-b-que down here you owe it to yourself to try it."

"So how is Bathroom Guy doing?" asked Rex.

"His name," said Five-O, "is Charlie Zsu. He is not Vietnamese, he is Chinese. He is from Charleston, South Carolina, and he has no record. Oh, and he has a real thick southern drawl, which kinda creeps me out. He has admitted to me that he was playing dumb when the cops came in. He tried to pass himself off as just some dumb Chinaman who did not speak much English, and had no idea what was going on. He is now claiming that he was just a customer at the shop. He wants to talk to the Detective in charge.

Rex and Kat had learned the fine art of interrogation years ago when they were working the Sexual Assault Unit. There you had to go one on one with a rapist, sexual predator, or child molester and get him to confess to his deepest darkest secrets. You had to do this without having any kind of handle on the suspect.

Many times, you were doing the interrogation without even any real physical evidence because it had not been processed yet. All you had was the word of the victim. They had learned all the tricks of reading and interpreting body language. They had learned the art of thinking quickly on their feet, staying one step ahead of the suspect, and responding appropriately to even the smallest change in the suspect's demeanor.

Contrary to popular belief and TV shows, the good cop/bad cop routine rarely worked. A skilled interrogator knew that he had to go into the room alone with the suspect. You had to know what props to bring in with you. You also had to be prepared to spend as long as it took. The idea was to keep the suspect talking and not asking for a lawyer.

Kat entered the holding cell. Since they had Mr. Charlie Zsu in Pre-Processing, it was not the most favorable environment for the interrogation. The holding cells were cinder block walls with a large reinforced glass window in the front so the PPC Sergeant could watch each room. The room they had Charlie Zsu in had a video camera in the corner that was barely detectable. Rex would be watching the video feed in another room and recording the interrogation.

Kat closed the venetian blinds on the front window, giving them a sense of more privacy. Charlie Zsu sat on a metal stool welded to a metal table bolted to the floor with his left wrist handcuffed to an eyebolt permanently affixed to a metal table. There was a matching metal stool on the opposite side of the table.

"Good evening Mr. Zsu, my name is Detective Sanchez. I am conducting the investigation into what went on at the P & L Auto Shop today."

Charlie Zsu cleared his throat and said, "Well ma'am, it is a pleasure to meet you." Five-O was right. The guy had a southern accent so thick you could cut it with a knife.

"Before we get started, is there anything I can get you? A glass of water maybe?"

"No ma'am, I'm fine, and please call me Charlie."

"O.K., Charlie. Do you know why you are here?"

"No ma'am, I don't, I was just at that auto shop as a customer. I was talking to the owner about getting some work done on my car."

"Charlie, if that is the case, then you will be out of here in a little while. But, just to be on the safe side, before we go any further, I'm going to advise you of your rights." Kat pulled out her department issued Miranda Card and read off from it.

"You have the right to remain silent. Do you understand?"

"Yes ma'am."

"Anything you say may be used against you in court. Do you understand?"

"Yes ma'am."

"You have the right to the presence of on an attorney before and during questioning. Do you understand?"

"Yes ma'am."

"If you cannot afford an attorney, one will be appointed for you free of charge, before any questioning, if you want. Do you understand?"

"Yes ma'am."

"So, Charlie, do you want to tell me what happened?"

"Yes ma'am. Like I said, I was just at that shop as a customer. All I wanted to do was talk to the owner about getting my car fixed."

"Why did you hide in the bathroom?"

"I had to use the restroom, and while I was in there I heard all this yelling about San Jose Police, and then I heard gun shots. Ma'am, I wasn't hiding, I was just too scared to even move."

"What did you need to get fixed on your car?"

Charlie looked up and to the left, a sign that he was thinking up a lie. "Somebody ran into my car in a parking lot and dented the fender. I wanted to know how much it was going to cost to get it fixed."

"That would be the silver SLK Roadster parked in front of the auto shop?"

Charlie did not say anything he just looked down at his shoes.

"The car that doesn't have a scratch on it?"

Charlie remained silent.

"The car that comes back registered to TVN Enterprises?"

Charlie still sat there staring at his shoes.

"The car that has mail on the front seat addressed to you?"

Charlie looked up at Kat with a lost look on his face. Kat knew that look, this was the first sign that he was looking for a way out.

"Look Charlie, the way this works is that you have to tell me what you know. I can't help you if you won't help yourself."

Finally, Charlie spoke, "Uh, it was my other car that I was there to talk to him about."

"Really Charlie? Because there is no record of you having any car registered in California."

Charlie looked down at his shoes again.

"You see that door Charlie?"

Charlie looked over at the holding cell door.

"The only way you get to walk out that door is by cooperating with me."

Charlie looked back down at his shoes. With his free hand, he picked imaginary lint off his pant leg.

Kat leaned forward and lowered her voice. "Look Charlie, we all make mistakes. That's why they put erasers on pencils. I think that what happened here was that you made a mistake is all. You are not a bad guy. And now you have a chance to erase that mistake."

"You don't know what you are asking me to do."

"Charlie, let me tell you what we do know. We know that Tran Van Nguyen is the man who runs TVN Enterprises. We also know that Tran Van Nguyen is into some serious crime like selling protection, forging credit cards and auto theft. The fact that you were driving a TVN car tells us that you are involved with Tran Van Nguyen."

"No, that's not true," Charlie wailed. "You don't know what you're talking about."

Kat kept her voice low and reassuring. "Charlie, it is true and you know it. As we speak, other detectives are out there collecting more evidence against Tran Van Nguyen. He is going to go down for everything, and we are going to add on the fact that he was in charge of a continuing criminal enterprise. Do you know what that means Charlie? That means a lot of extra jail time, Charlie. And if you don't cooperate with us, you're going to be sitting in a cell right next to him."

Charlie just sat there looking at Kat and blinking rapidly. That eye movement told her that he was just about ready to be pushed over the edge.

Kat picked up the notepad in front of her and drew a line right down the middle of it. "The way I see it Charlie is that this line divides the good side from the bad side and right now you are over here on the bad side." She tapped the left side of the pad with her pen for emphasis.

"But I think that basically you are a good person Charlie. I don't think you have crossed that far over onto the bad side. It's not too late Charlie, cross back over to the good side and let me help you."

Kat leaned back and looked at Charlie. She could almost see the wheels turning in his mind. Now was the time to back off and let Charlie think. Push too hard and he would shut down. He would either stop talking or worse, he would demand a lawyer. She had to let him sit there and think for a while.

Rex, who had been listening and watching the interrogation, knew that it had reached the point where it was time for him to play his part in helping nudge Charlie towards talking to them. He took a manila file folder and stuffed it full of papers. These papers had nothing to do with the case. They were the department phone directory, printouts from other prisoners that had been processed through PPC earlier that day and copies of some department memos that were lying about. Rex was making a prop. It didn't matter what the papers were as long as the file looked thick and official.

Rex took the folder to the holding cell, knocked on the door, and then quickly stepped in.

"Sorry to interrupt, but this information just came in and I thought you should see it," he said handing the file to Kat.

Kat made a show of slowly going through the file folder without letting Charlie see any of the papers.

"Oh," said Kat, "this is very interesting. Tran Van Nguyen's little enterprise goes much deeper than we first thought."

She rifled through some more papers in the file. "Look here, isn't that a photo of Charlie with Tran Van Nguyen?"

"I believe that was taken in front of the Loving Cup Coffee House," said Rex. "It's a little hard to make out, but we can enhance it and blow it up."

Chapter 29

Kat closed the file and handed it back to Rex. "Yes, why don't you get started on that?"

Rex left the holding cell.

Kat just sat and looked at Charlie for a long moment. Charlie was actually starting to sweat, and had developed a nervous tick in his right eye.

"Charlie, I'm going to be honest with you. With what we've got right now we could put you away for twenty-five to life. Right now, I am your only hope. When I walk out that door, it's all over. You go straight over to main jail and take your chances with your other buddies that work for Tran Van Nguyen. How long do you think it will take for someone to start talking? Or worse yet, how long do you think it will take before one of them decides you have already been talking to the police. These are some pretty hard-core gang bangers we are dealing with here. You are not a banger. You haven't been jumped into the gang. You are just the book worm who counts the money."

Charlie's head snapped up and he gave Kat a surprised look.

"What? You think we didn't know about that. I told you Charlie, there is a lot we already know about you. And we are finding out more every minute."

Charlie's eyes darted left and right as he looked for a way out. Charlie licked his dry lips and said, "O.K., I want a deal."

"You know how it works Charlie, I can't offer you a deal, but I can help you with the District Attorney. The DA wants to know three things. First, he wants to know that everything you tell me is the truth. Next, he wants to know that you cooperated fully and didn't hold anything back. Finally, the DA wants to know that you are sorry for what you did. You give me that Charlie and I'll do everything I can to work something out with the DA for you."

Charlie looked at Kat with pleading eyes. "You don't understand Tran will kill me. I've seen him kill someone already."

That last statement shocked Kat, but she did not let it show. If what Charlie had just blurted out was true, that really upped the stakes. She could not stop the interrogation now. Charlie was almost there, and she had to get him talking.

"Charlie, we will protect you, but you have to start telling me the truth now."

Charlie sat there hunched over the table looking at his hands for a long while. It was so quiet in the holding cell that Kat could hear him breathing. Finally, Charlie looked up at her and said, "O.K., what do you want to know?'

In a soft and soothing voice Kat said quietly, "Just start at the beginning Charlie. Tell me how you got hooked up with these people."

"My parents came to the United States when I was five years old from mainland China. They settled in Charleston, South Carolina. My father was a fisherman, and he got work there on the shrimp boats. I was the first in my family to go to college. I graduated from the College of Charleston with a degree in Accounting."

"How did you end up in San Jose?"

"Right out of college I got a job with Cisco. When I first moved out here, I was excited about my new job. But I was away from my family and friends and started feeling homesick. Some people from work took me out to the Bay 101 Card Room one night. There was a Texas Hold 'em Poker Tournament going on. One of my co-workers was playing in the tournament. He made $500 in just a few hours that night."

"Did you play cards that night or just watch?"

"I just watched. This was the first time I had ever been to any place where there was gambling. After that, I got my friends to teach me the card games. I was good with numbers and found that playing cards came naturally to me. I really liked the fast moving Asian card games like Pai Gow and Sic Bo, and the American version of Pai Gow Poker."

Charlie gave a little chuckle. "I even found myself playing in a Texas Hold 'em Poker Tournament a couple of months later."

"What did you do next Charlie?"

"In the beginning I was winning. I made some good money too. That was my play money. I spent it all on booze, women, and having a good time. But I couldn't stay away from the tables. The more I played, the more I wanted to play. Pretty soon it seemed like all I was doing was playing cards. When that happened, I started to lose and lose big. Now there wasn't any extra money. One day I played for twenty-four hours straight and lost my entire Cisco paycheck."

Charlie sighed and looked up at Kat. "That was bad. I was at rock bottom. There I was, one day after payday, two weeks to the next payday and I had lost all my money. I didn't even have any money in the bank because I had already gambled all of my savings away. I needed money, so I asked around and got introduced to some people that would loan me some money. There were always people hanging around the card clubs that were willing to lend people like me any money.

"The problem was I didn't put that money away or pay my rent or buy food. I went right back to the tables and gambled it away. Then I had to borrow more money. Then I couldn't pay them back."

"Then what happened Charlie, when you couldn't pay back the loans?" asked Kat.

"One night as I was leaving Bay 101, these two guys stopped me in the parking lot and forced me into a car. They drove me to a deserted parking lot behind a building in North San Jose, and they beat me up. They pushed me around and punched me in the stomach a few times. They told me I had two days to come up with the money I owed them. Then they drove me back to the Bay 101 parking lot and let me go."

"So what did you do then?"

"I called my parents and lied to them about how I needed some money to take some classes that would help me get a promotion at work. My parents wired me the money. Two nights later, I walked into Bay 101 fully intending to pay these guys off. I looked around for them, but they weren't there. I waited a little bit, just wandering around the tables and watching people play. But it was like that money was burning a hole in my pocket. I thought I could take that money and just play a little. Make some safe bets and win me enough money to pay off the loan and still have some walking around money."

"How'd that go?"

Charlie snorted. "How do you think? In a couple of hours, I'd lost all the money. I knew what would happen if I ran into those guys now, so I decided to get out of there fast. Just my luck, just as I made the front door, I met them coming in. They invited me outside for a talk. My mind was racing; I had to think of something or else these guys were probably going to start breaking arms and legs, or worse.

"I knew these guys weren't running this loan operation on their own, they weren't smart enough. They had to have a boss. If I could get to see their boss, then maybe I could work out a deal to work off my debt. You know, do some bookkeeping work for him or something. After all, he was a business man in the business of money, so I figured he must have books to balance."

"So what happened?"

"I don't know how I had the nerve to even do it, but as soon as we got outside I told them I wanted to see their boss. I said I had something for their boss that he would be particularly interested in. If I didn't get to see him they would be in trouble. One of them walked back into the club, and the other one stayed outside with me.

"After a few minutes, the one guy comes back to the front door and motions for me to come back in. He takes me into the restaurant and to a table in the back. That was how I met Tran Van Nguyen."

"Did you know Tran before you met him that night?"

"No, I had never seen him before. I didn't even know his name."

"So tell me what happened," said Kat.

"I introduced myself, and he said he knew who I was. He asked me to sit down at his table. I remember he was exceedingly polite and soft spoken. He came straight to the point asking me what information I had that was valuable to him.

"I was terribly nervous. I told him that I did not have any information but was interested in working something out with him to pay back the money I owed him. He asked me what I thought I could do for him. That was when I made my pitch. I told him that any smart businessman needed someone that could keep two sets of books. One set for his eyes only that would show exactly what each area of his enterprises were making. A second set that should show whatever profit or loss he wanted them to show. I told him that I surmised that his business was mainly cash. It was probably safe to say that he dealt in large amounts of cash. With large amounts of cash charging hands, it was easy for some of it to go missing. I explained that I had a degree in Accounting and was currently employed as an accountant at Cisco.

"It just so happened that Tran was looking to expand his business holding. He was also having some second thoughts about some of his employees and was suspicious that they were stealing from him. Tran liked the idea and gave me two weeks to put his books in order. If he was satisfied with my job at the end of the two weeks, my debts would be cancelled."

"And if he wasn't satisfied with your work at the end of those two weeks?"

"He really didn't say, but I got the impression that if he didn't like what he saw I would be cancelled."

Charlie was getting more relaxed and more comfortable as he got into his story. Kat found that all she had to do was keep nudging him along. There comes a moment in almost all interrogations where the suspect forgets he is talking to the police and is just telling his story. The more he talks, the more he wants to talk. He wants to brag about his accomplishments.

"So Charlie, you went to work for Tran Van Nguyen. What did you find out?"

"Tran told me to meet him back at the Bay 101 Club the next day and bring my calculator. I met him in the lobby, and he handed me a briefcase. We went into the restaurant, and were shown to a table in the rear. The briefcase held all kinds of sheets of paper showing money coming in and money being paid out from several different businesses. Tran told me to take all these receipts and organize them onto an Excel spread sheet showing his cash flow and also a profit and loss statement."

"What kinds of businesses? Do you remember the business names?"

"One was P & L Auto. Others were just described by the type of business they were like personal loans, or local business support, or commodities trade. Stuff like that. I assume you guys got my laptop from the auto shop. All the stuff is on there, and way better organized than when Tran first handed that briefcase to me."

"O.K. Charlie. However, let's go back to that first meeting. What happened after you got handed that briefcase."

"I don't know if Tran had any other set of books or any other way of keeping track of his cash before that, but what he gave me was a mess. But I was real eager to show him I knew what I was doing and could help him out. It only took me one week, and I had put a completely new set of books together for him. I gave all of his various enterprises names and set each one up as a subsidiary company of TVN Enterprises. I was then able to make data entries on all monies going into or going out of each company. I was finally able to show Tran where three of his employees, each responsible for a different company, were stealing money from him."

"And how did Tran take this?"

"Oh, he was very grateful to me. He told me that he wanted to make me his full time and exclusive bookkeeper. To show his appreciation, he threw a party for me that night at the Fairmont. There was lots of food, champagne, good whiskey, cocaine and some very talented female entertainment. I don't know, I guess it all went to my head. Tran told me I could have all of this all the time if I went to work for him. I was never going to have anything like this working for Cisco. I accepted his job offer."

"What happened after that Charlie?"

Charlie's eyes glazed over and he seemed to be staring off into the middle distance. Charlie's body was still in the holding cell, but it was as if his mind had left the room.

"What happened after that Charlie?" . . . "What happened after that Charlie?" . . . "What happened after that Charlie?" Charlie kept hearing that question over and over again, echoing in his head. Images formed in his mind and Charlie found himself sitting across the table from Tran in the Bay 101 Club Restaurant.

Chapter 30

"Charlie," said Tran putting down his coffee cup, "you have done an excellent job for me. Thanks to you, I now know for the first time where all of my money is. Play ball with me Charlie and you'll go a long ways in my organization."

One of Tran's men walked up and whispered something in Tran's ear. Tran's expression never changed.

Tran picked up his napkin and patted his lips. He smiled at Charlie. "Come on Charlie, I have a special meeting to go to, and I would like you there with me."

They left the Bay 101 Club and walked out to Tran's car. As they left the parking lot, Tran got onto Highway 101 heading south. It was early evening and just getting dark. Tran turned off on Tully Road and headed east. This was the area known as the Eastside of San Jose. It was an area of the city that had at one time been almost exclusively Hispanic. Now it was mostly Asian. Charlie relaxed in the passenger seat and listened to the car stereo. Driving to the Eastside was perfectly normal since all of Tran's dealings were with the Asian community in San Jose. This stretch of Tully Road was where a lot of Asian businesses were located.

When they got to Quimby Road, Tran turned right. They skirted the Eastridge Shopping Mall and continued across Captiol Expressway. This took them into the upscale residential area of the east foothills. Charlie thought that maybe they were going to someone's house. A lot of Asians lived in this neighborhood.

However, to Charlie's surprise Tran kept driving up into the east foothills. They had left all of the houses behind. They were the only car on a winding backcountry road at night. Charlie started to get nervous.

"Where are we going?" asked Charlie.

Tran looked over and smiled at him. "Relax, we are almost there."

They rounded another bend in the road, and Charlie saw two cars parked on the shoulder of the road. Tran slowed down and pulled in behind one of the cars. Tran got out of the car and motioned Charlie to follow him. As they walked towards the front of the car they had parked behind Charlie could see three men kneeling in front of the car in the glare of the headlights.

Tran put his arm around Charlie's shoulder and pointed towards the three men. "You see these three men here Charlie? I use to call them my friends. I used to trust them. That is until you showed me how they had been stealing from me. I thank you for that Charlie. You showed me that I should trust no one. You also showed me that I needed to be more firm in my discipline.

"Charlie, do you remember the movie we watched last night? The one about Al Capone and Elliot Ness? The Untouchables? That is one of my favorite movies Charlie. Did you know that? Not because of Elliot Ness, no, because of Al Capone. Al Capone built an empire and ruled it with an iron fist. That is what I am doing Charlie. I am building an empire. But I made a mistake. I thought I could trust all the people who worked for me. I thought that if I took care of them in a generous way, they would do the right thing by me."

Charlie felt his knees start to shake. His mouth went dry, and he started to sweat.

Tran continued in his soft voice. "I'm afraid I'm going to have to make an example of these three. People are going to have to learn that you do not mess with Tran Van Nguyen."

Tran slipped his arm from Charlie's shoulder and walked forward. Tran reached into the car and pulled out a baseball bat. He turned and faced Charlie while working his grip on the bat.

"Do you remember that scene in the movie Charlie? The one where Al

Capone is at dinner with all his people and finds out that one of his people have been cheating him?"

Tran took three fast, long strides over to the closest man on his knees and swung the bat viciously down on the man's head. The bat connected with the sickening thud of a ripe watermelon being broken open. Blood spray out, and the body slumped sideways. Tran continued to rain blows down on the man's head with his bat. He literally beat the man's head into a bloody pulp. The blows broke open the man's skull and bits of brain matter and blood sprayed out with each blow.

Charlie doubled over and sank to his knees. He threw up right there. He just kept heaving until nothing was left in his stomach.

Tran walked over to the next man in line. He lifted the man's chin with the bloody bat.

"Now you know what will happen to anyone else I catch stealing from me. I hope you two have learned your lesson. Make sure that it is a lesson learned by everyone in my organization."

Tran walked back to Charlie and gently helped him to stand. He took out his handkerchief and gently wiped Charlie's mouth and face.

"There, there Charlie. I know this is something you are not good with, but I wanted you to see the fruits of your hard work. After all, it was you Charlie who found my thieves. Come now, let's go back to one of my cribs and relax. I have a couple of women waiting for us."

Chapter 31

Kat stood over Charlie shaking his shoulder. "Charlie, are you all right? Come on Charlie, snap out of it. Charlie, can you hear me?

To Charlie her voice sounded as if it was coming from extremely far away. Then Charlie shook his head, blinked, and tried to focus his eyes on Kat. Her face was just a blur. He blinked again and Kat's face started to come into focus.

"I think I'm going to be sick." Charlie leaned over and threw up on the floor.

Kat moved back out of the way just in time.

Rex came through the holding cell door. "What's the matter with him?"

"I don't know. One minute he was talking and then the next he just seemed to fade out. Then he got sick all over the floor."

The PPC Sergeant, Sergeant Black, came up behind Rex. "What's the matter with your prisoner? Why is he getting sick all over my floor?"

"Sorry Sarge," said Kat, "I don't know what happened to him."

"All right, move him to another room and I'll call the paramedics." There had already been a few in-custody deaths at San Jose PD, and Sergeant Black was not going to have one on his watch if he could help it. "Let the paramedics check this guy out and see if he needs to go to the hospital or not."

They got Charlie moved to another room and gave him a glass of water. He insisted that he was fine and did not need to be seen by the paramedics.

Kat told him that it was standard procedure when any prisoner got sick. She told him to relax and left him in the new holding cell alone.

While they waited for the paramedics, Kat, Rex and Five-O had a conference about what they had found out from Charlie so far and where they needed to go from here.

"This guy is our golden goose on this case," said Kat. "He is the bookkeeper. He knows all the players and all the transactions. He cannot only nail Tran Van Nguyen for us; he can put his entire organization away. We have to keep him playing nice with us."

"We have to keep him alive," said Rex. "I mean we have to put him in some sort of witness protection, and I'm not sure how we do that. I can't remember it ever being done in the entire time I've been on the department."

"I guess you could always turn him over to me on federal charges," said Five-O. "That way I could get the US Marshalls involved and get him into witness protection that way. To do that I'd still have to go find an Assistant US Attorney, lay out the case and get them to sign off on it. And the case is still a much bigger local case than it is a federal one."

"He's still our guy, and the Chief is not going to want to turn him over to the feds," Rex replied. "I guess I better go find the Chief of D's and explain it all to him. I'm sure he will have an idea."

"Don't forget to let your Sergeant know that you are going to the Chief of D's" said Kat with a conspiratorial smile on her face and a touch of sarcasm in her voice.

"Yeah, right," said Rex as he left.

San Jose Fire and AMR paramedics showed up to check out Charlie. Other than the fact that his blood pressure was elevated, they could find nothing else wrong with him. Besides, Charlie insisted himself that there was nothing wrong with him and he wanted to continue talking to Detective Sanchez.

After fire and the paramedics left, Kat went back in to the holding cell to continue the interrogation. Charlie still looked a little pale.

"So Charlie, what happened there? You just seemed to fade away on me and then you got sick. I thought you were going to pass out."

"I'm sorry, Detective; I was just remembering the most horrible night of my life. It was the night that I realized that the only way I was going to get out this mess was if I died. Detective Sanchez, you've got to help me. I don't want to die, and I can't go on like I have been. I'll do anything for you. I'll tell you all about Tran's organization. I'll show how I set up his books. I'll show you everything. I'll even testify against him. Just please, please, you've gotta help me."

"Don't worry Charlie, I'll help you. My partner's working on that right now. So, do you feel like talking about this horrible night now?"

Charlie nodded his head and then retold the story of Tran beating to death one of his men while Charlie watched. He was so drained after telling her the story that Kat decided to take another break.

She stepped out of the holding cell to find Rex back in PPC.

"I was right. It has been so long since we've put anybody in protective custody that most everybody has forgotten how. Fortunately, the Chief of D's knows exactly what we need to do. He had to do this same sort of thing many years ago when he was a detective. He's in talking with the Assistant Chief to get the ball rolling. He said he'd come down here when he got things set up."

"O.K. Well you had better go back up stairs, give the Chief of D's a new update, and then you can go talk to Homicide. Charlie just described to me in detail a murder he saw Tran commit about two months ago. Tran beat one of his guys to death with a baseball bat for stealing from him. Charlie saw it all. It seems that Tran is a big fan of Al Capone and saw it in a movie. Rex, this guy Tran is a real psycho. Charlie has agreed to cooperate one hundred per cent. Even to testify, but he wants us to keep him safe."

Rex gave a low whistle. "This just gets better and better. Where did the homicide take place?"

"Somewhere on Quimby Road up in the foothills"

"That makes it the Sheriff's jurisdiction. I'll go update the Chief of D's and talk to Homicide. You go back in and see what else Charlie can tell us."

Kat went back into the holding cell, and Charlie continued to talk.

There was no need to persuade him anymore. Now that he had decided to cooperate fully with the police, the story came pouring out of him. Kat worked feverishly to take notes on just some of the high lights knowing that she would spend several hours going over the recording of the interrogation to get all of the details.

Charlie told Kat how Tran had moved extremely quickly after the incident on Quimby Road to consolidate his control over the Vietnamese street gangs. The two men he had let live had spread the story quickly, and Tran became known as a person to be feared. He quickly brought all of the Vietnamese street gangs under his control, consolidating their various criminal activities. Charlie said that Nick Lueong was Tran's cousin and his chief enforcer. Nick was just as ruthless as Tran.

Charlie continued with his description of Tran's organization. "Tran controls all of the loan sharking activity at both of the San Jose card clubs. He also makes money through hosting special betting parties. If a group of businessmen wants to bet on a sporting event or a horse race, they can do so through Tran at Las Vegas odds.

"What makes it so much better to bet with Tran rather than go to Vegas is that he organizes the whole thing into a lavish party. The businessmen are picked up in a limo and chauffeured to the house where they can watch the game they bet on. There is lots of good food and good booze. There is also good dope. All at no extra charge. And there are women. Beautiful, gorgeous women that serve the food and booze and provide whatever else the men want.

"These betting parties became very popular because the food was the best, the booze was top drawer, the dope was the purest, and the women were very talented.

"Unknown to those attending these parties was that all of the rooms in the house had hidden video cameras. Everything that was said and done was captured digitally. Tran has quite a collection of DVD's starring local and out of town businessmen and some local politicians."

"Do you know where those DVD's are now?"

"No, Tran and maybe Nick, were the only only ones who knew where they were kept."

"Do you know where any of the party houses are?"

"Only a couple that I have been to."

"What about the women? Do they live at the party houses?"

"No, they are kept elsewhere."

"What do you mean kept? Don't they work for Tran?"

"In a manner of speaking. You see, they are all Asian girls. They come from Vietnam, Thailand, Laos, China. You know, brought in from Asia."

"What do you mean brought in?"

"Tran has people in Southeast Asia. They look for pretty young girls and then offer them a better life in the United States, for a price. Only when they get here, they find out that they have to pay more money. They don't have the money and their parents don't have the money, so they have to go to work for Tran to pay off their debt."

"He turns them into prostitute slaves."

"Yeah."

"Where do they keep the girls?"

"I don't know. I just know Tran has several party houses in San Jose and Santa Clara, and that he keeps a couple of other houses where he keeps his girls."

"How old are these girls?"

"Between twelve and twenty."

"What else is Tran into?"

Charlie went on to explain how Tran had expanded into credit card theft and the passing of counterfeit checks. There was also the auto theft ring. Charlie confirmed that the auto theft area involved chopping and selling parts, auto cloning and title fraud. Charlie told Kat about Nick Lueong extorting the Vietnamese businessmen for protection money.

Finally, Charlie talked about the latest scam where Tran was supplying someone with counterfeit credit cards to buy cigarettes that would then be sold through some of the stores they were extorting. This scam was so new that Charlie did not know who was receiving the cards. Only Nick and Tran knew that information.

When Charlie was through, Kat had a pretty clear picture of the

Tran organization. Charlie had even signed a consent search form for his computer, given the passwords, and sketched out how the files were organized. Charlie had set up a full profit and loss accounting sheet for each phase of Tran's business interests. He was given various hand written ledger sheets or just scrapes of paper and notes. Each week he made the entries on his computer, balanced the books, and reported to Tran.

The only exception was the chop shop. Because the chop shop dealt in so much cash and because that was where the original and largest thefts that Charlie had discovered came from, Charlie went to the chop shop once a week to count and collect the cash and make sure there wasn't any money missing.

Charlie's story was not entirely new. The facts were that Asians loved to gamble, and some of them got into trouble because of it. They gambled more than they made. When they got in over their heads to the loan sharks, some of them were recruited into the criminal enterprises. They were used to pass counterfeit check or to run counterfeit credit cards through the super ATM's at the card clubs. These ATM's did not have the usual $300 to $500 a day transaction limit that all other ATM's had. You could get as much as $5,000.00 at one of the card clubs. The clubs gave the cardholder the money in chips so that they would then gamble giving the club a chance to win the money back.

The usual scam on the credit cards was to get hold of a stolen credit card before it was reported stolen. The poor guy that was into the loan sharks was recruited to "borrow" a credit card from a family member without the family member knowing it.

The crooks loaded up the credit card by paying off not only what was owed on it but also paying over the card's credit limit. This was usually done with counterfeit checks. Since bank laws required that there would be a zero float on payments being applied to a credit card, the card company had to apply to amount of the check to the card account immediately. The cards would show a positive balance for several days before the counterfeit check was returned. This allowed the cardholder to go to the card clubs and get a "cash advance" for the total positive account balance.

The gang banger handling them was right there with them when they were paid off. The poor guy holding the credit card had to give most of the money to his handler. He was paid a small amount in chips as payment for his services. He usually ended up losing whatever he was paid that same night at the card tables.

The handlers got their cut and the rest of the profits were passed up the chain. No one cared if the card passer was caught. They had intimidated them so badly about their family getting hurt if they talked that their silence was guaranteed.

That was why Charlie was such a rare find. Not only did they now have someone from the inside that knew the organization from top to bottom, they had someone that was going to testify if they could keep him alive.

As she waited for Rex to come back down to PPC, Kat wondered how this would all play out. The card clubs were the sacred cows of the city. She and Rex and some of the other detectives in Vice and the Gaming Enforcement Unit knew what was happening at the card clubs, but they had never been able to get approval to put an investigation together. The city depended on the income the card clubs were generating so much that there was even talk on the City Council of expanding their operations.

Chapter 32

Rex found the Chief of D's back in his office.

"Chief," said Rex as he knocked on the doorframe. "You got another minute?"

The Chief of D's looked up, waived Rex into his office, and motioned for him to sit down.

"What's up now?"

"Latest update, and it's a dozy. I was just back down to PPC and talked to Kat. Charlie has promised to turn state's evidence, even testify, if we can keep him alive. He is real scared, and if his story checks out he has a right to be. According to what Charlie told Kat he witnessed Tran Van Nguyen beat one of his guys to death with a baseball bat for stealing money."

The Chief of D's gave a low whistle. "Where did this occur?"

"Somewhere way out on Quimby Road a couple of months ago."

The Chief of D's reached for his phone and punched in a few numbers. When the phone call was answered, he asked for Sergeant Harris.

"Sergeant Harris, Chief Ortiz. Say, have you heard anything about a homicide of a Vietnamese male out on Quimby Road a couple of months ago?"

The Chief of D's listened to his answer.

"Yeah, I know that would be S/O jurisdiction. Have you heard anything from your counterparts in S/O Homicide?"

There was another pause while the Chief of D's listened.

"O.K., thanks."

The Chief of D's hung up the phone. "Nothing out of S/O Homicide. Sergeant Harris thinks that if it involves your current playmates, the body was probably taken someplace and dumped, and it hasn't turned up yet.'

Rex shook his head. "We'll probably find it after the first good rain in the Santa Cruz Mountains."

The Santa Cruz Mountains were a known place for dumping bodies. Almost every year, after a really hard rain, a hiker came across a body that had been washed out.

"You're probably right. So Charlie is willing to testify against Tran Van Nguyen, heh?"

"Chief, Kat has him eating out of her hand. Right now he is willing to do anything she asks. But we have to do right by him. He is scared. No, petrified with fear is more like it. And with this organization I can't blame him. If we can protect him, not just for tonight, but all the way up to and through a trial, there's no telling what he can give us."

"Well, like I told you, the last time we did this was when I was a young detective. It was on a murder for hire case I was working. Anyway, I can get the Chief to go along for a while. We are going to have to get the DA's Office involved for the long run. Since I'm probably the only one left that knows all the in's and out's about running witness protection, I'll run that part of the operation for you."

The Chief of D's stopped and smiled at Rex. "I'd forgotten how much fun it was doing real police work."

Rex walked back in to PPC to find Kat going over her notes. "You won't believe this, but the Chief of D's is taking personal charge of the witness protection end of our investigation. He said he was the only one that really knew how to put it all together anyway. He told me he had forgotten what fun it was to be doing real police work again.

"I think he is kinda jazzed about working on our case. All right, here is what is going to happen tonight. The Chief of D's has called back in the Vice Lieutenant and two of his detectives to take charge of Charlie. They are going to rent a hotel room and sit on Charlie tonight. Tomorrow we go with the Chief of D's to the District Attorney to see how we proceed from there. We are going to have to give the District Attorney a pretty detailed briefing so make sure you have your notes together."

"That won't be a problem. What about the homicide?"

"I was right, that is Sheriff's Office jurisdiction. Sergeant Harris is not aware of the S/O finding any bodies out on Quimby Road, so he thinks it is an unreported homicide at this point with the body dumped somewhere else. He's going to talk to S/O Homicide tomorrow. At some point they are going to want to talk to Charlie."

"O.K., that shouldn't be a problem," Kat replied. "You can also trot back upstairs and give the Chief of D's another bell ringer update. Tran is also into human trafficking. He is bringing young Asian girls, as young as twelve, into the country and turning them into prostitute slaves. Somewhere out there are some houses where he keeps them locked up. Charlie doesn't know where. We've got to find them."

Rex shook his head. This case was turning into something that was almost even too much for him to wrap his brain around. "O.K., I'll go back up and tell the Chief of D's the latest."

A half hour later, Rex trooped back into PPC with two Vice detectives in tow. Kat took them in to the interrogation room to meet Charlie. She explained to Charlie that the Vice detectives were going to be taking care of him for the next couple of days.

She stepped back out of the room and walked over to Rex. "Look," said Rex, "it's almost 2100. The Chief of D's is going to set up a meeting with the District Attorney first thing in the morning. He wants us to be ready to give a full briefing on our case. Let's knock off for the night and get in early tomorrow, say 0630?"

"That sounds good to me."

*   *   *

Rex pulled into his driveway at 2230 hours. His wife had opened the front door, and the dogs came running out to greet him. With the dogs in tow, he walked wearily to the front door. It had been an exceedingly long and draining day, and he was looking at an even longer one tomorrow.

Carmella met him with a loving kiss and an even bigger glass of Jack Daniel's and water.

"Hey sweetie, I figured you could use that."

"What, the drink or the kiss?"

"Both. Did you get super?"

"Yeah, out of a vending machine."

"You poor baby. Do you want me to fix you something to eat."

"Nah. It's too late to eat. Besides, I've got to get in early tomorrow and get back at it. I'll just have my drink, relax a little, and go to bed."

They walked on into the house and sat down on the couch in the Great Room.

"I've already fed the horses and the dogs," said Carmella, "so you just relax and tell me about your day."

"We caught a big break in the case today. We lucked out and caught the bookkeeper for the whole operation. Kat was able to flip him, and he is giving up everything."

"Wow that sounds good."

"It's great. The only thing is we've got to move fast. As soon as Tran van Nguyen finds out we got his boy, he's gonna run. We gotta try and find him and what's left of his organization and take it all down fast."

"Well you just be careful and don't forget to come home to me."

Rex gave her a big hug. "Of course I will honey."

Chapter 33

Rex was at his desk at 0615 hours the next morning and by the time Kat walked in at 0620 hours he had already burned three DVD's of Charlie's interview, one for him, one for Kat, and one for the District Attorney's Office.

"All right Cowboy," said Kat as she came waltzing in with her briefcase, a Noah's Bagels bag and a tray with two extra large Peet's coffees, "I've got egg mitt sandwiches from Noah's and extra large, extra strong coffee from Peet's."

"Oh goodie," said Rex rubbing his hands together. His face lit up with an impish smile. "This will help get the day started."

As they were eating their breakfast at their desks and discussing the case, Sergeant Alvarez walked into the unit.

"Well," said Alvarez, "you two are here early. What can you tell me about your case?"

Kat gave Sergeant Alvarez the Reader's Digest version of what they had discovered after the raid on the chop shop and the interview with Charlie. She let Alvarez know that they would be tied up for most of the day writing search warrants and meeting with the DA. Rex suggested that Alvarez attempt to set up a meeting with everybody involved so that they could all go over what they had and make sure they were all moving the investigation forward together. Alvarez agreed that a meeting was an excellent idea and would try to set something up for mid-morning.

After Alvarez had walked away, Rex said to Kat, "I figured if I gave her something to do she would stay out of our hair."

"Good idea," Kat replied.

The Chief of D's walked into their office area.

"Good morning. How are my two favorite detectives doing this morning?"

"Just fine Chief," Kat replied.

"That's good. I just checked in with the detail on Charlie. No problems. I'm going to call the DA about 0800 and set up a meeting for this morning to see how we are going to move forward with this investigation so you two keep yourselves available."

"Sergeant Alvarez was going to try and set up a task force meeting for mid morning," Rex told him.

"We'll have to move that back. I'll talk to her. What else do you have going on?"

Rex took another sip oc coffee before replying. "From Charlie's interview we know that Tran Van Nguyen has a safety deposit box at Bay 101 where he keeps emergency cash and maybe some passports. I'm working on a search warrant right now for that box. Kat and I will walk it through as soon as I have it written up and then serve it. We also know, thanks to Charlie, where two of the party houses are located. I'd like to get search warrants on those also. We should hit them simultaneously and as soon as possible."

"I agree," said the Chief of D's. "Get that search warrant on the box served as soon as possible. If he does have his running money in there, that should slow him down some. I'll call the Gang Unit and have them start working on the search warrants for the party houses."

At 0730 hours, Rex took a break from his typing and walked down the hall to Homicide in search of Sergeant Harris. He found him at his desk pounding away at his keyboard.

"Hey Cowboy, how's it going. That was a good piece of luck yesterday finding the outfit's bookkeeper at the chop shop. I made a call to S/O Homicide this morning. They don't have anything on a Vietnamese male murder victim who got his brains beat out. They would be very interested in talking to your boy."

"OK, we'll set something up."

"Also the two Glocks those guys had on them? Came from the same gun store burglaries down South. So these guys are tied in to Asian Organized Crime in L.A. County. You have stumbled into something really big and bad here. Not only are the bad guys really bad guys, but the administration is not going to like anything to do with Asian Organized Crime coming to light here in San Jose. You watch your back. Not only will the bad guys be gunning for you, but some in this administration will be also."

Rex thanked Sergeant Harris for his words of advice and walked back to his desk.

As he walked back into his office, he saw Kat on the phone. She held the phone away from her and told Rex to pick up line two because it was Porter Goss from Costco. Porter told them that he had downloaded all of the surveillance footage. He would be emailing them still photographs, and his initial report on the cigarette thefts that had happened on Saturday. Rex thanked Porter and hung up.

"You know," Rex said, "with all the twists and turns this case has taken I'd almost forgotten that it all started with cigarette thefts from Costco."

Chapter 34

One floor down in the PIO office, Dawn Summers was meeting with Sergeant Comstock.

"Dawn," said Sergeant Comstock handing a DVD over to her, "here is raw footage of the raid yesterday at the chop shop. Our video unit shot it from a surveillance van close to the action, and the Chief says that you are free to use any of it that you want." Comstock pushed the DVD across his desk towards Summers.

Sergeant Comstock sat back in his chair and touched his finger tips together in a peak before he continued. "There will be a full press release and interview in Room 314 tomorrow sometime around mid-morning, so everyone can file their afternoon and evening stories. We promised you an exclusive on this and you will get it. Prior to the press release, you will be able to interview the principal officers involved in this case. That would be Detectives Johnson and Sanchez, and Officer Tam.

"That way you can have you story ready to go. All we ask is that you don't break it until after tomorrow's news conference. This is a major crime bust in which the Department went all out to protect the community. I think you will be more than happy with the access we gave you to this case."

Sergeant Comstock sat forward and started playing with a San Jose PD logoed coffee mug on his desk. "As you know, there is a lot of paper work that goes along with a case of this magnitude. There have been some on-view arrests, and there will be more arrests later. You can appreciate the time constraints our detectives are under to get the paperwork filed for the on-view arrests. Because of that, I can't get your interviews set up until late this afternoon. I trust that will be all right."

"That will be fine," replied Ms. Summers, picking up the DVD. She was quite happy as a matter of fact. From the coverage she had already done of the two police shootings, she knew that this was a significant story. She had the exclusive for the complete story, and access to all the major players. What more could a reporter ask for?

After Dawn Summers left his office, Sergeant Comstock walked across the hall to the Chief's Office. The Chief's door was open. He was sitting at his desk reading a report. When he looked up at Comstock's gentle knock on his door, he told him to come in and shut the door.

"So," said the Chief, "where are we on this whole mess."

"I just had my meeting with Dawn Summers and gave her the DVD of yesterday's raid. I told her that she would get complete access to Detectives Johnson and Sanchez, and Officer Tam for interviews this afternoon," said Comstock

"You just make sure that you thoroughly brief those officers before they talk to the press. I want only one story coming out of this. That is that the Department became aware of a Vietnamese street gang that was trying to expand their criminal influence into the Vietnamese community. That it was I who directed the Department to bring all assets to bear on solving an issue that was a direct threat to the Vietnamese community. That because of the swift action of this Department we eliminated that criminal threat. San Jose is still the safest large city in America thanks to the efforts of its police department," said the Chief.

"Yes sir," said Sergeant Comstock. "What about the other crimes that have come to light during this investigation? A possible homicide, human trafficking, counterfeiting, and loan sharking? Not to mention the possibility of blackmail videos of prominent businessmen and maybe some politicians."

"We keep to our message," said the Chief. "It was a Viet street gang involved in selling protection and preying on the Vietnamese community. We will quietly clear up the rest in follow-up investigations after the press has lost interest."

"Understood Chief," said Sergeant Comstock. "I will personally see to it that the right message gets out. The main press conference will be tomorrow morning at 1100 hours in Room 314. I'll send out the notices later this afternoon. I'll have your press release and notes written up in plenty of time for you to go over. We will have the commanders of the various units involved in the investigation standing behind you. We should also have a good visual with a pile of cash, some cartons of cigarettes, and some guns."

"Good, good. Remember, I have to keep up my image as the Chief of Police that is taking care of all the different communities in this city, making it a safe place for them to live. When it comes time for me to run for mayor I want everyone to know what a great job I did keeping this city a safe place to work and live for all the many, varied ethnic groups that live and work here," said the Chief.

Sergeant Comstock left the Chief's Office and returned to his own where he called Rex, Kat and Sonny Tam and asked them to come down to his office as soon as possible. He knew he would not have any trouble with Officer Tam, but Rex and Kat might give him a little push back. However, he knew they would not give him any grief in front of a junior officer.

When all three were standing in front of his desk, Sergeant Comstock started.

"The Chief wants to express his appreciation for the outstanding job you three have done. Tomorrow he will be giving a press conference, and he wants all three of you up there with him.

"He also had another favor to ask of you. During your investigation Channel 2 reporter, Dawn Summers got wind of what was going on and came to me. We worked a deal out with her that she got an exclusive if she would hold off and not break the story until after tomorrow's news conference. She agreed. Part of the agreement involved giving her access to you three. She will interview you this afternoon here at the Department. The focus of her story is going to be how we discovered that a street gang was intimidating and extorting the Vietnamese community, and how you developed leads that lead to the two recent raids.

"Sonny, you can talk about how you have been trying to get the

Vietnamese community to trust us with your outreach to them over the past year. You can talk about how you have worked a patrol beat that primarily covers the Vietnamese business district on the East Side. How you have talked to business owners trying to get them to trust the police. You can say how you heard about the Detectives' investigation into the cigarette thefts. That a shop owner who was being extorted finally came forward and told you how he was being forced to sell these stolen cigarettes.

"Rex and Kat, you can talk about how this stolen cigarette case came to light with a report from Costco corporate security and how you developed the investigation with the aid of Costco corporate security in an example of the fine cooperation between the private sector and this police department.

"You can go on to talk about how your investigation soon centered on a Vietnamese street gang that was involved in the theft of the cigarettes, the theft of credit card account numbers, the extortion of Vietnamese businessmen and the theft of autos. You can explain how you brought RATTF into the investigation, and they will explain the stolen car aspect of the investigation.

"You can talk about the raids, but not in detail. Those are still open investigations of officer-involved shootings that have to go before the Grand Jury.

"The main thing is to provide Ms. Summers the background she needs for her in-depth report on how this Vietnamese street gang was terrorizing the Vietnamese community and endangering all of the citizens of San Jose.

"Are there any questions?"

Rex and Kat looked at each other and then back at Comstock. Finally, Rex spoke. "Is there anything else the Chief would like us to say?"

"No," said Comstock, "that about covers it. The three of you be in Room 314 at fourteen-hundred. I'll be there with Ms. Summers and her cameraman."

As they walked back to the third floor, Sonny asked Rex, "Did I miss something in there? Are we being told we can't talk about all this being something bigger with Asian Organized Crime?"

"You didn't miss a thing Sonny," Rex answered. "We were given a script direct from the Chief's Office that will tie in with what he says tomorrow at the press conference. Look, you're a good officer, and you have a future in this Department. Do what Comstock wants and just say it was a Vietnamese street gang behind all of this. Don't mention organized crime or any continuing criminal enterprise. Just play your part like you were told and everything will be all right. Welcome to the political side of a police investigation."

Chapter 35

When they got off the elevator on the third floor, Sonny headed back to the Gang Unit and Rex and Kat headed back to Financial Crimes where Rex picked up his search warrant.

"Let's grab a car and then go see if Judge Tobias has a few minutes for us."

Kat dangled a set of keys, "I've already got us a car."

They signed out on the board and headed for the Hall of Justice.

They found Judge Tobias in his chambers.

"Your honor, we have a search warrant here for a safety deposit box at Bay 101 belonging to Tran Van Nguyen who has been identified as the lead suspect in an on-going fraud investigation. We have a witness who has informed us that Mr. Tran Van Nguyen maintains this safety deposit box for the purpose of storing cash and passports. He has personally seen Tran Van Nguyen access this box on several occasions, placing bundles of money into the box.

"Our witness has told us that the money in that box all came from the proceeds of a criminal enterprise. Mr. Nguyen has become the focus of our investigation, but we have not filed charges against him yet. However, it is our contention that as soon as he becomes aware that he is the focus of a criminal investigation he will attempt to flee the area if not the country."

"That's good enough for me," said Judge Tobias.

With the signed search warrant in hand, they headed over to the Bay 101 Club.

When they walked into Bay 101, they went up to the main service desk, identified themselves, and asked to see the manager.

When the manager arrived, they explained the purpose of their visit and showed him the search warrant. The manager did not look happy but knew there was nothing he could do except cooperate with the police. He got his master key and led them behind the counter to where the safety deposit boxes were located.

Behind the main service desk was a bank of safety deposit boxes that Bay 101 rented to customers. The stated purpose was so that big winners could secure their funds in the safety deposit box. This way they did not have to walk around with large amounts of money on their persons. The Gaming Enforcement Unit, Vice, and Financial Crimes, had always suspected that the boxes were used for other reasons. This was the first time the police had ever had an investigation that allowed them to get a search warrant to get into any of the safety deposit boxes.

The manager unlocked the safety deposit box door and pulled out the box. Rex and Kat followed him to a private room. Once the manager placed the box on the table and unlocked it, Rex stepped forward and opened the lid. Inside the box were stacks of $100 dollar bills and four passports.

The $100 dollar bills were in bank bundles of 100 bills each. When Rex had counted out the money, there was $100,000.00 in cash.

The four passports were from Vietnam and were in four different names. The picture on each passport was that of Tran Van Nguyen.

Rex wrote out a receipt for the cash and the passports and placed it in the safety deposit box along with a copy of the search warrant while Kat bagged the evidence. They thanked the manager for his cooperation and left.

On the drive back to the department, Kat looked at Rex and asked, "So what's your take on what Comstock was getting at?"

"Simple," said Rex, "they don't want us talking about organized crime. They want the whole thing to look like it was just a street gang that was trying to branch out into other things beside straight street thuggery. They want it to be a local problem that the department jumped on and wiped out. That way the Chief looks good when he runs for mayor. End of story."

"So, are we going to let them get away with it?" asked Kat. "I mean, Summers is sort of our back door asset in the press. Why don't we leak something to her that blows holes in their story?"

"No, this time we are going to play ball," replied Rex. "Look, I don't particularly like this Chief. I don't think he is an effective leader, and I don't think he knows all that much about police work. After all, the majority of the jobs he had in the department were admin assignments. But I'm not going to get in a pissing contest with him either. We would both loose that one. And remember, that was also the advice of the Chief of D's. He is in our corner for now, and I'd like to keep him there."

"Yeah," said Kat with a sigh, "you're right. But that doesn't mean we can't continue our investigation. The Chief can have his news conference and make his big splash in the pan right now because the story is hot. But you and I both know that we have a lot more follow up to do on this case, more bad guys to find and more people to arrest. So we can just keep going. Your Sergeant isn't smart enough to know what we are doing anyway. If we just keep moving ahead and making arrests, they will let us go because they are afraid to say anything to us."

"Ah yes," said Rex with a mischievous smile, "so many bad guys, so little time."

Chapter 36

When they got back to the department, they went straight to the Chief of D's office. He saw them walking in to the outer office and waived them into his office.

"Hey Chief," said Rex, "we just got back from serving our search warrant on Tran Van Nguyen's security box at Bay 101."

"Find anything?"

Rex paused for a little dramatic touch and then dumped the bag of money and passports out on the Chief's desk.

The Chief of D's sat back and gave a low whistle. "Man, that is some haul. You guy's got back just in time, we've got a meeting with the DA in fifteen minutes. Bring this with you to show the DA."

The Chief of D's grabbed his suit coat and headed out of his office with Rex and Kat in tow. As they walked the two blocks over to the DA's Office, the Chief of D's said to them, "I hear you got a briefing from Sergeant Comstock about your participation in the press conference. Any problems there?"

"No sir," said Rex. "We'll play our part."

"Good. Look, I know there is a lot more to this investigation and that the Chief is rushing the press conference to get a certain message out. But if you play ball now, I can keep you on this case. This case has the potential for some really damning information coming to light. Information that some people would just as soon was never known, will be known."

"That is certainly true, sir," said Rex. "But Kat and I are just interested in catching the bad guys."

"So am I Detective. So am I."

They walked in to the office of the District Attorney of Santa Clara County. After handshakes all around, they sat down to their meeting. Rex gave an overall briefing of their case up to the last find of the money and passports. Kat gave a detailed briefing on her interview of Charlie Zsu. The Chief of D's explained how San Jose PD had Charlie Zsu in protective custody, and how he believed that Zsu's life truly was in danger.

The District Attorney quietly listened to all of it, taking notes as he listened. When the Chief of D's was through, the District Attorney sat back in his chair.

"This is quite a case you are putting together here. I agree that our main witness, Mr. Zsu, is probably a dead man if we turn loose of him. Rather than going the normal complaint route and issuing an arrest warrant from this office, I think we should go the Grand Jury route. That will allow us to keep the identity of Mr. Zsu under wraps for little while longer. I'm going to assign my top guy to this."

He reached for his phone and dialed. As soon as the person on the other end answered, the District Attorney asked him to come to his office right now.

Five minutes later, a slightly built man wearing glasses and a wrinkled grey suit walked in to the District Attorney's office.

The District Attorney said, "This is Assistant District Attorney William Henry. William, I'd like you to meet Detectives Johnson and Sanchez and Chief of Detectives Ortiz of the San Jose Police Department. They have brought to us quite an interesting case that I think needs your personal attention."

Once again they shook hands all around.

"I know this is tiring," said the District Attorney, "but if you could repeat to William what you just told me, I think that would be the quickest way to get this prosecution rolling."

So they went over it all again. When they finished telling their story a second time, Assistant District Attorney Henry looked at his boss.

"Grand Jury?" asked ADA Henry.

"Yes," said the District Attorney.

"Very good," ADA Henry replied. He looked back at the Chief of D's, Rex and Kat. "If you two detectives can come over to my office right now, we will get things started.

Sergeant Alvarez had phoned Rex while they were in the meeting with ADA Henry. She told him that she had set up a task force meeting for 1300 hours in the Detective Conference Room. They had just enough time to grab a quick lunch at the county cafeteria before the meeting.

When they walked into the Conference Room, they noticed that Sergeant Alvarez was not there. Neither was anybody from Special Ops. Only the Chief of D's, Officer Sonny Tam, Detective Pham and Sergeant Larry Quin from Vice was present.

As they took their seats, the Chief of D's spoke. "As you are all probably aware by now, there will be a press conference about this investigation tomorrow. That will signify the official close of this investigation. Before you say anything, I realize that there is a lot more to do on this case. However, some of the follow-up is going to lead us into some very politically sensitive areas. Because of that, I am taking personal charge of this investigation. All follow-up action will be approved by me before hand. You will not talk to anyone else outside of this group about the status of this investigation.

"Sergeant Quin, from Vice, is now your new team sergeant. He will be in charge of the day-to-day operation and he will direct your investigation. By the end of the press conference, tomorrow, you will be set up in your new home, off site, over at Narcotics and Covert Investigations. You will work out of there until this investigation is over. Sergeant Quin is getting your cars, computers and work space set up. Any questions?"

The four officers looked at each other in stunned silence.

When they left the Chief of D's meeting, Rex, Kat and Sonny Tam trooped down the hall to Room 314 where Sergeant Comstock was waiting for them. Dawn Summers and her cameraman were already set up and ready to go. They started with Sonny Tam.

Dawn Summers was highly professional in her interviews with no indication that she knew Rex and Kat other than from previous interviews.

From the start, it was easy to see that she was going for the story of the

Vietnamese community being preyed upon and victimized by their own. Rex could tell, or at least he thought he could tell, that she was not quite buying the solo street gang expanding their criminal influence, but she did not push or even ask any questions about Asian Organized Crime.

She knew that was Rex's pet theory for most of the financial crimes taking place in San Jose and the Bay Area. She had heard this theory from him in the past. She had also heard him say off the record that he thought the Department was not committed to investigating organized crime. The department did not want to admit that it even existed. However, she played it cool and did not go there.

After the interviews, they shot some stock footage of everybody sitting at their desks looking through paperwork or typing on their computer. Rex called it canned shots of detectives at work.

The whole thing was over in about an hour and a half. Sergeant Comstock seemed highly pleased with the way it had all gone. As he turned to escort Ms. Summers and her cameraman out Rex leaned over to Kat and whispered, "Good, now he can report back to the Chief what good little detectives we were."

Chapter 37

The alarm went off at the usual 0400 hours. Rex rolled over and shut off the alarm. He grudgingly crawled out from under the covers and put on his workout clothes. The dogs dutifully accompanied him down to the barn to feed the horses. When he got back to the house, he grabbed his bottle of water and headed for their workout room. Rex climbed on to his Ironman stationary bike and punched in an hour program. By the time he was done with his workout and headed for his shower; his wife was up and stumbling into the workout room.

Rex selected a black western suit with white shirt and a red power tie. That should look good on camera.

"Wow," said Carmella when Rex walked into the kitchen to pour himself a cup of coffee, "you're looking very sharp today. What's the occasion?"

"Today's the big day, the Chief's press conference on the case Kat and I have been working."

"Oh yeah, I forgot. Well, you'll certainly look good on camera. Now I want you to promise me that you will behave yourself."

"Hey, this is all the Chief's show, we are just window dressing."

Rex gave Carmella a kiss, told her he loved her, and headed out to his truck. An hour later he was parking in the employee lot across Mission Street from PAB. Kat was waiting for him as he walked into the unit.

"Come on," she said. "I've already got us a car and have signed us out on the board. Your Sergeant has been in and left with some of her friends for their morning coffee. I figured we'd get some breakfast at Bill's Cafe."

"Sounds good to me," said Rex looking his partner over. She was also dressed in an elegant but conservative black pant suit with a light blue blouse. She looked decidedly professional.

"I see you got the memo," said Rex.

"What memo?"

"The one about it being black suit day."

"Hey, got to look good for the camera," Kat said and flashed Rex a big smile.

As they were walking through the parking lot to their car, they ran into Mitch coming in to work and told him to join them for breakfast over at Bill's Cafe. He said he would get a car and be right there.

Kat and Rex had just finished ordering breakfast when Mitch came into the restaurant with Terry in tow. They sat down and ordered.

After ordering, Mitch looked at Kat and Rex and said, "So, today's the big news conference. How's that gonna go?"

Rex smiled and said, "Should be a real dog and pony show. The Chief himself will be giving the news conference, and the rest of us will be up there as props. I imagine he will pontificate on how the San Jose Police Department is the greatest department in the Universe and how he saved the day with this investigation."

"Speaking of which," said Mitch, "how's that going?"

Kat and Rex exchanged looks. Rex said, "It seems to have taken a strange twist. Yesterday, the Chief of D's informed us that he was personally taking charge of the investigation. He apparently fired Sergeant Alvarez and put Sergeant Quin from Vice in charge. We have also been moved off site to NCI."

Mitch whistled softly. "So, this has turned into some super secret, I could tell ya but then I'd have to kill ya investigation out of the Chief of D's Office."

"That's about the size of it," said Rex.

"Right after breakfast," replied Kat, "we have a meeting with Assistant District Attorney William Henry. He is handling the case personally at the direction of the District Attorney. We still have a lot of follow up to do and hopefully we will make some more arrests. That is, if this press conference doesn't send everybody into hiding. We know who the number one guy is, but I have a feeling he might be out of the country by now."

"We hit his safety deposit box at Bay 101 yesterday," said Rex. "We found a lot of cash and four Vietnamese passports with his picture on them, but with different names. I can't believe that was his only stash of money and passports in case he had to leave town fast.

"This guy is smart, and he seems to be the kind of guy who had all his options covered. By the way, did you hear that the two Glocks the guys at the chop shop were carrying also came from the gun store burglaries down South? Yet another tie in with Asian Organized Crime in Southern California."

"I don't suppose the boy wonder is going to mention anything about that in his news conference," commented Mitch.

"Hell no," said Kat. "We were told yesterday that the official story is that this was just a local Vietnamese street gang that was trying to expand its turf. There is no tie in to organized crime because there is no organized crime in San Jose."

"Wait a minute," said Terry. "Aren't you two the lead detectives? What do you mean you were told this was just a street gang?"

"Word came to us directly from the Chief's Office," said Rex. "We were to play ball with the Chief's version of what happened and his version is just what Kat said, a street gang, not organized crime."

"So now," said Terry, "he's dictating what we can tell the press?"

"In this case he is," replied Rex.

"I knew that he wanted to control his image, but this is ridiculous," said Terry.

"What can I say," said Kat, "it's the new San Jose way of controlling the image of the Chief and the Department. Play ball or suffer the consequences."

Kat and Rex drove straight to the District Attorney's Office after breakfast for their meeting with Assistant District Attorney Henry. They picked up their security badges on the first floor visitor's check-in area and headed for the elevators. They walked into ADA Henry's outer office right on time for their meeting. His secretary ushered them right into his office.

"Good morning detectives. How are you guys today?" asked ADA Henry. "Please sit down. I've been going over your interview with Charlie Zsu Detective Sanchez. Great interview, you really got him to open up. This is some powerful stuff. I've got us booked before the Grand Jury tomorrow. I know your Chief is giving his press conference this afternoon and I want to move quickly for an indictment."

An hour later, they walked out of the District Attorney's Office with their new instructions. Kat said, "I don't feel like going back to the office yet. We've got the news conference starting in an hour, so we are pretty much on hold until then. I don't feel like hanging out at my desk and being asked a hundred questions by your Sergeant. Let's go down to the Grind and get a real cup of coffee."

"Sounds good to me," said Rex. "You're right, back at the office we'd just have to explain what is going on to your Sergeant and watch her get nervous about the upcoming press conference."

So they headed down to the It's a Grind coffee shop on Skyport and ordered a couple of large latte's. They sank into the large winged chairs and discussed where they were in their investigation.

"So, what do you think of our new status as a super secret investigation unit for the Chief of D's?" asked Rex.

"I can certainly understand it," replied Kat. "We are stepping on a really big sacred cow if we investigate the card clubs any further. And, if those secret videos do exist, a lot of people are going to be very embarrassed."

"You're right there. At least we got rid of Alvarez. Sergeant Quin is a really no nonsense, sharp guy."

"So where do we go from here?" asked Kat.

"Well," said Rex, "we still have to go out and pick up the people that were using the skimmers for Lueong. Porter has some new information about the cigarette thefts last Saturday. In addition, there are the leads that ADA Henry wants us to followed up. Hopefully there will be some additional information there."

Kat shook her head. "There is still that file we found at Lueong's house on John Paul Mercado Reyes. We still have no idea who he is or how he fits in to the investigation, if at all. And we still don't know where Tran Van Nguyen is. Hopefully the mail cover on the TVN Enterprises mail box will turn up something."

"The Gang Unit still has to serve the search warrants on Tran's party houses," said Rex. "And there is still the human trafficking angle. Somewhere in the city are a group of young girls being held against their will and we have no idea where."

Chapter 38

They made it back to the Department at 1030 hours, in plenty of time for the news conference. As they were pulling into the police parking lot, they saw several news vans lining Mission Street in front of the Police Administration Building. All the major networks were there (NBC, CBS, ABC, FOX) as well as the Spanish and Asian TV stations.

When they walked into Room 314, there were six TV cameramen and another six or seven still photographers. There were TV news personalities standing around, radio news reporters and newspaper people. The podium was set up with the seal of the city of San Jose on it and the SJPD logo on the blue backdrop behind it.

Over to one side of the podium stood two VCET Officers guarding a table with several cartons of cigarettes, all the cash that had been seized from the chop shop and Tran Van Nguyen's safety deposit box at Bay 101, the seized passports, three Glock handguns, a shotgun, and an AK-47 assault rifle.

On the other side of the podium, Sergeant Comstock was positioning all the Department brass. Chief of Detectives Ortiz was there along with Captain Felder who was in charge of all the property crimes detectives. There were the Lieutenants who commanded Special Operations, the Gang Unit, and Financial Crimes. Sergeant Webber from RATTF was also there. The Chief of Police was standing behind the podium.

Rex felt someone come up beside him. "This is quite some show ain't it Cowboy?" whispered Five-O into Rex's ear.

"Were you invited to this shindig to?" asked Rex.

"No, I'm just gonna watch from back here," said Five-O.

Just then, Sergeant Comstock saw them and waved them forward. He already had Officer Tam in tow.

"I want you guys to stand right here, next to the Chief," he said, indicating a spot just to the right of the Chief.

When they were in place, the Chief started the news conference.

"For some time now the San Jose Police Department has known that certain elements within the Vietnamese Community have been preying on their own. We have worked very diligently to extend a helping hand to the law abiding Vietnamese Community to show them that they can trust this Department. We started by hiring more Vietnamese police officers and then began assigning those officers to beats that covered the Vietnamese Community. We also instituted outreach programs with our Vietnamese officers. I am here today to tell you that that program has finally paid off.

"Three weeks ago Detectives Johnson and Sanchez from the Financial Crimes Unit began an investigation into the theft of cigarettes using counterfeit credit cards. A Vietnamese street gang using counterfeited credit cards obtained the cigarettes in local Costco stores. The plan was to resell those stolen cigarettes through local Vietnamese mom and pop stores. The same stores this gang was extorting for protection. One of our Vietnamese officers, Officer Sonny Tam, had befriended one of those storeowners. When the storeowner came forward and told Officer Tam that he was being forced to sell those stolen cigarettes, Officer Tam brought that information to Detectives Johnson and Sanchez.

"Further investigation by these fine detectives disclosed that this gang was also involved in a recent spate of auto thefts in this city. A task force involving the San Jose PD Gang Unit, the Regional Auto Theft Task Force, San Jose PD Special Operations, and the U.S. Postal Inspectors was quickly organized under the Office of the Chief of Police to deal with this problem. Detectives Johnson and Sanchez continued as the lead detectives.

"Long hours of investigation led to the execution of several search warrants and the attempt to arrest several of the gang members. The leader of the gang, Nick Lueong, was shot and killed by the police when VCET officers tried to arrest him. When told to surrender he instead pulled a gun and started firing at our officers. They were forced to return fire to protect their own lives and the lives of others present.

"Monday afternoon a search warrant was served on an auto body shop in North San Jose that was being used as a chop shop in their auto theft operations. As our MERGE officers were attempting to serve the search warrant, two of the gang members that were there to guard the place opened fire on them and they were forced to shoot in self-defense. Both gang members were killed.

"However, through outstanding investigative work, Detective Sanchez was able to determine that one of the people picked up at the chop shop was the book keeper for the gang. She was able to elicit a confession out of him, and now Charlie Zsu is a cooperating witness in protective custody.

"Because of the quick thinking and diligent work of this Officer, and these Detectives, the back of a vicious gang has been broken. An end to the extortion of the Vietnamese Community has been brought about."

As the Chief was taking questions, Rex was wincing inside. First, there was the lie about pulling this task force together under the Chief's Office. Boy Wonder had not even known about the investigation until the first officer involved shooting.

Then there was that bit about Nick Lueong being the leader of the gang. They knew he was the number two guy, and the leader was Tran Van Nguyen.

Finally, the Chief had outed their star informant. They had promised Charlie Zsu protection in return for his cooperation and the Chief had just thrown him down in front of the press. The gang was by no means broken up as the Chief had asserted to the press. With it now known that Charlie was the one who talked to the police he would be lucky to still be alive at the end of the week. The Chief was seriously trying to stamp case closed all over this one.

The press conference ended and it was over. Rex just wanted to get out of the room, and he could tell from the look on Kat's face that she did too. However, they could not escape just yet. The Chief came over to them and started shaking their hands while the cameras clicked. He kept telling them what a terrific job they had done. The Chief proclaimed to the brass and others around that they were his two best detectives.

As Rex and Kat finally walked out of Room 314, Sergeant Alvarez was waiting for them in the hallway.

"I just wanted to remind you two that this operation is now over except for some mopping up. That means that there is no more overtime authorized. Since this is your Friday, you two take your usual weekend and you can start back in on Monday." After delivering her little speech, Sergeant Alvarez turned and walked away.

Rex looked at Kat. "Did she seem to take pleasure in telling us that we weren't authorized any more overtime?"

"It's the only way she has of showing her power, of proving that she is in command."

"I guess she didn't get the memo."

"What memo?"

"The one that said we didn't work for her anymore."

"Man, after everything that happened in there I feel like I need a shower," Kat explained.

"Yeah," said Rex, "they were laying it on pretty thick in there. You didn't just need boots to get through the horse pucky, you needed hip waders. Well, as my great grand pappy used to say, 'never assume malice where stupidity would suffice.' "

Kat chuckled at that one. "God, I couldn't believe all the lies he was telling in there. And the fact that he outed our one and only witness. Not only has he painted a big target on Charlie's back, but he has also made the job of the officers guarding him that much harder. I hope nobody gets hurt because of this. I've had enough of this place, let's go to lunch. Then we can get moved in to our new digs."

Chapter 39

Tran Van Nguyen was alone with his thoughts sitting at his table upstairs at the Loving Cup coffee house. For the past several years, Tran had been building himself an organization. He now had about thirty people working for him. His organization was into loan sharking at the card clubs, passing counterfeit checks and credit cards, illegal gambling, prostitution, human trafficking, and car theft.

As a teenager, he had been a driver in a Vietnamese street gang that had done several home invasions. They specialized in invading houses of wealthy Vietnamese and taking all the cash and jewelry in the house. He personally had never used a gun or gone into the houses.

This gang had graduated to armed robberies of delivery trucks bringing computer chips to the various companies in Silicon Valley. The precious metals in the chips made them extremely valuable just for that. But, they could also be sold on the black market in the Far East to countries like China. The only problem was that these chip heists brought a lot of heat. The local police had teamed up with the FBI and formed a task force to hunt down the people responsible. This had lead to most of the gang being caught.

Tran was one of the few that had not been caught by the police. Those that had been caught had gone to prison for a long time. The police got seriously upset with people sticking guns in peoples' faces and beating and raping them. The police organized and hunted the gangs down when they got too violent. All of the people caught were convicted on multiple felony counts and sentenced to long prison terms.

After his fellow gang members were arrested in San Jose, Tran had gone to Southern California to hide and let things cool down. He lived with a cousin in Westminster. This cousin was into counterfeit checks. He had taught Tran how to do it.

In the beginning, it was so easy. You went to Staples or Office Depot and you stole a small business check writing software program, complete with the blank check stock. You then got your hands on a check from some business, and with your computer, you simply made up a counterfeit check payable to yourself from the company. If you kept the amount small enough, it would not trigger the security alerts in the bank computers. You then went to several different branches of the bank the target company used and cashed your checks. You could easily make yourself $1,000.00 to $3,000.00 in a day. If you dressed neat and looked like you belonged, nobody ever questioned you.

As the scam progressed, they learned how to make better looking checks. They also learned to recruit other people to pass the checks so they did not have to enter the banks themselves and worry about being caught. Tran learned that he could make more money with a computer than with a gun.

The likelihood of being caught was also a lot less because it took so long for the crime to be discovered. If you stuck a gun in someone's face, demanded their cash and jewels, and left them alive, they reported the crime to the police as soon as they could. However, if you went to a bank and passed a counterfeit check, the crime was not discovered until that cancelled check made it back to the company the check was drawn on and they discovered that it was a counterfeit. That could take a month or more.

Even if you were eventually caught, it was just a simple theft, so the odds were you would not go to prison for very long, if at all. With a skilled lawyer, you could probably avoid any state prison time and just get probation.

Eventually Tran had returned to San Jose with his new found talent and his cousin. The local Vietnamese gang leaders had all been arrested, and a vacuum existed. The old leadership was doing time in state prison, and the local scene was screaming for some bright young man to step in and take over.

Tran considered himself that bright young man. He was the brains behind the organization. His cousin was the muscle. Tran had made connections with influential people in Asian Organized Crime in Southern California. He came back to San Jose to organize with their support and blessings.

Eventually Tran put together an organization that controlled Asian crime in the entire South Bay Area. They started with the passing of counterfeit checks and expanded into counterfeit credit cards.

The next logical step was loan sharking. There were two card clubs in San Jose. These clubs had a large Asian clientele, so they specialized in Asian card games like Pai-Gow. These games moved fast, and you could lose a lot of money in a remarkably short time.

The problem for many of the card players was that they loved to gamble, but did not have enough money to support their habit. There were gamblers that would lose their entire paycheck in a couple of hours. Then they would go looking for someone from whom to borrow money. Enter Tran's boys. They hung around the card clubs, playing a little, drinking at the bar, and eating at the restaurant. The word was quietly passed that if you needed money they were there to help you. Business was good.

As an outgrowth of his loan shark operation, Tran expanded into handling special party nights for gamblers who wanted to bet on various sports. He set up houses where the high rollers could lay down their bets and then watch the football game or horse race they had bet on. All the while being entertained by lovely young ladies. And if the gamblers wished to avail themselves of the talents of these young ladies, the bedrooms were available. Making sure that he had a never-ending supply of 'clean' young women had led Tran into human trafficking.

Of course, all of the rooms in Tran's party houses had hidden video cameras in them. Tran had quite a collection of DVD's starring local businessmen and a few local politicians.

Tran also expanded into the auto theft business. Tran first "inherited" an auto body shop from another Vietnamese man that owed him money from gambling debts. Tran had made him an offer that he could not refuse. The guy would continue to operate the shop with Tran as a silent partner. Tran would forgive all of his gambling debts. After getting the shop, Tran sent his cousin out to recruit several of the small Vietnamese street gangs that were boosting cars in San Jose and Santa Clara. These gangs were all organized under the Tran Van Nguyen umbrella organization, but each gang knew nothing about the other. Besides stealing cars for Tran, they provided the street muscle he needed.

With this added muscle, Tran had added the next logical enterprise to his organization, extortion. He and his cousin visited the Asian owned businesses in San Jose and offered protection to the storeowners. For a small monthly fee, they were assured that they would be protected, that nothing would happen to them, their family or their business.

Tran's organization was doing quite well and was bringing in a nice chunk of money each week. He had bought property. He drove around in a red Lexus IS C. He wore only designer suits.

Chapter 40

A few months ago, word had been passed to Tran that a Filipino man was looking for some counterfeit credit cards and IDs. Tran had his cousin set up a meeting at the Bay 101 Card Club. The meeting was to take place in the restaurant of the club over a late lunch. Tran got there about one o'clock and was shown to a secluded table in the back of the restaurant. Tran ordered coffee and waited. At 1:30 PM, his cousin came in with the Filipino man in tow. Tran's cousin brought the Filipino man over to the table and left.

"Won't you sit down please," said Tran.

The Filipino man sat without saying anything.

"Would you like some coffee?" asked Tran.

The Filipino man nodded his head,, and Tran signaled the waitress.

When the Filipino man had been served his coffee and the waitress had left, Tran said to him, "My name is Tran."

The Filipino man said, "I know who you are."

Tran replied, "Then you have me at a disadvantage because I do not know who you are."

"My name is John Paul Mercado Reyes. I need your help and your permission. I know that you run all things illegal in the Asian community. I have a proposition for you." Reyes took a piece of paper out of his jacket pocket and passed in over to Tran. "That is a license from the state of California to sell cigarettes. My plan calls for forging that license and making a Costco membership card and American

Express credit card to go along with it. With these, I plan to buy cigarettes from Costco."

"And what do you plan to do with these cigarettes after you have bought them?" asked Tran.

"I intend to sell them to you at a discount," replied Reyes. "It is said that you have many connections with small stores in San Jose. With so many connections, it would be easier for you to re-sell the cigarettes than me."

Tran studied Reyes. He was young, about mid 20's, and dressed conservatively in Chino's, a blue golf shirt, and a lightweight tan windbreaker. His hands were clean, and he had the appearance of a college student about him. Tran did not know much about Reyes. His cousin had asked around and had not been able to find out anything either, other than Reyes had been seen around Bay 101 for the past month. Reyes was an unknown and this made Tran wary. After all, Reyes could be an undercover cop.

"What makes you think that I can provide you with any of these things?" asked Tran.

"I have been coming to Bay 101 for the past month and quietly asking around. I know that you are the man to see if you need to borrow money. I know that you are said to have a great influence over the Asian shop owners in San Jose. I have also heard it said that in the Asian community, nothing illegal gets done without the approval of Tran Van Nguyen. I know you think that I might be a cop, but I am not. A few friends of mine have come up with this way to make some extra money, but to do it, we need your help and your blessing," said Reyes. "I am willing to answer any questions you might have of me."

Tran looked Reyes over again. Finally, Tran said, "Let's order lunch, then we can talk some more."

And talk they did. Tran found out that Reyes had actually been a college student. He was in the United States on a student visa. He had been attending San Jose State University until money stopped coming from home. Reyes did not want to go back to the Philippines; he wanted to stay in the U.S. But that would take money and Reyes did not want to get a real job. So Reyes and a couple of his friends had come up with the cigarette plan.

Tran still was not quite sure how he had come up with the plan, Reyes was a little vague about that, but as they were talking Tran could see the merits of the plan and realized that he could make a tidy little profit with minimum risk. Reyes told Tran he lived in an apartment on McLaughlin and Tully with a roommate who was also on a student visa from the Philippines. The roommate had also been attending San Jose State, but had dropped out. The roommate was still getting money from home, but as soon as his parents found out he had dropped out of school, they would cut him off. It was the roommate that was Reyes main partner in the cigarette scheme, because he also wanted to stay in the U.S. and realized he needed money to do that.

After they finished lunch Tran told Reyes, "I'm still not sure what I can do for you, but why don't we meet back here in two days to talk more."

They shook hands and Reyes left the restaurant. He did not see Tran give a barely detectable signal to a Vietnamese man hanging around the entrance to the restaurant. Nor was Reyes aware of this man following him out to his car. As Reyes got into his car, the Vietnamese man continued walking down the row of parked cars. Reyes did not notice him making note of his license plate.

With the car license plate number, Tran was able to run a check on Reyes. A girlfriend of one of Tran's gang worked at the main branch of the Department of Motor Vehicles in San Jose. She did favors for her boyfriend occasionally like running license plates and name checks. She ran the license plate of the car that John Paul Mercado Reyes had gotten into, and it came back registered to him.

The registration also showed him with an address on McLaughlin just as Reyes had said. The girlfriend then ran a driver's license check on him and got the same residence. All of this information was passed on to Tran. Tran then had the same gang member who had followed Reyes to his car hang around the McLaughlin apartment complex until he had seen Reyes coming and going from the apartment listed on his driver's license. Satisfied that Reyes was probably not an undercover cop, Tran set up a second meeting and sealed the deal on a new venture and partnership.

Still, Tran thought as he sat there finishing his espresso, there was something else to Reyes. Tran did not think he was a cop or an informant, but there was something else. There was something about Reyes that warned Tran to be careful with him. He decided to have his cousin do some further checking on Mr. John Paul Mercado Reyes.

After a couple of more weeks of checking, Tran's cousin, Nick Lueong, could find nothing else about John Reyes that showed him to be anything more than what he said he was, a former college kid on a student visa who wanted to make a quick buck.

Tran decided to try him out and ordered the counterfeit documents and credit card that John Reyes wanted. If this one deal turned out profitable, then there would be others.

Chapter 41

Reyes sat across from Tran Van Nguyen in an upstairs table at the Loving Cup coffee shop. He had just passed two envelopes to Tran. One contained money and instructions for the next set of forged documents and credit cards that Reyes would need. The other contained the keys, location, and license plate number of a van that contained the cigarettes they had just acquired from Costco.

Tran in turn, gave Reyes an envelope containing the cash payment for the newly acquired cigarettes. Tran then called one of his employees upstairs and gave him instructions for picking up the cigarettes.

After Reyes picked up his money from Tran at the Loving Cup coffee shop, he drove to Fremont to see his "banker." On the drive to Fremont Reyes's thoughts turned to Tran. He knew that Tran had checked him out before going into business with him and wondered just how much Tran had found out. Did Tran still think that Reyes was just the out of money college student from the Philippines or had he learned more? It mattered to Reyes because of operational security. It was crucial that Tran believed him to be the crook that he presented and did not find out his true identity.

It was true that Reyes had come to the United States on a student visa to attend engineering classes at San Jose State University. Things had changed for Reyes shortly after his arrival in the United States. Reyes had met another Filipino student in the engineering program who had helped him find his purpose in life.

Reyes had never thought much about religion or politics or even what he was going to do with his life after getting his engineering degree. This had all changed after his fellow student introduced him to Islam. He had invited Reyes to his mosque and introduced Reyes to his Imam, Saleh Muhannad Jazir. It was unknown to Reyes at the time of their introduction, but Jazir was a follower of Wahhabism. Wahhabism is the Saudi branch of Islam, established by Sheikh Muhammad bin Abd al-Wahhab. At its core, in addition to the known five pillars of Islam is the belief that there is a sixth hidden pillar which requires fighting the Jihad to spread Islam and to defeat it enemies.

Reyes found a connection with Islam and converted. He embraced the five pillars of Islam; the testimony of faith, the ritual of daily prayer, the obligatory almsgiving, fasting, and the pilgrimage to Mecca, a journey Reyes hoped to take one day. He found that Islam was not just a religion but was a total way of life. He found the fact that Islam had instructions on how one was to spend every minute of one's life immensely comforting. He felt that he was no longer just casting about aimlessly. His life was now peaceful and had substance. This order and meaning was found in the teachings of the Koran.

Reyes also came to embrace jihad. He came to know and hate the arrogant way of thinking of all westerners, but especially Americans. Through Jazir's teachings he began to understand just how the people of the Great Satan tried to defeat Islam and oppress the true believers. Jazir opened his eyes as to how powerful the Muslim nation had once been and how much greater it would be again once they had slaughtered the Great Satan and all the unbelievers who lived there.

As Reyes spent more and more time under the tutelage of Jazir, he became more radicalized. Reyes learned that for those not of Islam, there were only three choices; convert to Islam, remain in your own faith but submit to a tax and be subservient to Islam; or be put to death. Reyes came to hate the "Great Satan" and all Americans that were not of the Islamic faith. In time Reyes committed himself to jihad.

Reyes learned of the Abu Sayyaf Group in his homeland of the Philippines. The radical Philippine Islamist group, the name meant "Bearer of the Sword," had been founded in the late 1980s to seek complete religious and political independence for the Muslim island of Mindanao. Reyes wanted to go back to the Philippines and join his brothers in the fight, but Jazir convinced him there was a better way.

Jazir convinced Reyes that the jihad needed people in the United States, people that could be called on at a future date, people that could act now to raise funds for the world wide jihad and for the Abu Sayyaf Group. With Jazir's help, Reyes set up a terrorist cell in San Jose.

Jazir put Reyes in contact with Eljvir Nosair. Nosair schooled Reyes in how to set up his cell and how to protect it. It was Nosair who came up with the cigarette scam. He said it was based on something that had been done in North Carolina several years ago to raise money for Hizballah in Lebannon. Nosair told Reyes that it had raised several millions of dollars for Hizballah. The idea appealed to Reyes who saw himself raising several millions of dollars for Abu Sayyaf.

Reyes took the Fremont Blvd exit off 880 and continued on to the section of Fremont known as Little Kabul. He found a place to park to the rear of the Salang Pass Restaurant and went in through the rear entrance. Nosair had once told Reyes that he had developed a fondness for Afghan food while fighting with the Taliban in Afghanistan. Nosair thought the Salang Pass served up the best Afghan food. As Reyes entered the restaurant, he looked around and spotted Nosair at a back table in the "western" section of the restaurant.

Reyes walked over to the table and greeted Nosair. "As salaam alaykum."

"Wa alaykum as salaam, my brother, it is so good to see you again," said Nosair reaching out and shaking Reyes's hand. "Please, please, sit down. I have already ordered us some Turkish coffee and ice cream."

Reyes sat down and a waiter came with the coffee. When the waiter had left, Reyes took the envelope containing the money he had gotten from Tran out of his jacket pocket and slid it across the table to Nosair.

"Praise Allah," said Nosair, "is this the latest for our friends in Mindanao?"

Reyes nodded yes.

Nosair took the envelope and put it into his briefcase.

"You will see that it all gets to our friends?" asked Reyes.

"But of course," said Nosair. "I will see my hawalandar this afternoon and our friends will have their money by tomorrow."

Hawala was a way for them to transfer money clandestinely through an informal exchange. As Reyes understood it, Nosair had a working relationship with a man in Fremont known as a hawalandar. Nosair gave this man the money Reyes had just given him. The hawalandar would then make a call to another hawalandar he did business with in the Philippines. He arranged for that same amount of money to be delivered directly to their Abu Sayyaf contact. The money Reyes had collected never left the country and was thus entirely untraceable by the police. The books that the hawalandar in Fremont kept, such as they were, only dealt with the money he owed to the man in the Philippines.

Reyes asked, "You are sure that the authorities will not be alerted?"

Nosair smiled at Reyes. "My friend, I have told you many times before not to worry. The man I deal with has been in the Hawala business for many years and is very discrete. He keeps very little in the way of records, and there is nothing that can tie this money to you or me. On the other end, our friends in the Philippines are given their money personally by the moneyman in the Philippines. His records are about as little as the man here in Fremont. There is nothing for the Philippine government to find. This is the best and fastest way to get the money you are collecting for our great cause into their hands."

"All right," said Reyes.

"My friend," said Nosair, "you look worried. Is something wrong?" Nosair had run agents for Al-Qaida for years. First, he ran them in Europe and now in the United States. He knew that agents needed to be constantly reassured that everything was all right so that they kept their nerve.

"We serve Allah in a great cause, he will see that nothing happens to us," Nosair reassured him.

"Allah is great," said Reyes. "You are right Nosair, our cause is righteous, and He will see that we succeed against the Crusaders."

The ice cream came, and they enjoyed a pleasant half hour over their

Turkish coffee and ice cream. Nosair told stories about when he was in Afghanistan.

When they had finished their ice cream and were about to leave, Nosair reached across the table and took Reyes by the hand. "My brother, are you set to continue in our quest against the Infidels? Are you strong? Does the jihad still burn within you?"

Reyes looked at Nosair, and a calm seemed to come over him. "Yes my brother, I am ready. Tran had the new documents ready for me and we will make another purchase tomorrow. I shall have another delivery of money for you in a week, Allah willing."

"Allah is great," said Nosair as he stood up. "I will wait for your call." Nosair left money on the table, turned, and left the restaurant by the front door.

Reyes waited another ten minutes and then left the restaurant by the back door. He looked around the parking lot as he came out but did not see anything suspicious. He got in his car and drove back to San Jose.

Chapter 42

Tran Van Nguyen walked into Bay 101 and headed for the front desk. After the cops killed his cousin Nick and then took down his chop shop, he figured it was time for him to take a vacation. He wanted to get his money and his passports out of his safety deposit box.

He was just about to step up to the desk and request access to his box when he saw the club manager carrying a safety deposit box into the privacy room. He was followed by two people Tran recognized from television news as San Jose PD detectives. He hung back and watched. After a few minutes, the detectives walked out carrying a paper sack. The manager took the safety deposit box back to the rack and replaced it. Tran was not close enough to see the actual box number, but it was in the area of where his box was.

Tran was convinced that the detectives had just searched his safety deposit box. That meant that the cops had his money and his passports. Well, this was not the only place he had stashed his getaway cash and papers. He would swing by his alternate stash sites and then make serious plans to get out of town. There were just a few loose ends to tie up.

Two hours later Tran sat alone at his table upstairs at the Loving Cup drinking an espresso. Tran was composed outside, but he was seething with hatred inside. The police had killed his cousin, and someone was going to pay. Nick had taken him in years ago when Tran had to leave San Jose and lay low. Nick had introduced him to influential people in Southern California that helped him get to where he was today. It was having Nick working as his enforcer that made his entire organization work.

The cops seemed to be systematically taking his operation apart. It was just a matter of time before they started arresting some of his other employees. It was clearly time for him to leave town before the cops closed in on him.

He was also a little confused. He could not figure out how the cops had found out so much about his organization. He was sure that nobody on the inside had talked, especially after he had gone all Al Capone on the one employee that was stealing from him. How had the cops known so much and moved so fast? Well, that would be something to consider from somewhere safe, like a beach in Vietnam.

He hated the police for killing his cousin. He was also a little frightened. If the police knew that Nick was going to the store to deliver the cigarettes, then they must have been waiting for him. If they were waiting for him, they must know about the cigarette thefts. If they knew about that, how much more did they know about his organization? The cops must be on to him or at least have him under investigation. He had been exceedingly careful.

Nick was the enforcer and front man for his organization. Tran stayed in the background and did not have much contact with the soldiers in his organization. Maybe the police did not know who he was yet. No, that was not true because they had found his safety deposit box at Bay 101. They had to know who he was, and they had to be getting their information from someone on the inside.

Nick and Charlie Zsu were the only two people that knew about the safety deposit box at Bay 101. Nick was dead and Charlie was . . . ? Where was Charlie? Charlie had been going over to the chop shop yesterday to pick up the money. Had Charlie been there when the cops hit the place? Was Charlie in police custody? It did not make any difference. Charlie would not talk. Charlie was too scared to talk. Or would he?

Then he remembered that he had just given a new set of counterfeits to Reyes, and he would soon be making his cigarette buys. He had to get a hold of him and have him stop. But how? Nick had always been the one that set up the meetings. He remembered Nick telling him that Reyes did not even have a cell phone; at least he said he did not.

Reyes was extremely secretive, and he was the one that made contact with Nick when he was ready to deliver his stolen cigarettes. Oh well, that was Reyes's problem now. If Reyes was only able to get in touch with Nick, then the police could not trace anything back to Tran. The whole thing would stop with Nick and Nick was dead. Maybe he would not have to take that vacation and loose all that money. All he had to do was shut Reyes out, and that was all but done.

Then Tran thought that would not work either. Reyes knew him and had met with him. Tran remembered Reyes saying that he knew that he needed Tran's permission to go into business. He knew that Tran was the big boss and organizer. If Reyes got busted, he would talk to the cops and tell them everything he knew about Tran. Tran had to figure out how to get to Reyes and tell him to cool it for a while.

Tran's thoughts were interrupted by an announcement on the flat screen TV in the corner of the loft. When Tran was at his table, he always kept the TV tuned to KTVU Channel 2 because they had the best local news coverage. Tran saw that regular programming had been interrupted and a reporter in the studio was saying something. Tran grabbed the remote and turned up the volume.

"We now go live to Dawn Summers at the San Jose Police Department Headquarters," said the talking head.

The picture jumped and the screen filled with a live shot of Dawn Summers. "Thank you Ken. In just a few moments, San Jose Police Chief Ed Daniels will be giving a briefing on a major gang arrest that has occurred in San Jose. After weeks of almost round the clock investigation, the San Jose Police Department has taken down a large gang that was preying on the citizen's of San Jose. Chief Daniels has just stepped up to the podium, let's listen."

The camera swung, and the image of Chief Daniels filled the screen. For the next half hour, Tran Van Nguyen listened to the news conference. He showed no emotion. He did not even move a muscle. He just sat at his table with his jaw set.

At the end of the briefing and the question and answer session, the screen filled once again with the image of Dawn Summers.

"Well, there you have it Ken, a major gang with their criminal tentacles into many different criminal activities has been taken down by the brave and dedicated men and women of the San Jose Police Department."

"Dawn, I understand that you have some additional information about this investigation."

"Ken, I was given exclusive access to this investigation several days ago. Because of the sensitivity of the on-going investigation, I agreed to not report the story until today. Tonight on the six o'clock news, I will start my six part series that takes an in depth look into this investigation, the criminals involved and the victims. Back to you Ken."

"Thank you Dawn, we will be looking forward to that informative series."

Tran lowered the volume. He sat there, still as a statue for another minute. Then he slammed his fist on the table. He had his answers now. Charlie Zsu had betrayed him. After all, he had done for Charlie. Charlie would pay for his betrayal.

And those two detectives. They may not have pulled the trigger, but they were responsible for the murder of his cousin. They would pay also. They may have taken out some of his organization, but they did not know how big his organization was and how much influence he actually had. Tran would attend to his revenge before he left town.

While he never thought it would happen, Tran had made contingency plans for this day. He knew that eventually the police would bust up some of his operations. He had back up plans. The money and the passports in the Bay 101 safety deposit box were not the only money and passports he had. Right now, he had to move. If the cops knew about Bay 101, it would not be long before they figured out he also operated out of the Loving Cup, if they did not know already.

Tran Van Nguyen calmly got up and walked downstairs and out the front door. He got into his car and drove out of the parking lot. Tran drove for about an hour through the residential neighborhoods of East San Jose. He made several turns and doubled back on himself looking for a tail.

When he was sure that he was not being followed, he headed for his safe house in the Jackson and Story Road area. These were older small houses in a neighborhood that was mostly low income Hispanic and the turf of several Hispanic gangs. He had purchased a home about a year ago that he kept as a safe house. No one else in his organization except his dead cousin knew about it.

Several blocks from the safe house Tran pulled over and hit a speed dial button on his i-Phone. This remotely accessed the sophisticated alarm system of the house. Tran pulled up the entry log. It showed that the last person to enter the house was his cousin Nick, and that was two weeks ago. From his i-Phone, Tran accessed the security cameras. The cameras covered every room in the house and covered the entire outside perimeter. Tran scrolled through all of the cameras. All the rooms in the house looked normal. There was no indication that anyone had ever been there.

He scrolled through the outside cameras, which showed him the street in front of the house, the backyard, and the side walkways. There was no suggestion that the house was under surveillance. Tran punched in the code that deactivated the alarm system and pulled away from the curb.

The lawn was brown and dead, and the paint on the house was peeling, much like the other houses in the neighborhood. Tran hit the garage door opener and drove into the garage. He parked his red Lexus next to a nondescript older brown Honda Civic already parked in the garage. As soon as he parked, he hit the garage door opener again and closed the garage door. He got out of the Lexus and covered the car with a car cover. Tran then activated the perimeter alarm.

Tran Van Nguyen went into the house and to the back bedroom. He opened the closet door and looked at the double door gun safe. Tran punched in the combination on the digital key pad and spun the locking wheel. The safe contained cash, passports and prepaid burn cell phones. There were also four AK-47 assault rifles, two Remington auto loader shotguns, and six Glock Pistols.

Tran took out one of the Glock pistols, loaded it, and shoved into his belt. He then went back into the kitchen and sat down at the cheap table. The table held a computer and several flat screen monitors that showed the views of the perimeter cameras. It was time to prepare his revenge.

Chapter 43

It was Friday morning, and it should have been their day off. It would have been if they were still working for Sergeant Alvarez. Things had changed dramatically when the Chief of D's had decided to take personal charge of the rest of their investigation. Rex, Kat, Detective Phong from the Gang Unit and Officer Sonny Tam were moving into their new home at NCI.

NCI stood for Narcotics and Covert Investigations. It was an off-site location that housed the SJPD's undercover narcotics unit and the Hi-Tech Unit. They would work out of here and away from the prying eyes of the rest of the department and the press for the duration of their investigation into the Tran Van Nguyen criminal enterprise.

They had been told to bring all of their files with them. They had boxed up what they had and were now sorting through what they had brought over. They had been given a room to themselves in the NCI building. For the time being, their desks would be four tables that had been pushed together in the center of the room. On each table was a brand new armored Dell XPS laptop computer and a docking station.

As they were unpacking, Sergeant Quin wheeled a large white board into the room.

"Good morning everyone," Sergeant Quin called out. "How do you like your new home?"

There were murmurs of approval from everyone.

"This is as good a time as any, let's have a quick team meeting. Grab a cup of coffee if you want."

When they had topped off their coffee mugs, Sergeant Quin continued. "As you know, this team has been specifically formed to follow up the continuing investigation of Tran Van Nguyen's criminal enterprise. To follow up and arrest Mr. Tran Van Nguyen.

"The DA has convened a Grand Jury hearing today for the purpose of seeking an indictment against Mr. Tran Van Nguyen. Kat and Rex will be testifying before that Grand Jury this afternoon. I see no reason why the DA should not get his indictment. And that is why I say follow up and arrest Mr. Tran Van Nguyen.

"For those of you who don't know me or have not worked for me, let me say this. I love putting bad guys in jail. To that end, I will make sure that you have every available resource this department can muster to make that happen. We already know that Mr. Tran Van Nguyen is an extraordinarily bad guy. We are going to follow every lead and turn over every rock to find and dismantle every last part of his organization.

"According to what we already know, some of our investigation will lead us into some pretty sensitive areas. I don't care where your investigation leads you, I expect you to follow up on every single lead.

"All you have to do is keep me fully informed at all times and we will not have a problem. To do that we will try to start each morning with a quick briefing so we know where we all are in the investigation. But I'm not one to let briefings get in the way of police work, so if you can't be here I'll understand.

"Now as you can see, you have the latest department issued laptop computers at your desks. They are entirely wireless and tied into all the department, state and national data bases through an encrypted wireless router. Take them with you when you go into the field so that you can run anything from anywhere.

"Cars. Rex and Kat, you've got a Ford Explorer," Sergeant Quin said as he tossed a set of keys to Rex. Phong and Tam, you guys get a Ford Mustang. These are asset forfeiture cars and completely untraceable to the PD. These are all take home cars because you are all now on the clock 24-7 until we wrap this up.

"Communications. In the charger at each desk, there is a Nextel phone. We are programmed in as Group One on the push-to-talk groups. Get familiar with how they work and who else you can talk to. Keep them with you at all times. Any questions so far?"

Rex raised his hand, and Sergeant Quin nodded at him. "Are we still working with RATTF on the stolen car operation of Tran's enterprise?"

"Yes, they will be handling the entire stolen car case and turning over to us anything they find that is not related to stolen cars," answered Sergeant Quin.

Rex continued. "What about Postal? Can we bring Five-O into our group. Postal still has those pole cameras operating at the Loving Cup Coffee House and the mail covers on the TVN Enterprises mailboxes. And we could always use another Vietnamese speaker. Besides, Five-O gives us access to some really neat toys that might be useful down the road."

"Good idea," said Sergeant Quin. "Mostly we wanted to keep this in-house because of where it might lead. But I know Five-O, he's a good man and he can be trusted. Rex, why don't you call him up and see if he would like to join our merry little band of misfits."

They spent the rest of the morning going over what they had already discovered in the case. They hauled in three more whiteboards and made a timeline of the investigation so far.

When they were done with that, they looked at what leads they had and where they needed to go from here. They needed to pick up any of Nick Lueong's skimmer workers and squeeze them for any information they had. They decided the best way to do this was to split up in teams and go to each restaurant in Nick's ledger at the same time he would have gone there to swap out the skimmers.

They needed to get meetings with the Vietnamese business leaders to see if they could gin up any more support, or anymore information on the extortions. It was decided that Officer Sonny Tam would handle that. He would start working that angle the following week, after Tran Van Nguyen's indictment came down.

They still needed to find the young prostitutes Tran employed. They had no idea where they were being held. Detective Phong said that he had gotten search warrants for the two known party pads, and he suggested that they might find something in them.

Sergeant Quin decided to move on the search warrants that after noon. While Kat and Rex were testifying at the Grand Jury, he would take Phong and Tam and a VCET Team and hit both houses simultaneously.

While the rest of the team started planning the execution of their search warrants, Kat and Rex decided to head out for lunch and then on over to the Grand Jury.

Since the Grand Jury met in the County building, they decided to have lunch at the County cafeteria. They found a parking space by the police academy building and walked down to the basement cafeteria.

As they walked over to the Grand Jury meeting room, they saw the star witness, Charlie Zsu being escorted in by two DA Investigators. They had taken over the protection of Charlie from San Jose. They all walked into the witness waiting room together.

"How you holding up Charlie?" asked Kat.

"Just fine Detective Sanchez. Everybody has been treating me real nice." drawled Charlie.

Just then ADA William Henry popped into the room and told Rex that he was up next. After Rex testified it was Kat's turn, and then Charlie's.

When Kat was finished testifying ADA Henry told them they could leave. He would call them when the Grand Jury reached a verdict. They thanked him and stepped out into the hallway.

"Let's see if I can work this fancy gizmo," said Rex as he pulled out his Nextel. He turned it on, hit the push-to-talk button and called Sergeant Quin. Quin answered immediately. Rex told him they were done at the Grand Jury and wondered how the search of the party pads was going. Sergeant Quin told him he was standing in one of Tran's party pads and suggested the two of them join him. Kat jotted down the address and they headed back to their Explorer.

When they got to the house, they saw that it was a corner residence in a quiet neighborhood in South San Jose. The front lawn was green and recently mowed. The bushes and flowers were all nicely cared for. Sergeant Quin met them at the front door.

Inside everything was clean and neat. The furniture was nice but not extravagant. There was a well stocked bar in the living room. The most prominent feature of the living room was the 72-inch flat screen TV on the wall. There was a kitchen stocked with silverware, plates and linens, but no food. There were three bedrooms, each with a king size bed with satin sheets.

Sergeant Quin showed them to the garage. It too was neat and clean with no sign that any car had been parked in there recently.

"Right here is the brains of the house," said Sergeant Quin opening a cabinet door. Inside was a computer and two 12-inch flat screen monitors. Sergeant Quin hit the power button and the screens came to life. The left screen showed a multiple room shot of all the rooms, including the bathrooms, in the house. The right screen showed one of the bedrooms.

Sergeant Quin picked up a pair of headphones. "Each room is also wired for sound. You can watch the action in all the rooms on the left monitor and then switch to a single view of whatever room you want on the right monitor. You can zoom in on any action with this joystick. It is much the same as any loss prevention setup in any store. The cameras are all hidden in smoke detectors, clocks, fake books, things like that. Detective Phong and Officer Tam tell me that the other house is almost a mirror image of this one.

"I don't suppose they left behind any DVDs or paperwork or any other hard evidence," said Rex.

"Nothing that we've been able to find," said Sergeant Quin. "I've already cleared it for the Crime Scene Unit to come out and process each house for latent prints and any other biological evidence."

Rex looked at Sergeant Quin with newfound respect. "You do have pull. They usually don't come out for anything but a homicide."

"Not me, the Chief of D's."

Chapter 44

It was 10:45 AM, Saturday morning and Reyes was sitting in a minivan in the parking lot of the Costco at the Almaden Fashion Plaza. At the two other Costco stores in San Jose and the one in Santa Clara, other people in his cell sat in their van's and waited. They had figured out that the best day to do their cigarette buy was on a Saturday because that was when the stores were the busiest. Reyes had also figured out that even though his counterfeit Costco ID showed him to be a business member, it was better to wait until after 11:00 AM. That was when all the rest of the members were let in and the store got really busy. The game plan was that they would hit these four stores first and then move on to the stores in Sunnyvale, Mt View, Foster City, and Fremont. All the stores would be hit today. They all had two sets of forged cards and documents, so they could each buy the maximum number of cigarettes at each store. When they were all done, they would all come back to the storage unit on Story Rd where they stored the cigarettes until they delivered them to Tran Van Nguyen.

This would be their largest haul yet. Reyes had shuffled everybody around so that no one was going into a store that they had been in before just in case they were recognized by a store manager. Reyes was figuring that they should get about $200,000 for their cause after selling the cigarettes to Tran.

At 11:10 AM, Reyes pushed his shopping cart through the front door of the Costco. The person checking membership cards gave his only a fleeting look as she did everyone else's and smiled at him. Reyes smiled back and told her "Good Morning." Once in the store he started looking for a floor manager. Twenty minutes later Reyes pushed his full shopping cart out of the store. Everything had gone according to plan, and no one had seemed the least bit suspicious.

Reyes loaded his van and drove on to the next Costco store he had assigned himself. He repeated everything he had done at the first and walked out with a shopping cart loaded with the maximum amount of cigarettes he was allowed to purchase. At all the other stores, his other three cell members had made all of their purchases without a hitch. Later that evening they had all delivered their cigarettes to the Story Road storage unit. Reyes placed a call to Nick Lueong to arrange for the delivery of the cigarettes, but there was no answer.

Reyes had been trying to get a hold of Nick Lueong ever since Saturday. He had several hundred cartons of cigarettes in his storage locker, and he wanted to get rid of them and get his money. Nick Lueong was his only contact with the gang, and that was by cell phone. The problem was Nick was not answering his cell phone. Reyes did not know what was going on. Were they trying to cheat him somehow? That did not make sense. He still had the cigarettes and for them all to make money he had to get the cigarettes to Nick.

Reyes did not pay attention to the local news; it honestly did not interest him. Most of his free time was spent at the mosque studying the Koran or listening to teachings by the Imam. He did not know that Nick was dead, shot by the police. He did not know that Tran Van Nguyen's little criminal empire was on the verge of collapse. He only knew that he had something for them, and they owned him some money.

Therefore, on Monday morning he decided to seek out Tran Van Nguyen himself. The only places that Reyes had ever seen Tran Van Nguyen was in the restaurant at the Bay 101 Club and the Loving Cup Coffee House. He decided that the Bay 101 was his best bet.

Reyes looked all over the club but did not find him. So he decided to reach out to him. Reyes stopped every gangster looking Vietnamese male in the place and asked them if they knew Tran Van Nguyen. His ploy worked. Soon two tough looking Vietnamese males with slicked back hair, sunglasses, and black leather jackets came up to him and asked if they could talk to him outside. It was unquestionably not a request because at the same time they were quietly asking him to step outside they had taken hold of each arm and were directing him out the front door.

Reyes did not offer any resistance, he went willingly wherever they directed. This was what he wanted. He figured that if he bugged enough people and made them nervous some of Tran Van Nguyen's people would come find him.

Once out in the parking lot, the two gangsters turned him around and asked him, in a none to gentle manner, what he was doing asking about Tran Van Nguyen all over the club. Reyes told them that he had a business deal with Tran Van Nguyen and Nick Lueong, but he had been unable to get a hold of either one of them. It was essential that he talk to one of them as soon as possible. Reyes handed them a slip of paper. He told them that was his current cell phone number. He asked them to please ensure that Tran Van Nguyen or Nick Lueong got it. The two gangsters looked at each other and shrugged. Then one of them took the slip of paper and said they would see what they could do. They then turned and walked away back into the club.

Reyes walked out into the parking lot and got into his car. He had done all that he could do. He would have to wait for their call. He hoped that they did not take too long to call, because the number he had given them was for a disposable cell phone. He would be changing out at the end of the week. He had learned from Nosair that for security reasons, you should only use throwaway prepaid cell phones. You should not keep a cell phone for longer than a week. Less if you used it a lot. Reyes had gotten in the habit of buying a new cell phone every Sunday.

Chapter 45

By that same Monday morning, Tran Van Nguyen knew that he was in real trouble. Unlike Reyes, Tran not only watched the local news, but he read the local papers including the San Jose Mercury News and the Viet Nam Nhat Bao, the oldest and largest Vietnamese daily newspaper in Northern California.

Of course, Tran already knew about the killing of his cousin. Now he knew about the raid on his chop shop and the arrest of the shop owner and Charlie Zsu. The shop owner would keep quiet, at least for a while. He was too afraid that something would happen to his family if he talked.

Charlie Zsu was another matter. Charlie did not have anyone around that could be easily threatened. Charlie had been in it for the fun, the booze, the drugs, and the whores. Charlie would talk. Fortunately, Charlie did not know anything about Tran's safe house because Tran had seen this day coming and made sure Charlie did not know.

Charlie did know about Tran's organization or most of it anyway. Tran was thinking that he probably should have already left town, but there were still some loose ends to tie up. He had his passports and ID's in other names and could easily get out of the country.

While he was lost in thought about his escape plans, one of his cell phones rang. It was one of his boys at the Bay 101 Club.

"Hey boss, we just had a guy asking about you at the club. He says his name is John Paul Mercado Reyes and that he had a business deal going with you. Funny thing was he did not seem to know that Nicky was no longer with us. He gave us a cell phone number and we let him go. Hope we did the right thing."

Tran Van Nguyen assured him that he had and got the cell phone number from him. Tran had almost forgotten about Reyes. Of course, they were not going to be able to do any further business in the cigarette trade, but maybe he could be used for something else.

Tran still wanted revenge for the murder of his cousin. He wanted that Vietnamese cop who had been working so hard to get the Vietnamese Community to trust the police taken out. Take him out and that would put an entirely new fear into the community. They would see that Tran was untouchable.

He also wanted those two meddling detectives taken out. If they had not started with their cigarette investigation, none of this would have happened. Nicky would still be alive. It was their fault that Nicky was dead, and they had to pay for that. Maybe if he could make this all happen he would not have to leave town. Just lay low for a while and come back stronger than ever. Tran dialed the cell phone number.

Reyes answered in one ring. Tran gave him instructions to meet him at a Vietnamese restaurant on the Eastside of San Jose in one hour. Reyes was right on time. Tran was waiting for him at a table in the back.

"Sit down Mr. Reyes," said Tran. "You look a little upset. Calm down and tell me what is the matter."

Reyes sat down and said, "Look, we made the buy last Saturday and I haven't been able to get a hold of Nick. I've got a large shipment waiting for delivery, and I can't get a hold of you guys. What's going on?"

"You obviously don't pay attention to the news do you Mr. Reyes?" asked Tran. Tran went on calmly, "The police were waiting for Nick as he made a delivery of your stuff to a store in East San Jose. The police shot and killed Nick. They murdered him. Then Monday the police raided another operation of mine. I don't think that was a coincidence. I think they are investigating me and are starting to attack my various interests. I am going to have to suspend operations for a while."

"But what about my stuff?" asked Reyes. "What am I suppose to do with it? I can't move it without you."

"I suggest you just sit on it for a while until things cool down. We might be able to move it later. Meanwhile, you too are out of business because I can't supply you with any more documentation," said Tran.

"Wait a minute, we had a deal. I need that money. It's important," replied Reyes getting a little agitated.

"Do not be mad at me," said Tran. "If you are going to be mad at anybody it should be the police. You should be especially mad at two Detectives and one patrol officer. They are the ones responsible for this."

"They are getting in the way of our cause," seethed Reyes forgetting whom he was talking to.

Tran raised an eyebrow at the reference to a cause. This was the first time he had heard Reyes say anything about a cause. He had always thought Reyes was in it for more than just the money. Apparently, there was something else. So much the better thought Tran. People who were just crooks had no loyalty to anything. They were in it just for the money, and when things got tough, they usually disappeared. But someone that was in it for a cause was different. Tran did not know what cause Reyes was referring to but it did not make any difference. If he was raising money for a cause, than he was committed, people with causes did not stop. Tran could use this commitment to his own benefit. He could manipulate Reyes into taking revenge on the cops.

"Look," Tran calmly went on, "if you want to get back at anybody for this mess, it's those three cops. It is their fault we are stuck right now. It is their fault that you cannot move your product or make any more money. As long as they are investigating my organization, I cannot help you. As long as they are investigating, believe me, everybody else is going to shut down too.

"So you see I can't even send you to someone else. The cops are making it hot for all of us right now. The only thing that is going to help all of us is to take them out of the picture. You take out the cops and the people I do business with will be afraid again. They will understand their lesson that it does not pay to cooperate with the cops because the cops cannot protect you. They cannot even protect themselves."

"You think we should kill those cops?" asked Reyes.

"Take them out and it puts the fear back into everybody. Take them out and I can put my organization back into business even stronger than before. They are the ones causing us a problem and every problem has a solution," said Tran as he looked at Reyes, formed a gun with the fingers on his right hand, and pantomimed firing it. "I can help you, I can get you information on the cops, and I can get you guns, AK-47's. With my information, it would be a cinch. I can tell you where to be and when to take them out without any problem."

Reyes sat back and started thinking. He had always wanted to do more for the Jihad than just raise money. He wanted to strike at the Crusaders. He wanted to cause them pain and fear. According to his teachings, these cops were a legitimate target because they were part of the army that was fighting Islam. His teachings told him that as a soldier of Jihad this enemy had to be slain, that he needed to take his sword to their neck. He would have to talk to Nosair. He was sure he would be able to get the blessing of Imam Saleh Muhammad Jazir to carry the battle to the infidels.

The agitation was now gone out of Reyes voice. He seemed quite calm now as he said to Tran, "Your proposition interests me. Who are these people that have gotten in our way?"

Tran explained who Detectives Johnson, Sanchez, and Officer Tam were. He showed Reyes photographs of them in the Mercury News from the press conference. Tran also told Reyes that he had sources inside the police department that could get personal information on all three.

When Tran was done, Reyes told him, "I have someone I need to talk to first. Give me a phone number that I can reach you at tomorrow."

Tran wrote down a cell phone number for Reyes and watched as Reyes left the restaurant. He wondered whom Reyes had to talk to, but then shrugged and decided it did not matter. Tran smiled to himself. He had been right; a man with a cause is willing to do anything to whoever gets in his way. Tran just did not know how willing Reyes actually was to act and to what lengths he was ready to go.

Chapter 46

As soon as he left the restaurant and Tran, Reyes used his throw away cell phone to call Nosair. Reyes told Nosair it was an emergency and they had to meet as soon as possible. Nosair had handled agents enough to realize that the kid was spooked about something and realized that he had better see him right away. He set up a meeting at the Salang Pass Restaurant in one hour. Nosair also cautioned Reyes to take all the precautions against being followed.

As Reyes drove to Fremont, his mind was racing. He remembered something he had read in his studies of thirteenth century Asia. When Marco Polo had traversed Asia, he had heard many people tell about a shadowy leader of the Assassins known as the Sheikh of the Mountain.

In a valley, he had made a most beautiful garden, planted with all the finest fruits in the world and the most splendid mansions and palaces that were ever made. There were four conduits, one flowing with wine, one with milk, one with honey and the final one with water. There were fair ladies there and damsels, the loveliest in the world. These women were unrivalled at playing every sort of instrument and at singing and dancing. The Sheikh gave his men to understand that this garden was Paradise. That was why he had made it after all, because Mahomet assured the Saracans that those who go to Paradise will have beautiful women to their hearts' content to do their bidding, and will find there rivers of wine and milk and honey and water. No one ever entered the garden except those whom the Sheikh wished to make Assassins.

Reyes also remembered from his teachings that, around the time of the Crusades, there was a notorious sect of Ismaili Shi'ite Muslims known as the Assassins. They introduced assassination on a large scale to the politics of the Islamic world and the Crusades themselves. After carrying out an assassination, the Assassins almost always allowed themselves to be captured peacefully, even though this meant certain death. This story matched what Reyes had learned the Qur'an said about Paradise in his own studies.

The Ismailis thought of themselves as the exponent of pure Islam, which they were giving their lives to restore. The Qur'an said that the surest guarantee to Paradise is given to those who slay and are slain for Allah.

By the time Reyes reached Little Kabul he had made up his mind. He was ready to become a soldier for Allah. He was no longer satisfied with just raising money to support jihad. He wanted to strike back at the unbelievers, the Crusaders, who had stopped him in what he now saw as his trivial role of raising money for the Jihad. These cops deserved to die. They had insulted and opposed Muhammad and his people, and they deserved to die a humiliating death. Reyes was ready to smite the necks of these unbelievers.

When Reyes arrived, Nosair was again at a table on the Western side drinking coffee. After exchanging the customary greetings, Reyes got right into his problem.

"The cigarette operation is closed down. The cops have started investigating Tran Van Nguyen and are closing down his network. They have killed his number 2 man, his cousin Nick, who was my contact, and two other of his guards. He doesn't think the cops have figured out who he is yet. He assures me that the cops have no idea about me and my part in the cigarette operation.

"However, he says that the cops have made it so uncomfortable because of their investigation that he cannot even refer me to anybody else. Everybody is closing down their operations for now. I can't get any more credit cards and I can't unload the cigarettes we got this weekend. It's all because of those damn cops." As Reyes had been talking, his voice had gotten louder and louder. The stress he was feeling was showing.

"That is most unfortunate," replied Nosair in his most calm and soothing voice. He knew that he had to calm Reyes down. "We certainly could have used the money for our friends. Did Mr. Nguyen tell you anything else?"

"Tran thinks that if we were to strike back at the cops we could be back in operation sooner. He said that if we took out the three cops that were most involved in this investigation, it would put fear back into the community he controls. The Vietnamese community would be even more afraid of Tran because they would realize that the cops could not protect them," said Reyes.

"What do you think we should do?" asked Nosair, still keeping his voice calm and reassuring.

"I have been thinking about this as I drove over here. I have given it much thought. While I understand that it is important to be a part of a mission that collects money so that we may continue our glorious jihad against the Great Satan, I have come to the conclusion that I want to be a greater part of the Jihad. I think we should strike these cops now," replied Reyes.

"But they have not attacked us," said Nosair.

"Is it not the divinely ordained duty of all Muslims to fight until man-made law has been replaced by God's law, the Sharia, and Islamic law has conquered the world?" asked Reyes. "Are we not taught that anyone who insults or opposes Muhammad or his people deserves a humiliating death? These cops have opposed us. They are stopping us from achieving our goal of collecting money for the Jihad. After all, are not these cops just and extension of the army of Crusaders that has invaded our homeland? Have not scholars said that it is in accordance with logic and with Islamic religious law that if the enemy raids the land of the Muslims, Jihad becomes an individual's commandment, applying to every Muslim man and woman, because our Muslim nation will be subject to a new Crusader invasion targeting the land, honor, belief, and homeland?"

Nosiar was nodding his head in agreement. "I remember the great Ayatollah Ruhollah Khomeini saying that 'those who know nothing of Islam pretend that Islam counsels against war. Those who say this are witless. Islam says: Kill all the unbelievers just as they would kill you all. Islam says: Kill them, put them to the sword and scatter their armies. Islam says: Whatever good there is exists thanks to the sword and in the shadow of the sword. People cannot be made obedient except with the sword. The sword is the key to Paradise."

"I am ready to take up the sword for Allah," Reyes replied softly.

Nosair was thinking fast now. The young man's words had re-ignited the passion of the fight in Nosair. It had been many years since he had taken the fight to the Crusaders in Afghanistan. He longed to be in the fight again, to once more smite the necks of infidels with his sword. Yes, it was possible to strike back at these Crusaders. They had after all interfered with his money operation. They were enemies of Islam. Just by being cops, they were fair game because cops were just soldiers in their own land. They must not strike blindly. They must gather information and plan.

Nosair looked thoughtfully at Reyes. "Did Mr. Nguyen give you any information about the three cops he said were the prime interferers in his operation?"

"Yes," replied Reyes. "He has their names and pictures from the news. He also said he could find out more information about them so that we would know exactly where and when we could strike."

"Excellent," said Nosair. "What about the rest of your cell? Are they as ready to take up the sword as you are?"

"I have not talked to them yet, but they will follow where I lead," said Reyes.

"That is good," said Nosair. "Go back to Mr. Nguyen and get all of the information he can give you. Talk to your cell members and prepare them. We must plan."

Chapter 47

When Rex got into his new office on Monday and read his email, he found one from Porter informing him of the cigarette theft that had gone down Saturday. He forwarded the email to Sergeant Quin. Apparently Tran Van Nguyen's criminal enterprise was still very much active. Kat walked in with a bag from Noah's Bagels.

Rex had just taken his first bite when his cell phone rang. It was Five-O.

"Good Monday morning Five-O. What's shaking this early in the morning?"

"Hey Cowboy, got your email. I also just got the latest downloads from the pole camera covering the Loving Cup. Tran Van Nguyen was there on Thursday. Judging by the time stamp, he was probably watching your news conference. He walked out shortly after the news conference ended and hasn't been seen since."

"Son of a bitch," Rex swore.

"Looks like he is in the wind my friend," said Five-O.

"That sucks," said Rex

"Yeah, it sure does. I'll be over shortly so we can plan out the rest of the week," said Five-O and he disconnected.

It was the start of the week following the news conference. The team was going to follow the only solid leads they had. Using Nick Lueong's ledger, they were going to hit every restaurant where he had placed a skimmer and pick up the people working for him. Maybe they would have some information that would move the case forward.

The Crime Scene Unit had come up with some latent prints and semen stains at the two party pads they had searched. These would be kept on file until they had something to compare against them.

Late Friday evenings the Grand Jury had returned an indictment against Tran Van Nguyen on multiple felony accounts. After their morning strategy meeting, Rex made sure the SJPD Warrant Unit entered the no bail arrest warrant into the computer database. He also made sure Homeland Security had the latest pictures of Tran Van Nguyen on the off chance he had not left town and might try to fly out of San Jose International Airport or one of the other airports.

For the rest of the week they followed the same schedule that was in Nick Lueong's book hoping to find the listed employee still at the restaurant. They were incredibly lucky. Of the ten employees listed, they found five of them still working at the restaurant indicated. Four of those still had the skimmers that Nick had given them in their possession.

The only thing that the restaurant employees all had in common was that they were gambling addicts that had gotten in trouble with the loan sharks at the two card clubs in San Jose. When they could not pay off their loans, they were recruited by Nick Lueong.

He did not even have to worry about placing them because they already worked in the restaurants that were targeted. Nick had given each a skimmer and explained how to use it. He had given instructions on what type of credit cards he was looking for, only platinum cards. Nick would come by the restaurant once a week on the days indicated in his book and exchange skimmers with them. They were paid $40.00 for each card they skimmed. At first, the money was applied towards their loans. When the loans were paid off, they were paid in cash. None of them had anything else to do with Nick's operation. All they did was skim high-end cards. What Nick did with the information, they did not know.

When they talked to RATTF at the end of the week, they found out that they were doing about the same. A thorough search of the chop shop had turned up hundreds of stolen car parts. RATTF had been able to close over one hundred stolen auto cases throughout Santa Clara County by just matching up serial numbers on the car parts.

In addition, the records found in the office allowed them to discover several different auto body shops in Santa Clara County that had purchased stolen parts from the chop shop. They had closed down six other auto body shops and made several arrests. The records also allowed them to close the books on several car cloning and title fraud cases that lead to Oregon, Washington, Idaho, and Nevada.

It was now Friday night. One week after the Grand Jury had handed down their indictment of Tran Van Nguyen. The team had been busy. They had hit nine of the ten restaurants in Nick Lueong's ledger and picked up five of the people working for Lueong.

They decided to keep the pole cameras up at the Loving Cup Coffee House. Pictures taken were still being run through facial recognition and license plates were still being run. The leads were few, but they were leads.

However, they were no closer to finding Tran Van Nguyen, any other party pads, or any of the young girls Tran Van Nguyen was supposed to have working for him. So far, the people that the team and RATTF had arrested either were not talking or did not know anything about this part of Tran Van Nguyen's operation.

Rex, Kat, and Five-O were headed to Saratoga to the last restaurant listed in Nick Lueong's ledger. The restaurant employee they were after was Lisa Nguyen. Her name had come up at the start of the investigation. She had a prior arrest for passing counterfeit checks and it was thought that her boyfriend might be an employee of Tran Van Nguyen. The case had taken so many twists and turns that they had almost forgotten about her.

When they walked into the restaurant, Lisa Nguyen was standing at the maitre d's station. She was wearing a long, dark blue oriental style dress that clung to her body and had a slit up to her left thigh. Her black hair was pulled up in back and held in place by a black lacquered decorative Chinese style hair fork. Her dark, almond shaped eyes were highlighted by a dark blue eye shadow that matched her dress. She was quite stunning and beautiful.

Both Rex and Five-O stood staring at Lisa Nguyen, saying nothing. Lisa Nguyen stood looking back at them. She did not move or say anything.

Finally, Kat stepped forward and flashed her badge. "Lisa Nguyen, San Jose Police. We have a few questions for you."

"I've been expecting you," Lisa Nguyen replied. "I suppose this is what you are looking for." She reached under the reservation desk and pulled out a small black box which they all recognized as a skimmer.

"Is that yours?" asked Kat.

"Yes," replied Lisa Nguyen.

"Do you know what that is?"

"Yes, it's a credit card skimmer."

"Have you used it?"

"Yes."

"Lisa Nguyen, you're under arrest. Turn around and put your hands behind your back." Kat stepped forward and handcuffed her.

Chapter 48

Down at PPC, they got Lisa Nguyen situated in a room. It was decided that Kat would take the first run at her as she might find it easier to talk to a women.

After Kat advised Lisa Nguyen of her rights she held up the skimmer and said, "Tell me about this."

Lisa Nguyen's upper lip was trembling and she looked about to cry. "I'm so glad it's over. I only did it for my little sister. You've got to help her."

"What do you mean?"

"He's got my little sister. He is making her work in one of his party houses."

"Who's got your baby sister?"

"Tran Van Nguyen."

"O.K., let's start at the beginning," said Kat.

Lisa Nguyen told Kat how she had gotten into trouble gambling at the card clubs. She eventually started borrowing money from the loan sharks. When she could not pay them back, Nick Lueong had come to her with a proposal. He set her up with the skimmer as payback for her loans.

Somewhere along the line, Nick Lueong found out that Lisa Nguyen had a younger sister in Vietnam that she wanted to bring to the United States. Their parents were dead and Lisa was the only family the young girl had left. Nick Lueong told Lisa that he could get her sister into the country for a price.

Lisa Nguyen agreed to continue to work for Nick Lueong if he would bring her sister to the United States. Lisa got to see her little sister once when she was brought to San Jose. After that she was told that her little sister would have to go to work as a hostess for Tran Van Nguyen to pay off her debt for bringing her to the United States.

"Where is your little sister now?" asked Kat.

"I don't know, but my boyfriend does," answered Lisa Nguyen

"Who's your boyfriend?"

"George Pham."

"How does he know where your little sister is?"

"It's his job to pick up the girls and bring them to Tran's party houses," said Lisa Nguyen.

"How do we find your boyfriend?"

"I can make a phone call and set up a meeting," said Lisa Nguyen.

"You would be willing to do that?"

"I'd do anything to save my little sister."

Kat stepped out of the interrogation room and huddled with Rex and Five-O. They decided it was worth a try to lay in a duped call to the boyfriend right now and see if they could pick him up tonight. Rex called Sergeant Quin and filled him in. He said he would call the rest of the team and they would be at PPC in half an hour.

When Sergeant Quin and the rest of the team had arrived at PPC, Sergeant Quin went back into the interview room with Kat.

"Miss Nguyen, I'm Sergeant Quin. We appreciate your cooperation. Right now we are setting up a non-traceable phone for you to call your boyfriend."

"What kind of phone is that?" asked Lisa Nguyen.

"That is a phone that caller ID won't show is coming from the PD."

"That won't work. If he doesn't see that it is coming from my cell phone he won't answer."

"O.K., we'll do it right here from your cell phone. Where are you going to ask him to meet you?"

She told Sergeant Quin the name of a Vietnamese restaurant on Tully Road where they always met.

"That's fine," said Sergeant Quin. "Now, to make sure he shows up I want you to tell him that they caught you with the skimmer at the restaurant and they threatened to call the police. You were scared, so you ran. You didn't know what to do, so you called him. You need his help. Can you do that?"

Lisa Nguyen said that she could and they set up the recorder on her cell phone so they could record and monitor the call. Lisa Nguyen was very good. She had her boyfriend convinced right from the beginning and he eagerly agreed to meet her right away.

They came up with a game plan and they piled into their cars and headed for the restaurant. Lisa Nguyen rode with Sergeant Quin.

The restaurant was a typical strip mall restaurant tucked in between two other shops. There was not that much parking out front. The restaurant was narrow and long with windows across the front. Five-O, and Detective Phong and Officer Tam parked their cars as far away from the restaurant as they could and walked into the restaurant separately. The restaurant was practically empty and they were told they could sit wherever they wanted.

They positioned themselves at separate tables around the restaurant. They ordered coffee and took their time looking over the menu.

Sergeant Quin, and Rex and Kat parked their cars where they could see into the restaurant but not be right in front of it. Lisa Nguyen said that she did not see her boyfriend, so Sergeant Quin sent her into the restaurant.

Lisa Nguyen selected a table and waited. Five minutes later her boyfriend walked into the restaurant. Seeing her, he walked directly to her table without even looking around the restaurant. After he sat down, Lisa Nguyen gave the hand signal that let the other cops know this was her boyfriend.

Detective Phong had his Nextel open and up to his ear as if he was making a phone call. He keyed the push-to-talk button and said, "There's the signal, that's the boyfriend, move in."

Detective Phong closing his Nextel was the signal for the officers inside to move. Five-O got up and walked towards the boyfriend and Phong and Tam moved in on either side. Lisa Nguyen kept her boyfriend's attention focused on her by crying and acting very upset. He never saw the officers moving in.

Five-O had his Sig Sauer out and pointed at the boyfriend. Detective Phong grabbed the boyfriend's left arm and swept it behind his back and up forcing the boyfriend's face down on to the table.

"San Jose Police," said Detective Phong. "Don't move, you're under arrest."

Detective Phong patted down the boyfriend and handcuffed him. He did not have any weapons on him.

At the same time, Sergeant Quin, Rex, and Kat came through the front door wearing their raid jackets with their guns out.

"San Jose Police," called out Sergeant Quin. "Everybody just stay quiet and don't move."

Five-O repeated those instructions in Vietnamese.

Kat moved up behind Lisa Nguyen and took hold of her arm. "Lisa Nguyen, you're under arrest." This was part of the plan. They wanted the boyfriend to think that Lisa Nguyen was being arrested along with him.

Within moments, they had handcuffed Lisa Nguyen and her boyfriend and hustled them outside to their cars. The few customers and staff in the restaurant were still sitting there in shock.

As they put Lisa Nguyen into their Explorer Rex could not help himself. He tuned to Kat with that mischievous smile of his and said, "We come in the night, just like the body snatchers."

Within forty-five minutes, they were back at PPC. Rex and Kat took Lisa Nguyen out of their car first and walked her in to PPC in handcuffs in front of her boyfriend. They did this so her boyfriend would believe that she had also been arrested and was in custody.

Sergeant Quin and Five-O brought the boyfriend in a few minutes later. He could not see what room Lisa Nguyen was in.

Rex put together his prop case file, which had some real information and a bunch of filler paper, and entered the holding cell they had the boyfriend in.

"George Pham, my name is Detective Johnson. Can I get you anything like a cup of water?

George Pham just glared at him.

"Do you know why you are here?"

"No," said a sullen George Pham.

"Well then, before we get started I guess I should advise you of your rights." Rex made a show of taking out his reading glasses and putting them on. "Let's see. Just like in the movies. "You have the right to remain silent. Do you understand?"

"Yeah,"

"Anything you say may be used against you in court. Do you understand?"

"Yeah."

You have the right to the presence of an attorney before and during questioning. Do you understand?"

"Yeah."

"If you cannot afford an attorney, one will be appointed for you free of charge, before any questioning, if you want. Do you understand?"

"Yeah."

"So, George, let me tell you why you're here. Your girlfriend was caught using a skimmer at the restaurant where she works. The first thing she does when she gets caught is run to you. You have a prior for using counterfeit credit cards. The way I see it, you are the one that gave her the skimmer and she was copying credit cards for you. You want to tell me about that?"

George Pham just sat shackled to the table glaring at Rex.

"Your girlfriend is going down for a felony and so are you."

George Pham continued to sit there silently.

"If you want to help your girlfriend and yourself, now is the time. You see we also know that you work for Tran Van Nguyen."

That got a reaction. There was a sudden intake of breath by George Tran.

"Tran Van Nguyen is the one we are really after. Help us with information about him and I'll see to it that the DA goes easy on your girlfriend."

"I don't know what you're talking about. I don't work for nobody," said George Pham.

Rex calmly sat back on his side of the table and just looked at George Pham. Rex did not say anything he just continued to stare.

George Pham tried to be a tough guy and hold the stare, but he could not. Finally George Pham broke the connection and looked down.

Rex let out a sigh. "Look George, let's not start out by you lying to me. That is no way to help our relationship along. There is a lot we already know about you and about Tran Van Nguyen." Rex reached into his folder, pulled out a picture of George Pham and slid it across the table.

"That is you coming out of the Loving Cup Coffee House. That is one of Tran Van Nguyen's meeting spots. At the time this picture was taken, Tran Van Nguyen was at the Loving Cup Coffee House. Do you want me to believe that you just went there for a cup of coffee?"

George Pham stared sullenly at the picture.

"Look, we know that Tran Van Nguyen has a violent reputation. I can understand why you don't want to talk. But think about this. We already took out his cousin, Nick Lueong. We have taken down the chop shop on Kings Row. And while we were at it, we took out two of Tran Van Nguyen's guards. We are in the process of dismantling his protection racket. And we are taking off his party houses."

George Pham's head snapped up at that last comment.

"What's the matter George? You didn't think we knew about the party pads? We know all about them and that they are wired for video and sound. We know all about Tran Van Nguyen using those videos to blackmail people."

"I don't know what you're talking about," said George Pham.

"George, George, George," said Rex shaking his head. "We know all about the young girls Tran Van Nguyen uses in those houses. We know all about his human trafficking operation. What you need to understand is that you have a choice. Every day we are picking up people who worked for Tran Van Nguyen. Sooner or later someone is going to talk. That window of opportunity is closing fast for you.

"If you don't want to cooperate with us then I can guarantee you will be prosecuted as a career criminal. Do you know what that means? The DA will seek the longest prison sentence he can. You won't be going away for just a couple of years; you will be in state prison for up to twenty-five years. I can guarantee it."

George Pham sat back and looked at Rex. Rex could see that there was a crack in the tough guy shell. George Pham was starting to think.

"And what about your girlfriend? She'll get the same treatment. A career criminal in a continuing criminal enterprise. Twenty-five years, George. Think about it."

"No," blurted out George Pham. "She's not involved. She just had that skimmer. She doesn't know about anything else."

Rex decided it was time to push him. He slammed his open hand on the table and raised his voice. "Doesn't she George? Her younger sister is one of the whores in Tran's party pads. I'd say she is pretty damned involved."

"No," cried George. "She's a good person. The only thing she had anything to do with was carrying that skimmer. She had nothing to do with what her little sister is doing. Her little sister was forced into it. Lisa hasn't even been able to see her little sister since Nick brought her into the United States."

"So George," said Rex lowering his voice, "why don't you do something to help both of them. Tran Van Nguyen isn't doing anything to help you. He's running from us. We already seized some of his getaway cash and phony passports. He's running out on his entire organization. Tran Van Nguyen is all about Tran Van Nguyen. Come on man. Help yourself out here. Help you girlfriend. Help her little sister."

Rex sat back and let all of that sink in. He had given George Pham a lot to think about. It was time to let him think.

After several long minutes of silence, George Pham looked up at Rex. "You'll take care of Lisa and her little sister?"

"George," said Rex, "you help us and I will do everything I can to help them."

"All right then, what do you want to know?"

Chapter 49

It took the next hour for Rex to find out that George Pham really did not know that much about Tran Van Nguyen's operation. George was not much more than a gopher. Mostly, he ran errands for Tran Van Nguyen which included picking up his dry cleaning, and he brought the girls over to the party pads. In a way, Rex was relieved. While George had tried to play the part of the tough gang banger, he was not. This would make it a lot easier to talk the DA into giving him a break. Who knew, this might be just what George and Lisa needed to scare them out of the criminal life and into the straight life.

What George Pham did know was the location of the other three party houses and the house where the girls were being kept. After a quick conference with Sergeant Quinn, it was decided that the house where the girls were being held had to be hit that night. While Rex and Kat worked on a telephonic search warrant, Sergeant Quin organized use of the on-duty MERGE Team to hit the house.

It was a newer two-story house on the Eastside of San Jose. The house was located in an upper middle class neighborhood that was mostly Vietnamese. It was almost 2300 hours and most of the neighborhood had gone to bed. The MERGE Team had quietly worked their way into position up and down the street from the target house. They were in surveillance mode right now, waiting for Rex to show up with the search warrant. The District Patrol Team was backing up MERGE, taking the outer perimeter. As soon as MERGE moved in, they would block the street at both ends. Two patrol officers had also made contact with the house directly behind the target house and were now in the backyard observing the back of the target house.

Because of the past history of violent encounters with the Tran Van Nguyen organization, and because they did not know if the house was guarded or not, it had been easy for Rex to secure a no knock warrant.

Rex and Kat pulled up behind Sergeant Quin. “All right, Sarge, we’ve got the search warrant. We can hit it any time,” Rex told Sergeant Quin.

Sergeant Quin walked back to the intersection followed by Rex and Kat. Lieutenant Samson, the Special Ops commander, was standing there next to his SUV.

“O.K., Lieutenant,” said Sergeant Quin, “We’ve got our no knock warrant.”

Lieutenant Samson keyed his radio. “We’ve got the warrant in hand, go ahead and take it down.”

The MERGE team, which had been split in two, moved up to the house without making a sound. In the dark, in their black BDU’s, they looked like graveyard specters moving through the night.

The MERGE Team formed a tactical stack at the front door. The man at the front of the line held a ram. The hand signal that they were ready to go came from the back of the line to the man in front. As soon as the ram man received the signal he battered in the front door with the ram. One swing at the door lock and the door caved inward. The ram man stepped aside and the rest of the team entered the house calling out “San Jose Police” as they moved into the house.

The first half of the MERGE Team in took the ground floor. The second half of the MERGE Team through the door quickly located the stairs and moved upstairs. It was an explosive, dynamic entry. Once they hit the front door, they did not stop moving. If a door was closed, it was kicked open.

Close on the heels of the MERGE Team Five-O, Detective Phong, and Officer Tam entered the house. They called out in Vietnamese, “Police, get down on the ground.” Kat, Rex, Sergeant Quin and Lieutenant Samson were the last into the house.

The MERGE Team securing the ground floor kicked open a bedroom door and found a man and a women in bed. The women screamed and the man reached for the drawer of the nightstand.

A MERGE Officer quickly closed on him and stuck his M4 Assault rifle in the man's face. "Not so fast."

The man and the women were flipped over on their stomachs and their hands were cuffed behind their backs. The MERGE Officer retrieved a 9mm Glock pistol for the nightstand drawer.

As the MERGE Team upstairs moved down the hallway they came to a padlocked door. They kicked the door in splintering the door and the frame. Screams came from inside the room. In the dark bedroom lighted only by the tactical lights on their weapons, six young girls dressed in cotton nightgowns shrunk back against the far wall.

"Detectives," called out one of the MERGE Officer, "up here."

Detective Phong ran up the stairs. He saw the MERGE Officer standing in the doorway of a room. The door was kicked in and the doorframe shattered. Part of the doorframe still had a hasp with a locked padlock dangling from it. Inside were six young girls crying and holding each other in fear in the room. There was no furniture in the room, only six sleeping pallets on the floor. There was a large porcelain chamber pot in the corner, which was the only bathroom facilities the girls had.

The room was clean, but the conditions these girls were being held under were deplorable. Detective Phong found himself shaking with rage. He took a deep breath to calm himself and moved into the room.

He softly started talking to them in Vietnamese. "We are the Police. There is no need to be afraid. We have come to rescue you."

Down the hall, another door crashed open to more screams.

"Detectives, down here," called out another MERGE Officer.

As Officer Tam entered the bedroom, he was confronted with the same images Detective Phong had just seen. Six young girls, huddled against the far wall, crying and holding each other in fear. Just as Detective Phong had done, Officer Tam spoke to them in Vietnamese, trying to calm them down.

Within minutes it was all over and MERGE declared the house secure.

The girls were also starting to calm down. The couple in the bedroom had been allowed to get dressed and then had been separated. The woman was kept in the bedroom and the man was brought out to the living room. The man had claimed he did not speak English, so they had sent in Five-O to deal with him.

Sergeant Quin, Rex, and Kat huddled in the kitchen to figure out what they were going to do next.

"I'm going to call the Chief of D's and let him know what we've got," said Sergeant Quin.

Even though the Chief of D's was at home asleep, he answered his phone after only two rings. Sergeant Quin identified himself and then quickly told the Chief of D's what they had.

"Good job, Sergeant Quin," the Chief of D's told him. "Use whatever assets you need. I'll call the Homicide Lieutenant and tell him to roll out his Crime Scene Unit. I want that house gone over with a fine tooth comb. Call in whoever you need. I'll be down at PAB in an hour."

Detective Phong came into the kitchen. "One of the girls just told me she was Lisa Nguyen's little sister. She also told me she was twelve years old."

They all just looked at each other. They knew what she had been forced to do and they were disgusted by it. The best way they could help her now was to develop the most air tight case they could.

Five-O joined them in the kitchen. "That guy speaks better English than I do. He was just trying to run a scam."

Sergeant Quin turned to Rex. "O.K., Rex, you're still the lead detective on this. How do you want to handle it? The Chief of D's already has the Crime Scene Unit being called out to process the house. And he told me I was authorized to call out whoever I needed."

"Man," said Rex, "it pays to have friends in high places. I'm not use to having all these assets at my finger tips."

"Well just don't let it go to your head Cowboy," said Kat.

"Five-O, can you continue the interrogation of bedroom guy?"

"Sure, no problem."

"Kat, can you take the madam?"

"I can do that."

"We need to get all these girls down to PAB and keep them separated. We need to do an initial interview on them just to see who they are, where they came from, and how they ended up at this house. Phong, do any of them speak English?"

"Yeah. All of them speak a little English and some of them speak really good English."

"O.K., the Night Detectives can help us with the interviews of them."

Sergeant Quin picked up his cell phone. "All right then, I'll make the calls and get things rolling. Looks like our night just got longer."

Chapter 50

As the sun came up the next morning, the team huddled in the Detective Conference Room on the third floor of PAB. The man and the woman found in the house were not talking. They would not say for whom they worked and would only say that they were there to "look after" the girls. One interesting development was that the Glock that had been in the bedroom nightstand was also stolen in the gun store burglaries in Southern California.

The girls were another matter. Once they had calmed down and realized they were safe, they opened up to the detectives. There were a total of twelve girls. They ranged in age from twelve to sixteen. Most of them came from Vietnam, but a couple came from Thailand.

The story was the same. Their families had made arraignments to send them to live with other relatives in the United States. They were supposed to be heading for a better life. But when they got to the United States, they were not delivered to their relatives as promised, they became prostitutes for Tran Van Nguyen.

They were kept locked in their rooms except to eat and when they were needed at a party house. Then they were brought out and dressed in very fine silk oriental style dresses. Their hair was fixed and their makeup applied by the woman who the girls said ran the house.

This woman, the one found in the master bedroom, also instructed the girls how to be proper hostesses and how to act around the men at the party houses. They were taught how to properly serve the food and drinks.

At each house one girl was assigned to each player, and they were to take care of his every wishes.

The woman also schooled each girl in the many different ways to please a man sexually. Not only did she instruct them on exactly what to do, but they were forced to practice what they were taught on the man that stayed at the house with the woman.

At the party houses, if the man they were assigned to wanted to take them into a bedroom, they were to accompany him willing and perform whatever sex act he asked for. The only rule was that there was no swapping of girls allowed.

The older girls, who had been there a while, also talked of other girls that had been at the house but had been taken away. If a player was not satisfied with his girl or complained about something she had or had not done, that girl disappeared and was replaced by a new girl. The older girls did not know what happed to the girls who were taken away.

All of the girls had been told that it had cost a lot of money to bring them to the United States. Their families had refused to make the final payment. Therefore, to repay their debt, they had to work for Tran Van Nguyen. If they were good and worked and did as they were told, they would eventually earn their freedom.

All of the girls knew they worked for Tran Van Nguyen. They were all able to pick his photo out of a photo array shown to them. They had seen him often at the party houses entertaining his guests. Some of the girls had even had to sexually entertain him. However, they only saw him at the party houses. He never came to the house where they were kept as far as they knew.

None of the girls knew about the hidden cameras in the party houses. All of them were very embarrassed to find out that they had been secretly recorded performing various sex acts. Neither did the girls know whom the men were they had been with. They could only say that there had been a mix of Asian, White and Black males.

"So," said Rex to the assembled team, "we have very detailed statements from the girls of what they were forced to do. We have enough for charges of human trafficking, kidnapping, false imprisonment, pimping and pandering and I don't know what all else. But what we don't have is anything that gets us any closer to Tran Van Nguyen."

"O. K., folks," said Sergeant Quin. "We have been up all night and our brains are fried. Go home and we will take a fresh look at this Monday morning."

The girls were processed and turned over to the Children's Shelter as wards of the state. It would now be up to the feds to figure out their immigration status and what they were going to do with them.

As Kat and Rex walked out of PAB she let out a long sigh. "I feel sorry for those girls. They were looking for a better life and they got this. They are all broken. It's just so sad. We've got to get this bastard."

"We will Kat. We will."

Chapter 51

Reyes also had a busy week. He went back to Tran Van Nguyen and told him that he agreed with him. He would take out the three troublesome cops. Tran, good to his word, told Reyes that he would have information about their shift assignments, home addresses, and cars registered to them within a week.

Tran had a mole inside the San Jose Police Department. The sister of one of his boys had been hired as a records clerk a couple of years back. Her brother was not involved in gangs at the time, so it had not come up in her background investigation. Her brother had since become a soldier in Tran's organization. He was one of Tran's enforcers. They had never asked his sister for any information until now.

Tran called the brother and told him what information he wanted. Tran impressed on the brother that the needed information was extremely important. Failure to get the information was not an option. The brother knew Tran Van Nguyen's reputation for violence. The story of him beating to death a guy with a baseball bat was well known. It was often repeated in the inner circle of Tran's main employees.

That night, the brother went to see his sister. When he told her what he wanted she was incredulous. She could not believe he was asking her for that information. That information was confidential. It was against the law for her to give out that information. If anyone found out, she could lose her job. She could go to jail. She liked her job. She liked the people she worked with. She was not going to betray them; it was out of the question.

Then her brother explained who he worked for and what he did. His sister had not known or at least had not wanted to know any of this. Her brother explained how both of their lives depended on her getting this information. The man he worked for would not hesitate to kill either one or both of them if they did not bring him what he wanted. In the end, loyalty to family and a decidedly real threat of death won out. His sister agreed to get the information.

Personal information on police officers is restricted information with good reason. Police officers deal with bad guys all the time. For the safety of themselves and their families, they expect their department to safeguard their personal information like their home address. There is even a form they can file with DMV to restrict the release of information about the cars they own. However, no system can protect you from someone inside getting access to this information. Especially if that someone is a records clerk with knowledge of how to access the system and leave no trace.

Tran Van Nguyen had his information in three days. He knew what shifts the three cops worked, what their days off were, their home addresses and what cars were registered to them. In the same week that Rex and Kat had struck out finding any information about Tran Van Nguyen, he had found out all the information he needed about them to make them targets.

* * *

Reyes in the mean time had a meeting with his cell and informed them that they were going active. They would no longer be just passively collecting money for the Jihad; they were going to take the fight directly to the infidels. In the meeting, Reyes explained again to them that their study of Islam had taught them that the Qur'an's surest guarantee to Paradise was given to those who slay or are slain for Allah.

"Remember my brothers," said Reyes, "that in Paradise you will be dressed in fine silk and in rich brocade. You will recline on green cushions and rich carpets of beauty. You will sit on thrones encrusted with gold and precious stones. Paradise consists of gardens, with rivers of milk of which the taste never changes; rivers of wine, a joy to those who drink, and rivers of honey pure and clear. And the wine in Paradise is free from headiness so that those who drink it will not suffer intoxication there from. And remember that waiting in Paradise are voluptuous women of equal age. They are women of modest gaze, with lovely eyes, fair women with beautiful, big, and lustrous eyes like rubies and coral. These women are maidens, chaste, restraining their glances, whom no man before has touched. Allah made them virgins, and they will remain virgins forever." When the meeting was over, they were all ready to join Reyes as martyrs in the name of Allah.

When Reyes met again with Nosair he informed him that he had talked with members of his cell. They were all ready to become martyrs in the Jihad. Reyes also brought along the information on the three cops that Tran Van Nguyen had supplied.

"This information is excellent," said Nosair. "It is a great starting point and must be verified. What you and your fellow soldiers must do is go to their homes and watch. Learn more about them, about their neighbors, about the routine in the neighborhood. Go to their place of work and see what you can find there. Take pictures and make notes. But you must all be very careful, especially with the police officers. They are trained to watch for someone watching them. Do not linger too long in the neighborhoods or at the police station. Change cars amongst yourselves. We must build dossiers on each one of them so that we can plan the best attack."

Chapter 52

It was another Monday morning and the beginning of another week. Kat and Rex were brainstorming over breakfast at Bill's Cafe. Rex always liked starting Mondays with a big country breakfast at Bill's.

"You know," said Rex between bites of egg, sausage, and pancakes, "I hate to say it, but it looks like we have run out of leads on this case."

"I have to agree with you," replied Kat. "We are not any closer to finding *numero uno* of the organization, and we are no closer to identifying any more of his crew."

"There is still one thing that bothers me about all this," said Rex.

"What's that?"

"The surveillance photos that Porter sent us. All the perps in the photos don't look Vietnamese; they look more like they are Filipino. So, either our gang is a mix of Vietnamese and Filipino, which I have never heard of, or we have two different groups operating."

"What are you getting at?" asked Kat.

"I think that we have a group of Filipinos working the cigarette thefts. They went to a Vietnamese group for the counterfeit documents and credit cards. They then went back to the Viet gang to move the cigarettes after they stole them. We've heard time and again at the organized crime briefings at the U.S. Attorney's Office how the Vietnamese want to become the facilitators to all the other crime organizations and gangs. Why couldn't that be the case here? I think the Vietnamese are selling the counterfeit credit cards and documents to a Filipino gang in return for a share in the profits."

"Sounds plausible," said Kat thoughtfully. "But we still don't have any leads."

"We do have one lead left."

"What's that?"

"John Paul Mercado Reyes," said Rex with a smile.

"Oh, right," said Kat nodding her head in agreement. "The name on the file we found in Nick's house. But what are we going to do with that? We ran the name through all of our data bases and came up empty."

"Yep, but that name sounds Filipino to me. There is still one tried and true investigative method left to us," said Rex. "What say we go to the address listed in that file and do a knock and talk? We'll knock on the door, see who answers and try and talk ourselves into the place."

"I'm game if you are," Kat said with a smile. "Let's go back to the office and pick up the file."

"All ready ahead of you," said Rex. "I grabbed the file and a handpac before we left the office."

It was not often that Detectives took a handpac into the field with them and logged in on one of the police radio channels. Since you were mostly just talking with witnesses and victims, it was unlikely you were going to get into any trouble, so most Detectives did not bother. Besides, if something actually did happen there was always the car radio, and you also had your cell phone.

But Rex was kind of old fashioned when it came to this. Anytime he was going to go out into the field and contact someone unknown, especially if that person might end up being a suspect, he wanted to be logged on to the correct working channel, and have a handpac in case he needed to call for help.

Rex remembered a story told by some other detectives he was working with a few years ago. They had developed information that the suspect they were looking for might be living in a camper parked behind a Safeway store on the East side of San Jose. They had gone out to check it out. They parked their car in front of the store and went in to ask the store manager if he had seen a camper parked behind his store.

When he told them he had seen one off and on a couple of times they decided to take a look out back. They walked out through the loading dock. Sure enough, just down from the loading dock was a pickup truck with a camper on it.

As they were walking up to the camper to check it out, the door to the camper opened and their suspect stepped out. There was an awkward moment when the suspect and the two detectives stared at each other with nobody reacting. The suspect was looking like he wanted to run when one of the detectives identified himself as the police and told him not to move.

The suspect looked around again and realized that nobody else was there; it was just him and two guys in business suits. He turned and took off running. They could not shoot him because they had not seen a gun and he was not a threat. They had not brought along a handpac nor had they logged in on the radio. No one knew where they were or what they were doing. They chased after him on foot for a little while, but the suspect jumped a fence and disappeared.

Two guys in business suits were not about to go climbing over fences. All they could do was stand there and watch their suspect run away. After hearing that story, Rex vowed to himself that he would never be caught in the field unprepared.

They paid their bill and got in their Explorer. With Rex driving, Kat got on her cell phone, called Dispatch, and logged them on to the radio channel covering the area where they were going.

"Log on both badges as unit 24-0-1," Kat told the Dispatcher. "Put us in route to the Valley West Apartments, 1050 Summerside Drive, Apartment 192 on an attempt to locate. No need for a uniform and we will advise when we are on scene."

Forty-five minutes later Rex pulled in to the visitor parking lot in front of the apartment complex office. The Valley West Apartments was a large apartment complex that took up almost an entire city block on the Southeast corner of McLaughlin at Summerside. They went into the office and Rex flashed a smile and his badge at the girl sitting behind the desk.

"Good Morning," said Rex. "We need to know if you have a John Paul Mercado Reyes living in apartment 192."

"Is there a problem Detective?" asked the girl.

"Oh no, not at all," said Rex in his most reassuring voice. "Mr. Reyes may have been a witness to a crime and we need to talk to him. This was the last known address we had on him, so we just wanted to verify it before we went and knocked on the door. We wouldn't want to disturb somebody else now would we?"

The girl smiled back and typed something on her computer.

"Yes," she said, "A Mr. Paul Mercado Reyes is one of the people renting apartment 192."

"Thank you so much," said Rex. "Could you be so kind as to point us in the right direction?"

She gave them a map of the apartment complex and marked the location of the apartment. The apartment they were looking for was in the back corner of the complex. As they walked through the complex, they noted how empty it seemed. There was nobody out and about except for a couple of maintenance guys mowing the lawn.

As they were walking up to the apartment, Kat keyed the transmit button on the handpac and said, "Control, 24-0-1, we are 10-97."

After receiving a response from radio, they took up positions on either side of the front door. That was just habit after many years on the street. Even when you were not expecting a threat, you never stood in front of a door. For officer safety reasons you always stood off to the side as much as possible. You just never knew what was on the other side of that door.

Rex knocked on the door and waited. There was no answer so Rex knocked on the door again a little bit louder this time and called out, "Mr. Reyes, San Jose PD, we need to talk to you."

They waited and there was still no response so Rex hauled off and banged on the door. This time the front door popped open.

The door only swung open a couple of inches, but it was now plainly open. In a situation like this, the Detectives would have to enter and check things out. Someone could be injured inside and unable to come to the door.

Kat picked up the handpac again. "Control, 24-0-1, give us Code 33, we have an open front door and no response. We are going to enter and check it out. Also, start a beat unit this way."

Rex and Kat heard the alert tone come over the radio and the dispatcher say, "Code 33 on the channel. Code 33 for 24-0-1 on an Attempt to Locate at 1050 Summerside Dr, Apartment 192 with an open door. 5-1-Lincoln-3 respond to assist."

Rex and Kat drew their handguns and Rex pushed the front door all the way open. Rex then called out, "San Jose Police. Is anybody home?"

They got no answer and nothing moved.

Rex called out again, "San Jose Police. Come to the front door now."

There was still no answer and no sound from inside the apartment.

They entered the apartment with their weapons at the low ready. It was a two-bedroom apartment with a living room and a kitchen, so the search did not take long, especially since all they were looking for were bodies. There was nobody in the apartment and nothing looked like it had been disturbed.

As they holstered their weapons Kat got back on the radio and said, "Control, 24-0-1, its Code 4, nobody's here. Cancel Lincoln-3."

As Dispatch acknowledged their last transmission, Rex and Kat stood in the living room looking around.

Chapter 53

As Rex and Kat were entering his apartment, Reyes and his roommate were just pulling up in a van behind their apartment. The roommate was driving, and Reyes was just going to run in and get a camera before they took off again. He told the roommate not to park, but to just pull up on the side of the driveway and wait, he would be right back.

Reyes jogged down the sidewalk to his apartment. He was not actually thinking about anything. The apartment complex was his safe zone. Nothing ever happened around here, and he tended to let his guard down. As he walked up to his front door, he saw that it was open. Rather than disturbing or alerting him, he was just curious. Had he or his roommate forgotten to lock the front door? Rather than stopping, his curiosity drove him forward. Before he knew it, he was inside his own apartment staring at a man and a woman standing in his living room. They turned to look at him as he stared at them. It was a moment frozen in time.

* * *

As Rex and Kat stood in the living room looking around, they became aware that someone had entered the front door and was standing there looking at them. As they looked at the guy, they both recognized him as one of the people in the surveillance photos from Costco.

Rex smiled his winning smile again and said, "Hi, we're the San Jose

Police. We came by to talk to you and found your front door open." As he was talking, Rex started moving towards Reyes.

That broke the spell and Reyes turned around and bolted through the door with Rex and Kat in hot pursuit right behind him.

Kat grabbed the handpac again and keyed it, "Control, 24-0-1, Code 3 traffic. We are in foot pursuit Southbound through the complex."

The long alert tone sounded again and they heard the dispatcher say, "All units 24-0-1 in foot pursuit of a suspect Southbound through the Valley West Apartment complex. 5-1-Lincoln-3 and 5-1-Lincoln-2 respond Code 3."

Reyes was running as hard as he could back to the van. He reached the driveway/parking area at the back of the complex and turned left. The van was just a few feet in front of him with the motor still running. Reyes began yelling and waving his arms at his roommate. He ran up to the passenger door of the van and flung it open as the van started to move forward.

Reyes was pulling himself into the van as it was starting to drive away just as Rex ran into the driveway. Kat was right behind him. As Rex ran towards the van, it started to accelerate away from him.

He could hear Kat behind him on the radio. "Control, 2401, the suspect just got into a faded yellow Chevy Astro Van headed west out of the complex towards McLaughlin."

Rex continued to run after the van. It was heading for the exit, but there was an automatic gate across the exit and they would have to stop for and wait for it to open. Even so, the van had gotten so far ahead of Rex by the time it reached the gate there was no way he was going to catch up on foot. Rex stopped in the middle of the driveway and watched helplessly as the van turned South onto McLaughlin and sped away. He could hear the sirens of the fill units coming closer.

Kat ran up to him and asked if he had gotten the license plate. Rex was still trying to catch his breath and just shook his head no.

Kat got back on the radio. "Control, 24-0-1, suspect van last seen turning Southbound on McLaughlin. We didn't get close enough to get a plate. Van has at least two people in it, probably both Filipino males.

One suspect believed to be a John Paul Mercado Reyes, felony want for on view Grand Theft."

They stood there catching their breath for a minute and then turned back toward the apartment. After this turn of events, that apartment unquestionably deserved another look.

As they walked back to the apartment, they got a radio call from the District Sergeant asking where he could meet them. They told him to come to apartment 192.

Kat went directly back to the apartment and Rex walked out to their car to get an evidence kit. When Rex got back to the apartment, the District Sergeant was there.

"So," said Sergeant Taves, "what are you getting my troops into?"

"We've been working a cigarette theft case involving counterfeit credit cards," said Kat. "We developed a lead that the people living in this apartment might have been involved. We came down here to do a knock and talk. When we knocked on the door it came open, so we went in to make sure everything was all right. You know no dead bodies or anything. Anyway, just after we cleared the apartment this guy walks in. We recognize him from a surveillance photo as one of the perps we are looking for. As soon as we I.D. ourselves as the police, he turns around and runs off."

"O.K.," replied Sergeant Taves. "So do you have an arrest warrant on him and is it in the system?"

"No warrant yet," said Kat. "We think his name is John Paul Mercado Reyes." She leafed through her note pad. "Here is his DL info. If anybody stops him they can on-view him for felony grand theft and call us, we'll take it from there."

"Sounds good. I'll get a BOLO put out city wide and keep my guys circulating in the area. Maybe we'll get lucky." With that Sergeant Taves turned and left.

It took an hour of searching the apartment before they hit pay dirt. In a shoebox hidden under some clothes in a bedroom closet, they found counterfeit Costco membership cards, credit cards and state cigarette resale licenses. Kat recognized some of the store names on the state licenses as the same ones in the case file. The credit cards were excellent counterfeits.

Even the holograms looked real. Whoever had made these cards was an excellent counterfeiter. There were only four different names on the various credit cards and state licenses.

"You know what we are missing?" Kat asked Rex as she looked through the shoebox.

"No, what?"

"There are no I.D.'s in here," said Kat. "And we have the same four names appearing over and over. I'm thinking they used their real names and I.D.'s and had the rest made up to match the names. That way they didn't have to go to the extra expense and hassle of getting a counterfeit California Drivers License as well."

"If they did that," mused Rex, "these names will be in the data base. At least the DL info. Gives us another lead. Let's look around some more and see if we can find any other info about these guys."

As they took a second look at the apartment, they noticed a Qur'an on a bookshelf in the living room. There was also what appeared to be rolled up prayer rugs in each bedroom. A closer look at the bookshelf revealed that there was a book entitled "A History of Islamic Societies" by Ira M. Lapidus, another entitled "Muslim Resistance in Southern Thailand and Southern Philippines" by Joseph Chinyong Low and a third entitled "Muslim Rulers and Rebels: Everyday Politics and Armed Separation in the Southern Philippines" by Thomas M. McKenna. There were also books on Islamic History and biographies of historic Muslim figures from the IQRA on the bookshelf.

"So what do you think all this means?" asked Kat as they looked through the collection.

"I think it means our crook is interested in Islam and may be a practicing Muslim," replied Rex.

"You know what I mean," said Kat. "This has all the outward appearance of a possible connection to terrorists. Our crooks are Muslim, they are interested in armed insurrection in the Philippines, and they have been collecting a lot of cash through the use of counterfeit credit cards. We know that the Trade Center bombings were financed in part with counterfeit credit cards."

"No," said Rex slowly, "what we've got is some crooks who just happen to be Muslim. There is nothing here to verify they are involved in terrorism. If we say terrorism, then we have to turn our entire investigation over to the Joint Terrorism Task Force. We lose our entire case. The JTTF will sit on it for God knows how long and we will never know what happens with it because we are not cleared to know." Rex smiled at Kat. "Come on, work with me here. We're just two detectives chasing four bad guys that are using counterfeit credit cards, that's all."

"All right," replied Kat. "We'll go with that scenario for now. But you get a hold of Deputy Farnsworth at the Northern California Regional Terrorism Threat Assessment Center. You run all these names and all the information we have by him. Have him check RTTAC's databases. If anything comes back as terrorist related, we are handing it off to JTTF. Look Cowboy, I know you don't like the FBI much and neither do I. But, we are not equipped to handle a terrorism investigation and they are. If it is terrorist related, it has to go to them and you know it."

"Yeah," sighed Rex, "you're right. O.K. we have a deal. We continue with our investigation until we find a definite terrorist connection."

They collected up all of their evidence and left the apartment. On the way out, they stopped by the office. The same girl was still there.

She smiled at Rex. "Anything else I can help you with Detective?"

"As a matter of fact, I was hoping you could help us with one more small thing," Rex smiled back. "We need a copy of the rent application for Apartment 192."

"Well, I don't know," the girl started in. "This information is confidential and I could get is a lot of trouble."

Rex just continued to smile at her, and in his most reassuring southern gentleman tone said, "Oh, it will be all right. You see Mr. Reyes has turned out to be more than just a witness. He is now the suspect in a crime, and it might even involve his roommate. You see, we ran into Mr. Reyes at his apartment, but over our objections, he decided he did not want to stay around to answer any of our questions. I'm afraid we are going to have to go looking for him, and the application information just might help. I don't think you will be seeing him again because he left in a hurry, but just in case I'm leaving you my card with my cell phone number on it. Call me if you or any of the staff see Mr. Reyes again, please."

The girl took Rex's business card and handed him a copy of the rent application. Rex and Kat left and headed back to NCI.

Chapter 54

On their way back to their office they grabbed some lunch to go from Cosanteno's Market and ate at their desks. They worked through computer checks trying to match up the names on the cards with real people. At least they were only down to a search on two of the names. The other name on the Reyes rent application matched one of the four names on the credit cards, so they now had his date of birth as well. With that information, it was easy to find his CDL. Next, they were able to pull up his CDL photo and compare it to the surveillance photos from Costco. They had a second match. That was enough to obtain arrest warrants on Reyes and his roommate. Kat continued to work on trying to identify the other two crooks involved.

While she was doing that, Rex called Deputy Farnsworth at RTTAC. He and Kat had met Deputy Farnsworth a little over a month ago at a counter-terrorism class they had attended. They probably should not have been approved for the class, but Sergeant Alvarez had not quite understood the scope of the class when she signed off on their request. She just knew that it was their turn to go to an outside class. The class was mostly about recruiting and managing assets or in the vernacular of law enforcement, confidential informants. It was not just about any informants, it was about terrorism informants. Several agencies from all over the Bay Area had sent people, and it was a excellent opportunity to network. Rex and Kat were surprised to see how many other departments in the Bay Area actually had counter-terrorism units.

After class one day when Deputy Farnsworth had explained the data base he managed for RTTAC, Kat and Rex approached him to find out more. Chasing financial crooks is all about the money and to follow the money in the complicated cases you needed a powerful searchable database. That was something San Jose PD did not have. They wanted to see if they could work something out with Farnsworth.

The three of them started talking, and it started to sound like they might be able to do something together. Then Farnsworth asked them what agency they were from again, and when they said San Jose, he told them he could not talk to them.

"Are you kidding me?" asked Rex incredulously.

"No," said Farnsworth. "I was told that I could only talk to some Sergeant in the Intel Unit about anything involving counterterrorism."

Rex just looked at Farnsworth, speechless. But as always with Rex, the wheels were turning. "Wait a minute. Didn't you say that terrorism investigations were the sole responsibility of the feds and that the locals only got involved when they were working with the feds?"

Farnsworth nodded in agreement.

"And didn't you say that RTTAC data bases could also be used to track criminal enterprises across county lines and help multiple agencies coordinated their criminal investigations?"

Again Farnsworth nodded in agreement.

"Well then, there you have it. We are not talking about terrorism investigations; we are talking about investigations of continuing criminal enterprises."

Farnsworth looked at them for a moment and then said, "You know, I like the way you think, sounds like we can do business."

Ever since then Rex, Kat and Farnsworth had collaborated on putting together a database on continuing criminal enterprises involved in financial crimes in the Bay Area. It was still in its infancy because any decent database needed information and they were just getting the cooperation of other police departments in the Bay Area, but it had lots of potential. In forming another unofficial alliance with Farnsworth, Rex could also get Farnsworth to share some intelligence information on the terrorism front. More than what was put out in the unclassified warning bulletins.

That was what Rex was hoping for now. He gave Farnsworth all the information they had so far about who the players were and how they were committing the crimes. He also told him about what they had found in Reyes' apartment, and the potential Muslim tie in. Finally, Rex suggested that Farnsworth reach out to the Fremont PD Counterterrorism Unit. It was just a hunch on Rex's part, but one of the Costco's consistently hit was in Fremont and Fremont did have Little Kabul. Farnsworth said he would get back to him as soon as he came up with anything.

Next Rex called Detective Jones of the Fremont Police Department. He was the detective assigned to the Costco cigarette case in their city. Since Fremont was in a different county, they could not tie their case in with the San Jose case. If there were any charges filed in the Fremont case, they would have to be filed separately in Alameda County. Then it would be up to the two District Attorney's Offices to figure out what they wanted to do. Even though it was two different jurisdictions, that did not mean that Rex could not help a fellow detective and share what he had found. So Rex filled Detective Jones in on identifying Reyes and his roommate. He explained about finding the counterfeit credit cards and how they were working on identifying the other two crooks. Rex promised Jones a copy of their report.

As he was hanging up the phone, Kat came over to him waving a small piece of paper. "Look what I found in the bottom of the shoe box?"

Rex took the piece of paper and studied it. It was a receipt for a storage unit on Story Road. Crooks often rented such storage units either to keep stuff used in the commitment of their crimes or to hide the proceeds from their crimes. Either way, the storage unit was worth a look, but for that, they would need a search warrant.

"I already called the storage place and confirmed that the unit is still rented to Reyes," said Kat. "I'll start writing the search warrant."

Chapter 55

As Reyes jumped into the van, his roommate took off. Once out on McLaughlin they made a left on Story Road and then got onto Highway 101 going Northbound. They had heard the sirens approaching, but managed to get out of the area without seeing any police cars. Reyes was thinking fast. They had to get the van out of sight quickly. There was a friend, a fellow worshiper from the same mosque, who lived off Alum Rock Avenue. He had a house and a garage where they could hide the van. While this friend was not part of Reyes' cell, he would do anything Reyes asked. He told his roommate where to go and cautioned him not to speed or do anything else that would attract attention to them.

Fortunately, Ali was home. After they put the van in the garage, Reyes called Nosair and told him what had happened. Nosair said they should meet immediately at the Salang Pass Restaurant. Reyes borrowed Ali's car and took off for Fremont leaving his roommate at Ali's house.

When Reyes arrived, Nosair was once again sitting in the western section of the restaurant drinking a cup of Turkish coffee. After the greetings were exchanged, Nosair asked Reyes to explain to him in detail what had happened since they had met last week.

"Yesterday I picked up the information on the three cops from Tran Van Nguyen. We were going to start our surveillance today. We were on our way to the San Jose Police Department to take some pictures when I realized I had left my camera at the apartment. We went back, and I had Eman just wait in the van while I ran in to get the camera. The two police detectives were in my apartment. I didn't know what to do. I just turned and ran out of there. They ran after me, but I was able to get back in the van and Eman drove us out of there. We hid the van at Ali's house, and I borrowed his car and came here," explained Reyes.

Nosair thought over what he had been told while he sipped his Turkish coffee. "We will go forward with our plan. It is more important than ever now. I have a place where you can stay where you will be safe. Leave the van in Ali's garage, do not use it for now. I will arrange for you to borrow cars from others at the mosque. You will continue with your surveillance, but it must be completed quickly. We must strike the Crusaders quickly, but I need information so that I can make a plan."

Nosair made a couple of phone calls and arraigned for a place for Reyes and Eman to stay and for access to cars. Before Reyes left Nosair gave him instructions. They were not to do anything else today. Tomorrow, Eman was to take one of the cars and take pictures and notes of the San Jose Police Department. Reyes was to watch the female detective's house in the morning. He was to be there before she left for work. He was not to follow her but to see who else lived in the house and take note of the morning routine in the neighborhood.

Jamal was to do the same thing with the male detective. Kamil would watch the other police officer in the afternoon. Nosair emphasized to Reyes that he did not want any of the police officers followed. That was too dangerous. He just wanted information about what happened when they left for work. The others would make their reports to Reyes, and he would take the information to Nosair.

The following morning Reyes was in place on Kat's street by 0500 hours. He had parked across the street and up a few houses but behind another car already parked on the street. He had a good view of Kat's house. As he watched lights came on in the front rooms of the house. There was no other movement on the street. Apparently, the female detective got up much earlier than any of her neighbors did. By 0630 hours, the female detective walked out of her house, got into an SUV parked in the driveway and drove off. Following his instructions, Reyes did not follow.

He could see some lights coming on in other houses now as the neighborhood was starting to wake up. He stayed watching. He was curious because the lights in the front rooms of the female detective's house had remained on when she left. There was another car in the driveway. Was someone else there?

It was now almost 0700 hours and Reyes had been watching for two hours. A couple of other neighbors had come out of their homes, got into their cars and drove off. Nobody had even noticed him. Just then, a man and a young boy came out of the female detective's house. The man put the boy in the back seat of the other car and got in behind the wheel. As the man drove off, Reyes made a decision. He started his car and followed. Nosair had said not to follow the cops. He had not said anything about not following anybody else.

Reyes followed the man as he drove down residential streets. He did not head for any freeway or expressway. Finally, the car pulled into the driveway of a school. Reyes continued down the street, pulled over to the curb, and parked. He got out of his car and walked back towards the school. As he walked slowly past the school checking out the layout, he also noted the name: Santa Clara Christian School. Reyes turned and walked back to his car, he had seen enough.

The following evening Reyes was having dinner with Nosair at the Salang Pass. Nosair seemed extremely pleased with the information that Reyes had brought him.

"The police headquarters is out of the question," said Nosair. "The building is built like a bunker. Yes, you could get a car into the visitor parking lot and easily walk away from it. But when it went off all you would have is a large hole in the ground with remarkably little damage to the building. The parking lot is too far away and that concrete retaining wall and all that dirt behind it protect the building. Besides, we do not want to kill innocents. We do not even want to kill just any random police officer. We are after three specific officers. No, the police headquarters is not a target.

"The uniform officer, he is also a bit of a problem. He lives in a large apartment complex. I see that it has a security fence all around it. There is certainly no way to lie in wait for him either leaving for work or coming home inside his apartment complex. I am thinking maybe a car or a motorcycle outside. Then you drive up along side of him and shoot. That was how we did it in Afghanistan. We shall have to give that more thought. Keep watch on him.

"The male detective, I see he has a wife. He lives in a nice house on a large piece of property in the country outside of a little town called Hollister. According to Kamil it is a quiet neighborhood. Unlike compounds in Afghanistan where the house is surrounded by a high wall, this property has only a three rail fence. Maybe the same thing with him. Wait for him to leave for work, drive up beside him and boom. We will have to see. Kamil said that no one parked on the street, and he felt extremely vulnerable when he was parked out there.

"Now the female detective, most interesting. She has a young son that goes to a Christian school. How truly interesting. You remember what our brothers did in Beslan? How they took over that school? You see, we must not only remove these three Crusaders, we must do something that puts fear into the hearts of all the unbelievers. They must know that the Jihad is upon them, and they are no longer safe. They are not safe in their homes or at work. Their children are not safe in their schools. We must give many thanks to Allah for his kind gesture and choosing of us to perform the act of Jihad for his cause and to defend Islam and all Muslims.

"Ah my young friend, you do not approve of the last. I can see the objection in your eyes. You are going to tell me that Islamic law prohibits the killing of women and children. Well that is true unless they are aiding the war effort. The female detective as a member of her government's security force, is directly fighting against us. She is no innocent. And her young son? Is he not going to a Christian school? I submit to you that by going to a Christian school, he is learning how to become a future Crusader and, therefore, he is aiding the war effort against us. Besides, who has broken the law here? They have disobeyed all heaven and Earth's laws of war, to include their own laws. They have violated the law of war by supporting the Israeli occupation of Arab land in Palestine and Lebanon, and for displacing five million Palestinians outside their land. They have supported the oppressor over the oppressed and the butcher over the victim.

"So you see, they are the first class war criminals, and the whole world witnesses this. They have no values and ethics and no principles. They are a nation without a religion. On the other hand, we are a great nation, with a great religion, values, ethics, and principles, which we comply with and follow, and invite people to follow our ways.

"Remember what the Qur'an says. 'Fight those who believe not in Allah nor the Last Day, nor hold that forbidden which hath been forbidden by Allah and His Messenger, nor acknowledge the religion of Truth, even if they are of the People of the Book, until they pay the Jizya with willing submission, and feel themselves subdued.' Remember my young friend we have rediscovered the forgotten duty of Jihad. We will fight, we must fight, we are commanded to fight. In God's book, he has ordered us to fight the infidel everywhere we find him, even if he were inside the holiest of all holy cities, the Mosque in Mecca, and the holy city of Mecca, and even during sacred months.

"In God's book, verse 5, Al-Tawbah, the 9th chapter of the Qur'ran, says: 'Then fight and slay the pagans wherever you find them, and seize them, and besiege them and lie in wait for them in each and every ambush.' And we will continue to fight the unbelievers not until a peace treaty is signed or when negotiations have settled disputes, but when Allah's religion prevails, when Islamic law has been instituted over all of society.

"Come now, let us finish this wonderful meal and talk of things more pleasant."

That is what they did. When the meal was finished, Nosair gave Reyes further instructions. He wanted Reyes to concentrate his observations on the Christian school. He wanted to know all that he could about it. The time that school began, and the time that it ended. How long were the classes? How long were the breaks? How many teachers? How many students? What happened when parents dropped off their children in the morning and what happened when they picked them up at night? Was there any security? Nosair also cautioned Reyes to be careful in his surveillance of the school. He told him that Americans were particularly concerned about perverts hanging around their schools; as well they should be in a society that openly condoned immorality.

After Reyes left him, Nosair sat drinking his Turkish coffee. He was deep in thought and reminiscing about the good old days of the Jihad in Afghanistan and partly thinking ahead to the Jihad he was going to unleash. Nosair had been a bomb-making expert in Afghanistan, trained in the camps in Pakistan. Improvised Explosive Devices were his specialty. Mentally he was already making a list of the things he would need. As Nosair thought about it, he realized that he did not care about the killing of three American cops. They were nothing. Their deaths would not further the Jihad. The school was the thing. Take all the children and their teachers' hostage. Make demands for the release of political prisoners held at Guantanamo; in Baghram, Afghanistan; in the jails of the Jews. Of course, the Americans would not go along with this, but the American press would be giving it full time coverage while negotiations were on going. And then in the end . . . boom.

Chapter 56

That same morning Rex and Kat drove over to the Hall of Justice and went to the Chambers of the Honorable John J. Tobias, Superior Court of the State of California. They found the judge in his chambers prior to the start of the day's court calendar drinking a cup of coffee.

"Detectives, good morning, come on in, would you like some coffee?" Judge Tobias greeted them enthusiastically. "What can I do for you this fine morning?"

As they walked into his chambers, Kat could not help noticing with a smile the stuffed cartoon character looking buzzard holding a hangman's noose in its beak perched on the judge's bookshelf behind his chair.

"Good morning your honor," Kat replied back equally as cheerful. "We have a search warrant this morning for a storage locker," she said as she passed her Search Warrant over to the judge. "It is a continuation of our investigation into the cigarette theft investigation. We found a receipt for this storage locker in a shoebox in the apartment of one of our suspects. That shoebox also contained counterfeit credit cards and cigarette resale licenses that had been used in prior purchases of cigarettes from Costco. We believe more contraband and evidence will be found in the storage locker."

Judge Tobias said, "Let me take a minute to look this over." After having read through Kat's Search Warrant he looked up and said, "Everything looks in order." He then reached over to a tape player on his desk. When he hit the play button, the song 'Bad Boy' came on.

"Bad Boy, bad boy,
What cha gonna do when they come for you?
Bad Boy, bad boy"

As the song continued to play in the background Judge Tobias said to Kat, "Raise your right hand. Do you solemnly swear that the information contained herein is correct and true to the best of your knowledge?"

With her right hand raised, Kat replied, "I do."

"That should do it then," said Judge Tobias as he signed the Search Warrant. "Good Hunting."

As they left his chambers, 'Bad Boy' was still playing in the background.

They drove back to their office at NCI, grabbed an evidence kit and a handpac, and headed back out. Fifty-five minutes later, they were talking to the owner of the storage unit on Story Road.

According to his records, John Paul Mercado Reyes was still renting the storage unit. He had paid in cash and had paid for four months in advance. Rex and Kat explained to the owner that they had a Search Warrant for the unit and asked the manager for management's key to the lock. The manager consulted his computer and then went to a key rack and pulled a key, which he handed to them. He gave them a map of the complex showing where the unit was located.

When they found the unit, Rex tried the key, and it opened the lock. When they rolled the door up, Rex gave out a low whistle.

"I guess we can call Porter and tell him to come get his cigarettes," said Rex.

The nine foot by twelve-foot storage unit was stacked floor to ceiling with boxes of cigarettes. While Rex made the call to Porter, Kat started taking pictures of the contents of the storage unit.

When Rex hung up, he said to Kat, "Porter said he would have the manager from the nearest store over here with a truck in a few minutes. I'll go tell the owner to look out for them and let them in."

When Rex got back, Kat had already taken down a couple of the boxes, opened the tops, and photographed the cartons of cigarettes inside.

"What about fingerprints?" asked Kat. "They had to handle the boxes to stack them in here."

"I don't know," said Rex. "Let's call the Crime Scene Unit and see what they say."

Rex made the call and talked to one of the CSU Officers that was in the office. The Officer suggested that they select a representative number of the boxes and dust for fingerprints at the corners, where someone would have to grab the boxes to move them. If they developed any latent prints, they could protect them with lift tape and cut out that portion of the box. They could then bring in the cut out section to CSU, and they would photograph it and develop the prints. The detectives would then run these prints through the Fingerprint Unit to match against known subjects.

After Rex hung up with the CSU officer, he took off his suit jacket and rolled up his shirtsleeves. He then got some latex gloves and the fingerprint kit out of the Evidence Kit they had brought with them.

As Rex pulled on his gloves, picked up a fingerprint brush, and opened a jar of fingerprint powder he said, "Oh man do I hate dusting for prints. I always get powder all over me. And did you notice that after you've got fingerprint powder all over your hands your nose starts to itch. Then it starts itching so much you can't stand it, so you scratch it. Now you have a nose covered with black fingerprint powder. It never fails."

"Don't worry," said Kat. "When that happens I'll be right here to take a picture of you and your black nose."

Forty-five minutes later they were done. They had developed some decent looking latent prints and the Costco Manager had showed up to claim the cigarettes.

Chapter 57

Over the next week, Nosair was terribly busy. He instructed Reyes to contact Tran Van Nguyen and buy the four AK-47's and gave him the money for the assault rifles. He then went to several different beauty supply shops in Union City, Fremont and Milpitas and purchased hydrogen peroxide and acetone.

Spreading his purchases out among several stores he never had to buy a quantity at any one store that would have raised suspicions. His story was the same to each sales clerk. He had purchased a beauty shop for his daughter and was buying supplies for her shop.

In the same three cities, he visited sporting goods stores and military surplus stores and bought a quantity of thermal tablets, the kind used to heat food while camping. He also bought several backpacks at the stores.

Finally, Nosair went to grocery stores and bought citric acid. He now had all the ingredients he needed to make hydrogen peroxide bombs, an improvised explosive device with which he was particularly familiar. Next, he got a hold of another believer whose father was a farmer in California's Central Valley. As a farmer, it was easy for him to purchase sticks of dynamite. He was able to provide Nosair with twenty-four sticks. After Nosair knew how many sticks of dynamite he was going to get, he contacted another Islamic brother in Little Kabul.

Khalid was a tailor. He had lived and plied his trade as a tailor in Kandahar for many years. While in Kandahar, he had been known as a man that assisted the Taliban. It was not that he was a true believer in the

Taliban and their form of Islamic extremism; it was more a matter of life and death. The central government of Afghanistan was highly corrupt and had little control of the country outside of Kabul. The coalition forces were too few to provide real security for the area. The Afghan National Army and the Afghan National Police were almost nonexistent.

The coalition forces would come out of their heavily fortified bases and look for Taliban to kill and then go back into their bases. They did not provide security for the local people, protecting them from the Taliban. They just came through on their patrols and then they were gone.

The Taliban controlled the night. They had set up their own shadow government and collected taxes from the people. They said it was to protect them from the corrupt American lapdog government in Kabul. If you did not pay your taxes to the Taliban, you could be kidnapped for ransom. If you were not worth a ransom, you would just be beaten or killed.

What choice did a poor merchant have? He paid his taxes to the Taliban, and he did what they asked of him. Maybe it was just to make note of what time a coalition patrol came by his shop. Maybe it was just to let the local Taliban official know what the coalition troops had asked him when they stopped in front of his shop and talked to him. And maybe it was to sew up some special vests that some true believer would use in Kabul. Whatever it was, Khalid did what they wanted. After all, a man had to survive.

Two years ago, a cousin of Khalid had arranged for him to immigrate to the United States. He had helped Khalid set up a small tailor shop in Little Kabul. Khalid was a very happy man. He was away from the corruption, fear, and death of Kandahar, and he was doing modestly well.

Apparently, his old associations were not forgotten in his new home. A contact from those days, a man he had not seen in many years walked into his shop with a singularly specific order. Nosair asked Khalid to fabricate four vests. Nosair was highly specific about how he wanted the vests made. The vests that Nosair wanted were just like the ones Khalid had made in Kandahar. Nosair could not help but drop hints to Khalid about what was going to happen. After all, Nosair had known Khalid as a believer in their cause.

When Nosair came back to his shop a few days later to pick up the vests Khalid had been doing a lot of thinking. He knew that these were suicide vests that he had been asked to make, and he could not understand why here in America. If he were still in Kandahar, he would have no questions, but here in America?

Nosair had said that they were for a great strike at the Great Satan. Nosair had bragged that he was going to do something that would make the unbelievers terribly afraid. Khalid had decided to question Nosair to see if he could discover any more about what he was planning.

After the usual exchange of greetings, Khalid had invited Nosair into the back of his shop where he offered him a cup of coffee and showed him the vests. As Nosair admired the craftsmanship and praised Khalid for his meticulous work, Khalid tried to get Nosair to talk about what purpose he was going to use them for.

Nosair may have been a trained al-Qaeda fighter, but he had been out of the fight for a few years, relegated to money raising operations in America. He was a fighter at heart and was beginning to see himself as a sleeper agent who would never be activated. In short, Nosair was suffering from pride. He had a chance once again to strike at the Great Satan, and he was dying to tell someone about it. Besides, Khalid was one of them was he not? Nosair had heard about him in Kandahar and had even gone to see him a couple of times. He had always been tremendously helpful to the cause.

Khalid was able to elicit from Nosair that there was to be some sort of kidnapping on Monday of Christian children, one of whom was the son of a police officer. Even with his need to brag about being back in the fight, Nosair still was smart enough to maintain some operational security. Khalid could get no further information out of Nosair.

When Nosair left his shop with the vests, Khalid had more thinking to do. He was struggling in his mind to decide what was the right thing to do. He considered himself a good Muslim. He prayed seven times a day and faithfully attended his mosque. But Khalid was not a radical Muslim. Khalid abhorred religious violence and truly believed that Islam was a religion of peace. Khalid knew that Islamic law prohibited the killing of women and children.

* * *

Having now collected all of the material he needed, Nosair returned to his house to assemble everything he needed. He lived alone in a modest little house, in Fremont. The neighborhood was mixed with Hispanic, Asian and Arabic families. He lived a very quiet existence and doubted if any of his neighbors had ever taken notice of him. It was a typical working class neighborhood with everybody gone during the day to work and school.

After going over the additional intelligence Reyes had gathered for him, Nosair had decided that an attack on the Christian school, where the son of the female detective attended, was to be their course of action. Reyes and his three cell members would sweep into the school and take over four classrooms. One would be where the Crusader's young whelp was. It did not matter if the other classes got away, four would be enough for their purposes.

They would herd the teachers and their students into one classroom. Reyes and his accomplices would all be wearing the suicide vests made by his tailor friend carrying six sticks of dynamite each. Nosair would already have the hydrogen peroxide bombs assembled in the backpacks, and they would wire the classroom door and place the rest of the explosives around the room. All the wires would come back to a dead man's switch. One of the cell members would have to always be standing on it to keep the explosives from going off. If a sniper shot the person standing on the dead man's switch, the explosives would go off. If they tried to storm the front door, the explosives would go off.

Reyes would carry four cell phones, extra batteries, and chargers. As soon as they had the classroom secure and wired to explode, Reyes would start making his phone calls. One of the cell phones would be used solely to communicate with Nosair. The other three would be rotated and used to talk to the police and the news media.

After reporting to Nosair of their success in taking the classroom, Reyes would start calling the news media. He would have a script provided by Nosair. The script would have a list of demands, which included the usual demand for a release of prisoners. Nosair was not too worried about this list because he knew it would never be met.

Actually, the list of demands and the script was more for Reyes' benefit. It was to make Reyes think that this was actually the plan, to make a statement about Jihad and to get prisoners all over the world released. What Reyes would never know was that wired into the base of the dead man's switch was a remote detonator trigger by a cell phone. Whenever Nosair decided that the charade had gone on long enough, all he had to do was make one phone call and the bombs went off, killing everybody. Nosair smiled to himself as he started working on his bombs. Reyes and the others would die heroes, martyrs for Allah.

* * *

Deputy Sheriff Farnsworth had been working all of his databases and contacts extremely hard during the last week. He had found out that the IRQA, whose stamp was in the Islamic history books found inside Reyes' apartment, was just what it claimed to be, a nonprofit institution made up of educators, scholars and community workers who together possessed an extensive knowledge of the Islamic faith as well as up-to-date educational theories and teaching methods. They had an on-line presence as well and sold educational books. That was probably where Reyes got his. Nothing sinister there.

Farnsworth also found out that, in 1996, a group of young Lebanese men had carried out an operation where they would buy 299 cartons of cigarettes a day from the JR Tobacco Warehouse in North Carolina. They took the cigarettes to Michigan where they sold them. The scheme exploited the fact that the cigarette tax in North Carolina was only 5 cents, and it was 75 cents in Michigan. Each carload of contraband cigarettes yielded between $3,000 and $10,000. Over a period of a year and a half, the cigarette smuggling generated about $7.9 million.

The money was used to purchase equipment for Hezbollah, including night vision goggles, global positioning devices, mine detection equipment, radar, nitrogen cutters, blasting equipment, laser range finders, stun guns, naval equipment, sophisticated software, and cellular phones. The FBI and ATF had arrested the group in July 2000. It was not quite the same as Rex and Kat's case, but it was similar. If their crooks were sending money to extremist groups, than it would make it a terrorism case.

The one problem Farnsworth had was that none of names Rex had given him showed up on any watch list. Therefore, there was no way to tell one way or the other whether these guys were just crooks or involved in terrorism. Farnsworth communicated all this to Rex.

* * *

Meanwhile, Rex and Kat had been busy themselves. After combing through several DMV photographs, they had finally identified the last two members of Reyes' crew. Like Reyes and his roommate, none of them had anything on them in the criminal database.

So they went back to Five-O. They gave Five-O the names and asked him to run them by his ICE contact. Sure enough, all four had entered the United States on student visas and those visas had now expired.

Rex and Kat were back at their NCI office discussing the case over a couple of lattes.

"I don't like where this is going," said Kat. "First we have four Filipinos who came into the country on student visas and over stayed their visit. Then we've got at least two of them living together. Those two are Muslim with enough literature around their apartment to indicate that they are radicalized. Next we have them embarking on a scheme that is similar to one used in 1996 by other terrorists. More and more this case is looking like it has real terrorist ties. We've got enough for the arrest warrants on these guys. I say we file the criminal complaints and then dump it all of JTTF. We are not going to get any farther with this case than we already are. We don't have the resources. And besides, we've accounted for all the bad guys. Chalk it up as a win and let's move on. We got plenty of other cases stacking up on our desks."

"You're right," agreed Rex. "I wish we could have found Tran Van Nguyen and his DVD's though."

"Don't worry," assured Kat. "We will get another shot at him down the road."

* * *

Khalid had wrestled with his decision over the weekend. His was a tortured soul. He had prayed for guidance. He had thought long and hard about his beliefs and looked deep into his own soul. The one thing he had not done was talk to anyone. This was a decision he had to make completely on his own and no one must know about it.

Khalid had finally come to a conclusion. Khalid did not believe in Jihad. He liked his new country and was studying to become an American citizen. In America, people of other faiths were not his enemy. He felt that Muslims and Christians could live together in the world. Whatever Nosair was planning could involve the killing of innocent women and children. He could not let that happen. That was against Islamic law.

There was a police detective that he knew. The man had been to his shop a few times and he had shared a cup of coffee with him. On Sunday night, Khalid made a phone call to Detective Hale of the Fremont Police Department Counter Terrorism Unit.

Chapter 58

Another Monday and another big breakfast at Bill's Cafe to start the week off right. They had turned in the criminal complaint to the District Attorney's Office last week and then called JTTF. They had made a complete copy of their case file for the FBI. The hand off went about as expected. The FBI was terribly official and decidedly cold. They had accepted the file like they were being asked to accept someone's garbage. They had listened politely while Rex had given them a summary of the case and then thanked them and said they would be in touch.

"You know," said Rex, "Thursday's little meeting with the FBI is exactly why I don't like working with them. Here we go and give them everything, and they act as if they are doing us a big favor by even looking at it. Did you know that the most senior agent in the San Jose Field Office has only three years of experience? Those guys are still wet behind the ears. We know ten times more than they do about investigating a case. Yet they still act like arrogant pricks."

"Oh calm down," said Kat. "It wasn't all that bad. Besides, we both know a couple of agents in that office that aren't half bad guys to work with. We already got our arrest warrants out of it, let it go. Besides, we did a lot of good work on the cigarette case."

Rex nodded in agreement. The number of arrests and cases closed were truly impressive. Chief of Police and Sheriffs from all over the Bay Area were exceedingly pleased. A lot of good will with the citizen's of several cities had been garnered by the many stories in the press about not only the diligent work of Rex and Kat, but also the hard work of detectives and officers in other units and other police agencies. The inter-agency cooperation between police agencies and the Postal Inspectors in shutting down a major criminal enterprise had been touted by all of the news media.

Letters of commendation had been written and handed out and more were coming. An officer always liked to get as many letters put in his personnel file as possible. These letters were saved for a rainy day because one awe shit wiped out at least five at-a-boys.

“You're right,” said Rex. “We did get a lot done. The bad guys will eventually get picked up on our warrants. So, tell me about this new case.”

“It's a check kiting case. This guy is good; he's rolling accounts from one bank to the next, and living high on the hog on other people's money. He's out there buying teak furniture and Persian rugs with non-sufficient funds checks, if you can believe that. This guy not only has good taste, but he's ballsy.”

They talked about Kat's new case for awhile. Then their conversation turned to friends and family. They decided it was time to have another BBQ where they would drink beer, eat some grilled brats, smoke some fine cigars, and talk trash about certain people.

“Well,” said Rex, “I guess we might as well head back to NCI and start packing up.”

Since their investigation of Tran Van Nguyen had gone as far as it could, their special investigations unit was being closed down and they were going back to the Financial Crimes Unit.

“Yep,” replied Kat, “Its back to your Sergeant, the Clock Watcher.”

As they were paying their bill Rex's cell phone rang.

“It's Farnsworth,” said Rex checking the screen on his cell phone. “I'll step outside and take it while you pay the bill.”

When Kat walked out of the restaurant, she could see from Rex's expression that something was wrong. As a matter of fact, something was terribly wrong.

“What is it?” asked Kat. “What's wrong?’

“Did you take your son to school today?” asked Rex

"My husband did, why?" replied Kat not liking where this conversation was going.

"Get in the SUV," replied Rex. "I'll drive."

Rex ran to their SUV and started it up. Before Kat could even put on her seat belt, he was laying rubber out of the parking lot and heading North on the Alameda into Santa Clara.

"That was Farnsworth," Rex said as he drove and realizing that Kat already knew it had been Farnsworth that had called. "Last night one of the Detectives in Fremont's Counter Terrorism Unit got a call from a merchant in Little Kabul. This guy had information about a plot to kidnap some Christian School kids and one of the kids was the son of a cop. The Fremont cop got a hold of Farnsworth this morning. Farnsworth says that the only cops dealing directly with anything that is terrorism related in the Bay Area right now are you and me. That kidnapping is supposed to happen today. We are heading to your son's school. It's on Monroe right?"

Kat nodded yes.

"Call Sam Capalini and tell him what we've got. Tell him our intel isn't solid, but it is enough to act on. Fremont and RTTAC think it's real. Have him lock down the school and send uniforms. Tell him we'll meet him there. Then log us onto the radio channel and put us in route to a possible kidnapping."

Kat did as Rex had directed. She had worked with him long enough to trust him in a situation like this. She called Sergeant Capalini on his cell phone, and he picked up on the first ring.

"Sam," she said urgently, "I've got Code 3 info for you." She then laid out what they knew, where they were headed, and what they needed. "We're just passing your police department now," she ended.

Sam Capalini was a no nonsense kind of guy who was not afraid to make a decision. "O.K., Kat, I'll take care of it right now. I should have marked units on their way to the school in less than a minute. I'll be right behind you."

Next Kat dug out her Nextel and called Sergeant Quin. She laid out the situation to him in cryptic detail. She told Sergeant Quin what they knew and that Santa Clara PD had been contacted.

Kat ended the call, telling Sergeant Quin, "we are in route to the school now."

"Fine," said Sergeant Quin. "I'm leaving the office now and will be right behind you. I'll call the rest of the team and get them headed your way."

As they turned off The Alameda onto El Camino Real, Kat was getting them logged on to the District Sam radio channel. After logging on she said, "Control, put us in route to 3421 Monroe Street, Santa Clara on a possible Kidnapping. We have already notified Santa Clara PD and they are also in route."

As they turned off El Camino Real onto Monroe Street, Rex found himself coming up on a faded yellow minivan. "Kat, doesn't that van look familiar?" asked Rex.

"That looks like the van from the apartment complex. Get a little closer so I can see the plate." Rex slowed and dropped in behind the van. When they were close enough to read the license plate, Kat picked up the car radio mike and keyed it. "Control I need a rolling 10-2-8 on California plate 3-Mary-William-Tom-4-5-2."

The dispatcher acknowledged and within a few seconds came back with their returns. "24-0-1, that plate comes back clear to a 1999 Chevy Van registered to a John Paul Mercado Reyes at 1050 Summerside Drive Number 192, San Jose."

"Control," said Kat "be advised that we are following that van Northbound Monroe from El Camino. The R. O. of that vehicle and three accomplices are 6 F out of our city, and this van may be tied to the kidnapping. Advise Santa Clara and see if they can get a couple of units to assist."

As soon as radio acknowledged Kat, another voice came up on the radio.

"24-0-1 this is 50-26. Do not attempt anything with that suspect vehicle. Wait for Santa Clara PD to get on scene."

Kat and Rex exchanged a quick glance. "Great," said Kat, "Just what we need. Some dick head Patrol Lieutenant has to be on the channel and wants to tell us what to do."

Chapter 59

Reyes was driving the van with the three other members of his cell in the back. They had eight backpacks full of hydrogen-peroxide bombs, four suicide vests, and four AK-47's with plenty of ammunition. There was also another backpack with cell phones, wire and the dead man's floor switch.

Nosair had instructed Reyes on exactly how to set everything up once they had the four classes of schoolchildren and their teachers rounded up and all together in one classroom. Nosair told Reyes to make sure they wore the suicide vests. It made for better pictures for the press if they were all wearing suicide vests. It also made them look more menacing and so people would willingly follow their instructions. And it made them safer because the police would not shoot them if they were wearing the vests around the children.

Reyes went over his instructions in his head again. They were to pull in to the back school parking lot and park next to the first classroom wing across from the school offices. The child of the female detective would be in the first classroom. Reyes was to take that classroom. There were three more classrooms in the wing and the other three members of his cell would take those and herd everybody back to the first classroom. There was no security on the school grounds.

The Americans thought that all school grounds should be gun-free zones so they were not likely to encounter anyone who would stop them. If someone did try to interfere, they had been told to just kill them and continue.

Reyes saw the black SUV come up behind them very fast as if it was going to pass them. Then the SUV slowed down and pulled in behind them. Reyes was worried. He yelled for one of his guys to look out the back window and see if he could tell what the people in the car were doing. Jamal moved to look out the rear window. He started yelling excitedly that the car was right behind them and the male detective was driving it. Jamal recognized him from when he had done surveillance on him. He yelled that the female detective was talking on the car radio.

Reyes decided that the only thing to do was to race to the school and get there ahead of the police. They would not have time to take over all four of the classrooms, but they could at least get the first one. The female detective's son was in that classroom. That was the most important one to take over. Reyes stepped down on the accelerator and started speeding away.

* * *

As the van speed up and started to pull away from them, Rex sped up to keep up. "Well, I guess they made us," said Rex as he reached for the switch under the dashboard and turned on the emergency light and siren.

Kat got back on the radio. "Control, 24-0-1, the suspect vehicle has sped up and is trying to flee. We are in pursuit Northbound Monroe crossing Reeve."

"24-0-1, 50-26, negative, terminate your pursuit. Let Santa Clara PD handle it."

Kat was furious. No Patrol Lieutenant with his head up his ass was going to tell her what to do. She keyed the mike again, "Look jack ass, these people are on their way to kidnap my son at his school. We are not going to let that happen. If you've got something to say about it, get your dumb ass over here and help."

The Chief of D's had just walked into the Dispatch Center and was standing on the bridge when he heard Kat lash out at the Patrol Lieutenant. He said in a voice loud enough to be heard throughout the dispatch center, "On my orders, I want all available units to back up my detectives."

The dispatcher hit the alert tone and keyed her mike. "Attention all units, 24-0-1 is in pursuit of possible kidnap suspects just over the border in Santa Clara. Per Deputy Chief Ortiz, all available units are to respond."

Unknown to Rex and Kat was that when they first advised that they were following the suspect vehicle several District Sam patrol units had started to drift towards the San Jose/Santa Clara border, just in case. And when they heard her tell off the Patrol Lieutenant and say that the potential kidnap victim was her son, they had stopped drifting and actively headed out on an intercepting course.

When the fill request came, two of the units were already across the city limit into Santa Clara. Three of these units responded immediately.

"5-1-Sam-1 responding Code 3."

"5-1-Sam-2 responding Code 3."

"5-1-Sam-4 responding Code 3."

* * *

In the van, Jamal was yelling that the police were coming after them. Reyes could see that the unmarked police car had turned on it lights and siren and was gaining on them. "Jamal," yelled Reyes, "shut up, open the back door, and shoot them."

Jamal picked up his AK-47 and braced himself on the floor of the van. Kamil positioned himself to open the back door. When Jamal nodded his head that he was ready, Kamil laid down on the floor of the van, threw open one rear door and tried to keep it open. As soon as the door was open, Jamal started firing.

* * *

Kat and Rex saw the rear door of the van fly open and saw the muzzle flashes as they were being fired upon. Rex instinctively swerved their SUV to the left taking them out of the immediate line of fine. Fortunately, for them it is exceedingly difficult for even a practiced marksman to hit what he is aiming at from a moving vehicle and Jamal was not a marksman. All Jamal did was start spraying bullets as soon as the back door of the van opened. Even so, he managed to put one round into the upper right corner of the windshield and a second round ricocheted off the rear passenger door.

Kat was back on the radio, "Control, 24-0-1, shots fired, shots fired. They have automatic weapons. Code 30, Code 30."

Code 30 was rarely used if ever. In fact, Rex had only heard a Code 30 called once in his entire career, but he agreed that it was the right call this time because they were in deep do-do.

A Code 30 meant that an officer was in extreme danger and was asking for immediate help from everybody who was close enough to respond. Dispatch would immediately relay the Code 30 by simulcast to Santa Clara PD, CHP, and the Sheriff's Department. Within seconds, the request for help would be heard by every local and federal law enforcement agency in Santa Clara County.

The long alert tone sounded on the radio, and the dispatcher came back on. "Attention all units Code 30, shots fired. All available units respond Code 3 and stay off this channel. 24-0-1, what is your location?"

"24-0-1, we are still on Monroe crossing Scott."

Because of other traffic, Rex had to drop back behind the van again. As soon as they came into view of the open back door, they were shot at again. Another burst of automatic rifle fire tried to reach out and touch them. One round hit the windshield almost dead center and passed right between them and went out the back window shattering it. Two more rounds went into the right side of their SUV as Rex was able to once again swerve to the left out of the line of fire.

They raced across Scott Boulevard, a major thoroughfare, against the red light at 60 mph. Cars were slamming on their brakes and skidding all over the place. Rex was sure he had heard cars crashing into each other. It was unbelievable that they had made it through without someone crashing into them.

The next intersection was San Thomas Expressway. Thank God they had a green light when they went through because they were up to 70 mph now. Rex was doing everything he could to stay to the left of the van and out of the line of fire. All he could think of was, "Where the hell is the cavalry?"

* * *

Reyes could see the unmarked police SUV in the side view mirror and realized what the driver was doing. He kept moving to the left so that Jamal did not have a shot at him. Reyes started weaving the van to the left to try and pull in front of the SUV. But as Reyes pulled left, the SUV would immediately veer right and come up on the right side of the van out of the line of fire again. The van was rocking so much because Reyes was weaving back and forth, that when the SUV was briefly behind the van, Jamal could not get a shot. Finally, Reyes gave this maneuvering up and decided to just race to the school.

* * *

They crossed Bowers Road doing 80 mph. The light had just turned green for Monroe Street traffic, but the cars that had been stopped for the light were just starting to move. Rex watched the van swerve to the left and into oncoming traffic to get around the cars that were bunched up in front of him. As the van cut back to the right, it clipped the car it was trying to pass. The van started to swerve back and forth, and Rex thought the driver was going to lose control. But the driver of the van managed to get it back under control and continued through the intersection.

Rex had no choice but to follow the van into the oncoming traffic lane. Fortunately for him the van going through ahead of him, and the other drivers' hearing the siren, had caused drivers to slam on their brakes and try to get out of the way. Rex made it through the intersection without hitting anything.

Right after they crossed Bowers, Monroe Street made a sharp bend to the right, and the van had to slow considerably to make the turn.

"We're almost to the school," said Kat.

"We're not gonna let them get there," said Rex. "Hang on."

Chapter 60

Rex figured that their Ford Explorer out weighted the minivan. They were going too fast to perform a PITT Maneuver, forcing the van to spin out, but there was still the possibility of just plain forcing them off the road. Rex accelerated and moved up on the left side of the van. When they were even with the van, Rex turned into the van trying to force it off the road.

Metal screamed, and the van moved right from the impact, but kept going. At that point, Monroe made another sweeping curve to the left. Rex was forced to pull away from the van to negotiate the curve. Just as they were coming out of the left curve, Rex put the Explorer hard over to the right and into the van.

This time the impact was enough, and they moved the van almost to the curb. Rex could see a parked car just in front of the van and he kept the wheel hard over to the right forcing the van into the parked car. The driver of the van must have realized he was going to hit the parked car and slammed on his brakes at the last minute. There was a squeal of tires and more tearing metal and then the minivan crashed into the back of the parked car. Everything came to a sudden halt.

The van had been slowed to about 30 mph when it hit the parked car. The trunk of the parked car and the front of the van were caved in and looked like they were fused together. Rex had pulled away from the minivan just before the crash and glanced off the parked car. Rex had hit the brakes and swung the police car to the right coming to rest across the traffic lanes and in front of and to the left of the parked car.

As their SUV came to a stop, Rex popped his seat belt, kicked open the driver's door and bailed out. He was yelling at Kat, "Come on, get out, this way."

But there was no reason to yell. Kat was with the program and right behind him. They both stayed low and drew their weapons as they came out of their SUV. Rex moved to the rear of their SUV taking up a firing position at the rear bumper. Kat moved around to the front taking up a firing position over the hood with the engine bloc affording her some protection from incoming rounds. They were about twelve feet from the front of the minivan. They could hear sirens approaching from all directions.

As Rex peered around the back of the SUV, he could see the driver of the van kick the driver's door open and half step, half fall out of the van. As the driver came around the door, he brought his AK-47 up towards Rex and started firing.

Rex stayed collected and on target and put two rounds center of mass followed quickly by a round to the head. The driver dropped like a sack of potatoes. Then Rex ducked down behind the SUV as full automatic fire came at them from the left rear of the minivan. As Rex and Kat ducked behind their SUV, they could hear several rounds slamming into the side of their vehicle. Glass was flying all over the place as their windows were being shot out.

When the firing stopped, Rex did a quick pop up peek around the rear of the SUV, but did not see anybody. The shooter must have ducked back behind the van.

"Are you O.K.?" Rex yelled at Kat.

"Still in one piece," she yelled back.

Another bust of fire hit the rear of the SUV. Kat popped up over the hood and returned fire.

"They're trying to move up on the right side of the cars," she said.

"We just have to keep 'em pinned down 'til the cavalry gets here."

Rex did a quick peek around the back of the SUV. As he peeked around the bumper, one of the shooters popped out from behind the minivan and charged them, firing as he came. Rex rolled down into a prone position and emptied his seven remaining rounds into the shooter. The bad guy staggered forward a few more steps. As he turned to his left and started to fall, his finger was still on the trigger of his AK-47. As the barrel swung to the ground, rounds continued to fire and ricochet off the pavement. Rex felt a sudden stab of pain in his left bicep. He rolled himself back into a sitting position behind the rear tire and started to reload his Glock 26. But his left arm suddenly was not working. He looked down and saw that he had been shot.

He looked over towards Kat but could not see her because of the open car door. "I hope the cavalry gets here soon," he yelled over to her. "I've been hit."

"How bad?" Kat yelled back.

"Not bad," Rex lied, "Just in the arm. Reloading."

Kat popped up over the hood, fired off a couple of rounds at movement by the right front of the van, and then ducked back down. She was answered by a burst of automatic fire.

* * *

Jamal and Kamil were the only two left now. Kamil had taken up a position at the left rear of the van and Jamal was at the right front. They were not trained soldiers, but they were warriors for Allah. They had the fervor of the Jihadist coursing through their veins and they were intoxicated with the idea of sacrificing themselves for Allah.

Jamal moved back to the rear of the van and told Kamil to keep firing to keep the cops busy. While Kamil fired short bursts at the two cops, Jamal climbed into the back of the van and retrieved two of the suicide vests. He put his vest on and then changed places with Kamil so he could put on his own vest. If it was Allah's will that this was where they would make their stand against the Crusaders, then they would take as many with them as they could.

Jamal and Kamil switched places again. Jamal told Kamil to keep firing at the cops to keep them pinned down. He worked his way up the right side of their van and the wrecked parked car. Jamal figured that would put him within a few feet of the cops, and he could make a dash into them and trigger his suicide bomb, taking them with him.

* * *

Rex had managed to reload his Glock 26 one handed by holding it between his knees while he inserted a fresh magazine. As soon as he had the new magazine seated, he dropped the slide lock chambering a new round and was back in business. All the time short bursts of rifle fire had been slamming into their SUV.

While Rex was reloading, Kat had kept popping up and firing a couple of rounds at the shooter at the rear of the van. As soon as Rex said he was re-loaded, she popped a fresh magazine into her Sig. While she reloaded, it dawned on her that only one gunman had been firing. She wondered where the other one was.

* * *

Jamal had been working his way up the right side of their van and the parked car. He was now crouched by the right front tire of the parked car. He must have made it there unnoticed because no one was firing at him. Any firing from the cops was directed to the left rear of the van where Kamil was.

* * *

Kat heard the roar of a big engine behind her and then the screech of tires. As she looked to her right, a Santa Clara marked unit came to a sliding stop in the middle of the road parallel to their car. As the car came to a stop, the cop threw open the driver's door and came out low taking up a shooting position over the hood with his shotgun.

* * *

The screech of tires of the arriving cop car was Jamal's signal to move. He jumped up and ran towards the front of the disabled cop car, intending to run around the side of the car and put himself in among the cops. He had left his

AK-47 behind and was carrying the detonator switch in his right hand. As he ran forward, he was shouting “Allahu Akbar” “Allahu Akbar” over and over.

* * *

Kat heard the shout and turned back to see Jamal running towards her. She took in the suicide vest and the right hand held up in a fist in a split second and knew what was happening. She had seen enough photos in their training sessions to identify a suicide bomber when she saw one.

Kat thought, “This is insane. This can’t be happening. I’m staring into the crazy eyes of a suicide bomber on the streets of Santa Clara.”

Even though it was surreal to believe that she would have one of these maniacs coming at her, she did not stop to consider that. Her training took over, and she just reacted. Kat brought her 9mm SigSaur up on target and emptied all 15 rounds, center of mass, into Jamal’s chest.

* * *

The impact of fifteen 9mm semi-jacketed hollow points slamming into his chest stopped Jamal dead in his tracks. That is exactly what he was, a dead man standing. The bullets had blown open his heart, tore apart his lungs, and cut the carotid artery, but his brain was still functioning, telling him to move forward in the name of Jihad.

He looked down at his shirtfront and the front of the suicide vest as the red stain spread. He did not feel any pain. He was confused. His brain kept telling him to move forward, but his body would not obey. He sank slowly to his knees. As one last gasp of “Allahu Akbar” escaped his lips, Jamal joined the martyrs of Jihad that had gone before him as the thumb of his right hand depressed the triggering plunger.

* * *

As Jamal stagger and started to fall, Kat turned and raced in a low crouch around the car door towards Rex yelling “Bomb.”

Kat cleared the SUV's open driver's door just as an explosion roared in front of their SUV. The blast rocked the SUV. Fortunately, they were crouched down and covered by the body of the car. They could hear shrapnel whiz over their heads. Rex felt something burn the back of his right calf. Then there was silence.

They did not realize it, but the explosion had made them temporarily deaf. Rex's ears were ringing as he looked over at Kat. He could see that she was bleeding from a head wound. "Are you all right?" he yelled.

To Kat it sounded like he was a mile away in a tunnel. "I'm fine, just a little banged up," she yelled back as she dropped the empty magazine from her Sig and slammed home her last full one.

The sound of the boom from the Santa Clara cop's shotgun brought them back into the fight. He looked over at them and asked, "How many?"

Rex yelled, "I think we're down to one. By the rear of the van."

As they watched, two San Jose marked units roared up the street from behind the van. The units swerved into the on-coming traffic lanes and came to a stop broadside to and at about a 45 degree angle off the rear of the van. They were about 20 feet away.

Both San Jose cops took up firing positions behind their cars. One of the cops had popped his trunk as he exited his car. As the other cop lay down covering fire, he maneuvered to the trunk of his car and managed to pop up and lean in and grab a rifle case out of the trunk. Rex knew that rifle case contained an AR-15. Rex thought, "Good, we are finally getting some fire power." They now had the van positioned between them with units to the front and rear but angled off so there was no problem with crossfire.

* * *

As the San Jose marked units arrived behind him, Kamil was forced to move around to the right side of the van to keep under cover. A hail of bullets that hit the right rear corner of the van forced him to stay on the right side, where he could not see what was happening.

* * *

The Santa Clara cop was on his radio letting everybody know that San Jose had the East side covered. He needed the next unit in on the West side to come up the sidewalk and take up a position where he could see down the right side of the van. He also advised that there were two wounded officers and wanted fire and paramedics to stage at the school until it was safe to bring them in.

The second Santa Clara marked unit came in as directed and bumped over the curb and onto the sidewalk to their left. As the car started onto the sidewalk the front of the car was chewed up with a burst of automatic weapons fire. The car came to an immediate halt and the cop bailed out taking shelter behind his car. He had not gotten far enough over to be able to see down the right side of the van, but he was far enough over to cut off any escape route into the apartment buildings that lined that side of the street.

A third San Jose unit arrived on the other side just as two more Santa Clara units pulled up behind Rex and Kat. The last two Santa Clara officers came over to Rex and Kat at a low crouch. One of them said, "Come on, we're getting you two out of here and back to the paramedics."

They all four started to move back towards the Santa Clara cars when firing came from the van. It was immediately answered by the two Santa Clara cops still in their firing positions. Rex felt like his right thigh had just been struck by a baseball bat and he fell. One of the Santa Clara officers dragged him to safety behind the police car. With everybody keeping low, they opened the back door of one of the cars and Kat climbed in backwards. With her pulling and the other officer pushing, they unceremoniously loaded Rex into the back seat.

"Easy," said Rex, "don't ruin the suit, I just bought it."

Chapter 61

The Santa Clara officer climbed in behind the wheel and raced them to the staging area at the school, which was only a block away. The officer pulled right up next to an AMR Ambulance, and the paramedics were right there with a gurney. As they pulled Rex out of the back of the police car and put him on the gurney, he recognized one of the paramedics.

"Hey Frenchy," said Rex, "welcome to the party."

Frenchy looked down and saw for the first time who his patient was.

"Don't worry about a thing Rex, we're gonna take good care of you," Frenchy said with concern showing in his face.

As they wheeled Rex to the back of the ambulance, a Santa Clara Fire Paramedic was already cutting his pant leg away to look at his leg wound. Another Santa Clara Fireman grabbed Kat and walked her over to the back of the fire rig.

They cut away Rex's suit coat and shirt to get a large bore IV into him. They also started a morphine drip. They rolled him over and made sure there were no wounds in his back. The Paramedics worked quickly. Pressure dressings were applied to his wounds to stop the bleeding. He was hooked up to a monitor to check his vital signs. Frenchy talked to him, asking questions to assess how alert he was.

Kat did not say a word. She just looked at her partner. There was a lot of blood, and she could tell he was hurt bad. It looked like he had been shot at least twice and he looked like a mess.

"Come over here Detective," one of the other paramedics said to her. "You look a little banged up yourself. Let's clean you up and see what we can do for you." She sat Kat down on the back of the fire rig and started cleaning her face so she could find the head wound, and see how serious it was.

Since they were only a block away, they could still hear sporadic gunfire. "Damn," said the female paramedic working on Kat, "I haven't heard anything like that since I was in Iraq. What kinda bad guys did you take on today?"

Kat looked at her and said, "Real honest to goodness terrorists."

The paramedic just looked at her with her mouth open. It was not something she had expected to hear, and it took a moment for it to compute.

"You've got a nasty scalp wound," said the paramedic. "Here, hold this in place," she continued placing a large gauze bandage against the right side of Kat's head.

As Kat sat there holding the gauze to her head, she started to take in her surroundings. She saw that the front parking lot of the school was being turned into a staging area and command post. She also saw that some of the press had made it in and were running around filming and taking pictures. She saw that there was a TV camera trained on her. Sam Capalini loomed into her vision, blocking the camera.

"Hey kiddo," said Sam, "how you doin?"

"I'm O.K. Sam, but I'm worried about Cowboy. How's my son?"

"All of the kids are fine. We've got busses coming to take them all out of here. You guys stopped those bastards from getting here. You did good."

A large explosion interrupted their conversation. Everybody in the staging area ducked involuntarily and then looked around at each other sheepishly. They could see a hugh column of smoke rising up just a block away.

"What the hell was that?" asked the female paramedic treating Kat.

Sam Capalini was listening to the chatter on his handpac. After listening for a moment he said, "It seems that when the van slammed into that parked car it ruptured the car's gas tank. I guess gas has been spilling out the whole time. One of the rounds must have sparked it. The gas started burning and caught the car and then the van on fire. The one guy was still behind the van firing at the cops and wouldn't give up. As the fire started to burn, the van blew up, and that apparently took care of the last bad guy. There has been no more shooting. The guys are calling for Fire to come in and hose down the burning cars."

As Sam was talking, Kat saw Sergeant Quin. He walked over to gurney Rex was lying on.

"Hey Sarge," said Rex, flashing a week grin. "Glad to see you could make the party. Sorry about the Explorer."

"Don't worry about that Cowboy, we'll just take it out of your pay. You just hang in there 'til we get you to the hospital."

The paramedics working on Rex started to load him onto the ambulance.

The paramedic treating Kat said, "Come on Detective, you're going to the hospital too."

As Kat climbed into the back of the rig and sat down on the bench, Rex gave her a weak smile and a thumbs up. Then he looked at the other paramedic and said, "Hey Frenchy, what hospital are you taking us too?"

"VMC's the closest."

"Good," said Rex. "My wife's working the ER at Regional today. If you brought me in like this, she'd kill me."

The ambulance took off Code 3.

Chapter 62

When they pulled into Valley Medical Center Emergency, the District Sam Sergeant and two Officers met them. One Officer went with Rex and one went with Kat for security, and to collect and secure their weapons. Rex was wheeled straight into surgery while Kat was taken to an exam bed in the ER.

Kat had a pretty deep gash in her scalp that had probably been caused by shrapnel when the terrorist blew himself up almost directly in front of her. Her face had been cut by flying glass and she had two flesh wounds, one in her left bicep and the other in her left thigh. The doctor treating her told her that nothing was serious and that none of her wounds would require stitches. They were just going to clean them up and close them with butterfly bandages. The doctor told her that she would not be admitted.

Word had gone through the department like wild fire that two of their own had been involved in a shootout and had been taken to VMC. Within minutes, a steady stream of on and off duty officers from patrol and the detective bureau were showing up to donate blood. Kat did not need any blood, but those that had the same type blood as Rex were eagerly received and immediately taken up on their offer.

Of course, the news media were there filming everything they could. The San Jose Chief of Police, the Assistant Chief and the Deputy Chief of Detectives all arrived within minutes of each other. Internal Affairs had arrived, and the Press Information Officer, Sergeant Comstock, arrived to handle all press releases and set up a news conference. Finally, the Chief of Police for Santa Clara, Sergeant Capalini and two Homicide Detectives for Santa Clara PD arrived.

A turf war was shaping up. The shooting had taken place in Santa Clara, but the Detectives involved in the shooting were from San Jose. Santa Clara's Police Chief did not want to step on anyone's toes, but he was not about to give up any of his authority either. After a quick conference between the two Police Chiefs, it was decided that Santa Clara would be the lead agency in the investigation of the actual shooting with San Jose assisting and that all press conferences would be a joint press conferences. That settled, the two Santa Clara Homicide Detectives went in to do an initial interview with Kat.

After the Santa Clara Detectives were through, the three San Jose Chiefs crowded around her bed.

"You've had a busy day Detective," said Chief Daniels. "Are you all right? Do you need anything?"

"I'm told I'll be fine. All my wounds are superficial. Any word on how Rex is doing?" asked Kat.

"He's in surgery," said the Chief of D's. "That's all we know right now."

"Any word on my son?" asked Kat.

"Your son?" asked Chief Daniels with a puzzled look on his face.

The Chief of D's came to his rescue. "Her son was at the school and was the initial target of the kidnapping attempt."

"With all due respect Chief Ortiz," said Kat, "that was no kidnapping attempt. Those were flat out terrorists and I think they were going to first hold my son and the rest of his class hostage, and eventually kill them."

"Now," said Chief Daniels, "we don't know that they were terrorists. It is still too early in the investigation to jump to any conclusions."

"Chief," replied Kat, "when one of them comes running at me wearing a suicide vest, yelling Allah Akbar, and then blows himself up right in front of me, that's a terrorist."

Chief Daniels was disturbed with where this conversation was going. How could he explain that the safest large city in the United States had terrorists running around blowing themselves up? He needed to control the flow of information on this and fast. He had to put the right spin on this thing.

"Well, we will let the investigation take its course and see where it leads," said Chief Daniels. "Meanwhile, if there is anything you need you let us know."

As Chief Daniels turned to leave, the Chief of D's gave Kat a knowing wink and a smile and said, "You hang in there kid."

As the San Jose Chiefs were turning to leave Kat's bed, Rex's wife walked up with the Department Chaplin in tow.

"Kat, how are you doing? What are your injuries and are you in any pain?" asked Carmella.

Kat had to smile. That was typical Carmella. She had been an Emergency Room and Trauma Nurse for over twenty years. She was always the go to person among their small group of close friends and extended family for all medical questions. And now that take charge attitude of the ER Nurse came through.

"Carmella, I'm fine. All my stuff is just superficial. Didn't even need any stitches. But how is Rex, nobody seems to know?" replied Kat.

"That's because nobody knows who to talk to," said Carmella. "I just talked to the Charge Nurse, you know, one ER Nurse to another, and got the scoop. He is in surgery and doing fine. It looks like he's got a couple of through and through gunshot wounds, but nothing life threatening. And besides, he knows better than to die on me, I'd kill him."

Chaplin Ben just looked at Carmella and shook his head. He had met her only a couple of times and knew her to be a strong and capable woman. But he was still not sure how to take her.

Chaplin Ben turned to Kat, "I've talked with your husband and told him that you are all right. He has picked up your son and is taking him home. Is there anything I can do for you?"

"Can you get someone to bring me a change of clothes, so I can get out of here?" asked Kat.

"I'll get to work on that," said Chaplain Ben and he left her bedside.

Chapter 63

Sergeant Comstock had his hands full. The press was clamoring for a press conference. They wanted an update they could go live with. Working with the VMC Press Information Officer and both his Chief and the Santa Clara Chief and the Santa Clara PD Press Information Officer, he finally got everything put together for a press conference about an hour after arriving at VMC. Since Santa Clara was the lead investigating agency, the Santa Clara Police Chief got to lead off the press conference.

"Good afternoon ladies and gentleman, I am Chief Bill Jones of the Santa Clara Police Department. This morning at about 0730 hours, two Detectives from the San Jose Police Department, Detective Rex Johnson and Detective Katrina Sanchez received a tip of a possible kidnapping attempt at the Santa Clara Christian School.

"The target of this kidnapping was the son of Detective Sanchez. This kidnapping was a direct attack on Detective Sanchez's family in retaliation for a previous investigation in which a major criminal enterprise had been shut down that was operating in San Jose, Santa Clara, Gilroy, Mt View, Sunnyvale, Foster City, and Fremont. They immediately contacted the Santa Clara Police Department and requested our assistance.

"While Detectives Johnson and Sanchez were in route to the school to meet up with Santa Clara Detectives to exchange information and coordinate an investigation, they came upon the van carrying the suspects to the school. Recognizing them as police detectives, the suspects immediately opened fire on them with AK-47 assault rifles.

"The suspects attempted to flee from the Detectives, but continued in the direction of the school. While requesting additional units, Detectives Johnson and Sanchez pursued the suspect van keeping it under surveillance. With additional units on the way but not on the scene yet, and with the suspects now a little over a block from the school, Detective Johnson forced the suspects' van to the curb disabling it before they could reach the school.

"In the ensuing gun battle with the suspects all four suspects were killed. Both Detectives were wounded, and Detective Johnson has undergone surgery.

"During our preliminary investigation we have determined that the four suspects were armed with AK-47 assault rifles and were carrying suicide explosive vests and backpacks containing explosives. During the gun battle, one of the suspects charged the Detectives while they were pinned down behind their disabled vehicle and detonated his suicide vest in an attempt to kill the Detectives. Also during the gun battle, the explosives carried in the van were ignited and the van blew up.

"Background information known about the suspects, the suicide vests, the explosives they were carrying, and the nature of the foiled attack, leads us to believe that this was an act of terrorism. We have asked the FBI for assistance in this investigation.

"I would like to say here and now that without the heroic intervention of Detectives Johnson and Sanchez, we could have had a much more horrific and deadlier situation to deal with. They selflessly intervened, literally putting themselves in harm's way between those schoolchildren and the terrorists, to protect them.

"I would now like to turn it over to their boss, Chief Daniels of the San Jose Police Department."

Inside Chief Daniels was seething. He had not known that Chief Jones was going to say anything about terrorists. Now he would be forced to admit that terrorists had been operating in his city. How would that look when he ran for mayor? Terrorists had been operating in his city while he was the Chief of Police, and he had not known anything about it? That would not be acceptable. He had to get in front of this and spin it in the right way.

"Ladies and gentlemen, I too would like to praise Detectives Johnson and Sanchez for their immediate and decisive actions today. They are certainly the heroes of the day.

"This entire incident grew out of a fast moving investigation that these two Detectives launched just four weeks ago. As they pursued their criminal investigation, it became apparent that there were potential terrorist connections. They had just completed their investigation and turned the results over to the Joint Terrorism Task Force of the FBI when this morning's tip came to them.

"This morning's attack was a premeditated attack not only on the police, but on the community and upon our children. Detectives Johnson and Sanchez rose to the occasion and put themselves in harm's way thereby stopping something that could have been much worse. Thank you."

The next to speak was the Chief of Surgery at VMC.

"Good afternoon everyone. I am Doctor Ray Cherna, Chief of Surgery. Detective Sanchez has been treated and released for non-life threatening minor bullet and shrapnel wounds and other cuts and abrasions.

"Detective Johnson underwent surgery immediately after arrival at the hospital. He had been shot multiple times and had suffered from severe blood loss. Two of the bullets caused severe tissue and muscle damage which our surgical trauma team was able to repair. Detective Johnson is out of surgery and doing fine. His condition is serious, but stable. At this point we expect a full recovery. However, there may be a possibility of some future corrective surgical procedures."

After the Chief of Surgery spoke, the press conference was opened up for questions. The first newsperson recognized was Dawn Summers from KTVU Channel 2.

"Chief Daniels, you said that this morning's shooting came about as retaliation for an investigation Detectives Johnson and Sanchez had just completed. Would that be the investigation into the theft of cigarettes, extortion and auto theft that you said was just a Vietnamese street gang?"

Chief Daniels' was visibly upset by Summers' question as he stepped back up to the mike. "The Detectives' initial investigation indicated that the suspects were all members of a Vietnamese street gang that was preying on the Vietnamese community. Only in the follow up stages of the investigation, after the initial news conference, was the possible connection to terrorist activities uncovered. It was at that time that the investigation was turned over to the FBI. Because it was an ongoing investigation with the FBI, no further press releases were made so as not to compromise a sensitive investigation."

"Are there any other suspects?

"Not to my knowledge."

"Was this the only terrorist cell operating in San Jose?"

"You would have to ask the FBI."

"Do you know who this terrorist cell was affiliated with?"

"Again, you would have to ask the FBI."

"Thank you Chief," said Dawn Summers with a smile. She now had more of a story that she had originally thought. This one was going national, and she had most of the information exclusively. This story was going to do marvelous things for her career.

As she walked back to her news van, she also thought about how she owed Rex. He had been good to her, steering news stories her way. She knew what a vindictive prick Chief Daniels could be if you got on his bad side. She knew all about his desire to run for mayor. How he planned to use his carefully sculpted image as the police chief of the safest large city in America to get himself elected.

Daniels tried to portray himself as the steady hand guiding the San Jose Police Department in its quest to be a more modern, kinder and gentler police department, one that kept the city safe but dealt with all of its citizens, the honest ones and the crooks, with tolerance and understanding.

Rex and Kat were good detectives, but they did go against the grain, especially on this case. They had truly put themselves out there. It was not that they were heavy handed or anything like that. They were probably the smartest detectives she had met. They did not settle for the simplest or most obvious answer when they investigated a case. They took it all the way and dug deep. They found the conspiracies and the connections.

Chief Daniels did not like these connections, especially when they got in the way of his message. They exposed the fact that organized crime did exist and was operating in San Jose. Now these two had exposed that terrorism existed in San Jose. Daniels was not going to like this. He would use all of the tools at his disposal to shut them up.

However, if their story was already out there, then Daniels could not go after them. She made up her mind to do everything she could to help protect Rex and Kat. If they were the hero cops of the hour, of which there was no doubt that they were, then she would make sure it was clearly told in her news story tonight and the series that she already intended to produce. Daniels would not dare touch them if they were generating such good press.

Epilogue

In the bar at a luxury hotel in Bangkok, Thailand, he sat looking at his laptop screen. It was open to the Mercury News web site. The headlines of the lead story screamed out at him. "Hero Cops." Pictures of Detectives Johnson and Sanchez stared out from the screen at him. The story detailed how the two detectives had taken on terrorists in a major shootout and won, stopping an imminent kidnapping of schoolchildren.

He sighed and thought, "Good help is so hard to find. Well, after about a six month self imposed vacation, he would have to return to San Jose and take care of this problem himself. He would rebuild his empire. It would not be that hard. After all, he still had his DVD's of some very prominent businessmen and politicians being entertained at his old party houses."

Tran Van Nguyen shut off his laptop, closed it, and ordered another drink.

CPSIA information can be obtained at www.ICGtesting.com
Printed in the USA
LVOW081600171011

250873LV00002B/28/P